Unbelievably Kurt

Deborah Holness

Copyright © 2026 Deborah Holness

All rights reserved

The characters and events portrayed in this book are fictitious. Any similarity to real persons, living or dead, is coincidental and not intended by the author.

No part of this book may be reproduced, or stored in a retrieval system, or transmitted in any form or by any means, electronic, mechanical, photocopying, recording, or otherwise, without express written permission of the publisher.

This book is dedicated to:
YOU!
Thankyou for choosing this book to read. I hope you enjoy it.

Fiona: Your enthusiasm is contagious.

CONTENT ADVISORY: *This book is intended for mature audiences.*

The vocabulary, grammar and spelling of Unbelievably Kurt is written in British English.

Contents

Title Page
Copyright
Dedication

Chapter 1	1
Chapter 2	24
Chapter 3	48
Chapter 4	71
Chapter 5	95
Chapter 6	107
Chapter 7	123
Chapter 8	150
Chapter 9	175
Chapter 10	197
Chapter 11	213
Chapter 12	228
Chapter 13	247

Chapter 14	274
Chapter 15	298
Chapter 16	315
Chapter 17	337
Chapter 18	357
Chapter 19	371
Chapter 20	392
Chapter 21	408
Chapter 22	430
Chapter 23	448
Chapter 24	460
Chapter 25	480
Chapter 26	496
Epilogue	514
Bonus	524
Books By This Author	533
Marked by Stone	535

Chapter 1

"Ohmigod! Ohmigod! Ohmigod!" I double over where I'm sat on the couch, clutching my head in my hands, trying not to have a complete nuclear meltdown.

"Breathe," my best New York friend and housemate sits beside me, rubbing soothing circles on my back, "we can sort this."

I'm not a crier, never have been. My whole family are fixers, problem solvers others come to for advice when they can't see a way out of whatever hole they've fallen in to, but today, the tears burning the back of my eyes are all too real.

"I can't be." I say panicked.

"Hmm," Izzy's doubtful tone doesn't fill me with confidence. "What do *you* think is going on then?"

"The test, it's wrong. Give me another."

"Tina honey, I don't think…"

"Just give me the damn test," I scream impatiently.

Izzy clamps her mouth shut and hands me a

second test. Half an hour and two pints of water later, the result is the same and we've come full circle.

"Nooo!" I wail. "This can't be happening. "The tests are wrong. Where did you get them?"

"The pharmacy on the corner."

"Well that explains it," I say, exhaling in relief and immediately perking up. "They're out of date. Some of the stuff in there has been on the shelf for as far back as I can remember. I'm getting a false positive."

Izzy studies the back of the box, "No," she says helpfully. "These are well within their use by date."

"Nooo!" I sob, and this time the tears really do start falling. I grab the box out of Izzy's hand and lob it across the room in frustration. "What am I going to do?"

"Well, telling the father would be a good start. I assume it's the guy you slept with when you went back to Vermont for that wedding?"

"Kurt?" My girly parts perk up at the mere mention of his name. "It can't be, we used protection."

"Every time?" Izzy asks with a hint of suspicion.

"Uh huh," I answer dubiously, as I rack my brain trying to reassure myself as well as her. The memories of that day are so vivid I can recount every detail and I'm one hundred percent certain we didn't drop the ball.

"Well, who else have you slept with?"

"No-one."

"There has to be, you don't wind up pregnant unless you've actually had sex."

"There hasn't been anyone else, I promise," I raise three fingers to my temple in the Girl Scout salute. It's true. I'd been going through a bit of a dry spell since I'd split up with my last boyfriend almost two years ago. Correct me if I'm wrong, but I'm pretty sure a drunken snog with my hot new boss at a networking event—before I even knew he was married, or my new boss—couldn't have led to the tiny ticking time bomb now growing inside me. The thought makes me perk up again. "See, the test is wrong."

"Hmm," Izzy pretends to consider this information thoughtfully, even though I can tell she's still unconvinced.

"Spit it out?" I growl.

"What?" She answers nonchalantly.

I narrow my eyes at her. "Whatever dumbass notions are swirling around that brain of yours right now."

"I was just wondering the reason behind your fluctuating mood swings."

"My moods do not fluctuate!" I snap—then realize how that sounds and immediately slap on my sweetest, most innocent smile.

"Or the fact you've got a hair band holding your jeans together because you can't get them to do up properly."

"They shrunk in the wash," I tell her through gritted teeth. "I just haven't had a chance to buy a new pair yet."

"What about the fact I found several of my bras in your room?"

"They must've got caught up with my washing." I reply nervously.

"Oh, so it has nothing to do with the fact your boobs have gone up at least one cup size and you can't squeeze them into your own underwear anymore?"

I instinctively cross my arms over my chest. Damn it. The realisation makes the tears start flowing again before I can stop them.

"Look Tina," Izzy holds my gaze. "The sooner you face facts the better. You're pregnant. And if you haven't slept with anyone since that guy at the wedding, I'd say it was a pretty safe bet the baby is his."

"But we used protection."

"So you said." She looks at me sympathetically, "You do know mistakes happen. Condoms are only like, ninety-eight percent effective at the best of times. You're obviously walking proof of that. You need to decide what you want to do, then talk to the father."

"But he doesn't want kids. He doesn't even want to get married."

"Married?" Izzy looks at me horrified. "Who said anything about marriage? Let's just take this one step at a time shall we."

I burst out crying again.

Izzy wraps her arms around me and gives me a comforting squeeze. "I know it's a lot to take in. Especially since you've been burying your head in the sand for weeks. How about I run you a nice bath, order us a pizza…"

"with chocolate ice cream to follow?" I ask hopefully.

"With chocolate ice cream to follow," Izzy confirms, "then we find a suitably violent movie to help us forget all about this baby nonsense for a while. We can talk about it some more when you're ready."

"Ok," I sniff. *When I'm ready. How about never!*

Izzy gives me a warm smile, rubbing the tops of my arms comfortingly. "It'll be Ok. I promise."

I smile back even though my heart isn't in it, "Thanks Iz," I whisper despondently.

∞∞∞

I glance at the clock on my nightstand to see the neon green figures staring back at me. It's just past one a.m. which means it's just past eleven p.m. in California. It's not too late to call. Sleep won't come until I provide myself with some sort of solution for the way ahead.

Izzy tried to keep my mind off 'my situation' for the rest of the evening, but the terror kept pressing in like an unrelenting tide. There's no hiding from it anymore, I have a new life growing inside me and I'm scared shitless.

I lift the sheet, letting my gaze settle on the gentle curve of my belly. I'm showing already, and I can't be more than three months along. A warmth stirs in my chest—an undeniable certainty mingling with the realization that this is real. Whether I like it or not, it's happening. And suddenly, despite the fear, despite the unknown, one thing is certain: I'm keeping my baby.

I reach for my mobile, hand trembling as I scroll through the list of names in my contacts. I find *his* name and my heartbeat quickens as my finger hovers over the screen. For the first time in what feels like forever, I let myself hope. The thought of hearing his voice, steady and familiar, fills me with something dangerously close to comfort. Maybe things will be different when he hears the news he is going to be a daddy. I inhale, press call, and rush to sit up, anticipation crackling beneath my skin. The ring echoes in the silence as I close my eyes, waiting. Drawing on every ounce of my strength, until the line finally connects.

"You okay?" I immediately pick up on the concern in his voice, even though it sounds rough and breathless—oh, how I've missed it, how I've missed him.

I swallow hard. "Um, yeah. Can you talk?"

There's a long pause followed by some shuffling and heavy breathing accompanied by a low groan. I wait patiently for him to finish what he is doing and get back to me. The silence drags on for so long I almost think I've been forgotten. I'm just about to hang up when he forces out a little tersely, "Can it wait? I'm kinda busy right now."

And then, there's laughter. A woman's giggle, light and carefree followed by a masculine grunt of satisfaction. The sound punches the air from my lungs as my fingers inadvertently tighten around the phone. Of course. I should have expected it. I should have known he wouldn't be alone. But the thought doesn't make the reality hurt any less. Shame coils in my stomach as I hang up, my hands still shaking. I pull my knees to my chest, wrapping my arms around my body, holding myself together even as I feel like falling apart.

"Don't worry, Nugget," I whisper into the darkness, voice cracking. "We've got this. You and Me. It's just us now. Your daddy never needs to know."

∞∞∞

It was friday evening when Izzy staged her intervention—perfect timing, considering I rarely work Saturdays and I'd spent the best part of the last twenty-four hours buried in bed.

There's a soft knock before Izzy nudges my door open with her foot, balancing a tray stacked with sandwiches, fruit, and cartons of juice.

"How we doing?" She sets the tray down, then perches on the edge of the bed beside me, close and familiar, before forcing a grape between my lips.

I chew absently, staring at the ceiling. "I called him, Iz," I say finally, voice quiet. "Me and Nugget. We're on our own."

She stills before, "Jerkoff." The word shoots out before she can stop it, her tone sharp. "Want me to call him? Give him a piece of my mind?"

Her outrage is fierce—predictable and protective. "It takes two to tango, you know. He should be bending over backwards trying to make this right. Hell, he should be grovelling for forgiveness after buying the faulty prophylactic in the first place."

Despite everything, I laugh—a small, reluctant chuckle. Izzy can be terrifying when she's riled, though I suspect she's underestimated the size and ferocity of her opponent this time.

"Thanks, but no," I say. "He's not a bad guy. I knew what I was doing. I have no one to blame but myself."

She sucks in a breath and I brace, expecting a fight. But instead, her voice softens.

"Convince me," she says, watching me closely. She shifts, tucking her knees beneath herself, facing me head-on. "Tell me about him."

"Who Kurt?"

"The sperm donor," Izzy corrects, making me chuckle again.

It feels good to smile. Cathartic.

"He was always around when I was growing up. Maeve—my best friend…" I pause as Izzy raises an eyebrow. "Fine. My oldest and best non-New York resident friend." She nods, satisfied. "Anyway, her brother Jimmy grew up with both Kurt and Josh."

"Josh as in the Josh whose wedding you went to?"

"Yeah. Maeve and Josh got hitched. Kurt was his best man."

"Okay, go on."

I sigh, letting the memories surface. "When we

were younger, Maeve had a massive crush on Kurt. Everyone knew it—including me. So I never gave him the time of day. He wasn't my type back then anyway."

"Handsome?" Izzy prompts.

I roll my eyes. "Yeah, but too quiet, not my type. Always brooding. He dressed in black like, all the time. It was depressing, although it made him seem mysterious and dangerous in the kind of way girls couldn't resist. Trust me, he never lacked admirers."

"Smart?"

"Unbelievably. But never the type to brag. He'd sit back, watching people struggle to solve a puzzle they thought was impossible. Then, when he got bored, he'd stroll over, show them the answer, and walk off—leaving them scratching their heads."

"Kind?"

"I think he'd prefer something more like fierce. He despised bullies, the way they preyed on the vulnerable, the way they thrived on fear. Maybe that's why he chose the career he did. It was a way to stand between cruelty and those too small to defend themselves. There was never any hesitation in him, never a moment's doubt; stepping into a fight wasn't just instinct, it was his duty. Protecting the little guy wasn't something he did—it was just who he was. It helped that he always looked so mean and scary. Most of the time, someone only had to start a rumour that a certain person was on his radar, and it would be enough to make them rethink their life choices. He saved a lot of people from suffering—many whose names he never even knew."

Izzy smirks. "Sounds like Maeve wasn't the only one with a crush. Even if you refused to admit it."

"He used to flirt with me occasionally, but I always shut him down."

"What changed?"

I hesitate. "I went to visit Maeve before her wedding to Josh was even in the works. She was engaged to someone else, and I knew he wasn't right for her. We fought, and I lost my bed for the night. So I went to my brother's place—no clue that Kurt was back in town. Turns out Liam had already offered him a place to stay too."

Izzy's eyes widen in anticipation.

"Josh and Kurt left town to join the Navy's sea, air, and land division when I was sixteen. Our lives had gone in different directions and I hadn't seen either of them in well over ten years."

Her jaw drops. "He's a SEAL?"

I laugh. "Ex-SEAL. He and Josh just got out after fifteen years' service. Josh started his own security firm in L.A., and Kurt's his right-hand man."

Izzy lets out a low whistle. "What happened when you saw him again?"

I nod, remembering. "That night, when there was a knock at the door... he was the last person I expected to see. And let's just say—he aged well. Very well. Six foot three, all solid muscle. Sleeves of tattoo's that gave him an edge, you know what I mean?"

Izzy nods grinning. "And?"

"Liam, Kurt, and I ordered pizza, started reminiscing over old times. Then Liam's latest flame called, asking him to pick her up from work —her car was still in the garage my family owns, waiting for him to finish the repairs."

I pause, meeting Izzy's expectant gaze.

"So Liam left. And suddenly, it was just me, Kurt, and a crate of beers."

The silence between us stretches, weighted by memories.

"One beer led to another. And then..." Izzy prompts, eager for the juicy details.

"He seduced me," I say finally, "with the practiced air of a man who had spent years perfecting his technique."

Izzy raises an eyebrow.

I sigh, my lips curving into a half-smile. "Regardless, I don't regret a single second of that night. He gave me an unforgettable night of bliss— one that made me question everything I thought I ever knew about sex."

"That good, huh?"

I smirk.

"Protection?" She asks, her voice careful—searching.

"Always." I exhale slowly.

A beat of silence.

"What happened next?"

I swallow, my throat tight. "I woke up in the morning."

Izzy watches me, waiting.

I let the words settle before I finish.

"And he was already gone."

"Just like that?"

I nod. "I saw him again the next day when I went to make up with Maeve. She had a busy day planned so I agreed to stay one more night so we could have breakfast together the following morning. Kurt hadn't planned to, but—he ended up staying another night too."

Izzy's gaze sharpens. "And?"

I exhale slowly. "We both ended up at Liam's again. I was in the spare room, so Kurt took the couch. But as soon as Liam was asleep—he came to me."

Izzy doesn't interrupt, just watches, waiting.

"He apologized for leaving without waking me,"

I continue, "but he also made it clear—I couldn't expect more than a bit of fun from him."

I pause, swallowing the weight of his words before pressing on. "The job he does is... unique. The firm Josh created offers a bespoke service—his employees aren't just skilled; they're lethal. Sometimes, they step in where the authorities struggle, handling problems that require a different kind of resolution."

Izzy's expression darkens, absorbing this.

"He didn't think it would be fair to be with someone—knowing he'd constantly be putting himself at risk. Knowing that every time he walked out the door, he could be leaving someone behind, waiting, worrying if he'd even make it home."

The words hang between us, thick and heavy.

Izzy exhales angrily, crossing her arms. "Sounds like a noble excuse."

I let out a small, hollow laugh. "Maybe. But I can't pretend it didn't make sense."

Izzy's expression shifts—something between frustration and understanding.

"Deep down, I already knew we wouldn't last," I admit. "Me living here, him in L.A.—It was always just going to be a fling, nothing more. And once I made peace with that... we went for round two. We agreed it would be the last time."

Izzy lets out a breath, but doesn't speak.

I glance down at my hands. "The next morning, he was gone again—before I woke up."

Silence hangs between us.

"This time, I expected it. And it felt like…" I swallow, forcing the words past the ache in my throat. "…Like the last night was his way of saying goodbye."

"But the wedding?"

I sigh. "I know."

"Maeve and Josh got married on a raft. On a lake." I shake my head, exhaling. "And as soon as the vows were over, Kurt thought it would be fun to celebrate by wobbling it."

Izzy's eyes widen. "He didn't."

"Oh, he did. And one thing led to another, and—yeah. I went overboard."

She lets out a sharp laugh, but I groan. "The water was shallow, but that didn't make it any less humiliating."

"And Kurt?"

"Thought it was hysterical. But guilt must have kicked in, because he jumped in after me—threw me over his shoulder—and carried me off to 'help me get dry and changed.'"

Izzy's jaw slackens. "Oh my God."

I bury my face in my hands. "I was so embarrassed, Iz. Everyone was watching."

"Wait—where did he take you?"

I groan. "Thankfully, I had a room booked for me at the venue where Maeve got married, so at least we didn't have far to go."

"And?"

I swallow, remembering. "The second we stepped through the door, everything changed. Kurt paused, his fingers were still wrapped around my wrist, I remember his touch was warm, grounding somehow. I could feel my pulse starting to race.

I couldn't understand why he was still holding me, yet I didn't pull away.

Water was dripping from my hair, sliding down my back. I remember I shivered, though not just from the chill, and he noticed. The way he looked at me, Iz. He exhaled, slow, deliberate, like he was fighting something—like his restraint was slipping through his fingers."

Izzy sucks in breath as she waits for me to continue.

"He told me I was soaked, and I was. I felt a droplet of water as it slipped from my hair, tracing a path down my neck. His gaze followed it, lingering where my dress was clinging to my damp skin. My body suddenly felt on fire.

He told me to get changed. But neither of us moved. His eyes were boring into me, freezing me in place.

He stepped closer and it's like his gaze was telling me not to move. He brushed my wrist again, this time deliberate, tracing a path up my arm. The heat of his skin against mine was dizzying. I couldn't pull away.

His touch moved to my jaw, tilting my face toward his—hesitant, like he was giving me time to refuse.

When I didn't say anything, without warning, his lips came crashing down on mine. The kiss was beautiful, slow at first, exploratory—like he was memorizing me, mapping the curve of my lips. Then something shifted. His restraint suddenly crumbled and the kiss deepened—urgent and consuming.

His hands found my waist, and suddenly he was pulling me closer.

I didn't stand a chance."

I glance at Izzy, puzzled by her silence, only to see she's staring at me, leaning forward with her eyes wide, mouth open, completely enthralled by my story. Suddenly she snaps back to life, falling off the edge of the bed as she does so. There's a loud thump followed by a groan as she lands heavily on the floor. I roll to peer over the side of the mattress.

"Iz, you OK?" I snigger as I watch her rubbing her coccyx.

"Well, as nice as that all sounds, it doesn't excuse the fact that he turned his back on you when you needed him most."

"He didn't turn his back on me, Iz. I never told him."

"What? Why?"

I hesitate—just for a breath—before forcing a casual shrug. "It doesn't matter," I say, pretending like there isn't a sudden heaviness pressing down on my chest. "It's better this way. We want different things. If I tell him, I know he'll step up, or if he doesn't, Maeve will get Josh to make him. But that's not what I want. I don't want him in and out of my life whenever it suits him, just because he feels obligated. That would be too confusing for Nugget… and me."

Izzy inhales sharply. "Oh my god. You have genuine feelings for him, don't you? You're in love with him."

"What?" I scoff, but it feels flimsy—transparent. "No. I just think it's for the best."

Izzy narrows her eyes, like she sees right through me.

I push forward before she can call me out. "Please, Iz. Can we just keep this between us?"

"How?" She says. "You video chat with Maeve

nearly every week. Don't you think she'll notice when your belly starts expanding even more? She'll tell Josh, and Josh will tell Kurt."

"I'll keep it hidden. Make sure she can only see me above the waist."

"What about your family?"

"What do you mean?"

"You can't keep this hidden forever. Christmas is just around the corner. You'll have to visit them eventually, and don't you think your brother will tell Kurt?"

I press my lips together, then exhale slowly. "I'll avoid them all for as long as I can. When the time comes, they don't need to know who the father is. I'll fudge the dates a little. I just… need time. To iron out the details. To figure out how I'm going to survive on my own."

Izzy watches me carefully, as if weighing my words against a truth she knows I don't want to admit.

"I don't want you worrying about the rent," I say quickly, changing the subject. "I have some savings put aside. That's if you don't mind me staying. I know having a new baby around isn't exactly what you signed up for."

"Of course I don't mind," Izzy says, kindness softening her voice. "I just don't think you should be going through this alone."

"I won't be alone." I force a smile. "I have you."

"Babies are expensive. I really think you should reconsider."

"Iz, I've made up my mind. I'm doing this on my own. Like I said, I have savings to fall back on. I'll find a way. I'll work as late into the pregnancy as I can. That shouldn't be an issue—the firm I work for needs all hands on deck right now. Especially since one of the attorneys disappeared *mid-trial*, and they had to bring Steven in to replace him."

Izzy's brow furrows. "Wait—Steven? As in the guy you snogged? Damn, you really know how to pick 'em. But seriously—one of your old bosses disappeared? Just up and vanished?"

I nod, rubbing my temple with a deep sigh. "One day, Robert was in court, arguing for his client like usual. The next, gone. No warning, no explanation. And this wasn't just any case—it's one of the most high-profile trials we've ever had. No-one could reach him and the firm scrambled to keep things running, they got Steven in, filed for a continuance... but you should have seen the chaos.

Steven, he's sharp, with a reputation for winning at all costs. But he's no Robert. Before I actually met him, I asked around. From what I've heard, people find him unsettling—against the odds, he always keeps winning. Apparently, he never seems to put in the most effort—he's not the strongest, the fastest, or even the smartest of his peers. And yet... he never loses. No one knows how he does it. Maybe it's blind luck. Maybe being underestimated works in his favour. Either way, the result is always the same. No one ever sees it coming. He keeps his head down—until... Bam! Just when his opponent thinks they've sealed the case, he throws them a curveball. When the dust settles, he's always at the top. And he's far too young to be this untouchable. It doesn't make sense. He's climbed higher, faster than lawyers twice his age. It's as if the usual rules don't apply to him.

Some people admire him. Others don't trust him. Either way, it seems no one can stop him. Something about it all just feels... off."

Izzy leans forward, eyes narrowing. "Off? In what way? You don't think something happened to Robert do you?"

I hesitate. "I don't know. Maybe he walked away. Maybe the pressure got to him. But something doesn't sit right with me. For one, Robert was always so considerate, it's just not like him to disappear without leaving word. For two, the timing seems a bit convenient. Robert was holding his ground, he had the prosecution against the ropes—then suddenly, they introduced new evidence, the case started shifting in their favour, and poof. He's gone. Finding someone to replace him shouldn't have been as easy as it was. Steven seemed to be waiting in the wings, like his taking over had already been planned."

Izzy folds her arms. "You don't buy it."

I exhale, shaking my head. "Not entirely. But I'm just a Case Management Assistant, a small cog in a very large wheel. What do I know?"

Izzy studies me for a beat, then grins. "Was a case management assistant," she reminds me. "Didn't you say you've been offered a promotion?"

"The senior partner has asked me to be Steven's Executive Assistant for a while."

Izzy lets out a low whistle. "Not that I'm not happy for you but... isn't that quite a career jump."

I shrug, like it doesn't bother me. But it does. "It's temporary, apparently. As soon as Robert disappeared, his E.A transferred across to H.R. I've been asked to help keep things running smoothly while Steven settles in and gets up to speed with the case. I couldn't very well refuse, could I? Especially since I was told Steven requested me personally."

Izzy arches a brow. "And let me guess—nobody's questioning it because the orders came from the top?"

I force a casual laugh. "Not out loud, anyway."

"That must have been some kiss," Izzy sighs playfully.

I throw a cushion at her before exhaling heavily,

shaking my head. "None of it matters anymore. It's not my problem. I don't have time to dwell on it, not now. I'm sure Robert is fine, and we're just letting our imaginations run wild. I just need to keep my head down, do my job, and figure out what's best for me and Nugget. If they want to throw an extra thirty grand a year at me to do a job I'm barely qualified for while I do that, who am I to argue? And honestly? I'm gonna need all the money I can get right now."

"Just as long as this isn't a prelude to Steven wanting to chase you round his desk so he can try and have his wicked way with you," Izzy tells me seriously.

"How about I get one of those 'baby on board' signs and hang it round my neck," I counter. "That should be enough to keep him in check."

Izzy snorts. "Honestly, just slap Kurt's face on a T-shirt instead. From what you've told me, that should be incentive enough to keep Steven at bay."

"You're not wrong there." I say, before our eyes connect and we fall about laughing at the absurdity of it all.

Chapter 2

Monday morning arrives far too soon. I head into work early, grumpier than usual thanks to the decaffeinated beverage I'm clutching—swapped last-minute for my usual coffee, a decision I already regret.

I sigh, settling into my new desk. I'm sure this whole pregnancy thing is going to be a breeze—once my body has had a chance to adjust to the mornings naturally, without its usual stimulant.

Suddenly, the intercom on my desk buzzes, making me jump. I hadn't even realised Steven had arrived yet.

"Tina, can you come in for a second, please?"

Grabbing my notebook, I head to his office, knocking once to announce myself before stepping inside. I stand nervously before my new boss.

"Yes, sir."

I wait patiently as he scans the papers strewn across his desk, barely acknowledging me. Finally, he leans back in his chair, looking me over appraisingly before gesturing to one of the chairs in front of him.

I sit, pen hovering over paper, ready to take notes.

"You can put the notebook down, Tina," he says, catching me off guard. "And please, call me Steven. I think we've become far too acquainted to be so formal, don't you?"

I feel heat rising to my cheeks, and he smirks knowingly.

"I just wanted to clear the air after..." He coughs lightly into his hand. "What happened."

I knew we were all meeting at the bar around the corner to welcome the flashy new attorney drafted in to salvage the firm's reputation after Robert's abrupt departure. But feeling queasy—and not yet understanding why—I'd arrived late. I almost didn't go at all, but guilt pushed me to show my face before heading home.

When I finally arrived, the festivities were winding down. Some colleagues had already left, others were mingling with patrons at the bar. I chatted briefly with a few coworkers and was just about to leave when Steven took me to one side, offering to buy me a drink.

He was good-looking, easygoing, and chatty—not like the usual stuffed shirts at the company. It never occurred to me that he was the man we'd gathered to welcome.

We left together, both intending to hail a cab, but instead, we slipped into the alley around the corner and shared a heated kiss—one I now wish had never happened.

The next morning, when Steven appeared at my desk during his building tour, I felt the blood drain from my face. Only later did I find out he was happily married. That realisation had sent my stomach into knots, making me dash to nearest bathroom, but now I know my reaction wasn't just caused by guilt—it was fuelled by something more.

"I just wanted you to know—what happened… it's not something I normally do." Steven leans forward, resting his forearms on the desk. I think it was the thrill of the new job, combined with the fact that people were buying me drinks all evening. My wife and I… we've been having a few problems. Not that I'm using that as an excuse. I'm saying I slipped. It won't happen again, and I'm sorry. I hope it won't affect our working relationship going forward."

I study his face. He sounds sincere, but there's a glint of something—something duplicitous—that makes me doubt his honesty. Still, I need this job. So, I extend my hand across the desk.

"What do you say we forget it ever happened and start over? Hi, my name is Tina Collins—I'll be your executive assistant while you settle in. Pleased to meet you."

Steven takes my hand, shaking it firmly.

"I was hoping you'd say that. Steven Prentice. Delighted to make your acquaintance, Tina."

I nod toward the papers scattered in front of him. "Is there anything I can do to help?"

"Not right now," he sighs, the weight of responsibility evident in his posture. "I've got a lot to catch up on. The best thing you can do for me right now is keep interruptions to a minimum. Unless it's one of the suits from the top floor, make sure no one gets through. Maybe sort through my emails and set up my schedule?"

"I can do that," I reply, offering a reassuring smile as I rise from my chair.

Just as I'm leaving, Steven calls out and I turn expectantly.

"One more thing—I've got a lunch meeting at one. It'll probably take a couple of hours. If anyone asks for me, could you cover? Maybe say I just stepped out for some air, I'm in the restroom or something?"

"Why?" I laugh. "You're entitled to eat."

"You'd think so, wouldn't you?" He chuckles dryly. "I'm expected to have this entire case file reviewed by tomorrow. I doubt the people signing my paycheque would be happy to hear I sloped off before finishing—regardless of the fact that I'm supposed to be meeting a potential witness who claims to have pivotal information."

"Sure," I agree.

Steven smiles. "I knew we'd make a good team. As long as we're honest with each other from the start, we'll be fine."

Why did he have to say that?

My hand instinctively gravitates to my stomach. I could keep quiet about the pregnancy, but the truth would come out eventually, and then he'd likely be annoyed that I hadn't mentioned it sooner. Better to rip the band-aid off now and deal with whatever comes next.

"Um... there's something I need to tell you," I say hesitantly. "I found out yesterday that I'm pregnant."

His eyes widen as he absorbs the information. Then he breaks into a grin.

"Congratulations. I guess I wasn't the only one who slipped that night." He sounds relieved rather than shocked.

"I didn't slip," I retort indignantly. "The father and I... we're not together."

Realizing how that sounds, I start rambling.

"I mean, we were together—obviously—for it to happen. But we're not together together, if you know what I mean. Not that it was a one-night stand—more of a fling. And it wasn't some random stranger, he's an old friend. But I won't let it affect my work, though obviously, it will in some ways. I'll have appointments. And while I plan to work as close to my due date as possible, I'll need some time off after. But I *really* need this job and the extra money I'll be getting as your assistant. So I'm hoping it won't be a problem. But if it is, I'll—"

Steven raises his hand, and I clamp my mouth shut.

"Thank you for being honest with me," he says, a sly smirk playing at his lips as he rubs his chin thoughtfully. "You've just proved yourself to be the perfect choice for my assistant, and I won't be requesting any change. You're exactly the type of person I need in the role."

I smile—relieved, though slightly puzzled at his response—before heading back to my desk and getting on with the rest of my day.

By the time five o'clock arrives, I'm exhausted —and not really sure why. The tasks Steven set me hadn't taken long, and he still hadn't returned from his one o'clock appointment to give me more work. With time to spare, I spent the remainder of the afternoon researching pregnancy online, preparing myself for what to expect. I guess constantly closing down my browser and trying to look busy every time someone walked past had taken more of a toll on me than I'd realised.

It had been three months since the wedding, meaning I had to be at least twelve weeks along. When I read that my baby was approximately the size of a lime, my heart did a little flip. My hand instinctively settled over my belly in joy and wonderment, as close to a hug as I could give under the circumstances. I'd decided that no one in the office needed to know until it was necessary—my line manager knew, and that was all that mattered. I could do without the awkward questions and speculation that would follow as soon as my news became public knowledge.

Right now, my focus had to be on me and Nugget, starting with booking an appointment with my gynaecologist and replacing the noodle pots and fast food Iz and I usually dined on with a much healthier alternative.

After work, I stop at the store on my way home, and it takes much longer than I'd anticipated to decide what to buy. I'd never been much of a cook, and I hadn't realised just how much fresh food was available—or what paired well enough to make a decent meal.

After wandering aimlessly for about an hour, trying to figure out what to put in my basket, I decide I needed to do more research before frivolously parting with any of my hard-earned cash. In the end, I abort the mission, grabbing a burger and fries on the way home.

As soon as I get back, I kick off my shoes and flop onto the couch, putting my feet up on the coffee table and inspecting my feet critically. I'd read that swollen ankles could be a symptom of my condition, so I let out a relieved breath when mine look relatively normal.

A slight headache lingers, so I rest my head back and close my eyes with a deep sigh. I'm just starting to doze off when my mobile starts ringing from the bag I'd dumped beside me. I fish around blindly until my hand settles on the familiar shape, only opening my eyes once I'd lifted the device in front of my face.

When I see Maeve's name and picture flashing on my screen, I snap to attention—sitting bolt upright and smoothing down my hair before answering her video call. We had been best friends for as long as I could remember, instinctively knowing what the other was going through. It would take all my wiles to keep a secret as big as the one I was hiding off her radar.

Once I'm confident I look my usual unexpectant self, I answer the call jovially, carefully angling the camera so only my face is visible on her screen.

Hey," I call, "How's married life treating you?"

Maeve beams back, bouncing excitedly in her seat. "It's wonderful! I have news. You'll never guess. I wanted you to be the first to know," she pauses, "well, after Josh, of course... and Kurt—he was sort of there—and Mac..."

I'm not sure what she says after that—I kind of zone out the moment *his* name slips into the conversation. My mind drifts—back to the night of the wedding, to the moments after I had finished telling my story to Iz. To what happened next.

By the time we arrived at the post-wedding meal, the starters had already been cleared away. Then, after dinner, the festivities truly began. The mood was joyous and carefree—everyone determined to have a good time.

A man named Blake made a beeline for me, he was smooth, charming, and hot enough to survive hell in a heatwave. It felt good to be the one he wanted to flirt with. I was decent-looking, but not what I'd call stunning. Taller than average with blonde hair, but not the blue eyes I'd always craved —mine were more of a stormy grey. And while I envied my best friend's curves, my body had always been leaner. Though now, with my boobs suddenly expanding, I was finally starting to get the shape and definition I'd always wanted.

I was enjoying talking to Blake, a fact Kurt seemed oblivious to as he hovered around us like an annoying fly—interrupting every time things started to get interesting.

I managed to keep myself in check—until I accepted Blake's invitation to dance. That was when a rogue ice cube found its way down the back of my dress, making me squeal and flail around like some kind of deranged chicken. Mortified, I rounded on Kurt, who was chuckling, utterly unrepentant.

Livid, I slapped him—hard—across the jaw. Unfortunately, he had only just returned from a job that had left him with a broken arm and a face full of bruises. As he yelled out in genuine pain, guilt hit me instantly. The rest of the evening became a blur of tending to him, trying to make up for my outburst.

Somehow, the evening ended with us alone, back in my hotel room. And once we were there... his spending the night felt inevitable. That night felt different from the others somehow, not in way I could clearly define. We climaxed together, but as he buried himself deep the moment before he came, there was something about the way he looked at me. He made me hold his gaze as he stared into my eyes intensely, refusing to stop until he was sure he owned more than just my body. That night, he branded me. Imprinted himself on my soul. Left me wondering if I'd ever find anyone else capable of breaking his spell. He became a part of me that night—whether I wanted him to or not.

The following morning, I was surprised to find him still lying beside me. I'd never seen him look so relaxed, peaceful—one arm clamped me to his side, the other was raised and tucked behind his head.

I let myself admire the hard, toned physique I had spent the night exploring—just for a moment—before carefully extricating myself from his grip to take a quick shower and get dressed. If a few tears escaped, they mingled with the spray of the shower, washed away without a trace. My aching heart couldn't risk another goodbye after the incredible night we'd shared. Since I had booked an early flight back to New York from Vermont, I slipped away quietly, without any fuss. I didn't bother leaving a note. After all, I knew the score. Kurt had set firm boundaries the second time we hooked up—there was no need to make him think anything had changed on my part. It's just this time I happened to be the one leaving first.

If I'm honest, walking away felt unexpectedly empowering. It gave me a certain amount of control over my emotions—closure I hadn't realised I needed. I wasn't picking apart what I might have done wrong or the qualities I lacked that could have tempted him to stay. Not this time. This time, as hard as it was to do, I walked away with my head held high and the determination to find a man who truly appreciated me for more than the single night of pleasure he could take from my body.

Despite my best intentions, forgetting Kurt wasn't as easy as I'd planned. I tried to move on, severing all contact, believing it would help. But no matter how hard I fought to erase him, he still dominated my waking thoughts and haunted my dreams. The night Steven and I shared our kiss, I knew he wanted more—I could see it in his eyes, feel it in the way his hands lingered. But I couldn't. He was nothing more than a failed attempt to move past the man who still consumed me.

"Tina… Earth to Tina! I know it must have come as a bit of a shock, but it'll be fine, I promise." Maeve's words, laced with concern, drag my mind back to the present. I blink, focusing on the worry lines etched across my best friend's face.

Shock? What had I missed. I sit there, searching for an ambiguous response—something that won't reveal that my mind has been elsewhere, preoccupied by a certain sexy someone. But before I can conjure anything remotely eloquent, Maeve continues, yanking the rug from under me with such force that I jolt, as if she had reached through the phone and pinched me.

"I mean, we all knew it had to happen eventually, but when he turned up with her hanging off his arm, we all nearly keeled over. Kurt was always so adamant he'd never settle down. Hell, he never sees the same woman more than once, but honestly? He seems kind of smitten with this one."

"Smitten with who?" The words barely make it

past my throat as I force down the unexpected bile rising within me.

"Katrina. Honestly, have you not heard a word I've been saying?"

Suddenly, I'm wholly invested. "What? Where? When?" I ask, still trying to process.

Maeve sighs, exasperated at having to repeat herself. "Yesterday. At our apartment. Josh was cooking dinner for Jared and Mac, who were in town for the weekend. He invited Kurt, and well—he showed up with Katrina."

Jared and Mackenzie Jones own the place across from Maeve's apartment in Hollywood. Jared, an actor at the top of his game; Mackenzie, the ex-model who had effortlessly stolen his heart. They're blissfully married with four children—triplets and a five-year-old daughter who has the ability to charm everyone she meets. Mac works for Josh, keeping his professional life running smoothly so he can spend more time at home with his wife. They are good people.

Katrina, however—I'd never heard of her until now. Was hers the giggle I caught in the background when I called him the other night? A fresh wave of nausea washes over me.

"Tina, are you okay? You've gone a little green."

I nod numbly, focussing on my breathing so my body doesn't betray me.

Maeve's voice softens, the understanding in her tone palpable. "Honey, I'm sorry. I thought you'd find it amusing. You guys haven't spoken in months, and when Josh and I got back from our honeymoon, Kurt was so angry with you—I figured you two had run your course."

"He was angry with me? Why?" My brow furrows in confusion.

"He wouldn't say, but he was like a bear with a sore head for weeks—stomping around, making everyone's life hell. Even Josh couldn't get a straight answer out of him, but he wasn't overly concerned because the office had never run so smoothly. None of the guys dared put a foot out of line in case they had to face 'the wrath of Kurt'," she uses her doomsday voice before letting out a giggle. "And we're talking hard core ex-service men here, the kind who do five hundred press ups on their pinky fingers before breakfast and wrestle grizzlies just for fun. In the end we all assumed you two must have had a fight, then gone your separate ways, and we decided to avoid mentioning each of your names to the other until the dust settled. What happened?"

"Nothing."

"Something must have happened."

"Well… yeah. Something… happened, and it was epic. Then I left, came back to New York, and I assume when he woke, he got up and went back to

L.A. where it was business as usual."

"When he woke? Wait—you spent another night together, then just up and left without saying goodbye?"

"That's what he wanted," I snap, my throat tightening as tears prick at the back of my eyes. "He was clear about that after we... were together before. In fact, after the first time, when I woke the next morning, he was nowhere to be seen. Same as the second time we hooked up. So don't go getting all righteous on me—I was just following the rules he laid out. Unequivocally."

Maeve raises her hands in surrender, then lets them fall into her lap, twisting them distractedly. I narrow my eyes, recognizing the sign—she's about to drop more news I'm not ready to hear. She averts her gaze, then delivers the next blow.

"Let's not get stressed—it's not good for the baby."

My jaw drops, my bladder almost betrays me, and my mind scrambles to think of the best way to kill my loose-lipped roommate without ending up giving birth behind bars.

For a long moment, we just stare at each other. Then I whisper, "Does Kurt know?"

"I'm afraid so." Maeve tells me sympathetically.

Of course he does.

My stomach clenches so violently I feel like I

might actually throw up. "What does he think?"

She breaks out into a broad grin. "He's delighted."

"He is?" I ask, surprised. "Delighted in the genuine way, or in the 'if I don't make out I'm happy about it Josh is going to kick my butt' kind of way?"

"The former," Maeve giggles. I find myself grinning back as relief floods my body. Maeve presses on. "I know we always dreamed of having our babies at the same time so they could grow up together like we did, but it's not like this one was planned. And with you in New York and me in L.A.... it's going to make playdates a little difficult, don't you think?"

"I know. I'm sorry." Suddenly, without warning, I burst into tears.

"Tina. Are you crying?" The shock in Maeve's voice is unmistakable. And then—she's crying, too. Loudly. "It's not you that should be sorry, it's me."

"You? Why?" I croak between sobs.

"Because... because—"

Before she can finish, the door bursts open behind her, and Josh strides in, wrapping Maeve in the safety of his strong arms. "Baby, what's wrong?" he soothes, stroking her hair, holding her tight to his chest. I'm not envious at all.

His sharp glare lands on me. "Tina," he says, his

tone edged with irritation, like I'm the reason his wife is crying. But then his gaze softens, confusion flickering across his face. "You're crying."

No shit, Sherlock.

"Must be the hormones," I sniff.

"That's my excuse. What's yours?" Maeve teases, giving me a watery smile.

"You're pregnant?" The words spill out before I can stop them.

"Um... yeah. What did you think was going on?"

Our crying ceases almost as suddenly as it started. Maeve quirks an eyebrow at me, her gaze sharp and assessing.

Fuck.

I'm saved as someone appears behind them, carrying a four-foot brown teddy bear, with a large blue bow tied around its neck.

"What the fuck is that?" Josh growls.

"It's my godson's first gift."

"Are you trying to give the kid nightmares?" Josh grumbles. "And who said anything about you being a god parent?"

My breath hitches as Kurt bestows a rare smile at the happy couple, casting the bear over the back of the couch, where it lands beside a bemused Maeve—who immediately bursts out laughing.

"It might be a girl?" she giggles.

"Nature wouldn't be that cruel," Kurt chuckles, clapping Josh on the back. "Can you imagine? This one would never let her out of the house."

"I would," Josh counters immediately. Then, after a brief pause, he adds, "If one of us were with her." He gestures between himself and Kurt. They grin at each other and high-five.

Then Kurt's gaze shifts, noticing me for the first time. His smile vanishes instantly. What replaces it isn't just unreadable—it's cold. Hard. Like a wall slamming shut.

"Tina." The word is sharp, clipped—an accusation more than a greeting. "Why did you call me the other night?"

I sit motionless, caught off guard by his hostility, too afraid to speak lest my undulating emotions betray me.

Maeve glances between us, sensing the tension. "I think we should all get together over Christmas."

"You're not flying," both men bark in unison.

Maeve rolls her eyes. "Whyever not?"

"It's not happening," Josh states firmly, his tone leaving no room for argument.

"You're being ridiculous." Maeve sighs. "The doctor said my blood pressure is a little high, but other than that I'm fine. It's important we all get together. Whatever's going on between these two..." She gestures between Kurt and me. "Needs to be sorted. You are two of the most important people in this child's life, and I'm not bringing her into the world until all this awkwardness is resolved."

"See you've got the mom tone down already," Kurt snorts, clearly unimpressed, before turning back to me, addressing me like you would a naughty child. "Why. Did. You. Call. Me?"

"Tina can come to us," Josh tells his wife at the same time, crossing his arms defiantly. Maeve looks at me, an eyebrow quirked, waiting for a response.

"I can't come over Christmas," I reply instantly to Maeve, ignoring Kurt completely. "I promised my mom I'd go back to Vermont." In an effort to change the subject, I shift gears. "Wait—what do you mean your blood pressure is high?"

Maeve waves a hand dismissively. "It's nothing, really. Just a little higher than the doctor would like. He said gentle exercise is fine, but I shouldn't overdo it. I'm not on any medication yet, but I'm being monitored just in case."

Shit. I make a mental note to schedule a check-up first thing in the morning.

"Which means no flying." Josh crosses his arms, unwavering.

Maeve exhales in frustration. "Tina, could you come visit after Christmas?"

"Sure," I force a smile. "If I can get some time off work. Maybe I can meet Katrina." My voice is sweet, just enough to seem agreeable—yet a hint of annoyance lingers, impossible to mask. I have zero intention of going, but I can't resist throwing the jab to see Kurt's reaction. The sight of the oversized teddy bear and the protective instincts he's showing for someone else's child—when his own will never know that kind of care—cuts deeper than I expected. I appreciate him looking out for Maeve's baby, but watching him slip so effortlessly into that role for someone else stings more than I want to admit.

Kurt's eyes immediately cut to mine, the brief flicker of surprise breaking through his cool exterior. "Why. Did. You. Call. Me?" He barks again, his voice sharp and staccato.

Suddenly, three pairs of eyes are trained on me waiting for me to speak. When I don't respond Maeve gives me a gentle prompt. "Tina? You called Kurt? Why honey?"

I know none of them will let it go unless I give them a reasonable excuse, so I say the first thing that comes to mind. "It's silly, really. Robert Taylor—one of the attorneys at the firm I work for—walked out on a case, and now he's not answering his phone. No one can reach him, which is a bit out of character. He was always good to me, and I was worried. That's all. I guess I was calling for some advice."

"I'm sure it's nothing to worry about." Maeve reassures me sympathetically.

"Yeah. Yeah," I say dismissively, "I'm sure I'm just overthinking things. Anyhow, I have to go, speak soon." I blow Maeve a kiss and hang up before anyone can question me further.

As tears threaten once more, I pat my stomach affectionately. "Don't worry Nugget. You've got your uncle Liam. And I promise—I'll find you the perfect father figure as soon as I can. One that might actually crack a smile in your lifetime."

An overwhelming urge to hear Liam's voice takes hold, and I dial his number before I can talk myself out of it. I don't video call. He can't see me or he'll question the red eyes and sullen expression I'm sure I'm wearing. It's easier to fake happiness when the person you're fooling can't look at you directly.

"Hey, how's my little sis?" Liam's voice sails over the airwaves from Vermont, instantly lifting my mood.

"Good. You?"

"Yeah, just getting ready for a date."

"Really? Who dates on a Monday night?"

"Someone so hot he needs an eight-day week

just to manage all the attention."

"Yeah, but that doesn't explain why you're going out." I chuckle.

"Ha! Ha!" He's not offended. It would be stranger if we didn't fall into our usual banter. "What can I do you for?"

"Nothing, really. I just wanted to hear your voice." As soon as I say it, I realise my mistake.

Liam doesn't miss a beat. "Tina, what's wrong?" His teasing tone vanishes, replaced by instant concern.

"Nothing." I scramble for an excuse he'll find believable. "Unless you count the sudden realisation that you might be my favourite sibling. But don't let it go to your head—I can revoke the title at any time."

"Considering I'm your only sibling, the rank is a tad superfluous." His voice drops into mock solemnity. "Regardless, I'll cherish the moment while it lasts. But you should know, flattery won't get you out of telling me about whatever's actually bothering you."

"You're right." I sigh dramatically. "Bribery usually works much better."

"Tina." He's not buying it.

"I just need your help letting Mom down gently—I won't be home for Christmas this year." I say thinking on my feet again.

"Why?"

"Maeve has asked me to visit her in L.A."

"Can't you go after? If you're not here, I'll be made to suffer alone."

"Take one of your women." I giggle.

"To meet the parents?" He spits the words out like an expletive. "That could lead to all sorts of unwanted complications."

An idea strikes me. "What if we club together and send them on that mini cruise they've always wanted to go on? Not only does it solve the issue of what to get them for Christmas, but it also gets us both off the hook."

The silence that follows stretches for so long, I check my screen to make sure the call hasn't disconnected.

"Okay." Liam finally murmurs thoughtfully. "Though I'll miss you. We don't get to spend enough time together these days."

"I know." I say sadly. "But that'll change. I promise. I'm planning on taking some time off and coming home for the summer. We can hang out like we used to."

"I'd like that." Liam whispers affectionately. Then, in true Liam fashion, he raises his voice and sings, "But right now, I have to go—I promised Holly I'd pick her up ten minutes ago."

"Later, bro." I smile, then the words spill out before I can stop them, "Condoms are only like, ninety-eight percent effective. You know that, right? Be safe."

"Eww. Fourteen little words I never want to hear coming from my baby sister."

"Love you." I chuckle, wishing I could tell him I was speaking from experience rather than just trying to push his buttons.

"Love you." He calls back before hanging up.

Izzy always works late on Mondays, so I'm not surprised she's still not home. I take the rare opportunity to unwind with a warm bath and an early night. Sleep overtakes me with a half-written grocery list in one hand, and scribbled notes for quick and easy healthy recipes for expectant mothers in the other. There's one item on my list I won't find in any grocery store though. At the top of the page, scrawled inside a heart, underlined and highlighted by capital letters are the words: Buy Nugget the largest teddy bear you can find.

Chapter 3

The next couple of weeks pass by in a blur. Work is hectic as Steven's trial resumes, keeping me constantly running errands and fielding calls while he's out of the office in court. By the time I get home, I'm exhausted—more than I should be for someone in their early thirties. The doctor assures me I'm in optimum health; my fatigue is simply a side effect of Nugget's daily demands on my body.

Izzy manages to get time off work to accompany me to my first scan, and I'm grateful. Watching everyone else being fawned over by their partners would have been a painful experience to sit through alone. Instead, she has me doubled over laughing at her long and often hilarious list of baby name suggestions—a list she'd clearly compiled when she should have been working.

The scan revealed Nugget hadn't been conceived the eve of the wedding as I first thought. Since I was further along than expected, I quickly realised I must have conceived the first night Kurt and I spent together a couple of weeks prior. After the scan, my belly seemed to suddenly pop, and my bump became harder and harder to conceal beneath the loose-fitting clothes I was now used to wearing on a daily basis. I soon became the topic of conversation at the office— whispers died the moment I entered a room, only to be replaced by furtive glances.

I wished I had a story to appease the gossips. That I could openly share the wonderful night I'd spent with my baby's father—an old friend I'd recently reconnected with before we fell madly in love. I wished I could tell them he was thrilled to learn he was about to become a father, ready to stand beside me as we embarked on this journey toward parenthood together.

But I couldn't.

So, I held my tongue and pretended I wasn't bothered by the rumours constantly swirling around me.

As I stuck my baby's first picture to the fridge, it hit me—I hadn't asked Maeve when she was due. I'd been dodging her calls since we last spoke. I knew she felt guilty, convinced she'd hurt me by breaking our childhood pact to start our families at the same time, so we could share the highs and lows of pregnancy together. But I wasn't avoiding her for the reason she thought.

The guilt of knowing it wasn't her breaking the pact—it was me—sat heavy in my chest. I was stealing that chance from her by keeping my own pregnancy a secret, too afraid to admit the truth. I also knew she'd pressure me to book a ticket, to visit. There were only so many excuses I could give before she saw through me. And then what? Show up and give everyone a coronary at the sight of my expanding waistline, or watch jaws crack as they hit the floor at the ridiculous growth spurt my boobs had decided to go through.

And still, none of that compared to what I truly wasn't ready for—to face Kurt, to meet Katrina, to hear how wonderfully attentive he was being to his new girlfriend and impending godchild, all without my heart shattering into a million pieces.

Izzy offered to stay home with me over Christmas, but I knew she was looking forward to seeing her family back in Iowa. She suggested I go with her, but I hugged her and declined—I was happy to stay home alone. Or that's what I told her. This would be the first time I would be spending the festive season not surrounded by family or friends. Without alcohol to soften the edges of loneliness, I knew I'd have to keep myself busy.

Although I protested at first, she insisted we swap bedrooms, since hers was slightly larger and would better accommodate the baby paraphernalia I'd soon need. Before she left, we packed up our belongings, ready to move them when she returned. She made me promise not to do any heavy lifting in her absence, and while I agreed, I never mentioned my plan to redecorate my new room while she was gone. Nothing too extensive—just a fresh coat of paint on the walls and maybe some stencils where the crib would go in the corner.

Steven grants me Christmas Eve off as a thank-you for all the hard work I'd been putting in at the office. So, after waving Izzy on her way after work on the 23rd, I order myself some Chinese takeout and change into some old clothes. The leggings and T-shirt are stretchy and comfortable even if the waistband of the trousers rests just below my bump and the T-shirt clings to my new figure with the hem occasionally riding up to expose my burgeoning belly. I take the time to capture a few selfies, intending to get a baby book in order to document Nugget's journey into existence—one I could use to show him or her just how loved they were from the very beginning.

After, I head straight to the bedroom with the cans of paint and decorating accessories I'd hidden from Izzy under a pile of clothes in the wardrobe. I put the stereo on before covering the carpet with plastic sheeting and preparing to work under the watchful eye of the humongous grey and pink plush elephant I had chosen to purchase instead of a bear.

As I fill the paint tray, I chuckle, recalling the ordeal of getting the toy home. Back then, the thing was so oversized I could barely see over it. People on the street either dodged out of my way or laughed outright as I staggered along. And it was heavier than I'd expected. Eventually, I gave up and called Izzy. Together, we managed to squeeze it onto the subway, nearly knocking over a commuter in the process. The stares, the snickers, and Izzy's berating mumbles—I can still hear them now.

I barely finish my first paint stroke when a knock at the door interrupts me. Frowning, I set the roller in the tray, wipe my hands on a cloth, and go to squint through the peephole—impressed by how quickly my food has arrived.

The bag from my favourite restaurant is waved in front of my eyes, and my mouth immediately starts to water.

"One second," I call, scanning the room for my purse. It's right where I dumped it—on the chair. I grab it, forage for a tip, and absentmindedly fling the door open.

Immediately, a familiar voice yells, "Surprise!" Just as another growls, "No shit!"

I freeze, my heart pounding as I slowly lift my gaze—straight into my brother's shocked expression, his festive Santa hat absurdly out of place against the intensity in his stare, locked onto my stomach. Beside him, a man stands equally stunned, his gaze darting between my newly full breasts and the bare curve of my growing belly, and judging by the tight set of his jaw, he isn't admiring the view.

"Liam? Kurt?" The words catch in my dry throat, and I give a delicate cough, trying to restore my voice before squeaking, "W...what are you doing here?"

"I think the more pertinent question is: who the fuck knocked you up, and why the hell didn't you tell me?" My brother growls, his anger rolling off him in waves.

My gaze flicks between the two men. Kurt's eyes narrow with suspicion. "When are you due?" His sharp tone makes me shrink back, retreating into the apartment's safety. I know what he's really asking. Behind the potency of those bugged out, green eyes, I see his mind working—doing the maths, connecting the dots. Caught off guard, I have no idea how to answer.

So, I do the only thing a woman in my situation can do. I snatch the bag of food from Liam's frozen, outstretched arm before slamming the door in their faces, pressing my back against it as I try to control my escalating panic.

As my legs give way, I slide to the floor, my breath coming in ragged gasps. My hands shake as I clutch the takeout bag, the scent of food mixing with the nausea tightening in my gut. I ignore the muffled shouts and pounding fists, focusing instead on not throwing up or passing out.

When the voices and hammering finally subside, I swivel, pressing my ear to the door, hoping the two irate men have disappeared so I can go back to painting—pretending like this has all been some kind of vivid bad dream.

No such luck.

"Where the hell are you going?" Liam barks angrily.

"To buy a gun off the street," an equally terse voice quips. I can practically picture my brother's incredulous expression. The thought makes me choke out a giggle.

After a tense pause, Kurt finally follows up with, "Relax, you idiot. I'm going to find the super and *persuade* him to let us in. I would break the door down if it wasn't for the fact it would likely piss off your sister—and my arm is still weak from its last break."

"Shame, an unlicenced firearm could come in useful. When I find out who got her pregnant before abandoning her it's not going to be pretty." Liam growls.

"What makes you think he abandoned her?" Kurt snaps. "Maybe he didn't know. It's not like she's been advertising the fact she's knocked up to her family and friends."

"Why did you say 'didn't know'—instead of 'doesn't'?" Liam's voice turns low and threatening.

"What happened between you and my sister when you carried her off at Josh's wedding?"

I swallow hard against the lump rising in my throat.

"That's none of your goddam business." Kurt's voice comes back sounding just as dangerous.

The thought of Kurt's 'persuasion' tactics or my brothers temper earning me an eviction notice, has me scrambling to my feet. I can't afford to be homeless, not now. I swing the door guard across before hesitantly opening the door and peeking through the crack.

"I didn't conceive at the wedding." I whisper. It's enough to appease one of the angry men at least.

"Tina, let us in." My brother asks softly.

I'm just about to relent when Kurt steps forward adding angrily, "Or have your door broken down, your choice."

"Fuck you," I yell, my hormones getting the best of me. "Go back to L.A. and Katrina."

"Maybe I will!" He shouts back as I slam the door in their faces once more.

I brace myself waiting for the inevitable shouting. The threats. For Kurt's usual brand of reckless interference. But nothing comes. Silence stretches, thin as ice. This time, I snatch up the food still languishing by the door and head to the kitchen. Nugget is hungry. I'm hangry. I barely make it to the kitchen before the first crash comes—sharp and violent. The sound reverberates through every cell of my being. I pat my tummy, reassuring Nugget they are safe and there is no need for them to be afraid. It's nothing more than their daddy and uncle being overbearing halfwits. The second almighty bang follows like a war drum, echoing through the walls accompanied by the sound of splintering wood. I don't turn around. I already know my door is hanging off its hinges. But right now? Nugget and I have to be fed. I need to fuel our strength in order to brave whatever is about to come next.

A couple of minutes later, even expecting it, I still halt mid-step, taking in the devastation in the short hall off the kitchen as I emerge carrying my plate of food. A forkful of chow mein lingers between my plate and lips as I absorb the scene. My front door swings pitifully from one hinge behind the two unrepentant men standing before me, arms crossed defiantly.

Both stand with their feet planted wide, bracing for battle, but that's where the similarity ends. Liam, in his usual blue jeans and white T-shirt, radiates barely contained fury—his dark blond hair tousled, his angry blue eyes locked on me. Kurt, an inch taller, narrows his piercing green eyes at me while roughly dragging his hand through his deep brown, almost black hair. While my brother has his fair share of muscle, thanks to his frequent gym visits, his arms remain unmarked—unlike Kurt's, where intricate ink weaves a story from his wrists up to where it vanishes beneath the cuffs of his trademark black tee.

I swallow, throat tight. No-one speaks as we all eye each other warily.

"You need better security!" Kurt eventually states the obvious, a faint smirk ghosting his lips, at odds with the tension in his stance.

If there's one thing I'd learned growing up around these guys, it was their desire to confront issues head-on—going to war if necessary. They weren't above tackling each other to the ground and throwing a few punches to expel some of the testosterone surging through their bodies. Once some of that energy had been depleted, they'd likely shake hands and discuss the matter rationally over a beer or two.

Beyond irritated at the state of my door and not ready to face the barrage of questions I know is coming, I decide to do the one thing neither of them can handle. I choose to rise above their juvenile, prehistoric chest-beating. Taking the higher ground and the far more adult approach of giving them both the silent treatment.

I calmly resume eating my tea as I stroll over and plonk myself onto the couch, curling my feet up beside me and pointedly ignoring them both. I can feel their eyes following my every move, assessing me, waiting for me to strike like a coiled viper.

When I grab the remote and switch on the television—forsaking my usual crime documentary for the cheesiest romantic comedy I can find—a deep sigh breaks the silence, followed by the shuffle of discomfort. I know it's my brother. Romcoms are his worst nightmare.

"What's that smell?" Kurt's voice, accompanied by a couple of loud sniffs, cuts through the unease. I guess I've gotten used to the lingering paint fumes from the open can I abandoned.

When I don't respond, someone stomps off in search of the offending stench. I keep my eyes fixed on the film I'm only pretending to watch. My skin prickles, the hairs on the nape of my neck snapping to attention—a clear sign I'm still locked under Kurt's intense scrutiny while my brother tears through the apartment, throwing open doors and slamming them shut. The proof comes a few seconds later when Liam's voice rings out from the bedroom.

"Kurt, get your ass in here."

There's a brief pause before Kurt disappears into the bedroom and the door closes. Even as I strain to hear, only muffled voices filter through. I'm just debating whether to creep closer when the door flies open, and my brother storms back, throwing himself onto the couch beside me.

I know what they're trying to do—divide and conquer. Classic strategy. They're starting with the good cop.

"You know, you should have the window open when you're painting, especially in your condition. Paint fumes contain chemicals that can be harmful when inhaled."

I want to look over at him, but if I do, I'm afraid I'll crumble. Despite everything, I'm happy he's here. I've missed him more than I realised.

"And you should cover the can and tray if you're not going to be using them for a while. The paint was already starting to dry out."

I side eye my brother and he takes my fleeting glance as permission to make a grab for the TV's remote. I whip it out of reach and increase the volume of the film just to aggravate him.

"Seriously? I can feel my IQ dropping as I sit here."

It's funny, when we were younger, Liam was always telling me I talked too much and he wanted some peace and quiet. Now, as the silence stretches on, he feels the need to fill it.

"I bet you're wondering what I'm doing here?"

He nudges me gently on the side.

"Well, funny story." He goes on when I don't respond. "I missed my little sister, so I figured I'd fly to L.A. and surprise her, since she said she'd be spending the holidays with her best friend. Imagine my confusion when I turn up, only to be told she isn't there.

Obviously, I was worried—especially when I found out she hadn't been returning any of said friend's calls. Then Kurt tells me how she mentioned her boss had recently gone missing, and suddenly, everyone started freaking out. Maeve was ready to jump on a flight out here, Josh was completely losing it, insisting she couldn't leave. It was carnage."

I snort in amusement, unable to help myself. I can just picture my bestie facing down her new husband—so much bigger than her, just as terrifying as Kurt when riled, yet utterly devoted. No matter how intimidating he could be, one glance from her was all it would take to turn him into a big, squishy pile of mush.

"Anyhow, before there was any bloodshed, I said I would come here to find you and report back. Kurt insisted on coming too."

There's a long pause before he gets to the crux of what he really wants to know.

"Guess I now know the real reason you wanted to send Mom and Dad on that cruise. I take it they don't know they're about to become grandparents? I get that you needed time to process everything before letting Mom in on your secret—she's going to be over the moon. You know how long she's been waiting for one of us to finally crack.

Still, it stings that you felt you had to hide it from me. Let's be honest, you're actually doing me a huge favour—Mom's going to be so wrapped up with you and the baby, she'll finally stop nagging me about settling down so I can give her grandbabies."

Another pause.

"Who's the daddy, Tina? We should probably have a little chat—I need to warn him about what to expect."

And there it is—the question I knew was coming, woven seamlessly into the conversation like a well-placed trap.

I remain tight-lipped, feeling the sting of tears pricking the backs of my eyes. Eventually, Liam exhales in frustration and pushes himself to his feet. How can I tell him the truth when the father is blissfully unaware in the next room—and when the fallout might be more than I can handle tonight?

He disappears back into the bedroom, and more hushed chatter follows. The voices start to rise —frustration biting at each word, anger curling beneath every muffled syllable, still too indistinct for me to decipher. I brace myself, knowing the bad cop will be here soon.

Sure enough, a few minutes later, Kurt appears, yanking the television's plug from the wall before sinking into my brother's vacant spot on the sofa—exactly as I knew he would. My body tenses, I'm not sure if it's in anticipation of the interrogation I'm sure is about to begin, or simply from being in such close proximity to the man who always manages to reduce me to a tangled mess of nerves and reckless desire with a single glance.

When he says nothing, the silence is unnerving. I feel his gaze on me, assessing either me or the situation—I can't tell. I daren't turn to face him head-on—he's too skilled at reading people. Too skilled at reading me. Instead, I fix my eyes on the blank television screen, feigning indifference, waiting for him to make his move and mentally preparing my counter. After a few seconds, he exhales, slouching back and resting his feet on the coffee table, crossing his legs at the ankles.

"Yeah, she's here."

Not the words I expected. I tentatively glance sideways to see him on his mobile, likely phoning Josh to confirm I'm not dead in a ditch somewhere. I listen to the half of the conversation I can hear.

"I guess so. She's not really saying much."

"Probably something to do with the fact that her door fell off its hinges."

An indignant snort escapes before I can even think to suppress it.

"No, I'll be sticking around here for the foreseeable. Not just because the place isn't secure until the door gets fixed, but she's also covered her bedroom floor in plastic sheeting."

There's a pause while Kurt waits for Josh to reply. I wait for Kurt to explain I'm decorating and maybe that he is going to help me finish painting.

"I think she's planning to lure whoever knocked her up here so she can take them out. She might have thought about how to stop their DNA from seeping into her carpet, but probably not enough about how she intends to dispose of the body after. I'll have to stay and give her a hand since she looks about… three months gone I'd say."

I let out a deep groan, my eyes fluttering shut in dismay. The words barely leave his mouth before my own phone starts ringing. I shoot Kurt daggers not needing to look at my mobile to know its Maeve's name flashing up on the screen.

He grins, fully aware he's just outmanoeuvred me—and that my vow of silence won't last much longer.

"You gonna get that?" He taunts.

I snatch up the phone and answer, flipping him the middle finger.

"Hi," I whisper, my voice coming out small.

"Is it true?" Maeve screams in my ear. The pitch is so high I can't tell if she's thrilled or furious.

"Mmhmm." I side-eye Kurt, who's clearly paused his own conversation to listen in on mine.

"Tell me everything!" Maeve shrieks, then immediately launches into what feels like a conversation with herself. "Why didn't you say anything? Was it because of me? Were you worried about breaking our pact? I was nervous, but now —this is fantastic! I know we're not in the same state, but this is the age of technology. We can video call. All the time. Can you fly? You know Josh won't let me fly. Please say you'll visit. If you can't, I'll make him drive me to you. You know he won't let me do it alone. Who cares if it'll take a couple of days! Wait—who's the father? You didn't say you were dating. Is it that guy you snogged? Did you do more than snog? Are you together?"

In my left ear, Kurt growls. Maeve rattles on in my right.

"How far along are you? I'm due early July, so you must be later since you weren't seeing anyone. She's a honeymoon baby. Have you had a scan yet? What about symptoms? I'm craving ice—can you believe it? How lucky can you get, right? No calories attached. And hormones, don't get me started. I cry at the drop of a hat. Yesterday, I saw a puppy trying to pee. He cocked his leg against a tree, lost his balance, and toppled over. I was inconsolable—even though he wasn't bothered and scampered off happily. Oh, and since hitting my second trimester, I'm sooo horny all the time.

Every goddamn hour. Of every goddamn day. Josh doesn't mind so much, in fact he seems to be encouraging it, but I figured I should warn you—get your guy on standby. It's a shame you couldn't come for Christmas."

She pauses and my stomach sinks. I know what's coming.

"Wait." Her tone shifts. "Why did you tell Liam you'd be here and tell me you were going back to Vermont—when you've done neither?"

I open my mouth, but nothing comes out as I scramble for a response. Thankfully, Maeve answers for me.

"It's him, isn't it? You wanted to spend Christmas with your new guy. Tell me about him. Lay it on me—the whole Cinderella story."

"Yeah," a low voice murmurs beside me, simmering with dangerous tension. "Tell us all about this new guy, Tina."

I freeze. Kurt must have messaged Josh to put his phone on speaker—Kurt has been listening to Maeve's interrogation the entire time. I risk a glance at him. His thunderous expression could reduce lesser mortals to dust, and the grip on his phone is so tight I'm amazed it hasn't shattered.

"Um," I start carefully. Kurt tips his head, waiting.

"Can I call you back?" I finally venture. "Now

really isn't a good time."

"Oh… okay," Maeve doesn't even try to mask her disappointment.

"I'll call and explain everything soon, I promise."

"Tonight?" she asks hopefully.

Liam strides back into the room, looking merely moments away from spontaneous combustion.

Kurt subtly shakes his head. Liam acknowledges the slight gesture with a scowl before turning on his heel, stomping back off to the bedroom and slamming the door.

"Mmm… probably more like tomorrow," I counter, before we say our goodbyes and I hang up.

Kurt ends his call at the same time. Immediately, he moves so he is crouching before me, his arms braced on the couch either side of me, caging me in. His face hovers inches from mine, green eyes flashing with fury as he grinds out the words:

"Who is he?"

My mouth goes dry. I subconsciously roll my bottom lip between my teeth, knowing my time is up and I have to come clean.

"Who's who?" I giggle nervously, grasping at levity.

"Don't fuck with me, Tina." Kurt growls

impatiently.

"If I'd kept to that rule, I wouldn't be in this mess." I whisper, holding his gaze as the weight of my words sinks in.

The fierce green eyes soften dramatically, little lines crinkling at their corners as the edges of his mouth pull into a cheeky grin.

"He's mine." It's more of a statement than a question.

"She is." I confirm, smiling back.

The brief moment of joy shatters as his thunderous look returns. For just a second, I thought he looked happy—maybe even relieved. But as quickly as it came, the look's gone. My heart sinks. Maybe I was just seeing what I wanted to see.

"Who's the guy?" He barks in my face.

"What guy?" I ask, genuinely confused.

"The guy you're seeing. The one who thinks he's going to be raising my kid."

The devil in me can't resist.

"I dunno. Probably on a date with Katrina."

Kurt looms over me, snarling like a wolf, teeth bared. As fearsome as he looks—and as dangerous as he can be—I know he'd never hurt me. Even so, I'm exhausted from the drama. He'll have to get used to me having a guy around at some point, but that's an issue for another day.

"I'm not seeing anyone, doofus. Maeve only thinks that because she's assuming I conceived after her. But I didn't. I'm actually due a few weeks before her."

Kurt stiffens, his jaw flexing slightly. His expression shifts as something flickers behind his eyes—intense but unreadable. I've seen that look before, and I know he's piecing the puzzle together, slotting each detail into place.

"That means it happened…"

I nod. "That night we crashed at Liam's. The first night we… you know." I'm not sure why I'm suddenly shy.

"Fucked," Kurt supplies.

"I'd prefer we refrain from using that kind of language from now on," I mutter. "Around twenty-three weeks, the baby starts hearing external sounds. I know we're nowhere near that yet, but —no offense—you should probably get in some practice."

He smiles. Actually smiles. And it's a wonderful sight—even if he does look like he's laughing at me.

"I thought we were careful." His voice is softer now, almost pensive.

"So did I." I answer anyway. "Although, I've since learned condoms are only effective when used correctly ninety-eight percent of the time. There was a fair amount of alcohol involved that night, so… clearly, you couldn't handle it." I smirk, goading him. "You obviously suck at multi-tasking."

"I didn't hear you complaining at the time." The intense stare is back, but this time it's charged with something other than anger. As my pulse starts to quicken, Kurt smirks back arrogantly, "Maybe you distracted me with all your screaming."

"Proves my point. Like I said, you suck at multi-tasking." I shrug, victorious. "I'm surprised you lasted in the SEAL's as long as you did. You obviously crack easily under pressure." Kurt smiles again and I scramble out from under him, "Come with me," I say beckoning him.

"You taking me to the bedroom for a reenactment?"

"With my brother about to lose it in the next room?" I quirk an eyebrow at him.

"I thought you might be offering me the chance to prove you wrong and show you just how well I do work under pressure." He winks at me and I get a sudden flutter of butterflies in my stomach. "You'll have to keep the noise down though."

"Dream on," I reply, even though I'm a hairs breadth away from stripping him naked on the spot. He follows me to the kitchen where I point to the sonogram pictures I fastened to the fridge.

He stares at them wide eyed, before dragging his

hand down his face and swearing. "Fuck!"

"I know," I say rubbing his arm soothingly, "It was a shock for me too. Seeing her makes it all very real. I'll give you that one, but maybe now we can substitute the 'f' for a 'd' or something going forward."

"It's not the baby I'm worried about." Kurt growls locking me with his gaze, "It's figuring out which of us is going to break the news I'm the father to your ducking brother."

Just then, Liam bursts into the kitchen to join us. "Have you nailed it?" He barks at Kurt. "I've almost painted that entire fucking room while I've been in there waiting." Judging by the state of him, there's more paint on my brother than on any of the walls. A clear casualty of fierce, angry rollering, he's flushed and splattered in green, looking somewhere between the Hulk and the not so very jolly Green Giant.

"You could say that," Kurt grins, "Although it isn't polite to refer to your sister as 'it'."

Liam frowns and I glare at Kurt, stepping between the two men before the confusion on my brothers face lifts and the next world war starts in the kitchen of my tiny apartment.

Chapter 4

You know that moment when a twister hits the ground, threatening destruction, only for it to disappear moments later as the storm suddenly lifts? The sun breaks through, and though everything appears calm and serene on the surface, there's the undercurrent of repressed pressure, simmering and building, set to explode again when you least expect it. That's the feeling I'm experiencing right now.

Liam's jaw ticks as he clenches and unclenches the fists at his sides, his glare locked onto Kurt. His voice is a low, controlled growl, but the weight behind it is anything but restrained. "Did you do it on purpose? Because if you did, we're going to have a major fucking problem."

Kurt doesn't flinch. Without me realising he has manoeuvred us so he has me tucked up against him, my back to his front, his arm draped over my shoulder with his palm resting possessively over the swell of my stomach—like a silent declaration. "Sleep with your sister, or get her pregnant?" His voice is deliberately slow, edged with that insufferable smugness, like he's barely resisting the urge to smirk.

I try to push his arm away, a silent demand for him to stop goading my brother. But he doesn't move, so neither can I. "It was..." I pause, 'an accident' doesn't feel right. I don't want my child ever thinking they weren't wanted. "...unexpected," I correct. "And what sort of ridiculous question is that anyway? Kurt can you give Liam and I a few minutes alone?"

"No." The word is delivered with the finality of a door being slammed shut.

Cosmic!

"We..." I start, compelled to explain myself when no one else speaks.

"Stop right there," Liam interrupts, wincing like he's in actual pain. "You might scar me for life. I'm not emotionally equipped to hear my little sister talk about anything beyond hand holding—especially when the man in question happens to be one of my best mates."

Liam doesn't take his eyes off Kurt for a second. The tension stretches between them like a live wire, unspoken dialogue thick in the air. Finally, Liam exhales sharply, jerking his head toward me as if me being there is an inconvenience. "We'll talk about this later."

"Understood." Kurt doesn't hesitate. There's no

sarcasm. No bite. Just certainty. And somehow, the conversation ends there. Just like that.

Liam turns away with that simmering restraint only he can pull off, and Kurt, perfectly unfazed, releases his hold like the matter is settled. The next second, the pair of them are rummaging through my cupboards, tossing out critiques on my apparent lack of nutritional balance, as if my reluctance to grocery shop is the real crisis at hand.

"One of us needs to take her shopping," Kurt grumbles. "Unless you want one of these five-minute noodle pots for Christmas lunch." His eyes widen as he takes in Izzy and my secret stash. There has to be at least thirty squirrelled away for emergencies. A girl can only live on toast for so long.

"Craving." I toss out in embarrassment. Both men grunt like they don't believe me but have the decency not to pull me up on it either.

"You can do that. You're the one who thinks they're worthy of a Michelin star. I'll finish decorating the bedroom." Liam answers decisively.

"You can't cook, you mean." Kurt throws back.

"You can?" I asked surprised.

"No. When I was in the navy, I had a catering service on standby. They'd deploy every time I was hungry, jumping out of planes or swimming oceans dressed as maids or butlers whilst holding covered silver platters to be presented before me at my whim." Kurt deadpans.

"Wow. Sounds perfect. Where do I sign up?" I try to match his sarcasm. My comment rolls off him as effortlessly as waves from a shore.

"You already did. The minute you decided to let yourself get pregnant with my baby." He says it like he's absolving himself from any responsibility related to the conception. I'm seconds away from blowing my stack and calling him out on it, when he catches my eye and his mouth quirks enough to let me know he is teasing.

"What about the door?" Kurt asks, his tone firm but measured.

"Yeah, I broke it, I'll fix it." Liam sighs.

"You broke it!" I exclaim in surprise. I would have bet good money it would have been the other way round.

"I would've picked the lock." Kurt shrugs like I should have known this.

"A skill you could have mentioned before now." Liam mutters incredulously.

"Right that's settled." Kurt claps his hands together. "It's been an eventful evening and my son needs his rest. I propose we all have an early night. Tomorrow, Tina and I will go shopping. Liam, you'll stay here, get the door fixed and finish decorating the bedroom."

"Where's everyone going to sleep?" Liam scratches his head thoughtfully.

"Tina and I will take that room there. You can either stay in the one you've been painting or take the couch. Second thoughts, you better take the couch, you can see the main entrance from the living room and since you caved the door in, anyone could come waltzing through to burglarize the place."

"You are *not* sharing a bed with my sister," Liam shouts authoritatively.

"Why?" Kurt raises an eyebrow, looking at Liam like he has just grown two heads, "worried I might knock her up even more?"

"You're not going anywhere near her until you do the honourable thing and marry her."

"Fine." Kurt lobbies back, shocking both Liam and me into silence. "I'll marry her, but let's be clear—we'll be sharing a bed before then."

As the tension in the room hikes to an almost unbearable level, I feel the need to interject.

"Do I get a say in this at all?" I ask.

"No." Both men yell in unison before looking at me as if I'm the one that's lost their mind.

"Christ." I pinch the bridge of my nose. "I pity any poor fool stupid enough to try and break into this apartment tonight."

After some tense negotiations, it's decided I spend the night in my old bedroom alone. Liam stakes out what will eventually be my new one, and Kurt gets banished to the couch—too short for him to sleep on comfortably, but since Liam's hell-bent on punishing him, comfort isn't part of the deal.

We all turn in at the same time. Liam doesn't trust me alone with Kurt, and honestly, I feel the exact same about leaving the other two unsupervised. Kurt, as usual, seems unbothered by anything—except the fact that between my vigilance and Liam's stubborn refusal to back down, the couch is now hostile territory, and the chance of him getting any sleep at all is sliding from mildly unlikely to laughably impossible.

Eventually, we peel off to our assigned corners. Not that it helps me sleep. I should feel relief now that my secret's out, but instead I lie wide-eyed, every muscle coiled with tension. More than once I catch myself halfway out of bed, craving a glass of water I don't need—just an excuse to pass the sofa and sneak a peek at the man stretched across it. Each time, I force myself back under the covers, blaming baby hormones for the way my body pulses at the memories of what Kurt's body is capable of. Scenes steamy enough to fog the glasses of the harshest censor infiltrate my mind. If our prior antics were part of a movie, I doubt the crew could deliver a take without short-circuiting.

I twist and turn until finally, I prop myself up, mummifying myself in the covers to restrain the restless writhing. I stare at the ceiling trying to force images of Kurt from my mind until my eyelids finally begin to droop. I'm just slipping into that blissful, floaty space between thoughts and unconsciousness when the mattress dips at the foot of the bed. A weight shifts as a shadow crawls up the bed to loom over me. My mouth opens to scream, but a familiar mouth descends to silence it. The kiss is soft, deliberate—and maddeningly familiar. When my eyes adjust, Kurt's silhouette is hovering above me, the muscles on his naked torso flexing as he braces his arms on either side of my body. His knees part mine just enough for him nestle close without touching my belly. When he's sure I'm awake—and not about to shout for reinforcements like it's Code Red—he releases my mouth so I can speak. It takes me a few seconds to react as I drink in the sight of him, breathe in his scent. My heart starts beating double time at his close proximity.

"What are you doing?" I hiss, pressing my palms to his chest. I tell myself it's to stop him—but there's no force behind my touch. It's just an illusion designed to mask my craving for contact. "You're supposed to be on the couch. You promised Liam."

"I made no such promise," he replies, deadpan.

"I just let you two argue yourselves hoarse, playing along until your brother passed out. I was tired of him being a dick. And I wanted to talk to you. Alone."

"Don't call him a dick. He's just trying to protect me. And Nugget."

"Nugget?"

"When I first found out I was pregnant, I imagined the baby was about the size of a chicken nugget. The nickname stuck. I don't know why."

"Brilliant," he mutters. "My child is being likened to poultry. And the name probably came from your fascination with fast food and your firm refusal to use the oven."

"It's a term of endearment." I volley back, slapping his arm. "Wait! I have an oven?"

Even in the dark I can see the eye-roll.

"What did you want to talk about?" I whisper.

The wedding," he says. Just like that.

"What wedding?"

"Our wedding."

I burst out laughing before remembering my brother will go postal if he catches Kurt in my room. "We're not getting married," I force out as I try to stifle my giggles.

"We are. You're carrying my baby."

I can't stop another snort of laughter escaping. "Do you even hear how ridiculous you sound right now?"

"How so?" Kurt growls, his face close enough for me to see the determined quirk of his eyebrow as he challenges me.

"How can you be so hypocritical. Acting all righteous, pushing for a shotgun wedding just because I'm pregnant, but at the same time being one of the biggest advocates for sex before marriage I know. Christ, you're even dating another woman right now."

"I am?"

"Katrina. Have you forgotten about her already? That's just so typical of you." I sigh despondently. "I'm not doing this your way just because you storm in here throwing your weight around. That might work for you at work, but it's not going to fly with me. We can co-parent this baby without getting hitched. We just have to sort out the logistics so it happens in a way that suits us all."

"Suits us all? Who else are you including in this little delusional fantasy you're having." Kurt snaps. "This is between you and me. No-one else."

"I was referring to Nugget. Whatever decisions we make, we have to put her first."

"You think I wouldn't put *him* first? Is your opinion of me that low? Is that why you were hiding the pregnancy? What were you going to do, avoid everyone for as long as you could then manipulate the dates a bit so I'd never think the baby was mine."

My silence speaks volumes.

"Fuck's sake." Kurt rolls to lay beside me, dragging his hand down his face in frustration as we both stare up at the ceiling. "How fair is that?"

After about a minute's silence I reach out and take the hand resting beside mine on the bed, meshing my fingers with Kurt's, relieved when he doesn't pull away. "I'm sorry," I mutter. "I never meant to hurt you. I did try and tell you. That's the real reason I called you that night. But you were… busy, and I realised If I told you the truth, you'd do exactly what you're doing now. Take responsibility and step up in a way you never asked for. Maeve says you're smitten with Katrina. This doesn't have to change things for you. You never wanted to get married or have kids before. I guess what I'm saying is. You don't have to be involved just because you feel responsible."

"I am fucking responsible."

"Ducking, if you please." I say trying to lighten the mood.

"You think you have me all figured out, don't you?"

"Pretty much. I've known you a long time—it's

not that hard to do."

"Is that so." There's a long pause. Then: "I want to you to answer one question, and I expect an honest answer."

"Shoot."

"Why'd you run out on me the morning after Josh's wedding?"

"What?" I ask confused. I thought the answer was obvious.

"You heard."

"I had a flight to catch."

"And you couldn't wake me before you left?"

"Like you did me the other two times we were together?" I bite back.

"That night—after the wedding" he whispers. "It was different. The next morning, I woke up alone. You weren't there. I didn't like it."

"Call it karma. You set the rules—I was merely playing by them."

That night, the connection between us ran deeper than I'd ever believed possible. That's why I was convinced it was the night I conceived. I just hadn't realised he'd felt those emotions too. I wasn't sure he was capable.

"Is that why you were so mad when you got back to L.A.? Maeve said you were being a tad tetchier than usual."

"She did, did she?" His tone is terse, but I can sense his underlying amusement, probably at the description he knows I've dumbed down.

I decide to push my luck a little further. "I'm surprised she could tell the difference actually. I think you're more than a tad disagreeable even on a normal day."

This time I get a snort of mirth, then a moment's silence before he drops his voice thoughtfully, "You know you're the first woman that's ever run out on me."

"Try sprinted," I joke.

"I didn't like it." He repeats slowly.

"What are you saying? I'm not psychic."

"I think you've made that abundantly clear." He rolls onto his side so he is facing me, nudging me so I tilt my head to look at him. "So I guess I'm going to have to be crystal clear going forward."

"Hit me," I giggle.

"You and I will be getting married. You will be moving to L.A. so we can raise our son together as a family surrounded by our friends, and I will have to let your brother take a shot at me for his ill-conceived notion that I seduced you and stole your innocence. Which by the way, I know was taken a long time ago by Toby Macnamara in his parent's bed, when he pretended to be sick so they'd go visit his grandparents without him."

"You did seduce me, and I don't even want to think about how you know about Toby. You're right, we will be raising our daughter together. But, I won't be moving to L.A. when I have a job that I need here in New York. Nor will we be getting married. I'm not going to marry you just because you've suddenly decided it suits you. When I get married it's going to be out of love, not obligation. You. You never spend the night with the same woman more than once. Hell, half the time you don't even bother to ask their name."

"Yes I do."

"Name one."

"Tina Marie Collins," he says with a smirk. "And last count I spent four nights with her."

"Three," I correct him.

"Four," he corrects smoothly. "Since you lured me back here to ruin you all over again, it'd be rude not to oblige"

That smug smile. That maddening certainty. I open my mouth to toss something sharp back at him—some clever jab about him being delusional or ego-drunk—but the words don't come.

Because for a split second, I'm not thinking about his arrogance or his warped sense of how he believes our future will play out. I'm remembering that night. The weight of his body on mine. The way he'd looked at me, like I wasn't just some passing distraction.

And now here he is, lying beside me like he belongs, talking about marriage, about wanting to be a part of our baby's life, like he means it.

He can't possibly mean it.

Can he?

I swallow the lump rising in my throat and mutter, "You're impossible."

"Only for everyone else," he says, softer now. "For you, I'll be inevitable. I will get what I want. In fact, you'll be the one proposing to me."

"Dream on." I chuckle.

He squeezes my hand and it sends a surge of electricity up my arm where it spreads slowly across my body, firing up every nerve ending within me.

"How's the pregnancy been on you? What have I missed?"

"Not much, considering I didn't even realise I was expecting until a couple of weeks ago. I've had slight nausea at wildly inappropriate moments, I'm exhausted pretty much all the damn time, and my boobs have taken on a life of their own. I've gone up three cup sizes."

"I had noticed." He quips. "Are they sore?"

"Not really."

"Shame. I was going to offer to kiss them better."

My body shivers involuntarily.

"You know, Josh says Maeve's turned into a nymphomaniac since she hit her second trimester. How are you faring in that department?" He delivers the line so seriously it takes everything in me not to burst out laughing again.

"It's not a problem I appear to be having at the moment," I smirk, rolling onto my side so we're facing each other. The air between us thickens.

"If it does become an issue, how do you plan on handling it? Because I'm not exactly thrilled with the idea of you sleeping with anyone else while you're pregnant with *my* baby. Might give him PTSS. He's probably already riddled with anxiety thanks to that ridiculous nickname you've saddled him with."

I giggle despite myself. "Guess I'll have to cross that bridge if and when I get to it. I can take care of things myself if necessary."

"Hmm, I'm not sure that would be a good idea. You've already told me you're exhausted pretty much all of the time. I think you should let me take the strain."

"Excuse me?" I'm almost certain I know what he's implying, but until he says the words out loud, I'm not sure I'll believe him.

He doesn't blink. Doesn't miss a beat. "I'm saying, you should let me help you out. If there's a job going—especially one that involves your pleasure—I'm more than qualified for the position."

"You want to be my sex slave?" I'm full on laughing now. I just can't help myself. "Can I get that in writing?"

"Maybe." He bestows me with a rare thing. A cheeky grin that lights up his face making it even more handsome. "But only on the understanding that we're mutually exclusive, at least until after the birth. Then we'll review the situation."

"You're serious, aren't you?" I widen my eyes in surprise. I'd expected him to demand I stay away from other men, but hadn't anticipated his offer to fill the void. I've no intention on seeing anyone, Nugget comes first right now, but that doesn't mean I can't have some fun at his expense. "What if I get the urge and I'm at work?"

"I'll come to your office and we'll find an empty stock room." He gently pushes a stray strand of hair behind my ear. It's a subtle gesture that ramps up the tension between us. Especially when his touch lingers, his fingers gently tracing the contours of my face, my neck, and then my shoulder, before skilfully gliding down my arm leaving a trail of fire in their wake.

My brain misfires and I lose my train of thought. "I'll think about it." Is the best I can come up with.

"I understand," Kurt smirks, inching nearer.

"You need to perform a practical assessment before you make your decision. Make sure I'm able to cover all the positions you need me to."

"Positions?"

"As you get bigger, we'll need to get creative. Luckily for you I have an extensive repertoire," he deadpans. "I'll provide a demonstration now and you can evaluate me. But I'd appreciate it if you could keep the noise down. I'd prefer not to have your brother impeding my performance."

I open my mouth to respond, but the action is construed as an invitation. Kurt's lips crash down on mine, stealing both my breath and the words I hadn't yet found. It's not long before we're both naked and any sheets between us have been discarded.

What starts as a slow and gentle tease, soon descends into a passionate encounter fuelled by unyielding desire spiralling out of control. I'm desperate and almost begging by the time Kurt decides to put me out of my misery. I hook my legs around his hips urging him forward, but just as he is about to give me what I need, he stops cold.

"What?" I pant.

He locks eyes with me to make sure he has my full attention. "Should I wrap it?"

"I think that ship's sailed, don't you?" I say impatiently, tightening my legs around him, prompting him to finish what he started. He doesn't move.

"I've never gone bare before... not once... with anyone," He murmurs.

"Ooh, another first for me," I quip—only to be met with a flat, unflinching stare that dares me to keep talking.

"I didn't want to presume. And I need you to know that Josh insists everyone at the firm undergo a full work-up every six months. Because of what we do, he needs to be sure we're all in optimum mental and physical health before sending us out into the field. I had my check up two weeks ago and I've not been with anyone since. I'm clean."

For what I'd bet is the first time in his life, he almost looks vulnerable. I reach up and gently stroke the back of his head, tracing slow, soothing circles across his scalp—my way of letting him know I've heard him, and that I understand.

"I've been poked, prodded and tested like you wouldn't believe since the pregnancy was confirmed. There's been no-one else. I'm good to go," I whisper.

He jerks his head in acknowledgement before looking at me with such tenderness it makes my heart weep. He leans down and kisses me, not with urgency, but with the kind of care that says he's in no rush to be anywhere else. It's a kiss meant to be felt—not just on the lips, but everywhere. He lines himself up again, releasing my lips so he can rest his forehead on mine.

"Fuck," he moans as he pushes inside me. "You feel…"

His words die as he kisses me again, but what follows is a night so perfect I'm sure I'll wake to find it was only a dream. The hours stretch long and tender, wrapped in warmth, filled with passion, and surrounded by the quiet certainty that somehow, in all this chaos, we've found home in each other. If only for a short while.

The morning arrives far too quickly—though technically, the day's already begun by the time Kurt and I fall asleep, still tangled in a mess of limbs. A sharp knock on the bedroom door jolts us both. I freeze, knowing exactly who's outside and what he's discovered. Kurt feels me tense and kisses my forehead as I call out, "Liam? Is that you? What's wrong?"

"Kurt better not be in there with you," Liam growls through the door.

I'm about to answer when Kurt beats me to it. "He's not," he says, attempting to mimic my voice —though it still sounds unmistakably like him.

I groan and elbow him in the ribs. "Why did you have to do that? It's too early for you two to be at each other's throats."

"Kurt. Get your ass out here now!" Liam bellows.

"Go away! You're stressing out my pregnant girlfriend!" Kurt fires back, completely unapologetic.

"I'm not your girlfriend," I mumble sleepily.

"Um, yes you are," he says without missing a beat. "We're sleeping together and have agreed to stop seeing other people. What would you call that?"

"Mutually exclusive fuck buddies," I reply. "Besides, I only remember you *auditioning* for the role of sex slave, I'm pretty sure I never actually agreed to give you the job, let alone consider you for a promotion."

"Well, you did."

"When?"

"Just before you came on my cock for the second time last night."

"Oh," I mumble. I don't have much of a defence —even if I don't remember it, it's probably true. At that point, I'd have agreed to just about anything.

"Kurt. I'm gonna count to three and come in. You'd better be fully clothed and nowhere near my sister."

"For fuck's sake," Kurt snaps. "I'm marrying into a family of loonies."

"We are not getting married!" I retort, stunned

he's still clinging to that ridiculous plan. I was sure he'd come to his senses by now.

He gently untangles us, making sure I'm covered, then storms across the room—unabashedly naked—and yanks the door open. "This ends now!" he bellows, glaring at my brother. "I won't have you upsetting Tina while she's pregnant."

"Fine!" Liam snarls. "Put something on, and we'll finish this."

"Why do I have to get dressed first? The size of my dick intimidating you?" Kurt slams the door and begins rifling through the mess of clothes on the floor, swearing the whole time. He's like a category five hurricane tearing through the room—but I'm not afraid. Not for me. Just for my family.

"Please don't hurt my brother," I whisper, trying not to laugh as he nearly topples over while wrestling with his boxers.

"He's not some delicate flower," Kurt snaps. "He can handle himself. Funny how you never seem that concerned about me."

"You've got skills he doesn't," I reply. "It wouldn't be a fair fight, and you know it. He's a mechanic—not a former SEAL with combat-honed reflexes and years of tactical training under his belt. He fixes engines. You spent over a decade learning how to take people apart."

Kurt exhales and sinks onto the bed beside me. "Liam'll be fine. I'll let him take his shot, then I'll hand him a reality check. What happens after that—I can't say. But this I can promise you, we'll both walk back in one piece. And afterward, your brother? He'll know exactly where I stand—so we can put all this ridiculous posturing to rest."

He lays a hand gently over the covers on my belly. "Whether he likes it or not, you're having my baby—and I will be in my son's life. In yours too... when I finally decide to accept one of your proposals."

"Oh, so now I'm not only going to propose, but I'm doing it more than once?" I ask, incredulous.

Kurt ignores both my tone and my words, though I'm almost certain I catch a flicker of a smirk. "Liam's a good guy, and I respect him for looking out for you, but he can either accept the reality, or get run over by it. He'll come around. I just need to convince you both I'm not the surly, hard-hearted womaniser you think I am. Not anymore."

"Good luck with that," I challenge.

He leans in and brushes a soft kiss over my lips, removing his hand from my stomach to dip his fingers beneath the sheet splayed across my chest. He cups one of my boobs and gently starts massaging it. Just as I let out a soft moan of anticipation—Liam starts pounding on the door again.

"What's taking you so long?" Liam shouts, fury rising.

"Christ." Kurt murmurs the word against my lips, smiling. Then, yells: "I'm coming!" Before winking at me and dropping his voice once more, "and not in a good way. We'll pick up where we left off later.

He stalks out of the room, leaving me both turned on and terrified. My body's on fire, wired by the promise he didn't need to say out loud. But my mind's racing, conjuring every possible version of the confrontation I know is inevitable—and unfolding just a few feet away.

I scramble out of bed, throw on yesterday's clothes (half of which are inside-out), and dash to the living room... only to find both men have vanished.

Following them would mean leaving my apartment wide open. I might as well roll out a welcome mat that says *Come in and rob me, I'm feeling festive*, since Liam still hasn't fixed the front door. So instead, I curse both of them—loudly and creatively—before apologising to Nugget for the unexpected profanity.

The irony is completely lost on them: they've stormed off to knock five bells out of each other in my honour, yet somehow failed to provide the bare minimum of protection against strangers. You'd think after all the head-butting, their chivalry would extend to basic home security. Apparently not.

I plonk myself down on the couch, hoping they'll sort out their differences quickly and return—preferably in one piece and still on speaking terms—so we can spend Christmas Eve in something vaguely resembling harmony. My knee bounces like it's trying to escape, and I check my watch every few seconds as I wait.

And wait.

And wait.

Chapter 5

Seven hours.

That's how long I stew—worried out of my mind—until the pair of them swagger back through the hole where my door used to be, laughing and joking as if the discord of the past twenty-four hours never happened.

Kurt has a fist-shaped bruise blooming on his jaw and a ripped shirt. Liam's sporting a split lip and walking with a slight limp. But instead of offering answers—or, I don't know, any kind of apology for abandoning me and scaring me witless—Liam tosses out a flippant "It's sorted," while Kurt adds an eye-roll, an amused smirk, and a snarky "I'm on probation."

Furious at their lack of empathy and entirely unsatisfied, with seemingly no hope of garnering any further information, I send them both to Coventry. Again.

Thanks to a case I helped Robert out on a few months ago, I already know minors can legally emancipate from their parents, so I take to the internet to see whether thoroughly peeved sisters can do the same with their idiot brothers. When the answer turns out to be no, I make a mental note to bring it up with Steven at work—to see if there's anything else suitably contrary I can do. If not, maybe I can start some sort of campaign to amend the Bill of Rights or something—whatever it takes to bring long-overdue justice to aggrieved little sisters everywhere.

As far as Kurt's concerned, I make it quite clear he's sleeping on the couch tonight, much to Liam's amusement. I also privately rescind the job offer I can't recall making—in writing, no less, since we're no longer on speaking terms—by scribbling *you're fired* on a napkin and slapping it on his chest just as he moves in for something that looks suspiciously like a cuddle. Although realistically, I know my mind must be playing tricks on me. PDA has never once featured on his radar with any of his past hook-ups—so why break the pattern for me?

While Liam finally gets around to repairing the damage he caused breaking into my apartment—unapologetically whistling, as if kicking down a door is a perfectly acceptable means of entry under any circumstance—Kurt and I go shopping. Not that my presence is really required. I mostly trail behind him like a reluctant duckling while he plays domestic god, piling our basket high with vibrant produce like we're starring in some sun-drenched advert for contented couples.

Then come the bribes: my favourite flowers, my go-to chocolate—placed gently in the cart with a wink and a smile, peace offerings wrapped in cellophane and cocoa. Romantic? Maybe. Sweet? Almost. But I know Kurt too well to mistake it for anything deeper than a tactical manoeuvre. Charming, yes. Transparent? Even more so. And no—I'm not biting.

Not even when he showcases the muscles I know far too well, swinging the many heavy bags in one arm while surreptitiously reaching for my hand with the other. I let him take it—not because I want him to, and certainly not because the way our fingers entwine lights up a warm glow in my stomach. I tell myself It's a test of his resolve. A push to see if he'll step outside his comfort zone... for me. Not because I want this. Not because I need this right now. Just—because I don't want to seem petty. That's all. When he holds it like it's something precious, coveting it like he's never going to be ready to let it go, he surprises me. As his thumb ghosts over the back of my hand tenderly, I almost start believing in the dream he wants more than just the baby growing inside me.

Back home, he surprises both Liam and me with a perfectly presented pasta dish for tea. I lean on the doorjamb, watching him swan around the kitchen in the apron I bought and never wore —expertly wielding the knives purchased more for show than practicality, brandishing a wooden spoon like it's some kind of magic wand. I can't tear my eyes away. He moves like he belongs there —as if he's my own personal chef. And he knows it —offering me the occasional soft smile or a wink as he chops and stirs like a master.

My brother and I are stunned by the quality of the food Kurt effortlessly whips up—our curious glances shifting to shell-shocked awe with the first forkful. The flavours meld and burst in our mouths, drawing soft hums of surprise and delight. It's so pleasurable, so unlike anything I'm used to, I feel almost untethered—like I'm having some bizarre, out-of-body experience. I briefly wonder if maybe, it's not just the food that is messing with my head.

As I savour the first bite, the words slip out, unintended and without thought. "You'll make someone a great husband one day," I muse aloud. Liam nods in agreement, too immersed in his mouthful to respond properly.

"Is that your first proposal?" Kurt asks, arching an eyebrow with faux solemnity.

"What? No!" I bluster, while he smirks and Liam chuckles into his plate.

Later, the men vanish into the bedroom, touching up Liam's rather patchy paint job, before dragging me back into conversation by stubbornly rearranging the furniture under my watchful eye. They switch out the boxes Izzy and I had already packed, determined to get everything *just right*—although I suspect it's more of a ruse to keep me talking.

The day passes faster than expected, and before long I'm spent. I'd hoped to make the place feel a little more festive, maybe even pick up a tree now that I wasn't spending Christmas alone. But my energy's depleted, so I head to bed early, leaving the guys sprawled across the sofa, watching crime dramas and setting the world to rights over a few beers.

You'd think that after spending most of his adult life taking orders—where failure to follow instructions could result in his immediate demise—Kurt might have respected my very clear directive to spend the night on the couch.

And yet, sometime in the small hours, I feel the warmth of a body curling in behind me, spooning close. As a large hand slips over my hip to rest protectively on my stomach, I lie still, feigning sleep, pretending not to notice. Because I know if I acknowledge it, I'll have to acknowledge him. And admit to the fact that I'm all too willing to go back on my word just to keep him close.

Besides, having him here, like this, gentle and attentive, feels less like a breach of boundaries and more like the universe offering me a gift I'd be a fool to refuse.

A gift that keeps on giving, apparently—because

on Christmas morning, I wake to the hazy shock that what I'd taken for an erotic dream is, in fact, stone-cold reality: Kurt, in Liam's discarded Santa hat, with his head buried between my thighs, driving me to the brink of the most decadent, dizzying pleasure I've ever known. Just as I'm about to reach the pinnacle of bliss, he stops to look up at me. When I grab his head desperately trying to force it back to where I need it the most, he chuckles. The soft vibration flowing through my body like a caress determined to ramp up the tension already coiled within me.

"Can I have my old job back?" He murmurs, kissing me softly...there!

"Gah!" I moan, torn, tormented, and dangerously close to agreeing to anything as I try to writhe against him seeking relief.

A flick of his tongue is all it takes for me to surrender completely.

"Yes!" I scream.

Kurt just smiles, wry and satisfied, pressing his lips exactly where I need him to—sending me spiralling into an abyss of ecstasy, the single word of affirmation tumbling from my lips like a mantra until I'm sated.

As I float down from my high, I'm vaguely aware of Kurt planting a kiss on my forehead, warm and feather-light. "Merry Christmas," he chuckles. "I'll go make you some breakfast."

I manage little more than a contented sigh before flipping over, snuggling into a pillow, and drifting back off to sleep once more.

One woman's heaven turns out to be another man's hell. When I eventually drag myself out of bed sometime later to join Kurt in the kitchen, my brother is no-where to be seen.

"Where's Liam?" I ask absentmindedly, trying to steal the mug of coffee Kurt is gripping with all his might.

"Decaf for you," he reprimands, while nodding to some paper pinned to the fridge next to Nuggets picture. I rub the sleep from my eyes as they try to focus on the words scrawled in familiar handwriting.

I've gone for a walk. A long one! I know how babies are made—I don't need an auditory reminder—especially from my little sister. I'd like some noise cancelling headphones for Christmas please and if I've left it too late to ask for new ones, just leave yours on the bed, second hand is fine.

"Shit," I mutter as Kurt sidles up behind me, handing me my own freshly brewed cup of Joe. He slides his arms around my waist, chuckling, as he bends to nibble my neck.

"You know," he murmurs, "the note says a *long* walk."

I smile, leaning into his touch. "I thought *you*

were supposed to be at *my* beck and call. Not the other way around."

"Thought I'd get a head start, since I need to go back to L.A. the day after tomorrow."

The words hit me like ice water. I don't mean to tense—but I can't help it. I knew this moment would come. The dream life I'd been building in my head, crumbling. I thought I'd at least have until after New Year's before it collapsed. "Oh," I murmur, slipping out of his arms. No point torturing myself with promises of what can never be. The longer we keep pretending, the harder it'll be on both of us.

"Hey. I'll be back," Kurt says gently, sensing my mood shift. He steps in front of me and lifts my chin, forcing eye contact.

"I know," I whisper. He will be—but when? That's anyone's guess. And asking for a specific date? With the kind of work he does, that's only setting myself up for disappointment.

"Come with me," he says suddenly, like the idea alone might fix everything. "You can catch up with Maeve."

"I can't. I'm due back at work the day you leave," I try to sound upbeat.

"Take some vacation."

"It's not a good time."

"Why not?"

"Because things are really crazy right now."

"Even more reason to take a break. I don't want you getting stressed out or overdoing it—it's not good for the baby. You've got to take better care of yourself."

"I'll be fine," I snap. I hate that his concern seems aimed solely at the baby. I try to pull away, but his lips crash down on mine—and just like that, I'm a goner. Jerk.

When I'm suitably relaxed, my body melting into his, Kurt pulls back—just enough to keep me nestled close. My cheek rests sideways against the safety of his broad chest, his steady heartbeat grounding me. Almost lulling me into a trance so peaceful, I'm afraid I'll never want to wake.

"Why are things so crazy?" he asks softly, stroking down my spine to keep me languid.

"We've a huge trial underway. I've been temporarily promoted to executive assistant for the lead attorney." I pause, pressing my fingers into his shirt. "My boss has been great about giving me time off when I've needed it, but I don't want to push my luck. He offered me the position before he found out I was pregnant and I'm grateful he let me keep it after I came clean. This gig pays way better than my old job, and I need to bolster my savings before I go on maternity leave considering I want to take a few months off after the birth."

"How much better?"

"About 30k a year." Kurt lets out a low whistle. "Why'd they pick you?"

I have a sneaking suspicion it's because I snogged my married boss and now he either feels guilty—or he's nursing a crush. But instead of poking the bear, I shrug and go with the safer answer: "I like to think it's because I'm good at my job—not just because he pitied the single woman barely holding it together, scared witless about becoming a first-time mom."

Kurt bristles slightly, then hums thoughtfully into the top of my head. "Hmm."

"What's that supposed to mean?" I tip my face up, frowning at him.

Whatever thoughts he's harbouring, he's not inclined to share them. When he catches me watching him, his expression shifts—and so does the subject.

"I've got to head back and check in with Josh about a few things," he says, smiling down at me.

"And see Katrina?" I try not to balk at the words. Maybe Maeve was wrong about him being smitten. Maybe she was just the last in the long line that came before her. My heart sinks when he answers—casually, as if it's nothing

"Yeah, Kat too. We were heading out to lunch when Liam showed, throwing the other proverbial cat amongst the pigeons. I owe her an apology...

and an explanation for bailing on her. He shrugs, then adds, "But I need to see Josh more urgently—he's got too much on his plate right now. He's been trying to take a step back from the business since he found out Maeve's expecting. Decided he needs to stick to her like Velcro. The timings not great since he's still getting the firm established. We need to hire some more people to keep up with the demand. You wouldn't believe how many frightened people are out there needing the kind of help we can provide. Me suddenly skipping town didn't help his cause, though I'm sure Maeve's grateful. I think he's driving her crazy following her around 24/7 and she could use a little break from him." He chuckles, but I'm not laughing. I force a smile anyway—because that's what you do when you're not the one being stuck to like Velcro and arguing would make me look exactly as fragile as I feel.

"Hey! Please tell me you're both decent," Liam yells, stepping back in the front door. 'It's so cold out there, I swear I just saw a penguin flipping off the wind."

"I'm gonna jump in the shower," I tell Kurt as Liam appears, still bundled in his coat and blowing into his hands. I pass my brother my half-empty mug, the remaining coffee still warm. He grips it with both hands like it's a lifeline.

"Need any help?" Kurt calls after me, his tone unmistakably suggestive.

"Nah, I'll be fine." I don't turn. I don't want him to see the tears sparking in my eyes, the mess hiding behind my smile. I need to put some distance between us. Take some time to get ahold of my emotions. "You can practice your culinary skills again," I say with feigned enthusiasm. "Start prepping dinner for later. Nugget wants the full works—she expects all the trimmings."

"You got it," he calls back. If he is disappointed, he doesn't let it show.

Right after him there's a snort and bemused, "Who the everlasting fuck is Nugget?"

"From now on you say duck instead of dropping the F-bomb. I don't want you swearing around my kid." Kurt replies tersely.

Then, an incredulous snigger and, "Dude, who the *duck* are you? You're *ducking* quackers!"

I can't help a reluctant smile as I hear Kurt snap, "Better. Although you can lose the sarcasm or you and me, we're going to have another problem!"

Chapter 6

The next two days are a confusing mix of emotions. Kurt is the picture-perfect expectant father, trailing after me wherever I go, fussing as if I'm about to go into labour—when I've only just entered my second trimester. He feeds me constantly—healthy, nutritious meals prepared by his own two hands—and takes care of all the housework. All I have to do is say 'jump,' and he'll ask 'how high?' without missing a beat — even if his willing response is delivered with the usual grumpy disposition he carries off so well. He refuses to let me lift a finger, insisting I keep my feet up and relax so I can focus on nurturing his heir.

It's baffling, honestly. Liam finds the whole thing hilarious and keeps daring me to request increasingly ridiculous things, just to test how far Kurt will go to keep me happy. I know I shouldn't indulge in such mischievous schemes—but seeing a man like Kurt, someone who never yields to anyone, completely at my mercy? It's a novelty that's fast becoming an addiction.

As lovely as it is to feel like the centre of his world, I'm a realist. I've not forgotten he's on 'probation' with my brother, which means he is probably just trying to stay in Liam's good graces, and I know this tender devotion has an expiration date. He's still leaving. And with my emotions in a state of constant flux, I'm afraid it's going to hurt more than it should when he does. Keeping up a charade short-term is easy enough for anyone. However, if he were to stick around, I'm sure cracks in this new and unexpected persona would begin to appear. Maybe then I could start weaning myself off him slowly—I'm sure at some point my heart would be willing to let him go.

For now, I've drawn boundaries—to protect myself. I repeatedly dodge his amorous advances, even though he makes resisting a nearly impossible task. Excuses are easier to find throughout the day, but every night my willpower is pushed to its limit. Despite my feeble protests, he wraps himself around me, his muscular, naked body a protective barrier—against what, I don't even know. It feels too good. Safe. But also... almost like a lie. Because I know when he leaves, Nugget and I will be left to navigate life alone again, with no shield, no promises—it'll be just the two of us, left to figure out the way forward as best we can.

In the early hours of the 27th, I'm woken by a series of feather-light kisses across my face. As my eyes flutter open, I see Kurt fully dressed, leaning over me as he sits beside me on the bed.

"What's up?" I croak sleepily.

"Nothing," he whispers, brushing a few loose strands of hair away from my face. "I have to go. I didn't want to leave without saying goodbye."

Not fully awake, my brain doesn't censor the retort as it slips from my lips: "Makes a change."

His features barely flicker. He stares at me for a few moments before murmuring, "I *will* be back."

"I know," I reply evenly, with about the same level of enthusiasm I gave the last time he uttered those same words.

As my eyes crash shut again, I feel one final kiss pressed to my forehead. Then there's nothing but silence, and the expectant dread of waking up alone. And a little afraid. Afraid that without him to lean on, I'm going to fail spectacularly at this game called life. One which feels like a round of Russian roulette—played with nothing but the loaded expectations of my impending motherhood.

"He'll call," Liam throws an arm over my shoulders, tugging me into a sideways hug as he plonks himself onto the sofa beside me.

"Who?" I try to sound impassive but I'm fooling no-one.

Liam gives me 'the look,' "He'll call."

"It's been three days."

"He might be away on a job. He told you how much work Josh has on, right?"

"Mmhmm."

"Well then." Liam gives me a squeeze. "He still found the time to have all those groceries delivered for you, and he sent me a list of easy to prepare meals to make sure you are eating properly."

"Wait," I blink at him, momentarily stunned before shrugging out of my brothers hold. "He messaged you?"

Liam averts his gaze knowing he has inadvertently said the wrong thing.

"Liam?" I warn as I stand, hovering over him, trying to look intimidating.

"Uh huh," Liam murmurs sheepishly.

"When did he message you?"

"This morning," There's something in his tone that makes me think I'm not getting the whole story. I kick him in the shin and glare at him until he gives me what I need, "and yesterday." More glaring. "Maybe the day before that, too."

"So. You're telling me he has been in contact with you every day since he left, but he couldn't find the time to pick up the phone and speak to me once."

"Um."

I don't hang around to hear Liam's excuses. I don't want to fall out with my brother when, ultimately, he isn't the problem. The problem's mine. I should've known better than to let myself get swept up in some romantic pipedream.

Heading to the bathroom, I lean against the sink, the sting of disappointment sharp in my chest. I should've seen it coming. Once Kurt got back to L.A. and his life there, checking in on me would be just another box ticked off of his to-do list.

Liam's heading back to Vermont after New Year's. Working in a garage owned by our parents meant he was able to take a little extra time off to spend the holidays here with me, but with our parents away he needs to get back. Prove to Dad he's responsible. Capable. Ready to take over when the old man retires. I don't want us to spend our last days together fighting. I've missed him too much for us to part on bad terms. Plus, Nugget needs him. She needs a solid male role model in her life, someone she can rely on.

As I sit on the edge of the bath waiting for it to fill, my mobile starts to ring. Kurt's name glares up from the screen. My thumb hovers, then I swipe to reject the call. My chest tightens—not with joy, or curiosity, just the jagged throb of disappointment. It's obvious Liam gave him a nudge. If Kurt can't be bothered to call me of his own free will, I can't be bothered to answer.

The phone rings again a few seconds later. I stab decline and switch it off entirely. Stubborn as hell, I know Kurt. He won't quit until I cave. But tonight? I'm not in the mood to deal with him.

Work was chaos this week. Steven reluctantly granted me New Year's Eve off so I could squeeze in an extra full day with Liam before he flies out. I ran myself ragged making sure everything was in order before I left.

As the bubbles in the bath water nudge the brim, steam curls lazily upward, fogging the mirror and softening the sharp lines of the cramped bathroom. The scent of lavender and sandalwood lingers in the air — heady, but soothing. I test the water with my fingers, it's warm and inviting. The soft bubbles rich, frothy and everything I've earned after the mess of this week.

I twist off the taps, tug at the hem of my jumper, and just as I'm about to undress there's a sharp knock at the door.

"Um… Tina?" Liam's voice filters through the closed door, muffled and hesitant. "I've got Kurt on the phone. He says he couldn't get through on your number and he wants to speak to you."

I roll my eyes and smirk. Not many people have

the gall to cut Kurt off, and doing so has likely ignited his inner tyrant. "Now's not a good time," I sing through the door. "I'm just about to get in the bath."

There's a pause before I hear Liam's voice again, strained and clearly repeating me: "Yeah, she says... What? No, I'm not doing that!"

There's a few muffled curses, then another knock.

I shuffle back from the door so it's not obvious I've been eavesdropping. "Yeah?"

"You... decent?" Liam calls. His embarrassment drips through every syllable. "Kurt wants me to check a few things before you get in the water."

"No, I'm naked," I lie with theatrical flair. If Liam opens that door, he'll dump the phone in my hand and vanish, pretending Kurt isn't barking threats at him. Where's the fun in that? "What does he need to know?"

I hear Liam sigh. One of those long, tired ones that say he's regretting his entire life. Then:

"Right. He says don't use that fancy-smelling, soapy stuff that makes all those bubbles. You're to use Fragrance-free only as your skin might be sensitive from the hormonal changes. And you need a bath mat. So you don't slip. Because he's not here to help you."

I bite my lip to hold back a giggle. "Is that all?"

"I *wish* it were," Liam mutters. His voice flattens, like he's reading from a tragic screenplay. "The water temperature needs to be between thirty-seven and thirty-eight degrees Celsius. And you're not supposed to be in longer than fifteen minutes." He pauses. "I'm meant to set a timer."

"Oh, well you can report back: I have an abundance of sweet-smelling bubbles, zero bath mat, a broken thermometer, and absolutely no intention of getting out before I'm good and pruney. Also, I don't give a flying duck what Kurt thinks about it."

"You wouldn't want to… tell him that yourself?"

"Nope."

A sudden, shrill screech shreds the moment. The buildings fire alarm.

"Shit!" Liam yells through the door. "Tina — we need to get out!"

I don't question him. Maeve almost died in a house fire years ago. The memories of that night haunt me as I throw open the bathroom door. Liam ends his call with Kurt and glares at me —still fully dressed —before grabbing my hand, leading me out of the building where residents are already gathering on the street, shivering and cranky. The cold evening air bites at us, and Liam wraps a blanket he grabbed from the back of the couch around me and Nugget.

There's a lot of murmurs and whispering as everyone stares up the building. With the absence of any smoke or flames it's hard to imagine where the fire is originating from. A fire engine pulls up to the curb, klaxons wailing. Three men and two women jump out. Four gear up and head inside the building while the fifth pushes us all back and out of harms way.

"Eight B." One of the men yells as he disappears.

Liam and I stare at each other perplexed.

"Eight B? That's my apartment." I say confused. "We didn't have a fire, I need to let them know they're heading to the wrong location."

"I'll go," Liam tells me, as he starts pushing his way through the throng to the front. "Wait here, I don't want you getting squished."

Twenty minutes later everyone is making their way back inside when I pass by the building's super.

"What was the problem?" I ask as he wraps up his conversation with the fire chief.

"False alarm," he replies gravely. "There was some kind of systems failure or electrical fault that triggered the sensors outside of your apartment. I'll have to get someone in to check out the wiring, run diagnostics to make sure it doesn't happen again."

I nod in relief and continue on my way,

following Liam back to my apartment. "That water should still be good; I'm going to jump in the bath to warm up." I tell Liam as I slip past.

When I head into the bathroom, I'm surprised to see the tub has been drained.

"Liam?" I scream and my brother comes running.

"'Sup?"

"Where's the tap?" I point to the void where the hot water faucet should be.

"How the f... duck should I know?" He looks at me bewildered as he is alerted to a new message on his mobile. Pulling out his cell he announces "It's from Kurt," before he reads the message and turns the screen toward me. Fourteen little words precede a flood of laughing emojis...

Tell your sister to enjoy her bath!
If she wants to play... Game on!

As my shock gives way to anger Liam begs a hasty retreat, "Perhaps I'll make us some hot cocoa to warm us up instead."

"How? How did he do it?" I yell, storming after my brother.

"Do what?" He has his back to me but I'm sure from his tone he is stifling a laugh.

"Set off the alarm. Cut off my hot water." I growl. "And I'm sure my bubble bath was missing."

Liam turns and shrugs, almost in awe, "I don't know for sure, but I do know Josh has a guy at his firm who is a pretty skilled cybersecurity expert. I bet it wouldn't be a stretch for him to hack the system to set off the alarm. As for the tap, he must have either called in a favour or paid someone to sneak in and steal it after we evacuated."

"You're joking?" I look at Liam incredulously. "Surely that's illegal."

Liam shrugs again, trying to mask the slight smirk he's sporting by dragging his hand across his lips. "I have to say he is taking his new responsibilities seriously. I never thought I'd see the day that man was brought to his knees by a woman."

"I know I keep referring to Nugget as 'she', but 'she' *might* turn out to be a 'he'." I reply, assuming he is referring to the cargo I'm carrying.

"I wasn't talking about the baby." Liam gazes at me softly. "He's in love with you… you know that, right?"

I roll my eyes so hard they nearly do a backflip. "Harrumph." I snort unimpressed. Not sticking around for an emotional ambush, I stomp off to shower. We don't mention Kurt again for the rest of the evening. Liam stages a mutiny against the orders I'm sure he was given by ordering in a pizza, a subtle peace offering to cheer me up and make sure he is firmly back in my good graces. Then, while carb-loading like reckless athletes, we bicker over the remote like we used to when we were kids. It's a championship bout and the most fun we've had together in ages. I head off to bed so happy and relaxed I'm asleep almost the moment I lie down.

It's a high pitched scream that wakes me in the early hours of the morning. Leaping out of bed I sprint across the hall and snap on the light in the second bedroom to find a near naked Izzy beating my laughing brother around the head with a pillow.

"Iz?" I cry as I rub the sleep from my eyes, "What are you doing here?"

Izzy stops pummelling Liam who reclines back in the bed smirking like a cat that has had the cream.

"I didn't want you to be alone on New Year's," she pants. Her heavy breathing a testament to the force behind her blows. Not that Liam seems overly affected. Her eyes skate scathingly over my brother's arms. "I take it from the lack of tattoos you're 'the brother'?" She addresses Liam like a schoolteacher reprimanding a naughty child.

"Guilty." Liam answers like an unrepentant man facing the gallows.

I look between my brother's smug grin and Izzy's thunderous glare.

"What's going on?"

Izzy looks across at me, a rosy hue on her cheeks.

"When you messaged to say Kurt had left, I assumed your brother had gone too so I hightailed it back here so you wouldn't be alone for New Years. When I cracked open the door of your old room and saw you sleeping soundly, I came in here, stripped off and climbed into bed assuming it would be empty. I didn't bother with the light." She pauses momentarily to glare at Liam before continuing, "Let's just say I got a bit of a shock when I rolled over, crashing into a naked man."

Izzy glares at Liam again who bursts out laughing.

"Wait. If you were in the dark, how did you know it was a naked man?" I ask frowning.

Izzy puts her hands on her hips and raises her eyebrows at me while she waits for my still dozy brain to catch up.

"Eww." My face scrunches up as I try not to imagine how they inadvertently connected. Some mental images should never be born. I blink hard, hoping to erase the horror unfolding behind my retinas. "Liam you need to shift to the couch."

"Forget it." Izzy grabs the pillow she was using as a weapon, clutching it to her chest like a barricade. "You stay here, I'll take the sofa."

Liam smirks throwing back the covers beside him, an unsubtle attempt at seduction, "No need, there's plenty of room for two."

"In your dreams," Izzy blusters wide eyed.

"You will be." Liam counters with a smile before moving to slip out of bed. "I'll take the couch."

"Whoa!" I exclaim. "At least wait until your baby sister has left the room, she doesn't need to see 'little Liam' it could scar her for life."

"Right." My brother freezes.

"Wasn't *that* little," Izzy whispers, a flicker of begrudging admiration betraying her embarrassment. As Liam grins and tosses her a wink, she grabs a blanket from the foot of the bed, muttering, "Seriously. I'll sleep in the living room tonight, and you..."—she jabs a finger at Liam—"...can wash those sheets tomorrow." She turns to leave—and promptly stubs her toe on the edge of the dresser. "Ow!" she yelps, hopping on one foot before whacking Liam one last time with her pillow. "This is all your fault."

Liam barely flinches, fielding the blow with his arm as Izzy groans.

"Totally worth it," he laughs, earning himself a middle finger from Izzy. He opens his mouth, ready to sling another witty retort, but snaps it shut when I shoot him a warning glance.

I take Izzy's arm and lead her out of the room. She limps beside me in mock injury, her dignity trailing somewhere behind her. "I'm sorry, Iz," I mutter. "I wasn't expecting you back until next week."

"I know—I wanted to surprise you."

"Instead I guess I surprised you... or at least my brother did," I chuckle. Izzy catches my eye and we both start to giggle. "Take my bed," I offer.

"And make you sleep on the couch in your condition. I don't think so. Besides you need a good night's rest because we're going out later."

"Out?"

"Yep, one of the girls I work with is having a party and I scored us an invite."

"I'm not sure. I mean I can't leave my brother on his own, New Years eve and on his second to last night here."

"We'll take him with us," Izzy answers decisively and if I'm honest a little too eagerly. She catches the flash of curiosity in my eyes and reels herself back." "I mean, you have to go," she side eyes me hesitantly. "It's your last New Year's before the baby arrives. I get that you also want to spend it with your brother so it makes sense for him to join us."

"I don't know." I want to go, but I'm not sure that Kurt would approve. I give myself a mental slap. Why should I care what he thinks when he'll probably be spending the evening with Katrina. As my jealously spikes, spending the night sofa surfing suddenly loses its appeal.

"Please." Izzy pleads, giving me her best faux pout.

"Sure." I say firmly. "You'll have to help me find something to wear though." I cast my eyes down to my baby bump.

"That's my girl," Izzy gives me a squeeze as she smiles in triumph.

Chapter 7

When Izzy said she'd scored us an invite to a party, I pictured an evening of drinks and dancing at some nearby brownstone. Liam and I should have known better—especially when Izzy insisted we go last-minute shopping.

I understood why she needed me along. After all I'd asked her to help me find something to wear, and it soon became apparent I couldn't squeeze into anything fancy I owned. Surprisingly, it wasn't my expanding waistline causing trouble —it was my chest. Liam, however, was a different kettle of fish. One glance inside the carry-on he'd brought was enough for Izzy to declare, in no uncertain terms, that his wardrobe was unfit for the occasion. And just like that, she demanded he join us.

I'd laughed until my ribs hurt, telling Izzy she was being wildly optimistic. There was no way she'd convince him to tag along. My brother hated shopping and I'd seen countless women try to get him to join them on a spree by using all sorts of questionable tactics. Imagine my surprise when he folded like a cheap deckchair—right in front of my eyes—without a hint of resistance. She may have won that battle, but she wouldn't win the war. If Izzy thought she could get him into anything besides his usual casual wear, I figured she was dreaming—and told her so.

She took my words as a personal challenge.

I was stunned when we arrived home a few hours later: Liam ready to be dressed head-to-toe like he was heading to a celebrity gala. I could count on one hand the number of times I'd seen my brother in a suit, let alone a tux. Right then and there, I decided my roommate must be skilled in the dark art of voodoo—and wondered whether she could use her powers to successfully cleanse my mind of a certain someone. Especially since all the time I was getting myself ready, it was tearing me apart wondering where he was and who would be the lucky recipient of his kiss when the ball dropped at midnight.

After sprucing ourselves up and donning our new threads, we all leave the apartment dressed like stars about to hit a red carpet. Our cab pulls up outside one of the swankiest hotels in Times Square, and by the time we step into the penthouse —complete with a sweeping terrace overlooking the neon chaos below—I realize this is no ordinary gathering. This is the kind of event people name-drop for years.

Izzy throws her arms around a sweet blonde in a baby-blue dress, her eyes wide with the kind of innocence you only get away with when you're beautiful. "Clara!" she beams.

"You made it—I'm so glad," Clara says, though her gaze stays locked on my brother, who's already fiddling with his collar like Izzy has him in a choke hold.

"Is it okay I brought an extra?" Izzy asks, glancing between Clara and Liam with a soft crease in her brow. "This is Liam," she announces with a dramatic flourish, before smoothly planting herself between them. "I didn't know he'd be staying. He is Tina's brother." Izzy uses me to divert Clara's attention, "and this is Tina."

"Of course—welcome," Clara replies, pulling me into a hug. For all the luxury draped across this penthouse, she feels surprisingly grounded. Charming. Sweet. Just Liam's type.

I glance over, but he doesn't react. He's still too busy shuffling around trying to get comfortable.

"I love your dress," Clara says, her smile warm.

"Thanks." It *is* a triumph. Izzy tore through my closet like a gleeful hurricane, dismissing things with an enthusiastic "No. Never. Nope." and the occasional "Burn this." The winning piece came from our Macy's trip—a deep V-neckline that draws just enough attention to my new cleavage, skilfully distracting from the bump tucked beneath soft, flowing fabric cinched beneath the bust. Faux crystals shimmer along the hem, catching the light from the chandeliers like a wink from the universe. I feel elegant. The most radiant I've felt in years.

Liam doesn't agree. The neckline makes him twitchy, and the sparkly sandals—a chunky two-inch heel—might as well be stilts in his mind. He clutches my elbow every few steps like I'm about to tumble into a passing tray of champagne flutes. I grab two and hand one to him, the other to Izzy.

"Wait, let me get you one," Clara offers, ever the attentive host as she reaches for the tray.

"No, it's okay."

Her eyes widen as I smooth the fabric over my belly until realization dawns. "Oh, let's go and find you something else."

She slips her arm through mine, gently steering me away with a wistful glance over her shoulder. "Save me a dance later," she murmurs coyly.

If I were a betting woman, I'd put money on the fact she wasn't talking to Izzy.

As we weave our way through a crowd of elegantly dressed guests, I'm certain I recognize a few faces.

"Is that Judge Simmons?" I whisper in Clara's ear.

"Yes," she giggles. "He's a guest of my father. And

before you ask—no, that is definitely not his wife."

"I take it she's not his daughter either, based on how he's groping her ass."

Clara laughs. "She was introduced as his cousin from out of state. She must have a pretty extensive family—she's been to more than one of my parents' parties. Each time she's on the arm of a different guest, and each time they claim they're related. She never corrects them, they pay her enough not to."

"She's an escort?" I gasp, even though I'm shocked my curiosity's piqued.

"And a shrewd one," Clara surmises. "Always chasing the money. Tried to get her hooks in my old man once. Unfortunately for her—he and mom are solid. My parents were childhood sweethearts, together long before dad hit the big time. That one..." she jerks her head toward her guest, "...couldn't turn dad's head, despite all the 'specialist' services she was willing to provide. When she wouldn't take no for an answer, Mom stepped in and they had words. Battle lines were drawn. Like I said, my parents didn't come from money. My mom grew up on the streets—she doesn't suffer fools gladly, and she knows how to fight dirty if she has to."

"Sounds like there's more than one shrewd woman in the room," I say, smiling. "I'd love to meet your mom—I really think I'd like her."

"I think she'd like you too," Clara says, smiling broadly.

"So this is actually your parents' party?"

"You didn't think I could work with Izzy and afford a bash like this, did you?" Clara chuckles, but there's no bite in it. "My dad's a venture capitalist. He's made an awful lot of money over the years—pissed off a fair number of people doing it, too." Her voice drops to a whisper. "That combination tends to attract some very influential 'acquaintances.' Not all of them good. Mom turns a blind eye to the guests' plus-ones to keep them happy. When they're happy, they relax, let their guard down—and it's easier to spot anyone trying to take advantage."

"Acquaintances? Not friends?"

"Why do you think I wanted Izzy to come tonight?" A flicker of something—bittersweet—crosses Clara's face. "Most people here want something. If it's not money from my father, it's information from one guest to use against another. I can guarantee almost everyone here has a hidden agenda. I needed a few people around I could trust. It gets exhausting, always being on your guard. I figured if Izzy was here, I might actually have some fun."

"That's... sad," I say, a pang of sympathy catching me off guard.

"It's fine," Clara replies, smiling just enough to

lift the mood. "You came. That already makes tonight better. And you brought your brother. If you tell me he's single, you might've just become my new best friend."

"He's single," I chuckle. "Though fair warning—he's pretty committed to staying that way. And he lives in Vermont. He's just visiting and heads home the day after tomorrow."

"But he's here now," Clara murmurs mischievously. "Would it be a problem for you if he and I got to know each other a little better tonight?"

"No," I smile. "It wouldn't be an issue for me at all."

"Good." Clara glances around as we pause by a table laid out with artfully arranged canapés, bottles of water, and fresh juice. "Will you be okay if I go check on him? I'll send Izzy over to keep you company."

"So you two can be alone," I raise an eyebrow.

She rewards me with a shrug—cool, innocent, and far from convincing. "I'm sure I don't know what you mean," she says with a smirk, turning on her heel and slipping into the crowd.

I'm on my fourth canapé and second glass of juice with still no sign of Izzy when a man sidles up beside me.

"You look about as comfortable at this thing as I

feel," he says, voice gruff but friendly.

I glance over and smile, tilting my head upward when I realise he's much taller than I'd first assumed—definitely somewhere over six foot. He's broad, too. Out of place without a jacket, the sleeves of his crisp white shirt rolled to the elbows. Yet with his commanding presence, I doubt anyone would dare call him on it.

The top few buttons of his shirt are undone. From what I can see of his chest and forearms, he's clearly physically fit. An intricate tattoo of roses entwined around Latin script peeks from his open collar. I can't make out the full phrase—just one word: *vidi*. As I wonder what else is hidden beneath the fabric, my hormones suddenly perk up, deciding to make their presence known.

The stranger's hazel eyes glint as they regard me curiously from a face framed by a mop of chocolate-brown hair and a neatly trimmed beard. I've never been much of a fan of facial hair, but it suits him—accentuating his strong features, making him seem both soft and a little scary at the same time.

"My friend seems to have abandoned me," I reply jokingly.

"I take it your friend is a 'she'?" he ventures casually.

"Yes," I frown confused. "How did you know?"

"Because no guy would leave you stood here alone and looking as you do. Any random male could walk up and try to whisk you away." He throws me a cheeky wink and I feel myself blush all the way down to my toes. The unexpected heat that floods my body catches me off guard. With Kurt currently on the opposite coast, now is not the time for my hormones to start running rife.

"Tina," I extend my hand for shaking and he accepts it, holding on for a beat longer than necessary, letting his thumb graze the back of my hand as he gifts me a name that suits him to a 'T'. "Bear."

"Bear," I repeat with a smile. "Like the animal."

He chuckles—a low, guttural sound that rumbles through him and sends a shiver down my spine. "Indeed, though I promise I only bite on special occasions… and when I've been invited to do so."

I laugh—slightly breathless, flustered by his being so forward. "And here I thought I was going to be the wild one tonight."

His gaze holds mine, warm and slow-burning. "Maybe you will be," he says, voice dropping half a register. "Maybe we could take a walk on the wild side together?"

The warmth bubbling in my chest spreads quicker than I expect. The crowd fades to a blur. He leans a touch closer—not enough to invade my space, just enough to draw every nerve to attention. I catch a hint of his cologne—woodsy and clean, like the way he looks. It feels nice to be appreciated, even if I know the moment will be fleeting, doomed the second he notices the secret I'm concealing beneath my dress.

"Tina?" A familiar voice slices through the haze, sharp and unexpected.

I turn so fast I nearly slosh my juice. My stomach does a somersault.

"Steven? I didn't expect to see you here." He looks immaculate. Tailored in his tux. Handsome and composed as his eyes skate over me before locking with those of the man mountain beside me. The twitch of a half-smile dances at the corner of his mouth, like he knows something I don't.

Bear straightens beside me, the flirtiness pulled taut like a sail in the wind. He offers a polite nod, but says nothing.

Steven gives me a brief smile—just enough charm to be civil, just enough restraint to be calculating. "Small world." He slugs back a tumbler of brown liquor he is holding. "Fancy my executive assistant being here. I thought you would be at home resting since you're expecting and all." He arches an eyebrow, amused. "Friend of yours?" His gaze shifts back to Bear. The atmosphere thickens, it's a subtle change, but unmistakable. There's the flicker of understanding before Bear takes a step back, obviously repelled by the sudden newsflash of me being with child. Neither man says a word, but their eyes lock with just a little too much awareness. I get the feeling there is more going on here than meets the eye.

"This is Bear. We were just getting acquainted." I reply jovially trying to lighten the simmering tension.

Bear's smile tilts. It's no longer natural, it's even and controlled. "Nice to meet you," he says smoothly. But the words are loaded and sound like a test.

Steven nods, just once. "Likewise." His tone is clipped, professional, but also... false.

I glance between them, sensing something—it's almost like the two men know each other but are pretending not to. History, maybe. Or unfinished business. Whatever it is they're dancing around the issue, refusing to name it, but I know it's there. And suddenly, I feel like an intruder—wrong place, wrong time—through no fault of my own.

"Do... you two know each other?" I ask cautiously.

Bear's response is swift. "We've crossed paths," he says it like it's a closed door.

Steven nods again, but this time he's looking at me, not Bear. "Nothing significant."

And just like that, the mystery tightens its grip.

Something's off—I feel it crawling under my skin, making me itch to run. The maternal instinct I didn't know I had is suddenly screaming at me to get the hell out of Dodge. I spot Izzy weaving through the crowd and wave, silently thanking my lucky stars for the perfect excuse to escape.

"Iz, over here."

Izzy waves back and joins us, a frown pulling at her features. I'm certain she senses the tension—until she speaks and her concern reveals itself to be something else entirely.

"There you are," she says, clutching my arm and steering me away from the men flanking me. "You need to come quickly. I think Clara may have the hots for Liam."

"Liam?" Steven's curiosity gets the better of him.

"My brother," I call over my shoulder as Izzy pulls me across the room. "Nice meeting you, Bear."

Bear gives me a chin tip as I retreat. His arms are crossed defensively, head cocked to one side, listening as Steven whispers something in his ear. Then Bear smiles. The sudden, easy expression makes the exchange seem... almost friendly.

It's a far cry from the stilted conversation I witnessed moments ago, but I have to push the thought aside. Izzy's voice cuts through my musings with the exaggerated flair only she can muster. Apparently, my brother's chastity is on the line—and that, according to Izzy, urgently demands my full attention.

"Look at them." Izzy spits as she points to Liam leaning casually against a wall listening intently to whatever Clara is saying. The scene isn't anywhere as risqué as Izzy was portraying moments ago. "Clara clearly has the hots for Liam," Izzy repeats, eyes wide with scandalous urgency.

"You say that like it's contagious." I answer with a smirk, "Izzy, have you got a crush on my brother?"

"What? No!" Izzy replies affronted. He's a creep."

"As I recall it was you that climbed into his bed uninvited and groped him. Not the other way around," I giggle.

"He didn't have to grope me back. Anyway, don't be gross. Your brother's innocence is hanging in the balance here."

"Pretty sure Liam gave up his innocence the same year he discovered hair gel."

"Well, us New Yorkers are in a tougher league than the girls he is used to."

"Iz, you're from Iowa." I giggle.

Izzy waves a hand at me dismissively, "Look at her, she's circling him like a hawk in heels. I'm not saying she's dangerous exactly, but I definitely think he has bitten off more than he can chew here."

"You're saying Liam's in mortal danger?" I laugh, whatever Izzy's seeing is lost on me.

"I'm saying we need to intervene before she offers him an appetizer and calls it foreplay. Look! Look at that." She tells me incredulously shaking my arm.

"What?"

"Clara making sex eyes at your brother in front of all these people. I just saw her lick her straw while maintaining aggressive eye contact."

"Oh no. The straw lick?"

"With tongue flourish."

"God help us."

"That's why I came to get you. Intervention is required. Preferably with a cattle prod, or at least a firm distraction."

"You want me to launch myself between them like a chastity grenade?"

"You said it, not me."

"Okay, I'll play along. What's the plan?" I know Izzy's listening, even if her gaze is locked on my brother.

"I think we should stick to him like glue for the rest of the evening," Izzy says, side-eyeing me warily. "I invited you here so you could mingle and meet some new people…"

"I'm not very good at striking up awkward conversations with strangers."

"Could've fooled me. When I found you, you seemed to be doing okay." Izzy raises an eyebrow. "Anyway, so you can go ahead and enjoy yourself, I'll take the first shift. Maybe ask Clara to introduce you to a few people—tear her away from your brother for a bit. He looks bored."

"Does he?" I chuckle.

Izzy ignores me and presses on. "Then just before midnight, if you've been separated, you come and find Liam and me. If Clara is making a beeline for Liam when the ball drops to welcome in the New Year, I'll save him by kissing him myself." She says it like she's volunteering for a root canal.

"Very magnanimous of you," I laugh, slowly shaking my head. I don't know how my brother does it. He's been here barely a week and already has two women vying for his attention. I only hope it doesn't end in tears.

"I think so," Izzy replies seriously, then announces, "Good plan."

I arch a brow. "Good plan?"

We watch as Clara leans in, fingers brushing Liam's arm. He smiles down at her, and she giggles —soft, flirtatious, the sound laced with something that dances between interest and invitation. Izzy stiffens beside me, and a moment later, something inside her snaps.

"C'mon, quick," she hisses, grabbing my hand and dragging me back toward Liam.

"Clara," Izzy calls as we approach, "Tina wants to speak to you."

"I do?" I mutter under my breath.

"Yes, you do," she growls back.

Clara turns expectantly as I scramble for an excuse.

"I... er—"

"Didn't you want to ask Clara if she knew the men you were just talking to?" Izzy nudges me gently in the ribs.

"What men?" Liam frowns, ever the protective brother. Everyone ignores him.

"Oooh, you've found a prospective contender for a smooch at midnight!" Clara claps her hands and wiggles her eyebrows. Liam doesn't look impressed. "There are some pretty fine, single guys here. I think my parents are optimistically hoping I'll fall for one and settle down. Being an only child puts a lot of pressure on me to provide them with a future heir. That said, they've made sure I have the lowdown on nearly everyone here so I make good choices—if you know what I mean." She leans in conspiratorially. "Show me who you're interested in and I'll tell you what I know."

"Tina," Liam's voice slices through the noise, "I don't think Kurt—" He stops short, stunned, as Izzy raises her hand in front of his face to silence him.

"Kurt isn't here," I snap, annoyed that my brother has just managed to ruin a fun moment by filling my head with thoughts of Kurt again—and what, or who, he might be doing.

"Who's Kurt?" Clara asks, bemused.

Liam grabs Izzy's hand, catching her off guard. He spins her into his side and holds her close so she can't interfere again. Izzy sighs wantonly and makes a half-hearted attempt to wriggle free.

"Her fiancé and the father of her baby," Liam says tersely.

Clara looks to me for clarification. I hold up my left hand and point to the absence of a ring on my fourth finger. "Father of my baby, yes. Fiancé, no. In fact, he's probably out seeing in the New Year with another woman as we speak."

"Well then," Clara links her arm through mine, "What's good for the goose…"

"Tina, I forbid you to go trawling this party looking for some random hookup," Liam growls solemnly.

Clara, Izzy, and I all stare at him in shock—then burst out laughing.

"Good one," I wheeze, trying to catch my breath.

"I mean it," Liam says, a little panicked now, realizing he's in a situation he can't control. "There's something you should know—"

"It can wait," Clara giggles, sweeping me away into a sea of people. I glance over my shoulder to see Izzy animatedly blocking Liam from following. Once we're out of earshot, Clara leans in and whispers, "Is it wrong that I found your brother's Neolithic display of overprotectiveness totally hot just then?"

"Yes," I chuckle.

"Just so you know, I don't usually gossip about our guests," Clara says seriously. "It's just—dating in New York can be a minefield. And when the chips are down, we girls need to stick together. Especially since you've got a little one on the way."

"Thanks," I reply warmly. "I appreciate it. Although I'm not really looking to date anyone. The men I was talking to—one was my boss, the other a stranger who was flirting with me until he appeared and things got... weird. I got the sense they knew each other, but they were being really cagey about it. I just wondered if you could shed any light. Since I work with one of them, I'd hate to find myself in the middle of something without realising."

"I hear you," Clara says, squeezing my arm in solidarity. "What are their names?"

"Steven Prentice and Bear."

"Sounds like the title of a children's book," Clara giggles. "I don't recognise either name, but if you point them out to me I might be more help. I'm much better with faces than names." She winks. "And if we just so happen to find you another nice guy while we're searching, it wouldn't be such a bad thing, would it? It's always good for a girl to have options."

"Clara, I'm *really* not looking to date anyone right now," I repeat. She nods vaguely, which I take as confirmation she's choosing to ignore my protests. We plunge into a dizzying carousel of introductions—mostly to eligible bachelors who are handsome, upwardly mobile, and clearly handpicked for my benefit. All look like they've just stepped off the cover of GQ, with tailored suits, confident smiles, and job titles that sound suspiciously made-up.

Clara provides a running commentary on each one, offering unsolicited insights into their careers, family histories, and dating repertoire. She beams at them like a proud talent scout, whispering things like "He owns three properties" or "His mother's a nightmare, but he's worth it."

For the rest of the room, her commentary is less curated. She forgets names, skilfully prompting guests to offer them up mid-conversation, all while delivering an alarming amount of personal detail—recent divorces, financial losses through questionable investments, and allergies where intolerances might cause social embarrassment.

It's like watching a gossip columnist moonlight as a party host with mild amnesia. Great fun all the same.

I'll admit, as a single, unwed mum-to-be, I was a little intimidated to meet Clara's parents. I half expected judgment—or worse, a quiet decree to keep their daughter away from me. But they couldn't have been nicer. Maybe it was a polished front, but I didn't think so. Especially not after her mom invited me to join them for brunch one Sunday. That kind of gesture felt genuine—and an invitation I was determined to accept.

We're so busy working the room, time flies. Steven and Bear seem to have disappeared, and while I now know far more than necessary about the rest of the attendees, I'm still none the wiser about their connection.

As the atmosphere shifts with midnight fast approaching, I heave a deep sigh. "I don't think we're going to find them," I whisper to Clara. "I'm feeling a little warm. I'll grab a juice and head out to the terrace for some air. I want to get a good spot to see the ball drop."

"You're not going to invite any of the guys I introduced you to? I'm pretty sure you had more than one interested party. Michael was very interested—and I know for a fact you're just his type."

"Even with a baby on board," I laugh, patting my stomach affectionately.

She shrugs and smirks at the same time. "I'm sure you could think of a way to win him round."

"Thanks, but no thanks. My life is complicated enough right now." As nice as it would be to share a kiss with a handsome man at midnight, I'm not ready to deal with the fallout if Kurt finds out. Not that I should be letting him be a concern.

"Suit yourself," she smiles, unperturbed. "Although I understand it, I don't share your need for abstinence. Will you be OK if I go and top up Liam's glass for the countdown?"

I know I should save my brother from a potentially volatile situation, and Izzy did ask me to help distract Clara the moment she was poised to strike, but I'm tired and need a break from circulating. Besides, as much as I love Izzy, I like Clara. I figure this is a problem Liam needs to handle without any interference from me. "Sure."

Clara smiles and disappears while I grab my drink and head outside. The cool air is a sharp contrast to the warmth inside. I find a spot overlooking Times Square and lean on the balustrade, waiting for the countdown to begin and the fireworks to start.

The crowd outside is electric. The air hums with anticipation. I sip my juice as the cold bites at my cheeks. It's a relief to grasp a brief moment of solitude. I may be surrounded by people but no-one's eyes are on me, no-one is wanting to converse, there's no pressure to perform.

"There you are. I've been searching for you." I sigh and turn to see Steven pushing through the crowd, a glass in each hand. He offers one to me, and I shiver, wishing I'd had the forethought to grab my jacket.

"You're cold," he says, shrugging off his own and draping it over my shoulders. His fingers linger as they brush my arms—it's too intimate, even for a chivalrous gesture.

"Thank you," I say, forcing a smile. No need to seem churlish. "You were looking for me?"

"You know it's unlucky not to share a kiss with someone to welcome in the New Year." He delivers the line like it's gospel—a hard, unyielding fact. "I thought, since we've shared one in the past, it'd be less awkward than relying on a stranger to save us for the year ahead." He smiles, but there's something off—a gleam in his eye that doesn't match the warmth in his voice. My stomach tightens as my maternal instinct flares again, whispering that something's not right. With both hands full, I can't stop him when his hands slip beneath the jacket, settling on my hips. I stiffen, trapped by the weight of his touch and the glass I didn't ask for. "You know you've blossomed over the last few weeks," he murmurs, his eyes roaming my body—particularly my chest. "Your soft curves are becoming a distraction."

I try to take a step back, but his grip tightens. "Your wife not here tonight?" I ask, voice sharper than I intended. If he's here alone, I'll wager it's not by accident.

"No," he says, like it's a joke. "I'm here alone."

"Even so," I say, trying to sound in control, though I feel mocked. "I really don't think it's a good idea." The countdown begins.

Ten.

Nine.

Eight.

Steven grins, like the shouting revellers have drowned out my protest.

Seven.

Six.

"Let me go," I demand, voice rising as I try to twist out of his hold.

Five.

Four.

He leans in, completely ignoring me until I hurl a drink in his face and he reels back, shocked, wiping liquid from his eyes. Then his expression hardens. I try to flee, but the crowd has closed in —cheering, oblivious, caught up in the evening's festivities. I'm trapped in plain sight, and no one sees me struggling to escape.

Steven grabs me again, his fingers digging into my flesh. "Tina, you know you want to."

Three.

Two.

"No!" I scream, panic rising. I twist my head from side to side, desperate to dodge his advances, but he grips my chin to hold me in place. His hold is so firm, I feel the imprint of his fingers burning into my skin.

Fear blinds me to the sudden silence, to the way the crowd parts beside me, to the shift in atmosphere. It darkens—like a tornado hellbent on destroying everything in its path is about to touch down right beside me.

One.

As Steven closes in, he is wrenched away so violently he stumbles and crashes to the ground. I turn, breathless, expecting to see my brother. But Liam isn't my saviour. My heart leaps, not from panic but from the kind of joy that steals breath and bends time.

Other than Josh's wedding, it's the only other time I've ever seen him in a suit. Even with fury etched across his face, he looks devastatingly handsome—and every woman in the room seems to notice.

"When a lady says no, she means no!" Kurt spits, shrugging off his jacket and rolling up the sleeves of his shirt as he circles Steven like a cage fighter about to defend an undefeated title.

The whole terrace watches, captivated. The pyrotechnics behind us are a distant second to the fireworks unfolding right here. "Kurt, no," I whisper. He glances at me—just for a fraction of a second. Enough to tell me I won't be able to stop what's coming.

Steven drags himself to his feet and rounds on Kurt. "Who the fuck are you?" he yells. "This is none of your business, friend." The word *friend* drips with contempt.

"Oh, I think it is my business," Kurt replies. "Since that's my girl you were trying to force yourself on. *Friend.*" He throws the word back with equal venom.

His girl—Not just an incubator for his child. The words hit me like a jolt, fierce and tender all at once.

Steven narrows his eyes. I pray he walks away while he has all his limbs intact instead of saying something stupid. But when he pulls back his arm, I know his fate is sealed. A series of loud bangs startles the crowd as fronds of cascading light fill the sky. Kurt blocks the punch, grabs Steven's arm, twists, and flips him to the ground. Embarrassed, Steven launches himself again. This time, Kurt swings first. His fist connects with bone in a crack that makes me wince.

Steven reels back, blood pouring from his nose. He wipes his face then stares at his hand like he doesn't recognize the red streak staining it. "You *really* shouldn't have done that," he sneers.

Kurt raises an eyebrow, daring him to continue. When Steven doesn't, Kurt steps in. "I'm sure I'll live. Which is more than I can say for you if you go near my girl again."

Steven laughs—a cold, maniacal sound that sends a chill down my spine. "Is that so?" he replies, composure regained. "With a temper like yours, I bet you've made a few enemies. I suggest you watch your back." His eyes flick toward me, and Kurt steps between us. "Don't worry," Steven calls. "I won't hold this against you. I'll see you at work bright and early Friday morning."

Kurt watches him retreat, then glances at me. "The hell you will," he mutters. As soon as Steven disappears, the crowd loses interest and resumes their celebration. Kurt strides over to stand before me. I open my mouth, but I'm not sure where to begin. He places a finger gently on my lips. "I don't want to talk about that jockstrap tonight. I didn't get all dressed up and travel over two thousand miles to get into an argument with you."

"Why did you?" I ask, breathless. His proximity makes every cell in my body vibrate with longing.

"Kat told me it's unlucky to start the New Year without a kiss. I came for mine—from you."

I smile. And as the fireworks reach their grand finale behind us, I give Kurt exactly what he came to collect.

Chapter 8

"Will you quit doing that," Kurt grumbles as he sidles up behind me, wrapping his arms around my waist and nibbling my neck.

"What?" I giggle.

"Disappearing on me. I woke up reaching for you and all I found was air. It throws off my whole morning mojo." He nips me playfully and I squeal at the sudden sting. "I had plans for you this morning." Something firm and familiar presses into my back—Kurt's version of a wake-up call.

"Are you naked?" I ask as I continue making my morning coffee without turning.

"Maybe." Kurt chuckles resuming his coveting of my neck. "Well, you better put some clothes on. Izzy could be up at any second and Liam could be home soon."

"So? Liams seen me naked before and as for Izzy... it'll help her realise where she needs to set the bar. I think It would be helpful to know what to aim for, boyfriend wise"

"And you think you're the best example of that?"

I tease, prompting Kurt to tickle me mercilessly until I admit the truth: Izzy would be lucky to find anyone who stacked up to Kurt in the looks department. She could do without the ego, though.

"Morning. Nice ass."

Kurt spins us both so I'm shielding him from a pair of eyes neither of us were expecting to see.

"Clara?" I blurt—half surprise, half accidental introduction.

Kurt ignores me as he accepts the compliment and whispers "Told ya," in my ear. He extends his hand around me for shaking as he introduces himself. "Kurt. Baby daddy."

"Thought as much," Clara chuckles. She is definitely doing the walk of shame in last nights clothes with her hair mussed and no make-up.

"You stayed…" I venture carefully. "In Izzy's room?"

"I did," Clara's cheeks tinge pink before she rushes to leave. "Gotta dash, I'll be in touch about brunch.

"Where did Liam end up?" I glance over my shoulder at Kurt. "When we left the party, Izzy promised to get him back here safely and he clearly never slept on the sofa last night."

"Babe. He's a grown man. He doesn't need his irresponsible baby sister micromanaging his movements or his love life." Kurt kisses me on the tip of my nose to soften the blow of his character assassination.

I frown, "I'm not irresponsible."

"Says the girl who got herself knocked up and is refusing to marry the father," Liam enters the kitchen, fresh out the shower with a towel wrapped around his waist. He fist bumps a grinning Kurt on his way to the cupboard to grab a mug for his morning beverage.

"Where did you sleep last night?" I demand to know.

"Izzy's room." Liam smirks at me—or Kurt, I'm not sure which—from over the top of his freshly poured brew.

I feel the soft vibration of Kurts chest against my back as he lets out a chuckle and fist bumps my brother again.

"Then where's Iz?" I ask confused.

"Here." Izzy appears, entering the kitchen with a yawn.

"Well, where did *you* sleep?" my brow furrows so hard I think my face might crack.

"I didn't." Izzy casts a mischievous, sultry smile in Liams direction.

"I don't understand." I look between my brother and my friend, confusion knotting in my chest.

Kurt bursts out laughing behind me.

"Clara just left," I murmur, as if saying it aloud might help clear the haze.

"Clara and Izzy had a brief interpersonal conflict requiring third-party arbitration last night. They couldn't quite decide who should get my first dance at the afterparty," Liam explains, with the gravitas of someone recounting a peace treaty. "Since I was clearly the source of tension, I suggested we all come back here to resolve the matter. In an effort to mediate, I got *in between* them to help facilitate the negotiations that ultimately led to a mutually satisfying conclusion for all parties concerned."

It takes longer than it should for the penny to drop. Liam's overexaggerated diplomacy, Izzy's sudden inability to meet my eye—

"Eww!" I hurl a tea towel at my brother. "You disgust me."

I storm off to my room, a laughing Kurt trailing closely behind in an effort to shield his modesty.

"Ow." My foot slams into a suitcase I hadn't noticed — not surprising, given how Kurt and I had barrelled through the bedroom door last night, a tangled, breathless mess of limbs and heat. "Where the hell did that come from?"

"It's mine," Kurt says, matter-of-fact. "Dropped it off before I came to find you."

"How? You don't have a key." I blink at him, thrown.

Kurt sprawls across the bed, hands laced behind his head, grinning like a man with secrets.

When he doesn't answer I change tack — instinctively knowing I won't like the response to my last question. "Why is it here?"

"Because I'm moving in. And I couldn't find a single space in your closet you hadn't already filled."

A slightly hysterical laugh bubbles out of me. "You're joking?" I splutter, though I'm pretty sure he's not. When Kurt quirks an eyebrow it's the only confirmation I need. "You can't just move in." Even as I say it, my mind and body are already betraying me — a warm glow flickers in my chest, right where my heart should be. If he's moving in, it means he's staying.

"Why not?"

"Because I share this place with Izzy, for starters. It's not only my decision."

"Izzy won't mind," Kurt says, breezy as ever. "And if she does, I'll ask Liam to perform sexual favours until she agrees. Maybe you could invite Clara over again to help."

I grab a pillow and whack him with it. "What if I mind?"

"Look, it makes sense. We're getting married.

Having a baby. It's the next step. I'll move in until we relocate to L.A."

"We are not getting married," I say — for what feels like the millionth time.

"Only because you haven't proposed yet." He grins. "Ask me now. Go on, I dare you."

I ignore him. "And I told you before, I'm not moving. I'm back at work tomorrow."

Kurt's smile fades. He pins me with a look. "About that..." His voice drops. "Any chance I can persuade you to quit."

"None." My answer is immediate and firm. I'm not stupid. Kurt might be showing flashes of boyfriend-and-father potential, but that doesn't mean it'll stick. I need to keep my independence for as long as I can. Build up my savings like I planned. There's no way he gets to hold all the power, manipulate me into relying on him so when he leaves, I'm stranded.

"Sure?" His voice turns mischievous and my eyes are immediately drawn to below his waist as he takes himself in his hand. He starts to stroke himself and I'm suddenly at odds with my decision.

I shake some sense into my head and turn away so I'm not tempted to change my mind. "Yep." The word's meant to be final — but I hope he doesn't hear the slight waver in my tone.

His chuckle tells me he did. I hear him shuffling behind me, and I pretend to rearrange a drawer in my dresser, fingers grazing fabric I don't register. "Right then. That's what I thought you'd say."

I glance over my shoulder to see he's tugged on a pair of sweatpants. "I need to make a quick call. Then I'm telling Izzy I'm moving in."

"Asking... asking Izzy," I say again, firmer this time. "And if she says no—"

But he's already halfway out the door, smiling. "Then we both move out and find a place together."

The door clicks shut before I can respond. And just like that, he's rewritten the ending I was trying to write.

The following day rolls around before I'm ready, and before I know it I'm already tearfully saying goodbye to my brother in the kitchen before heading to work. Liam, Kurt, and Izzy all stare at me, bemused — like they've never seen me cry before. Stupid hormones.

New Years Day, the four of us never ventured out. Instead, we spent the day cocooned in blankets, bellies full from the feast Kurt whipped up — herb-crusted roast lamb, buttery potatoes, the freshest veg money could buy, and enough dessert to feed a small army. We watched movies back-to-back, flinging popcorn at each other and bickering over which film deserved the top spot. Izzy kept trying to sneak spoilers, Liam fell asleep halfway through everything — rookie mistake, since Izzy took it as an open invitation to test out her makeup techniques. He woke up looking like he was about to headline a circus—but not before Kurt and I had taken a few pictures purely for blackmail purposes, of course. The kind of ammo you save for milestone birthdays or wedding speeches.

Liam swore revenge on Izzy, but it was a half-hearted threat. I knew my brother — his outrage was all for show. Izzy seemed to know it too. She just grinned at him, unapologetic, twirling a makeup brush like it was a weapon she knew exactly how to wield.

Liam scowled, but to the trained eye, he was fighting back a smile. If not that, then it was his eyes that betrayed him — warm, lingering, far too soft for someone supposedly plotting payback.

Kurt caught my glance and raised an eyebrow, the corner of his mouth twitching like he was counting down the seconds before calling Liam out.

It was one of those days — beautifully chaotic, unforgettable, and perfect in its own way.

Liam swore he spent the night on the couch,

but when I mentioned getting up for a glass of water and finding him missing, both he and Izzy suddenly looked suspiciously shifty.

"Are you ready?" Kurt asks once I finally get the waterworks under control.

"What for?" My head snaps in his direction just as the words I fear most tumble from his lips.

"I'm taking you to work."

Shit.

"Worried I won't know the way?" I quip, trying to quell the swirling dread pooling in my stomach.

"No. Thought I'd give that idiot you work with the chance to apologise for assaulting my knuckles with his face," Kurt deadpans.

"What idiot?" Izzy asks, wide-eyed.

"Steven," I answer without thinking.

"You told him about the kiss." Izzy speaks directly to me, ignoring everyone else.

Suddenly the room shrinks as Kurt's anger engulfs it. "She better be talking about the one that didn't happen on New Year's Eve."

Izzy backs out of the room, tossing me an apologetic look and mouthing *"Sorry",* as she disappears dragging Liam with her. Kurt rounds on me, gently pressing me against the kitchen counter, his hands braced on either side — caging me in. I can feel the tension radiating off him as he lowers his face so close to mine, every breath he takes is almost shared.

"Well?" His eyes blaze with fury as I try to look anywhere but at him.

I know I'll never be able to demand total honesty from him if I'm not willing to reciprocate.

"Remember when you weren't speaking to me after the wedding, before I knew I was expecting," I mumble, "before we... reconnected?"

"Hmmm." Kurt growls, unimpressed.

"I went out after work and I met this guy. He was fun and flirty. I didn't know he'd turn out to be my boss — or that he was married. I was lonely and pissed at you for never calling after we'd spent that incredible night together, and my hormones were all out of sync," I ramble, then sigh. "We kissed." There's a weighted pause before I continue. "He wanted to take things further... but I couldn't."

"Why?"

I don't want to admit the truth, to wear my heart on my sleeve and give Kurt the satisfaction of knowing he owns me. But in order for me to be honest, I don't have a choice.

"Because he wasn't you," I whisper, mad at myself for being weak and handing him the ammunition he could use to slay me.

"That's the right answer," Kurt growls. "Anything else I need to know?"

"No. That's it. I swear."

"Good. Look at me."

It's a struggle, but I force myself to meet his gaze. The fury in his eyes has morphed into something else — understanding, familiarity. He locks me in his gaze before he speaks.

"Based on the fact we've already established I need to leave no room for ambiguity in any communication with you, I'm going to spell things out. Neither of us can go back and change anything about our past, but the future is yet to be written. Right here, right now, you're mine and I intend on doing whatever it takes to convince you to keep things that way. Nobody gets to touch what's mine. Period. I don't share — not when it comes to you."

"And..." Kurt cuts me off. He knows what's on my mind before I even elocute it.

"In case you still haven't noticed, I'm yours, princess. You own every part of me — mind, body, and soul—and have for as far back as I can remember. There's nothing I wouldn't do for you. I'd take a bullet for you. My only mission now is to make you happy, protect you, and show you I'm here not because of the baby, but because of everything that came before him. Because of us. There's no one else. Never will be, all the while we're together. I don't need anyone else. I don't want anyone else. The quicker you propose and tie me down, the sooner I'll be able to sleep at night...

knowing you feel the same way about me as I do you."

"You're mine?" I blink, unsure if I've heard him right.

"For as long as you'll have me. I'm hoping forever," Kurt says, sincere and steady. "Any question spring to mind you want to ask me right now? You don't have to go down on one knee."

It's too much. My emotions collide with my hormones, and I can't think straight. "What's the time?" Not the question he was hoping for — but it's all I've got. "I can't be late for work. After the other night, there's already a good chance I'm about to get fired."

Kurt sighs and steps back, his expression unreadable. "I hope you do." Then, as I reach for my bag, he adds, "But in case you don't… there's a few things you should know."

"What do you mean?" The solemnity of his voice makes me stop in my tracks.

"After you mentioned your old boss had gone missing, you stopped answering Maeve's calls. Then Liam showed up in L.A. expecting to find you there — and mild concern turned into blind panic. The two of us rushed down here, convinced something had happened to you. Josh even got the guys at his firm to start running checks so that by the time our flight landed, we had some idea what we might be walking into."

"What sort of checks?" I'm not sure whether to be touched by Kurt's concern or furious that my privacy might've been violated.

Kurt hesitates, clearly aware he's on thin ice. "We just wanted to make sure you were okay. Josh asked one of the guys we work with — Foxy — to check your recent card activity. When we saw you'd ordered takeout from your go-to Chinese not long before Liam and I showed up, we realised we might've blown things a little out of proportion."

"You think?" I say, incredulous, eyes wide and hands on hips. "Just so you know, any guy I eventually decide to marry has to respect my boundaries."

"Noted." Kurt tries — and fails — to bite back a smile.

"Anyway, Josh had already asked Axel to make some enquiries as to the whereabouts of Robert Taylor back when you first raised concerns about not being able to reach him. Before your card transaction gave you away, we figured that if you had gone missing, maybe you were with Robert."

"Missing as in 'in trouble' missing, or missing as in 'you lost your shit when you thought I'd sloped off for a dirty weekend' missing?" I ask, one eyebrow raised.

"Don't even joke about it." Kurt growls. I'm not sure which scenario bothers him more, but I can guess.

I roll my eyes. "Did you find him?"

"Not yet. And that's not a good sign. We can usually find anyone at the drop of a hat, but this guy... let's just say he's being elusive. And that's not all." Kurt's voice drops a notch, the protective edge sharpening. "After that tool you're working for and I got into it the other night, I got Josh to check him out. It's raised a few red flags we're looking into."

"What sort of red flags? What are you getting at? You're looking into the firm I work for?" I stare at him, horrified.

Kurt steps closer, wraps his arms around me, and presses a gentle kiss to my forehead. "It's nothing for you to worry about. I promise — no one will ever know we've been snooping unless we want them to. All I'm saying is, until we find out what happened to Robert... trust your instincts. If something feels off, proceed with caution."

"Kurt," I pull back to look him in the eye. "You're really starting to scare me."

"Relax. I'm not about to let anything happen to you. I've got your back — I'll be watching the entire time. Just do your job and come home. Don't get pulled into anything that feels over and above what you're expected to do."

"Watching? How? You can't be with me every second of the day."

That smirk again.

I start patting myself down. "Have you bugged me? If you have... I swear... I'll..."

Kurt bursts out laughing, shaking his head. "I would never dare." Then his expression shifts, the laughter fading. "But I want us to set up a code word. Not because I think you need one right now — just in case. If you're ever in a situation where you can't say it outright but need my help, I'll know to come running."

"I can think of a couple of good words," I deadpan.

"Hit me." Kurt clearly doesn't catch the sarcasm.

"Paranoia?"

"Try again." His tongue plays behind his cheek as he gazes down at me.

"Idiot? Overprotective? Overbearing?"

Within seconds, he lifts me onto the kitchen counter, nudging my legs apart with his knee so he can step between them, closing the distance.

"Orrrr," he drawls, "we could go with sexy? Handsome? The reason you're about to be late for work?"

He kisses me until I start seeing stars, then pulls back just enough to whisper: "Humour me. Josh made Maeve do the same."

"Let me guess," I say, breathless. "Her word is

'cactus'?"

Kurt looks at me — and we both burst out laughing, remembering the day Maeve bought a tiny cactus to decorate their new home. She'd left it on a chair, and Josh hadn't checked before launching himself into it. She spent hours picking needles out of his butt cheek.

"Got it in one." Kurt grins. "So, beautiful... what's our word gonna be?"

"Coconut."

"Coconut?"

"Remember when I was fifteen and we all went to the fair?"

"When handsy Andy kept trying to grope your ass?"

I giggle. "And you, Josh, and Liam threatened to disembowel him if he stepped out of line."

"He didn't deserve you," Kurt mutters.

"Anyway," I laugh, "you spent all your cash trying to win me that giant panda because I really wanted it — and Andy refused to try because he said it was a waste of money since the coconuts were clearly glued to the stands. You kept hurling balls at the coconuts and even though you hit them time and time again they wouldn't fall. You left empty-handed and in a foul mood, but the next morning I opened the door and found that same panda sitting on my doorstep... clutching a coconut."

I didn't think Kurt was capable of blushing, but his cheeks definitely tinge pink — visible even beneath the dusting of stubble.

"I didn't think you'd remember that."

"It's one of my favourite memories. Even if no one ever admitted how he got there. Plus, the word fits — your hard shell protects a sweet, soft interior. And you're kinda hairy right now. You could use a shave."

"Is that so?" Kurt rubs his cheek against mine. The bristles scratch just enough to tickle, making me giggle and squirm.

"Stop it," I laugh. "I don't want to go into work with beard rash. Questions will be asked."

"Let them ask. And when they do, you can tell them the truth." Kurt's eyes darken — and I recognize that look.

"Which is?"

"My fiancé had his wicked way with me as I was about to head out the door."

"We're not engaged," I chuckle.

"Tomato, tomahto," Kurt murmurs before his lips find mine again, this time with an intent that leaves no room for doubt.

∞∞∞

There's nothing like an unscripted quickie in the kitchen to put a smile on your face and a spring in your step on your way into work after— especially when the source of your pleasure is gripping your hand like you might suddenly disappear.

As we approach my office block, the usually quiet street is humming with activity.

"Shit!" I exclaim. "Something must've happened."

I try to break into a run, but Kurt's grip — and his maddeningly calm demeanour — keeps me from sprinting ahead to gauge the situation. It's only when we reach the building's lobby and find the building's security team checking bags and scanning employees with handheld wands that I finally get to ask what's going on.

"Maddie," I call to one of my colleagues, who seems more intent on checking out Kurt than listening to me. "Maddie!" I call louder, snapping her out of her trance.

She finally tears her gaze away from Kurt and offers a sheepish wave. "Oh, Tina. Hi." It's more apology than greeting.

"What's going on?" I ask, as Kurt stands beside me — suspiciously unfazed and silent.

"Some kind of security breach over the holiday," Maddie says. "Someone tried to hack into our systems."

"Tried to?"

"From what I gather, they couldn't get past the firewall — but they came close. Probably just some bored kids mucking around to see how far they could go. Even so, it's made the powers-that-be twitchy. They've hired in a specialist from out of town to revamp the system."

"If it was a cyber-attack, why the increase in physical security?" I nod toward the bag searches and body scans happening a few feet away.

Maddie shrugs. "Who knows? You're likely to find out more than me, since the senior partner personally fast-tracked you into your new position."

It's a subtle dig, but it stings. Kurt knows it — I feel his thumb brush soothing circles against my palm.

I tilt my head and smile, just enough to show teeth. "He fast-tracked results, Maddie. I just happened to deliver them."

Kurt lets out a low chuckle, and Maddie's expression falters.

"Smart move," Kurt adds, voice calm but pointed. "I'd bet you're the best investment they've made in years."

Maddie blinks, caught off guard. I don't miss the flicker of uncertainty in her eyes.

At least I can quash one office rumour. "Maddie, I'd like you to meet Kurt." I present him like an offering. "My…" I falter.

Kurt fills in the blank. "Fiancé and father-to-be."

"Y-you're getting married?" Maddie stammers, her shock almost comical. "To him?"

I don't want to lie, so I wrap my arms around Kurt in an intimate gesture that lets Maddie draw her own conclusion.

"Luckyyy," she breathes under her breath — just before she's called away. She scurries off, no doubt to fuel a fresh round of gossip.

"This is as far as you go," I tell Kurt once she's gone.

I try to step away, but he pulls me back in. "Seems we have an audience."

I glance around. Maddie hasn't wasted any time. A gaggle of employees is huddled around her, watching Kurt and me with their mouths open like we're the newest chart-topper on Netflix.

I move in for a hug — partly for show, mostly to whisper in Kurt's ear. "I guess I owe you for giving me my reputation back. Until this morning, I was potentially the slut who got promoted after letting her boss knock her up on his desk."

"Anything to oblige," Kurt murmurs. "Although I could do without the visual — unless it's some sort of kink fantasy you want me to fulfil later."

He smiles, then gently spins me, dips me, and kisses me with the kind of passion that should be reserved for private moments. When he rights me, our audience squeals and cheers in appreciation.

"Get out of here, you goofball," I bluster as my cheeks flame. I straighten my clothes and pat down my hair.

"Laters," he grins, winking as he walks away — leaving me standing in the middle of the floor, watching him go.

The closer I get to my desk, the more my heart sinks. I'm hoping Steven has already left for court. I'm disappointed to see his office door open — and him seated at his desk inside. The moment he spots me, I'm summoned into his lair.

"Tina." It's not a greeting. It's a verdict waiting to be delivered. A purple bruise blooms along Steven's jaw, and his nose is looking more than a little bent out of shape. I know he should be the one apologizing to me, but nerves make me speak first.

"About the other night…" I begin.

Steven smirks like he's already worn me down, reclining in his leather chair as he waits for me to start grovelling. Suddenly, pride gets the better of me. I swallow the undeserved apology on the tip of my tongue and opt for a more direct approach.

"When I told you to back off, you should've walked away."

Steven's brow creases — an infinitesimal gesture, but I catch it. He throws his pen down on the desk.

"Who was he?" he snaps.

"My fiancé," I lie. "And the father of my baby. We recently got back together and decided to make a go of things."

"I see." Steven doesn't look impressed. His beady eyes scrutinize me thoughtfully.

"So I guess you wouldn't want me having him arrested and incarcerated for assault. I have more than one witness ready to testify it was an unprovoked attack."

My heart starts pounding. Losing my job is one thing — losing Kurt is another altogether. I have no choice but to fight fire with fire.

"And I guess you wouldn't want your good name besmirched for unsolicited advances," I counter. "I had more than one friend at that party who saw me clearly trying to push you off before they witnessed a good samaritan intervene," I bluff.

Steven's face turns beetroot red. His eyes try to eviscerate me. He opens his mouth — likely to deliver my termination — when Carter Shaw, the senior partner, appears, tapping on the door frame.

Steven's irritation morphs into charm so fast it's dizzying.

"Knock knock," Carter calls jovially, blissfully unaware of the simmering tension. His companion is more astute, glancing between Steven and me with narrowed eyes that linger on my boss.

"Carter," Steven schmoozes, standing. "What can I do for you?"

"Just wanted to introduce you to Steven," Carter gestures between the two men. "Ah... Steven." He chuckles, as if the shared name is the funniest thing he's heard all week. "This could get confusing."

"Not really," the new guy interrupts, shaking my boss's hand. "Steve Fox. Most people call me Foxy. If you do the same, it'll negate any confusion."

I perk up instantly. The name rings a bell, but I can't place it.

Steven doesn't offer his name again. He just asks pointedly: "And what do you do, Mr. Fox?"

"Mr. Fox is an elite security consultant here to overhaul our computer systems following the attempted breach," Carter explains. "We were lucky to get him; he's one of the best in his field. He lives in L.A., but just happened to be vacationing in the area."

"Not 'one of the best'—'the best'," Foxy corrects, with the certainty of a man who can back it up if challenged.

"That's... fortuitous," I murmur under my breath, as I continue to wrack my brain, chasing the elusive flicker of recognition.

"Isn't it?" Carter claps Foxy on the back. Steven's look says otherwise. "If he hadn't accidentally collided with my wife last night when we were out for dinner, we never would have met or been able to secure his services."

Carter and Foxy share a look of camaraderie, one that suggests a negative experience was resolved successfully over a few glasses of scotch and a handshake that promised discounted IT expertise.

"Anyhow," Carter continues, "I just wanted to introduce you. Whatever he needs to plug any holes in our defences, he gets. I want you both to give him whatever access he needs."

Steven smirks. "If he's that good, he shouldn't need our help," Steven quips, trying to be funny. "He should be able hack our system, bypass any security to take what he needs."

Foxy doesn't blink. "He could," he says, voice flat, edged with quiet menace. "But that would be unethical." Then, with a stony expression and razor-thin smile he drops his voice, "Nasty mark on your face. Looks like your charm offensive finally met its match. You should be more careful. In your game, I bet you mix with all sorts. Upset the wrong person, and you could find yourself in a whole heap of trouble."

Steven snorts and throws himself back in his chair. "Whatever. Just see my assistant if you need anything," he sneers. "Tina can be quite accommodating when she chooses to be."

If his words are supposed to be a veiled slur on my character, any offense is surpassed by the happy realisation that I must still have a job.

"Nice to meet you, Mr. Fox." I extend my hand with a smile, and he shakes it warmly.

"Foxy," he tells me with a cheery smile backed up by a wink.

"Yes you are," I mutter, drinking in his tall, athletic frame and devilishly handsome good looks.

Chapter 9

After Carter has given Foxy a tour of the building, ensuring all the staff know they are to give him their full cooperation, I'm surprised when they both head back to my floor and the corner of the office where my desk is stationed right outside Steven's door, facing the room with its side aligned parallel to his office.

"What can I do for you sir?" I ask Carter as the pair approach, laughing and joking like they have known each other years.

"My man Foxy has decided he needs to set up in this area of the building," Carter claps Foxy on the back. "He needs to optimize signal triangulation for cross-platform latency reduction. It's critical for maintaining real-time data integrity across the building's decentralized nodes." Carter beams like he is suddenly the proud owner of a computer science degree.

Foxy doesn't miss a beat. "Exactly," he says solemnly. "Wouldn't you agree this spot—right here—is where the building's electromagnetic topography converges in a rare harmonic pocket of flux density allowing the fibreoptics to maintain their technological integrity.

"I would. I would." Carter nods enthusiastically.

I know for a fact Carter's assistant is still tasked with typing up Carter's handwritten notes and he still maintains a manual diary. He switches his laptop on every morning to create the illusion of computer literacy but the last time it 'crashed' it had simply run out of charge. Despite the confident delivery, even I know what I just heard is a load of twaddle. I glance at Foxy, who gives me a cheeky smile—the kind that offers an ulterior motive. I'm flattered, but I don't need any more attention right now. The last thing I need is a jealous Kurt assaulting anyone else at the company.

"Wouldn't you be better off downstairs, closer to the servers and the mainframe?" I quirk an eyebrow so Foxy knows I'm onto him.

Foxy grins all faux-innocence and charm. "Ah, that's a common misconception. Proximity to the servers is irrelevant when the task you are assigned to relies on your seamless integration into a sweet spot which just so happens to resonate from the general periphery of the exact space in which your desk is located."

I blink, as I try to ascertain if he is flirting, unhinged, or just dangerously good at improvising nonsense to hide a hidden agenda.

"In other words," he adds, voice dropping just enough to make it personal as he glances at me before casting his eyes out the window behind me then to the closed door of Steven's office. "I like the view."

I quirk an eyebrow. He's already watching me again with that grin—the one that says *yes, I'm full of it, and yes, I know you know.*

"That desk over there is vacant." I point to one the far side of the room. If he is flirting it's best I make it clear I'm not interested. Plus, it would be distracting to have someone so attractive working too close.

"Thanks," Foxy winks as he and Carter amble away chatting more techno-nonsense.

My mobile chimes and a message from Kurt flashes up on the screen:

Lunch

I check my watch to see it almost one o'clock before messaging back.

> *I might skip it today. There's a new guy starting and I think I should keep an eye on him. I've got an energy bar in my desk.*

I've barely hit send before the phone pings again.

> *It wasn't a request. I'm in the lobby waiting and if I don't see your sweet ass wiggling in my direction in five— I'm coming up to get you.*

I roll my eyes, but a giggle slips out anyway.

You think you can get past security?

Within seconds I get the reply that has me out of my seat and dashing to the elevator.

You think I can't? GAME ON.

The elevator pings as it hits the ground floor and the doors slide open. My heart stutters when I see him across the foyer, leaning on a pillar, the cuffs of his black T-shirt straining against the muscles of his tattooed biceps. His thumbs are hooked in the front pockets of his black jeans, and his piercing green eyes sparkle with mischief as they track every step I make in his direction.

"Hi," he murmurs, kissing my cheek. "See you decided you had time for lunch after all."

I give him my best look of infuriation as he takes my hand and leads me out of the building and down the road. "Where's your coat?" I ask as I try to wrap mine round me tighter. The sun is shining but the temperature is barely above freezing.

Kurt chuckles and leans across to kiss my temple, "You worried about me?"

No, I just don't want this child growing up thinking common sense skipped a generation and frostbite is a fashion statement. She's already got half your genes to contend with—let's not stack the odds. Let's give her a fighting chance at avoiding hypothermia."

Kurt's lips twitch. "I'm way too hot to get hypothermia. And if our baby inherits my good looks, he'll be just fine."

I sigh, dramatic and long-suffering. "If *she* inherits your ego, we'll need to move to a bigger place just to contain it."

My joy at thinking he's taking me to the burger joint I usually frequent is short-lived when he ducks into a small place I've never noticed before—probably because everything on the menu looks like it was curated by a wellness influencer that has a personal vendetta against anything with flavour. The air smells like kale and regret and I half expect to see a line of rabbits waiting for a table.

I glance at the menu. One dish promises to 'nourish my soul' with its fermented beetroot and something called activated quinoa. My soul would beat Kurt around the head with said menu—if it weren't made of recycled paper, which makes it about as impactful as whatever culinary disappointment is about to land in front of me. The devil on my shoulder is egging me to storm out in search of fries to salvage its dignity. The devil sitting across from me is grinning, blissfully unaware he could be about to be stabbed with a fork made from recycled bottles. Hasn't he noticed I'm growing a human. I deserve carbs, not edible regret.

"Have you decided yet?" Kurt asks, smirking like my pained facial expressions are the best source of entertainment he's had in a long while.

"Um…" I scowl at him and smile at the waitress waiting to take our order. "Sorry, it all looks so…"

"Healthy," Kurt supplies, clearly enjoying my discomfort. "We'll have the turkey, quinoa, and black bean salad. Twice." He snatches the menu from my hands, snaps it shut, and hands it to our server—presumably so she can use it to catch her drool before it lands on him.

"Drink?" she asks, batting her eyes. I'm unsure if she's offering us one or asking to take my date out for one.

"Water for me," Kurt says, glancing over.

"And for your… sister?" his new groupie ventures hopefully.

"I'm not his sister," I growl, wrestling my hormones into submission and omitting the word 'bitch' at the last second. "I'm his pregnant fiancée."

"No she's not," Kurt replies casually. I swear my jaw hits the table. "It's true she's carrying my baby, but we're not engaged."

"Really," the waitress drawls, her interest blatantly obvious. With her long flowing skirt and one too many bangles, I bet her names star—or something equally astrologically blessed.

"I'll have a lemonade," I say through gritted teeth. "Not the still, freshly squeezed variety—I'll take the one loaded with sugar and carbonated with gas."

"Coming right up."

"You hypocrite," I snarl as soon as moonbeam—or whatever her name is—disappears.

"What?" Kurt shrugs, maddeningly nonchalant. "I didn't think you wanted to get married."

"I..." I blame baby brain for the fact that, in that moment, words fail me. Maybe I wasn't sure about marrying him—but I was damn sure I didn't want him advertising that uncertainty to other interested parties, implying he'd be back on the market for all and sundry as soon as our 'mutually exclusive fuck buddy' arrangement expires.

"Got a question you want to ask me?" He smiles like a chess champion who's just declared check. "Pretty sure the answer would be a positive one. Yes, I do, or something similar."

"Do you want to sleep on the sofa tonight?" I snap, voice tight with something I refuse to name. When Kurt sniggers, I make a countermove—not out of strategy, but impulse. "The new guy who started today? He's very handsome. We kind of hit it off. So much so, he's requested a desk on my floor."

"That's nice." I was expecting a flash of jealousy

or at least a flicker of interest. Instead, Kurt leans back in his chair, smiling like he anticipated the move. It's almost as if he's laughing at me. Jerk!

I throw a napkin at him just as our drinks arrive. I reach for my lemonade, only to find it ceremoniously substituted with the glass of water. When the food arrives seconds later, I stare at the bowl like it's contaminated.

"It's good for you," Kurt chuckles, forking a spoonful of green leaves peppered with little round black things that look suspiciously like the droppings I used to clear out of the neighbour's rabbit hutch when I was pet sitting as a kid. "Packed with nutrition. Exactly the kind of meal that fuels growing babies."

"Worst lunch date ever," I moan, jabbing the food suspiciously with my cutlery and counting the seconds until I can get back to the secret stash of chocolate-covered contraband in my desk drawer.

An hour later, Kurt walks me back to the office. Annoyed and still hungry, I try to avoid physical contact en route. Kurt just chuckles before catching my hand, firmly entwining his fingers with mine and refusing to let go.

When we reach my building and I try to pull away, he tightens his grip.

"Do I get my kiss goodbye?" he asks, biting his cheek to keep from laughing.

"Do you have a quarter pounder with fries in your back pocket?" I reply haughtily, trying to shake free.

One swift, resolute tug has me wrapped in his arms and quivering with anticipation before his mouth lands on mine.

"Oh lord," I murmur when he lets me come up for air.

"What?" he chuckles.

"You've jump-started my hormones. Now I'm going to be horny all afternoon."

"Really?" he growls, eyes darkening. "We can't have that, can we?'

I barely have time to blink before he's steering me around the side of the building, past the bins and into the shadowed alcove usually reserved for deliveries.

"Kurt—"

"Shh."

His mouth finds mine again, hungrier this time, and when his hand slides between my thighs, I forget all about being late. He backs me against a door, lips grazing my neck.

"You said you were hungry," he murmurs. "Let me feed the craving I actually sparked."

Somewhere in the distance, a delivery van honks—probably en route to this very spot, stuck in afternoon traffic. I'm not normally so adventurous. Usually, my sense of propriety would kick in, tangled with the fear of getting caught. But I don't flinch. In the safety of Kurt's arms, I'm on fire. And too busy relishing how good it feels to be wanted like this—like I'm the only thing on his menu.

My body, overrun with need, takes control. Kurt matches my urgency as my hands fumble with his belt, unfastening it before working to free him from his jeans. When he lifts me effortlessly, I wrap my legs around his hips, locking them at the ankles for support. I can't tell you how good it feels to be with a guy who has the physical strength to do that so easily, despite the extra weight I'm carrying. It makes the moment even more intoxicating.

Once any obstacles have been shoved aside and we're in position, he claims me. Gently at first, then faster, harder. Over and over until my pleasure peaks. I bite Kurt's neck—hard—desperate to muffle the scream clawing its way up my throat. He grunts but doesn't complain. If I were a vampire, I swear he'd let me suck him dry.

Then time folds in on itself, until the only thing that exists is the way he's looking at me—like *I'm* a craving *he'll* never shake. If I were braver, I'd admit the truth right now: it's not that I don't want forever—it's that, despite his words, I'm terrified I won't be enough to make him stay. Instead, I pour every swirling emotion into one final kiss before he sets me down and we hurry to regain a more dignified composure.

I walk back into the office on shaky legs, lips swollen, blouse misaligned, wondering if I could wipe the smug smile off my face long enough for anyone to ignore me having a nap on my desk.

Best lunch date ever.

On autopilot, I drift to my desk, likely sporting the dazed, goofy look of someone who's just committed a major sin undetected. Without looking, I pull open the drawer, rifling for my smuggled stash of sugar-coated shame, when a voice slices through my X-rated thoughts.

"Well, someone looks like they had a productive lunch."

Snapping out of my post-coital trance, I find myself staring into the eyes of a certain foxy guy. I glance around the office. The desk I'd originally assigned him has been dragged across the room and parked back-to-back with mine, which has also been rotated ninety degrees to make space. I'm still in front of Steven's door—but now with my back to it. Instead of being able to scan the room to deflect attention before it strikes, I'm perpendicular to the action. Better view of the window, worse view of everything else. I freeze.

"What the hell? Does Steven know you've rearranged everything?"

"Nope." Foxy answers, head down, tapping away at a keyboard in front of three monitors that have magically materialised in the time I've been gone.

"I don't think he'll like it. I can't see who's approaching his door unless I sit twisted sideways—and that's not exactly conducive to typing."

"Hit Control, Shift, forward slash."

I log on and do as instructed. My screen flickers to life, now split with a picture-in-picture view of the room—I can see as much as before, only now, no-one knows I'm watching.

"You've been busy," I say, impressed. "But wasn't that a lot of work just so you could 'sit where the building's electromagnetic topography converges in a rare harmonic pocket of flux density to allow any fibreoptics to maintain their technological integrity'?" I parrot the load of bull Foxy was slinging around earlier back at him.

He lifts his head to smirk. "I told you—I like the view here."

"I'm not sure you should be staring at me all day. I don't think my boyfriend would appreciate it." I enunciate *boyfriend* just enough to make the point.

"Who says I'm looking at you?" Foxy grins.

I glance behind me. "I don't think Steven's closed door is likely to hold your attention." I volley back. Could the guy be any more obvious? I sigh and resume my quest for hidden candy.

"If you're searching for your snacks, I'm afraid I ate them."

"What?" The word bursts out, panicked and indignant. I scramble to check the drawer—hoping for a morsel, a crumb, anything to soothe the sugar-starved gremlin I've become.

"I didn't get the chance to nip out earlier. Needed the calories after shifting all this equipment around. Carter's not as young as he used to be—it was only fair I did the lion's share."

"Carter helped you?" I fall back in my seat, stunned. The man barely makes his own coffee. If he thought he could persuade his assistant to lift it to his lips, I'm convinced he'd try.

Foxy smiles like I should know he is a man not to be underestimated before throwing me an apple. "Peace offering."

I stare at the offending item like he has just tossed me a grenade.

"Fruit?" I snarl. "What sort of gift is that? Here's a thought, you could have eaten this instead of pilfering my emergency chocolate."

"Sorry." Foxy's eyes glint with mischief as he tries not to laugh, "I was so busy setting up I forgot I had it, then I got distracted. I happened upon the feed for the outside surveillance system and the camera focused on the west side picked up some very interesting footage."

"Oooh," I lean forward conspiratorially and whisper, "Spill, what did you see?"

Foxy leans over his desk, our eyes locking as he lowers his voice, "there was a couple in the delivery bay, 'getting it on.'"

Fuck. My. Life!

As Foxy flops back in his chair laughing, my face flames so hot I fear the fire alarm might go off.

"Don't worry," he says after a beat of enjoying my mortification. "Once I realised who it was, I scrambled the feed to stop anyone watching something they shouldn't and erased the footage."

I cough to clear the sudden lump in my throat before wheezing, "Thank you."

"Welcome." Foxy smiles. "Perhaps you could do me a favour in return. Your boss left shortly after you, and I really need to get into his office... to check if there's any malware on his hard drive."

"How can I help?" I ask, confused.

"He locked the door. Said if I needed anything, to ask you. Do you have a key?"

"No. I didn't even realise he had one. It's never been locked before—not even when his predecessor worked there. Can't you just hack in? Carter said you could use whatever means necessary to make sure we're protected."

"I tried." Foxy pauses, thoughtful. "He must've

unplugged the system. He's either worried someone unauthorised could get in remotely to view his files or..."

"He has something to hide," I automatically finish for him.

Foxy smirks. "Exactly. What's he working on right now?"

"As far as I know, he's solely tasked with managing the Jasper Knox case."

Foxy lets out a long, low whistle. "As in Knox Developments—*where vision and value collide.* I've seen that on the news. You know I'm not from around here... isn't he the property developer linked to the death of a single mother and her child?"

"I'm not sure I should be talking about it," I reply, sympathetic but cautious.

"It's okay," Foxy throws me another one of his winning smiles. "Do you think Carter would grant me full access to his systems without asking me to sign some kind of NDA? I'm bound to stumble across something confidential eventually—even if only by accident."

Weighing the odds, I decide he probably has access to far more information than I do, so it can't hurt to share the basics. Most of what I'm about to say has already been reported publicly one way or another anyway.

"You're right. Jasper Knox is the founder and CEO of Knox Developments, which buys urban spaces in prime locations that are in dire need of modernisation. He flips the real estate, creating bespoke luxury accommodation for celebrity clients—think rooftop gardens, state-of-the-art biometric security systems, helipads, that sort of thing. He's at every charity gala, in every lifestyle magazine, and constantly praised for his visionary renewal projects, which span New York State and have recently started to bleed into both New Jersey and Pennsylvania."

"Let me guess—the case only hit the big leagues because the victim was a celeb? Or was it because Knox is a rich twat?" Foxy's unexpected turn of phrase makes me giggle.

"Neither, actually. By all accounts, Knox is charming and charismatic. He's also a philanthropist, taking a hefty slice of the profits from Knox Developments and funnelling it into his subsidiary company, Urban Future Initiatives —*Because everyone deserves a shot at greatness*. That company builds affordable housing, then secures grants and donations to help subsidise low-income families. He helps people who otherwise wouldn't stand a chance get on the housing ladder, giving them the opportunity to fulfil their dream of home ownership"

"If this guy is such a saint, why did he get arrested?"

"When Camila Ramirez and her son perished in a house fire, it was a tragedy that hit the headlines. The property she lived in was part of an Urban Future Initiative project, and her brother Carlos was so distraught he blamed the firm for her death. Drunk and grieving, he went to the media slinging accusations—claiming he had proof the company had been cutting corners on the builds and that Knox knew but did nothing. Authorities had no choice but to investigate, and Knox was ultimately arrested. He didn't seem overly bothered. As he was being led away, he stated that while he was deeply sorry for what had happened, he was confident a full investigation would vindicate him of all charges. The fire, he said, had been caused by an electrical surge from the grid—a random, unforeseeable event—and he had documentation proving that neither he nor the company were at fault, as all building regulations had been followed to the letter."

"What was your take on it?"

I think for a second.

"Robert Taylor reviewed the initial evidence thoroughly before taking the case. He's one of the top defence attorneys in the US—which is probably why he was approached in the first place—but he's also known for having a strong moral compass. If he'd suspected any foul play, I doubt he would've touched it.

Honestly, I don't think anyone here believed the case would ever see the inside of a courtroom. Everyone assumed it would get thrown out. It didn't. I'm still not sure why. The prosecution must've had just enough to push it through.

From what I understand, they presented their case—but Robert dismantled their witnesses at every turn. Then, on the final day, just as he was preparing to mount his defence, the prosecution introduced a last-minute witness—along with new, unexpectedly damning evidence. He was granted a day to verify its authenticity.

But when court reconvened, Robert never showed. He's been missing ever since.

Carter had to personally request a continuance, and Steven was hastily drafted in to take over. He's known for winning at all costs and blindsiding the opposition when they least expect it. Maybe that's why someone tried to hack our system—and why he's switched off his hard drive. If he's still reviewing crucial information stored locally, he might be worried about it falling into the wrong hands.

I do know he's been leaving the office regularly to meet with some kind of informant. Every Thursday he's in, he leaves at noon sharp and never returns until the following day. He must go straight home after, because no one's ever seen him anywhere else."

"Where does he go?"

I shrug. "He's never said. And I always got the feeling that if I asked, he wouldn't tell me—so I never did."

"Interesting." Foxy switches off his monitors and stands with purpose—enough to make me ask:

"Where are you going?"

"Meeting my buddy for a burger."

"Ooh, if I give you the money, can you bring me back a quarter pounder with cheese? Actually, make that two. One for each of us." I point between my face and my baby bump.

"Sure," Foxy chuckles, waving away my offer of cash as he walks off. "Don't touch my keyboard while I'm gone."

"As if I would," I call after him.

If he brings me back what I asked for, I might propose to him instead of Kurt.

Twenty minutes later, I've caught up on all my tasks. With everything grinding to a halt over New Year's and Steven nowhere to be seen, I'm left twiddling my thumbs. I stretch and wander over to Foxy's desk. There's no clutter—just three monitors, a keyboard, and a mouse. I'm intrigued by the need for three screens and glance around furtively. He may have said not to touch his keyboard, but he didn't say anything about the monitors.

I switch on the first. Lines and lines of code roll across the screen. Panicking, I hastily switch it off before I disrupt whatever magic it's in the process of weaving.

I hesitate, then cautiously power up the second. The screen fills with unrecognisable gobbledegook. This time the script is static, the cursor flashing at the end of a line, waiting for Foxy's command. I switch that off and snap on the third—and largest—screen.

Little boxes fill the display, each showing a live video stream. When I recognise the delivery bay, I realise I'm watching the feed from the security cameras dotted around the building. I bury my head in my hands, embarrassment taking hold once more.

I'm just about to power it down when I spot Foxy leaning against a wall in a sheltered corner near the front entrance. He's chatting with someone just out of frame. Intrigued, I watch as he accepts a bag and retrieves a burger. I immediately start to salivate, mesmerised as he tucks in heartily. I can almost smell the sharp, caramelised sweetness of the onions and taste the unapologetic pre-saturated fat of the meat. Don't even get me started on the molten cheese—creamy, sinful, and exactly what my rabbit-food lunch lacked. It's food porn of the most graphic variety.

When he's done, he licks his fingers, screws up the empty bag, and laughs. Sure he's about to head back inside—and excited I'm about to receive my share of the food I've just been lusting over—my finger hovers over the power button. It drops in surprise as Foxy's mysterious friend steps into full view.

Fury bubbles up inside me as I see Kurt popping the last gratifying piece of his own burger into his mouth. And suddenly, it clicks. That's why the name 'Foxy' struck such a chord. Kurt mentioned it in the kitchen this morning. They know each other. That's for sure.

I have a minor battle with myself, trying to decide who I'm angriest with. Myself, for not picking up on their connection sooner. Foxy, for pumping me for information and not admitting he knew the guy he caught me with on camera. Or Kurt—for cheating on me with my favourite fast food restaurant.

Once clarity hits, it's the gift that just keeps giving. That's what Kurt meant when he said he'd be watching. That's why Foxy rearranged the furniture to sit opposite me. He's spying on me for Kurt. That's why Kurt wasn't jealous when I mentioned Foxy at lunch. Is that why my sweets disappeared and got replaced with an apple? Has Kurt recruited him into the nutritional narc squad?

Either way, if they want to play...

I switch off the monitor and mutter, "Game on, douchebags," under my breath. Then I calmly return to my side of the desk with two hours of free time to plot my next move.

Chapter 10

It was remiss of Foxy to leave his cell languishing on the break room counter that afternoon. I waited for him to return and collect it. When he didn't, I picked it up with the express purpose of returning it to him. *Honest.*

How it found itself switched off and therefore untraceable before being buried under a pile of tea towels in the drawer next to the sink—I'll never know.

"Are you sure you haven't seen it?" Foxy asks for the umpteenth time, dragging a hand through his hair in frustration as he flops into the chair opposite me. He's been running around the building for twenty minutes now.

"Not recently." I'm not lying. I haven't seen it in at least the last half hour. It's a shame mobile security has come so far. I could've had great fun sending his 'buddy' a few imaginative texts. Or maybe reshuffling the names and numbers of his female 'acquaintances'—just enough to ensure when he calls *Bootylicious Barbie* to ask her to pop round and polish his confidence, he ends up inviting his mom to boost his self-esteem in ways no son should ever suggest.

"If this is about the burgers, I'm sorry. It's not my fault my buddy met me outside and I didn't get the chance to grab you one."

"I told you. It's okay, I understand," I reply sweetly, smiling with just enough venom to throw him off guard. "Look, I'm sure it'll turn up... eventually."

"It's kind of important I find it now," Foxy says, half pleading, as if he suspects my innocence is entirely performative. "The guys I work for expect to be able to reach me at all times."

"Really?" I plant my elbows on my desk, steeple my fingers under my chin, and regard him with interest. "Tell me about them."

"What?" There's a flicker of panic in his tone.

"The guys you work for," I repeat. "If you're that worried they'll lose it just because you misplaced your mobile, they must be pretty scary."

Foxy looks at me like I'm a mystery he's not equipped to solve. He answers carefully. "Not much to tell. They thrive on efficiency, that's all."

"What about your buddy—the one you met at lunch? Tell me about him."

Another guarded answer. "What do you want to know?"

"What's his name, for starters?"

Foxy squirms. "I mostly just call him the 'b' word."

"Beelzebub?" I quip, without missing a beat. "Where'd you meet?"

"We were in the Navy together. When we got out, we both ended up working for the same firm." He may not be admitting the full truth, but at least he isn't lying to my face.

"Hmm." I rise and walk around to perch on his desk. I grab his bicep, giving it a squeeze. He jumps like I've tasered him.

"I bet you were a SEAL. You're fit enough to be a SEAL."

"Elec…" He coughs, and I smile to myself as his throat goes dry. "Electronics." He offers the word like it explains everything, neither confirming nor denying anything.

"Are you single, Foxy?" I purr, letting the seduction drip. I'm pretty sure he is—his phone's screensaver was bland and generic.

"Um… yeah," he murmurs, definitely nervous now.

I fight to hold back my smirk. "Then you're coming home with me tonight."

"What… No… I…"

"Hush." I press a finger to his lips, relishing his

discomfort. I'm fairly certain thoughts of Kurt—and what he might do to him if he took me up on my perceived offer—are flashing through his mind right now. "I insist."

"Y... You have a boyfriend," he stutters. *Bingo!*

"It's okay. I'm pretty sure he'd be up for a bit of fun too." Foxy's eyes go so wide they nearly eclipse his entire face. I pat my pregnant belly and fake a yawn. "I could use a hand keeping him amused tonight. I don't have as much energy as I used to since he knocked me up."

Rendered speechless, Foxy just watches me, slack-jawed, as I lean in provocatively and whisper, "Why don't you just send your bosses an email explaining you're not on your cell right now?"

"Right... yes." He swallows audibly. "Why didn't I think of that?" He scrambles for his keyboard, and I saunter back to my chair, satisfied I've managed to leave him rattled.

"And you call yourself an expert," I taunt, putting my head down and getting on with my work—pretending not to notice the subtle glances of fear and confusion aimed in my direction for the rest of the day.

At half five, despite his repeated protests, I link arms with a very apprehensive Foxy and drag him home with me.

Kurt's already there when we arrive, I hear him

scrambling about in the adjoining room as I open the front door. Foxy trails in behind me, visibly uncomfortable, unsure whether he's walking into a honey trap or a dinner party.

"Hope you've cooked enough for three," I chirp, dropping my keys into the bowl with a little more force than necessary.

"Shit." I hear Kurt murmur before calling back, "I thought Izzy was out tonight."

"She is." I reply jauntily.

"Great!" Kurt's voice lowers, deep and sultry. I guess he assumes the third party I'm talking about us our baby when he growls, "Get in here, I've got something simmering that's guaranteed to satisfy you."

Foxy and I enter the living room to see Kurt lounging on the sofa like he owns the place. He is naked, with a rose between his teeth and sign covering his essentials. I huff out a laugh as I read: Tonight's menu: tight buns, plenty of meat, and a whole lot of sauce.

Kurt sees Foxy and his eyebrows shoot so high I fear they will have to be peeled from the ceiling. Foxy looks like he's trying to disappear into the wallpaper. I'm not sure if he is embarrassed or afraid Kurt will whip out a gun and shoot him for laughing.

"What the hell?" Kurt spits the rose from his

mouth like it's toxic. He seems more bothered by being caught with *that* than by his nakedness. His eyes lock on Foxy like a hawk. "Did you two come together?"

Foxy chokes on air. "Uh—no. I mean—yes. I mean—she invited me. She insisted."

"Oh, I did," I say sweetly, brushing past them toward the kitchen. "He's new in town. It would've been rude to leave him to fend for himself… not when I could offer him something *hot*."

Kurt's jaw tightens. Foxy's eyes dart between us like he's watching a live grenade roll across the floor.

"Drink?" I offer Foxy, as I meander off leaving the two men muttering in low, growling tones to each other.

One glance around the kitchen, and my mind's made up. "I hope you like dessert, Foxy. Looks like Kurt whipped one up earlier." I lift the chocolate cream pie languishing on the counter. No pause. No mercy. "I'm sure you do. You know, it's funny — You both have such similar taste in everything else. Burgers. Friends. I pause dramatically before adding, "secrets."

Foxy freezes. Kurt doesn't blink as I re enter the room. I look between them before deciding Kurt is the one pulling the strings here, Foxy is just doing *his* bidding.

"Thankyou baby, it looks delicious." I smile, slow and sharp before leaning over the back of the couch and launching the pristinely presented pie in his face.

Kurt blinks, slowly wiping cream from his lashes, still sprawled on the couch like a dethroned king. I stand over him, pie dish empty in my hands, the scent of cocoa and humiliation thick in the air.

He opens his mouth, voice low and dangerous. "Tina, I was trying to protect you, there's—"

I tilt my head, smiling like I'm about to let him finish. "Things I don't know?" I cut in, smooth as silk.

Then I press a finger to his lips, smearing a bit of leftover filling across them. "Shh," I whisper. "Dessert's talking now. You had your chance."

I drop the tin on his lap with a satisfying *clang*, turn on my heel, and vanish out the door before he can spit out another syllable.

Foxy looks like he's about to have a stroke, poor guy.

As the door clicks shut behind me, I switch off my mobile and don't look back. Let them stew. I have better things to do—like hailing a cab and finding someone who's turned flipping burgers into an art form, and who doesn't believe in portion control when it comes to fries.

I'm not sure how I end up in the window

seat of Flippin' Scrumptious, a high-end burger joint facing The Obsidian, one of Knox's latest indulgences in the hospitality industry. The hotel looms across the street, all black mirrored glass, gold signage, and uniformed porters buzzing around like bees—collecting or depositing suitcases into waiting cabs. It oozes opulence and charm, but it's also prime dinner entertainment. I sit back, devouring my feast, watching the comings and goings of the guests like it's theatre.

I'm halfway through washing down my second burger with a large glass of orange juice when the hotel doors slide open and someone I recognise steps out.

Steven.

He's got a woman on his arm—tall, polished, the kind of beauty that looks expensive even in daylight. It takes me a beat to place her. Judge Simmons' 'cousin,' from Clara's party.

I watch like a voyeur as they embrace. Not politely. Not platonically. But with the kind of familiarity that doesn't belong to a happily married man with a wife waiting at home.

Steven hails a cab, plants her inside with a final grope of her ass, and slips the driver a wad of notes. With no other taxis lingering, he starts scanning the street.

My instincts kick in before logic does and I duck behind a menu like a child playing spy.

Peeking over the top, I watch him as my pulse ticks faster. Has he been here all afternoon? With her? What were they doing?

Eww. The possibilities make my stomach churn.

A black SUV glides up beside him and he climbs in without looking back. From where I'm sitting, it's hard to tell—but I could've sworn the driver was Bear.

And just like that, they're gone.

I sit frozen, the taste of orange juice suddenly sharp and unappealing. Was it Bear I saw? Why did I hide? And why does it feel like I've just witnessed something I wasn't supposed to?

I'm still turning over the answers when I walk back through the door at home and find Kurt—fully dressed and pacing like a caged tiger, ready to tear into the first person he sees. Foxy's nowhere in sight. Either he left, or Kurt's made him disappear and buried the evidence. Guess I'll find out at work Monday—either Foxy clocks in with all limbs accounted for, or HR starts sniffing around due to unexplained absences.

I brace myself for war, only to find myself being scanned from head to toe before being pulled into a pair of strong arms that feel like home—and a siege—all at once.

"Where the hell were you?" Kurt growls, affection laced with fury as he kisses the crown of my head. "I was going out of my mind."

"So was I. I needed sustenance. Something a bit more substantial than a bowl of bland promises masquerading as contentment. I'm a woman who hungers for things that don't come pre-approved."

"Is that so?" Kurt pulls back, a different kind of hunger flickering in his eyes. "Then I can definitely help you out."

I press both palms to his chest and shove —gently, but with intent. The action's purely symbolic. It's like trying to move a mountain.

"I'm fully satisfied for the moment, thank you. Unless you're offering answers as to why Foxy —the one you said works for Josh—is suddenly cozying up at my workplace. And why neither of you thought to mention your connection to me."

"Quit your job." The words fire out, sharp and sudden. But they're not a demand. Not really. More like a plea dressed in bravado.

"I can't. Not right now—I need the money."

"You can if you let me take care of you."

"What is this, the 1920s? Should I start watching reruns of Downton to learn my place?"

Kurt bites the side of his cheek as he tries not to laugh. "Not at all. I fully expect you to go back to work full-time after the birth to finance my early retirement, that way I can live out my days as your stay-at-home boy toy slash childminder."

I huff out a laugh. We both know there's about as much chance of that happening as Pythagoras rising from the grave to disprove his own theorem.

"Would it even count as childminding if it's your own kid?" I ask, an eyebrow arched. "Or would it just be you stepping into your role as a parent?"

"Semantics," he smiles softly. "I'd do it. If it meant you'd agree to walk away from that firm. Right now."

Something in his voice—low, certain, almost reverent—makes my chest ache. I want to believe him. I almost do.

"I'm not ready," I whisper. "Not yet."

He nods, an unspoken understanding lingering between us for a few seconds before he brushes his knuckles down my cheek tenderly.

"Then if you have to go... the less you know, the better."

"Or...If you told me what you believe is going on, I might be able to help."

He studies me for a moment, then shakes his head slowly. "No."

"Is this a 'because I'm a woman' thing?" I ask, exasperated.

He smiles, clearly trying not to laugh, which only aggravates me more. "No," he repeats. "It's a 'you're my girl and carrying my baby' thing. It's your job to keep him or her safe, and it's mine to do the same for you."

"But surely it'd be in my best interests to know what's going on. What if we want more kids someday?" The words spill out fast and unfiltered. It seems logical to me. Kurt, however, cocks his head, confused.

"What? I don't follow."

"I should get the option of protecting my interests too." I wave a hand vaguely in the direction of his groin. "I could play a pivotal part in helping keep you safe and all your parts in full working order." A huge smile creeps across his face until he's beaming brighter than the sun. It's disconcerting—he doesn't usually show emotion so freely.

"What?" I snap, assuming he's focused on the immediate gratification his parts can offer rather than the bigger picture. I brace for some crass comment about his superior sexual prowess. But his next words throw me.

"That's the first time you've openly admitted to my face you can potentially see a future with me."

My mouth flaps silently, automatic and useless. I'm pretty sure I resemble a goldfish after a live electrical cable has been tossed in its bowl. I scramble for words, knowing this moment needs careful navigation on my part.

"I... um... just..."

"Can't live without me?" Kurt ruffles my hair affectionately and cocks an eyebrow, smug. "Understandable."

I roll my eyes. "Yeah, right. It's just—Liam and I are close. I'd like Nugget to have a sibling someday. It'd be easier if both kids had the same father, you know? Less complicated."

"Sure. While I appreciate your... concerns," Kurt's lips twitch with amusement. I can tell he doesn't believe a word of the excuse I'm trying to sell him. Whatever. "I've got plenty of other people I can call on to watch my back if I need to. Highly skilled, lethal people. You don't need to worry about me." He pauses, then leans in and plants a kiss on my lips—soft, deliberate, and far too brief. "But I appreciate the fact that you do." His voice drops, low and serious now. "The less you know, the easier it'll be for you to keep things business as usual at the office. Start poking around in matters that don't concern you, and you'll draw attention. The wrong kind. And if that happens, you won't just be putting yourself at risk—you'll make it harder for me and Foxy to stay under the radar while we work through the anomalies that surfaced the moment we began digging into your boss and Robert Taylor's disappearance."

"What anomalies?" I rest my hand over the curve of my belly. He covers it with his own. "Kurt, you're scaring me again."

"Don't worry," Kurt says gently. "I'm not about to let anything happen to my girls."

"Girls?" I blink. "You're finally coming round to the fact this baby might not be a boy?"

"Honestly?" He shrugs. "I'll be happy either way. Half of this child is made of you, so it'll be perfect no matter what."

A lump rises in my throat. I swallow hard, wondering if maybe—just maybe—leaving my job wouldn't be the worst idea. Whatever this is between us, I'm not ready to risk losing it.

"Am I in danger?" I ask apprehensively.

"With a boyfriend like yours?" Kurts expression darkens, it feels ominous yet oddly reassuring. "Never. He'd do just about anything to keep you safe. Including keeping eyes on you at all times to ensure you're protected."

"Didn't do such a stellar job earlier, did he?" I tease, nudging his chest. "I managed to lose you and your shadow. Foxy hiding in a corner somewhere, reevaluating his life choices?"

"Probably. If he's finished trying to explain to Josh how he lost both his mobile and his credibility in less than twenty-four hours." He chuckles.

"Um… the mobile. I might have an idea as to where it could be," I mumble guiltily.

"There's a surprise," Kurt mutters, a hint of awe in his tone.

"You weren't too hard on him, were you?" I whisper.

"Me?" Kurt taps his chest like I've just insulted an angel. "Nah, I know who he's been having to deal with." He swats my ass playfully. "I should have warned him not to underestimate you. How'd you figure us out?"

I'm just about to tell him when I decide it might be good to harbour a small, harmless secret of my own. Keep him guessing.

"You're the one with the high IQ—you figure it out," I tell him, walking away with a backward glance and a smirk. "Oh, and if you and your elite task force are still struggling to find out where and with who Steven's been hanging recently when he's not in court. I can probably point you in the right direction."

"What? You saw him?" Kurt chases after me, spinning me round and demanding answers, "Where?"

I grab his T-shirt, pulling him in, almost close enough to kiss. "I see you're craving information, it just so happens I've suddenly got a craving too, but for something else entirely, something only you can provide. How about we trade?"

Kurt smiles against my lips. "Sounds like a

fair deal to me," he says, as I'm already walking backward, leading him to the bedroom like a puppet on a string.

He kicks the door closed behind us, and in that moment, I feel like I hold all the cards. The trick is knowing when to play them—and when to let him think he's winning. Tonight, I'll let him think he's playing an ace as he pumps me for information. Tomorrow? He'll realise I stacked the deck for my own ends—and his ace was my joker all along.

Chapter 11

"I… um… found this in the break room. Must've fallen into the drawer." I slide Foxy's mobile across the desk toward him first thing Monday morning.

I'd hoped to arrive before him, leave the phone on the desk, and plead ignorance—like the cleaners had found it and handed it in over the weekend or something. But Kurt made me late when he insisted on helping me shower. He made out it was purely out of concern for my safety, but some of the positions we adopted blew that theory straight out of the water. Not that I was complaining—until I noticed the time on the bedroom clock and realised I wouldn't just miss my chance to play innocent, I was running so late Kurt had to email Foxy to cover for me until I arrived, dripping with guilt but glowing like someone who'd just aced most of Kurt's unscheduled oral exam. Fortunately, since I flunked the time management module, he's making me retake the whole thing again. I grab a notelet and, grinning like a buffoon, jot down: amend tomorrow's morning alarm call.

"Switch itself off at the same time, did it?" Foxy grunts, eyes glued to his monitor.

"Must've," I reply nonchalantly, retrieving the cake box I'd dropped on my desk earlier then extracting a freshly made chocolate cream pie.

Foxy glances up. His eyes widen. "Am I going to end up wearing that?"

The wariness in his voice makes me smile. I remember Kurt's words from Friday night—*lethal, my ass. The man's scared of a dessert.*

"Peace offering." I slide the pie toward him. "I made Kurt get up at three a.m. He made it fresh."

I giggle at the two full moons staring back at me. "He willingly got up at three to make a pie for you to bring to work and gift to me?"

"Well... not exactly," I admit sheepishly. "He got up at three to go to the store and get me the olives I was craving—which is weird in itself, because I usually can't stand them. Anyway, before he left, I asked him to grab the ingredients for the pie too. He must've assumed it was another craving, came home, and whipped it up while I was sleeping so it had time to chill before I woke. I was actually going to ask him to make one today so I could bring it in tomorrow. Thought you might appreciate it since you missed out on dinner the other night."

Foxy flops back in his chair, blowing out a long breath. "He's different around you."

"Different good or different bad?" I ask, intrigued.

"Jury's out," Foxy replies thoughtfully. "He's smiling. That alone's got people rattled. The boss doesn't do content—he does control. Always barking orders, always one step ahead. And when he's calm like this? It's not usually peace— it's pressure building. Like he's winding up for something big, and we're all just waiting to see who gets caught in the blast radius. No one wants to be the poor bastard standing wherever the hammer's set to land."

He exhales. "I was sure he was going to rip me a new one Friday night—for losing my phone, blowing my cover, and letting you run right past me, out the door, with no clue where you'd gone. But all he said was, if I let on he'd been seen with a rose between his teeth and getting pied by his girlfriend, he'd bury me."

He pauses. "Unfortunately, by that time I'd already forwarded a picture of him naked and dripping with cream to Josh. Thought it might placate him before *he* chewed me out instead."

"Did it work?"

"I'm alive and in one piece, aren't I?" Foxy grins —then his smile drops. "Although probably not for much longer once Kurt finds out what I've done. You can bet your life no amount of begging will convince Josh to keep his big mouth shut. Which is fine for him, since he's about the only guy in the world who can bait Kurt and live to tell the tale."

"I didn't see you take a photo," I frown, trying to recall the moment.

"Have you forgotten I'm an expert in surveillance."

"Hmm." I smile and cock an eyebrow, unconvinced.

Foxy catches my drift and scrambles to explain. "Losing you was an exception."

"We'll see." I chuckle. "Although your job should be easier now—you don't have to resort to subterfuge. You can just ask me what my plans are."

Our hushed conversation is cut short when Steven forgoes the intercom and bellows my name from behind the closed door of his office. I roll my eyes at Foxy and stand, grabbing my notebook and a pen.

"Um..." Foxy starts.

"I know, I know. Don't let on about our connection outside the office." I whisper.

"He said you were smart as well as beautiful," Foxy adds with a wink. I feel myself blush.

"Who?"

It's Foxy's turn to roll his eyes. "Who do you think? Try to leave the door open when you're in there."

I knock once, then bounce into Steven's office—ignoring Foxy's veiled warning, too focused on the quiet thrill of knowing Kurt's been talking about me. Not just talking, but describing me as both smart and beautiful.

"You wanted to see me?"

"Shut the door," Steven barks from his throne.

I turn, flash Foxy a surreptitious apology, and do Steven's bidding before sliding into the chair opposite him.

"You can lose the notepad. We both know why you're here." He reclines, eyeing me like a viper sizing up lunch.

"I'm sorry," I frown, feigning cluelessness. "Where's this going?"

"Steven Fox."

Panic coils in my stomach, but I tamp it down, keeping my expression neutral. "What about him?"

Steven pauses, lips pursed, then continues. "What do you know about him?"

"Not much more than you. Carter brought him in to audit our systems. He's single. And judging by the parade of girls constantly orbiting his desk, they're hoping he won't stay that way."

"What about you? Are you taken with him?"

"No." I scoff at the absurdity of his insinuation. "In case you've forgotten, I have a boyfriend."

Steven grunts as he steeples his fingers under his chin, assessing. "Why did he rearrange the office to sit where he has?"

"You'd have to ask him." I shrug. "Carter signed off on it while they were deep in techno-babble. I tuned out somewhere between 'firewall' and 'data integrity.'"

Steven leans forward, hands dropping to the desk, pinning me with a stare that's hard to read. I glance around, pretending to be unfazed, and spot his computer—still off.

"Is your system down?" I ask, seizing the opening. "Want me to grab Foxy? I'm sure—"

"No." The word snaps out like a whip—it's the kind of response that draws eyes. Realising the misstep, he reins in his tone. "It's not broken," he adds, more softly.

He reclines again, visibly relaxing. "I don't need to tell you how important this case I'm working on is. Millions are at stake. Until Mr. Fox finds and patches any vulnerabilities in the company systems, I can't risk an outsider accessing sensitive data that's stored on my device."

"Oh, I get it," I nod. "You should let Foxy run a scan though—just to make sure your computer's protected and there hasn't already been a breach.

I think he tried on Friday after you left. Carter might've asked him to start with your desktop since the Jasper Knox case is our biggest yet. But when I got back from lunch, Foxy said your office was locked. He asked if I had a key, which of course I don't—since it's never been locked before."

Steven's eyes narrow. I try to lay a trap, catch him out in a lie.

"That could've proved tricky. If you'd called from court needing a file, I wouldn't have been able to get in and retrieve it for you."

He rubs his chin, deep in thought. It takes him so long to respond I half expect him to mention seeing me across the street when he left the Obsidian that night.

"Can I trust you, Tina?"

The question lands heavy. Loaded. Like the wrong answer might cost me more than just my job.

"That depends."

Steven tilts his head, waiting.

"As long as you don't ask me to do something I'm not comfortable with—yes."

I hope he thinks I'm referencing his party-night advances. When he rubs the fading bruise on his jaw, I know I've hit the mark. He sits bolt upright, all business.

"Very well. I locked the door because you weren't around to keep an eye on things. Tell Mr. Fox he can access my system tomorrow—under supervision. Until then, it stays offline. I'll be leaving for court at one again today and getting a spare key cut for you while I'm out."

I blink, feigning confusion. "Sorry, I thought your schedule had you here all day. Court's not due back in till tomorrow."

"Yes, well, there was a last minute change in proceedings and with my system down, I couldn't update it. That'll be all."

He bows his head over a plethora of paperwork, dismissing me without ceremony.

"Coffee?" I offer, trying to keep the conversation alive.

When there's no response, I know my dismissal is confirmed. I gather my things and head back to my desk where I scribble a note on a post-it and pass it to Foxy like a schoolkid dodging detention.

Steven's heading out at one. Said court, but I don't buy it.

Foxy reads it, tears it into confetti, and drops it in the bin without a word. Seconds later, Steven's door opens. He hands me a list of demands.

"Did you tell him?" he asks, jerking his chin toward Foxy.

"Not yet," I say, squirming as Foxy glances

up. "Steven says you can overhaul his system tomorrow."

"Under supervision," Steven adds, clipped.

"Fine by me," Foxy mutters, bristling but not biting. "Might be out all afternoon anyway."

Steven cocks his head. "Why?"

"Emergency dental." Foxy rubs his jaw for effect.

"Then I'd cut down on the sweet treats if I were you," Steven says, eyeing the chocolate cream pie languishing on Foxy's desk—already missing a generous slice.

As soon as Steven disappears again, my phone buzzes. I see Kurt's name and snatch it off the desk to read his message.

> *Thanks for the heads-up. But stop trying to help. We've got this.*

I glance across at Foxy. He's pretending not to notice, his phone untouched beside him. It takes me a beat to connect the dots.

"You emailed him, didn't you?"

Foxy feigns confusion, all innocence. "Sorry?"

His smirk tells another story. I sigh and fire back a middle finger emoji to Kurt. Seconds later, Foxy stifles a laugh.

"Care to share the joke?" I ask, raising an eyebrow. I'm pretty sure Kurt forwarded my reply with a remark of his own.

"Be more than my job's worth," Foxy says, grinning. "How about I make you a drink instead?"

"Fine."

The rest of the morning passes in a blur of quiet tension on my part. Foxy's morning is all relaxed banter and easy charm until he leaves at half twelve for 'the dentist'. Not long after, Steven follows, locking his office door behind him.

"When you've finished the list I gave you, you can head out," he calls over his shoulder. "Go shopping for the baby."

"You won't be back?" I ask, surprised. "Or need me here while you're in court?" I know Kurt warned me to stay silent, but I can't resist prodding the snake hoping he'll give *something* away about his plans.

Steven stops, turns. "Maybe, maybe not. Either way, I'll manage until tomorrow. Things might start to get hectic again—I want you rested in case they do." He digs into his pocket and tosses a folded wad of notes onto my desk. "Buy yourself something nice."

The cash lands with a soft thud. A bundle of new, crisp bills.

I hesitate, staring at them like they're toxic before pushing them back toward him. "That's not necessary."

He shrugs. "Call it a belated Christmas bonus.

Take it or leave it. But I want you out of here as soon as you're done, and I don't want to see you again until tomorrow. Are we clear?"

Something about the way he says it makes me pause. It makes his spontaneous act of generosity feel more like a payoff than a gift. But I shrug the thought off—for now.

"Sure," I reply, grateful. When it's busy, the days seem to stretch endlessly. A few extra hours of freedom feels like stolen treasure.

The time, I'll take. The cash—I'm not so sure.

I grab the notes and without counting them, shove them to the back of my drawer, before switching off my phone, and dropping it in beside them.

No distractions. No noise.

The sooner I finish, the sooner I'm gone. If I keep my head down, I'll be out and enjoying myself by two.

As I attempt to slide the drawer shut, something catches and it refuses to close. I aimlessly shuffle the contents, trying to free the obstruction, but the drawer stays jammed.

With a sigh, I drop to my hands and knees and peer into the narrow gap. Something catches my eye—the torn corner of a crumpled piece of paper, barely visible in the shadows. It's wedged deep behind the drawer, trapped in the runner like it was trying to hide.

Armed with a ruler and a little patience, I manage to push the document loose so it drops behind the drawers. After some careful wiggling and a fair bit of swearing, I prise it out from behind the bottom drawer so it doesn't cause any more problems.

The satisfaction at a job well done is short-lived.

I smooth out the paper. It's a single sheet of A4 —torn, crumpled, and covered in rows of numbers, each nine to twelve digits long. No headings. No context. Just data, meaningless on its own.

I rummage around some more, hoping to find something that might explain the figures —but come up empty-handed. I think back to the documents I've been working on. Nothing matches. No correlation to anything I can recall. I figure it must've been caught up in the items Steven gave me by accident—or, more likely, left behind when my predecessor cleared out her desk. Quietly overlooked until now.

I pause, my fingers hovering over the trash. Then, at the last second, I shove the battered paper into my bag. It'll probably amount to nothing, so there's no need to waste any more time on it now. I'll reprint it at home later, when I'm relaxing with my feet up, a mug of decaf in hand, and a favourite movie playing in the background. Then I'll ask Steven about it tomorrow—before I throw it away.

After powering through my tasks in record time, I manage to sidestep the office gossipmongers—or more specifically Maddie, who's been far too curious about my movements since meeting Kurt—to slip out the door just after two, leaving behind a half-drunk coffee and a tissue any seasoned investigator would notice. Embossed with the fresh imprint of a kiss in my favourite shade of pink, it's just enough ambiguity to keep her guessing, and a quiet warning wrapped in gloss—one any rival would recognize: the man is mine.

Instead of heading straight home, I catch the subway to Tribeca, heading to a boutique baby store known for its hip-hop onesies and indie designer gear—where I pick up a couple of cute outfits for Nugget, before spending an hour being thoroughly terrified by a sales assistant who insists I need everything: from a mini sound machine that blasts whale sounds for "soothing vibes" when labour is in full swing, to a stress ball for Kurt, because apparently *he'll* be suffering too.

I leave with enough impulse purchases to realise the cute little backpack I was planning to use as my hospital bag is nowhere near big enough—but quickly resolve that's a problem for another day.

I pat myself on the back for remembering to grab a loaded hot dog from a street vendor—just in case the food police are home when I get in. After finding a place to perch and eat my spoils, I figure I'd better call Kurt and check in. With Foxy out of the office, I'm surprised he hasn't already text demanding proof of life. I rummage through my bag, expecting the familiar buzz or glow of my phone. Nothing. It's only when I turn the whole thing out beside me that I realise—I accidently left my mobile in my desk drawer.

With a deep sigh, I weigh my options. Head back to the office now, laden with shopping bags after what will undoubtedly be perceived as an extended lunch, and brave the catty comments that'll ripple through the place like a Mexican wave at a concert. Or wait until the daytime crowd thins out and sneak in later to collect it —quietly, discreetly, thus dodging any awkward questions over where I've been lurking since that suspiciously cheerful hall-pass escape.

Leaving it overnight isn't an option—not if Steven needs to reach me. He's not exactly a tyrant when it comes to out-of-hours demands, but let's be honest: I'm being paid a helluva lot to stay sharp. And my boyfriend did almost break his jaw. I'm walking a tightrope, and I know it.

Steven may have said he could manage without me for the rest of today, but I seriously doubt that declaration was meant to stretch into tomorrow morning as well. If he heads into court and tries to reach me before I'm back at my desk, I don't want to be the reason the biggest case in the firm's history goes belly-up.

After careful deliberation, I decide to head home for now. If Kurt's around, I'm sure he won't mind coming back with me later. And if I can squeeze in a quick nap, we could even make a night of it—maybe dinner out, or a cinema trip followed by a late supper.

The thought pleases me… until I spot the crumbs from my recent snack and realise that if I don't start curbing my appetite, I'll be the size of a house before the pregnancy even gets a proper look-in.

Chapter 12

"Hi honey, I'm home." I burst through the door to my apartment just before 4 p.m. Kurt appears before it's even closed behind me, grabbing the bags I'm carrying. He doesn't look happy.

"What are you doing here? You're supposed to be at work. I was going to leave in an hour to come and meet you."

"You didn't know I was missing?" I tease. "I was half expecting helicopters circling with searchlights when you realised my phone was switched off."

"You switched your phone off again?" he growls, distinctly unimpressed, as I round the corner into the living room—only to stop dead.

The whole room has been rearranged. The TV's been shoved to one side, revealing a blank wall now moonlighting as a makeshift display board. Pictures of individuals, scribbled notes, and obligatory red string are tacked up like something out of a crime drama. The sofa's been repositioned to face the wall, where two of the largest, fittest men sit like they've just endured a PowerPoint on espionage—if PowerPoint were a collage of printed photos and handwritten arrows. They turn as I enter, tracking my grand entrance with a mix of amusement and expectation, like I'm either about to step up with a laser pointer and deliver the answers they've been waiting for—or go full postal on Kurt for the sheer number of thumbtacks stabbed into my wall.

I hear someone mumble, "my money's on the one in the dress."

One of the men—tall, tactical, and probably capable of folding me into a suitcase—springs to his feet. "You must be Tina," he says, extending a hand like we're at a networking event and not standing in front of what looks like a serial killer's Pinterest board. "We've heard a lot about you." He laughs, and I can't tell if that's a good thing or a bad one.

"And you are?" I ask politely.

"Not important," Kurt snaps, glaring at the man until he drops my hand.

"Don't be rude," I bite back, earning stifled chuckles from both guests.

"She's seen us now, boss. Might as well come clean." The second man I recognise instantly —from Josh's wedding. He and I were getting on famously until Kurt decided to intervene by putting that ice cube down the back of my dress.

He's hotter than I remember, looking like he could bench-press the sofa with his pinky fingers. Probably while reciting the national anthem backwards and continuing to make direct eye contact.

"Blake!" I squeal, abandoning all formalities as I run over to hug him. "It's so good to see you again."

"Is it?" Kurt growls, clearly unimpressed by what he deems an unnecessary display of physical affection.

When Blake stiffens under Kurts watchful eye, I glance back over my shoulder and throw Kurt a warning glare of my own.

"Fuck's sake, Tina." Kurt drags a hand through his hair, exasperated. "They were supposed to be gone before you got here."

"Why?" I ask, bewildered.

"Because they're being paid to work and blend in unnoticed—not flirt with my pregnant girlfriend," Kurt snaps, shooting Blake a look that could curdle milk. "And while we're at it, I'm pretty sure Blake doesn't appreciate being manhandled every time you see him. You're making him uncomfortable."

I turn to Blake, mortified. "Oh my god, I'm so sorry. Did I make you uncomfortable?"

"Nope," Blake replies, flashing a shit-eating grin at Kurt.

"You already know the smug-looking fucker,"

Kurt mutters through clenched teeth, before gesturing to the other man. "The ugly one—that's Ace."

Ace flashes me a smile so dazzling it could power a small village. My stomach dips, confirming that Kurt's description is wildly inaccurate.

"Language," I scold, patting my belly.

Kurt looks suitably chastised, but only for a second. "Just saying. You don't need to be making heart eyes at every man who walks through the door. You've already bagged the most genetically blessed specimen in the room, so maybe your overexcited hormones can lay off the rest."

"Excuse me?" I bite back. My tone laced with a mix of annoyance and genuine confusion.

The room goes quiet for a beat—just long enough for me to register the flicker of amusement on Blake's face as he coughs into his fist, and the way Ace suddenly finds the ceiling fascinating as he stifles a laugh. Kurt looks like he's aged five years in thirty seconds—and possibly developed a twitch.

"Are you okay?" I ask, concerned.

"I think he must've spotted a few grey hairs in the mirror this morning," Ace leans in to mock-whisper in my ear. "His ego can't handle it."

"I'll show you just how much my ego can

handle," Kurt's voice drops low and threatening, "if you'd like to step outside right now."

"Kurt, stop being ridiculous." I try to diffuse the situation before he combusts. "Would anyone care to explain why my wall looks like a ten-year-old's art project?"

Kurt sighs heavily, then defiantly dodges the question. "Would you like to explain why you're home from work early?"

His tone makes me bristle. "No."

It's obvious from their reactions that Blake and Ace have never witnessed anyone use that word against Kurt before. I can practically feel them holding their breath, waiting to see how he'll react. Kurt senses it too, and his tone softens.

"Babe. Please can I see you in the kitchen for one moment?"

I pause, considering his request. It's also evident from Blake and Ace's expressions that they expected me to immediately bow to the king's command. Fools. Eventually, I turn to our guests with a smile.

"May I offer you a hot beverage?"

"Um…" Both men glance at Kurt, unsure if they're allowed to answer. Kurt raises his hands emphatically, as if granting royal permission. The whole scene is quite amusing.

"A coffee would be nice, if it's not too much

trouble," Blake answers first.

"Same, thank you," Ace murmurs.

I stalk off to the kitchen, Kurt hot on my heels.

After a moment's hesitation, Blake calls out, "Got any chocolate cream pie to go with that?"

Behind me, I feel Kurt's step falter. Then, as we disappear into the kitchen, both guests burst out laughing.

"I'm going to f—ducking kill Foxy," Kurt growls, closing the door behind us. He leans back against the frame, watching as I busy myself making drinks for the men in the other room.

"So?" he growls again when I don't speak.

I pause, glance over at him. He pushes off the wall and comes to stand before me, resting his hands tentatively on my hips as he gauges my mood. He's right to be cautious—I'm mentally assessing whether I'm about to rip off one of his arms and beat him around the head with it.

"So?" I echo, using his own word back at him with a raised eyebrow.

"Babe, why are you here?" Kurt sighs, trying to distract me with feather-light strokes down my sides.

"I live here."

"Smartass." His hands slide down to cup my butt cheeks, pulling me into a body full of warmth and familiarity.

"Stop trying to distract me with your masculine wiles." He feels so delicious I'm practically purring now.

"My what?" He chuckles, the deep rumble in his chest sending pleasant vibrations through me.

"Never mind." I push away from him. With Blake and Ace just a few feet away, now is not the time to get too carried away. "Just before he left to go to…" I raise my index fingers to air-quote, "'court,' Steven gave me the rest of the afternoon off once I'd finished my assignments. I wanted to get away quickly, so I turned off my phone and threw it in the drawer to avoid distractions. I forgot to grab it before I left, and I really need to go back and get it. I thought maybe you'd like to come with me—and maybe we could grab dinner, catch a movie or something?"

"Like a date?" Kurt grins like I've handed him a winning lottery ticket.

"Um… sure." His sudden cheeriness throws me off. I eye him warily until I realise he's probably already planning to find a restaurant with the same kind of culinary inadequacies as last time. I add a quick disclaimer. "But only if I get to choose where we eat."

Kurt crowds me again, leaning down to kiss the tip of my nose. "Don't you trust me?"

"After last time?"

"As I recall, lunch didn't end so badly."

Warmth floods my body as the memories resurface. Kurt starts nibbling my neck and I'm momentarily lost in the sensation, tilting my head to give him better access—until I regain enough control to push away again, this time putting real distance between us.

"No you don't, Mister." I grab a wooden spoon from the worktop and wave it like a sabre. "No funny business while we have company."

Kurt smiles. "Are you sure? You're looking a little flushed—and like you're about to swallow me whole. I'm sure the boys won't mind waiting while you take your fill."

"And on that subject..." I seize the segue into safer territory. "What are Blake and Ace doing here?"

"They're here to help."

"Help with what?"

Kurt crosses his arms, his demeanour shifting. "Business."

"I hate it when you do that," I sigh.

"Do what?"

"Shut me out." My voice drops to a whisper.

"Babe..." He steps toward me, but I raise the spoon defensively.

"No." I wave it to keep him at bay. "I know you worry about Nugget and me, but we're tougher than you give us credit for. Just so you know, I could never marry someone who doesn't trust me."

"I do trust you."

"Just not enough to tell me what's going on—even though I might be smack bang in the middle of it. You want me to let you in? Then you need to do the same. No secrets. I want to share everything—the fabulous, the good, the bad, and the downright ugly. If you're serious about building a future with me, then we have to be a team. No exceptions. I won't settle for anything less."

"Even if it makes it harder for me to protect you?" His voice is low, uncertain. His expression says it all—like I've asked him to choose between whatever affection he has for me and duty.

Time to play my ace. Literally.

"Look at Josh and Maeve. He confides in her."

"How do you know?" Kurt looks genuinely shocked.

"She told me. Don't worry, she never shares more than she should. What I'm saying is, he trusts her enough to confide in her—and vice versa. They work through things together. He doesn't keep her in the dark. That's why they're solid. If our roles were reversed, I bet he'd tell her what's going on, no matter how bad it is. Because he knows she'd never put either of them at risk unnecessarily—and she knows he'd die before he'd ever let any harm come to her."

Kurt and Josh are close enough for him to know I'm not lying.

"Maeve isn't you," Kurt counters.

"What's that supposed to mean?" I ask, baffled. Maeve is like a sister to Kurt. He'd never let anything happen to her, and if he tries to convince me otherwise, he'll have one hell of a job doing so.

"She sees things a little differently than you. She went through one hell of an ordeal last year, and it gave her a whole new perspective on Josh and the work we do. She listens to him because she knows how fast shit can get real. She's been in the thick of it and learned from the experience. It gave her a wariness and understanding you only get from being thrust into a life-or-death situation firsthand."

He pauses, then continues more gently.

"You say you want to know more about the work I do—but do you really? Do you really want to know how fucked up this world can be? Carry the weight of those dark images in your head? Worry every time I go out on a job? It's not all sunshine and roses in Maeve's world, no matter how much you think it is. Right now, you're innocent—focused on our baby and all the good times ahead. I don't want to be the one that ruins that for you."

"Surely that should be my choice," I say firmly, then soften. "I appreciate what you're trying to do, but it's not what I want. If you're never going to let me be there for you the way you are for me... then maybe we need to stop pretending this is ever going to be more than two people who care about each other but aren't really walking the same path."

Kurt hangs his head, the weight of his internal struggle visibly dragging him down.

"What if..." His voice is almost boyish, uncertain. He looks at me with eyes that seem far too vulnerable for someone who usually stares down fear. "What if I let you in and you don't like what you see? I'm not the same kid you knew growing up. Not anymore. I've seen things... done things..." His voice trails off, swallowed by the silence.

And suddenly, it clicks. He's not just protecting me—he's protecting himself. He's afraid that if I get too close, I'll see something about him I can't unsee. That I'll walk away anyway.

"Kurt Reginald Callahan," I say, steady and sure. When he winces at the use of his second name I smile, run at the guy with a machete, he doesn't flinch, throw his full name at him and he starts to crumble. "Whatever you've been through in the years we were apart may have changed you—but who's to say it wasn't for the better? We've all faced trials that shaped us. Our pasts don't have to define us; they're just lessons life throws our way. What matters most is the way we respond to life's challenges: the way we grow, the way we choose to move forward.

You're not the same boy I knew—no. But the man standing in front of me has just as much integrity, and he's stronger for the battle scars he carries. I know that heart of yours is still huge, even if you see it as a weakness and hide it behind that fierce, guarded exterior."

I move close enough to cup his cheek in my hand, forcing his tortured eyes to connect with mine—hoping he'll see how much love for him is simmering beneath the surface, waiting to be set free.

"I won't lie—there might be things you tell me that I won't like. And let's face it, we both have tempers. I'm sure we'll have our fair share of emotional blowouts. But I know you well enough to believe there's always a reason behind what you do. A good one."

I pause, letting the weight of my words settle.

"I can't promise we'll make it—who can? But I do know this: we won't stand a chance if you're not even willing to try and open up to me a little."

Kurt stares at me, deep in thought.

I tap his temple with my index finger. "What's going on in here?"

He smiles down at me.

"Do you promise to behave yourself? Not get all bull-headed and interfere when I specifically tell you not to?"

I draw a cross over my heart with my finger. "I promise."

"And do you promise to stop flirting with other men right in front of me?"

I giggle. "I was not flirting."

"You so were."

"Is that why you got all cranky?"

"I was not cranky—I was jealous. Two totally different emotions. And I need to know that if I take you back in there"—he jerks his head toward the living room—"I won't have to castrate Blake with your melon baller."

I laugh out loud. "I don't have a melon baller."

"Well, I'm buying you one tomorrow," Kurt growls. "Just in case." He opens the door and extends his hand, I take it. With his free hand, he grabs the two coffees I made and pulls me out of the room.

"Let's get this over with. Then I can kick the pair of them out and punish you."

"Punish me?" I frown, confused.

"For flirting with another man."

"I wasn't flirting," I reiterate.

"So you don't need me to punish you?" Kurt asks, brow quirked and eyes gleaming with mischief—more promise than threat.

"Well... maybe I was a little," I admit with a smirk.

"That's what I thought," he says seriously as we re-enter the living room, having ignored our guests for far too long.

"Make room, Tina's joining us," Kurt announces as he hands out the drinks. Ace and Blake shuffle to either end of the couch. I grab my laptop and squeeze into the narrow gap between them. It's a snug fit—and judging by Kurt's expression, not one he approves of.

"Just pretend I'm not here," I sing happily. "I have something I need to type up."

"Do you mind?" I gesture to Blake's lap, hoping to use it as a makeshift table.

"Be my guest," he replies, amused, as I lay down the crumpled piece of paper I retrieved from my desk and smooth it out on his legs.

Kurt coughs in annoyance. I glance at him and realize his eyes are fixed on my wandering hands rather than the task I'm looking to complete. I bite my lip to keep my smile from escaping and pretend to concentrate as I begin replicating the lines of code.

Ace looks at Blake over the top of my head. "Told ya."

Blake sighs, retrieves a fifty-dollar note, and hands it to Ace. Ace waits until Kurt's back is turned, then leans in to whisper in my ear, "I knew you had him whipped."

I'm not the only one who catches the way Kurt's posture stiffens before he turns and pins the other two men with a stare that screams: *fuck with me and I'll seal your fate.*

Blake and Ace wisely decide they want to live to fight another day. They settle back in their seats, giving Kurt their full attention.

"As I was saying," Kurt begins, "Steven Prentice is still holed up in the Obsidian with an unknown female. Early thirties, approximately five-seven, auburn hair. He checked into room 222 but didn't register her as a guest, so that's all the intel we have for now. Foxy will get a picture when she leaves, and we'll send it to Axel to work his magic."

I recognize the description and raise my hand tentatively. All three men turn to me in bewilderment.

"Do you need the bathroom?" Kurt asks incredulously.

"What? No!" I bluster.

"Tina, you don't have to raise your hand to

speak. You're not in school," Kurt grumbles, while the other two hide their smiles behind their coffee mugs.

"Sorry. I wasn't sure what the etiquette was," I mutter, embarrassed.

"What did you want to say?" Kurt asks. He sounds cross, but I catch the amused twinkle in his eye.

"Only that, um… the description fits a woman I saw him with the other night."

"The night you gave the boss and Foxy the slip?" Ace adds with a grin.

"Um… yeah."

"Do you know who she is?" Kurt's speaking to me but levelling Ace with a death stare at the same time.

"Sort of."

"Either you do or you don't." Kurt's tone is tight, barely controlled.

"If it's who I think it is, I met her briefly on New Year's Eve."

"At the party the boss gate-crashed before beating up one of the guests?" Ace adds helpfully. Blake nearly chokes on his coffee as he tries to suppress his laughter.

I glance at Kurt, who now looks like he's considering a second use for my new melon baller.

243

He tips his head, urging me to continue.

"Yes," I mumble to a grinning Ace. "She was there with someone I recognized. He introduced her as his cousin, but I found out later she was an escort—which made sense, since he was being a little handsy. Then the other night, I saw her leaving the Obsidian with Steven, and I got the impression they too were more than just good friends."

"What gave you that impression?" Kurt challenges.

"Oh, I don't know," I reply with a hint of sarcasm. "Could've been the way he stuck his tongue down her throat before feeling her up and bundling her into a cab, thrusting a wad of cash at the driver."

"That'll do it," Ace chuckles, while Blake muses, "She could be the link."

The other two murmur in agreement. I wait for someone to clue me in. They don't.

"Do you know anything else about her?" Kurt presses.

"Not really. I think I overheard someone at the party call her Cassie, but I don't know if that was her real name. Someone else said she's money-obsessed—that there's not much she wouldn't do for a fast buck."

"He could've paid her to tamper with the jury,"

Blake suggests. "If she got compromising photos of one or more of them, she could be setting up a blackmail scheme."

"Who? Steven? Jury? What jury?" I parrot. No one answers—they're too deep in thought.

"We need to find out who this woman is and what she's capable of," Kurt states.

"Has this got something to do with Judge Simmons?" I ask, noticing his photo pinned to my wall as part of an eight-person lineup. Suddenly, I have the room's undivided attention.

"Why'd you ask?" Kurt voices the question on everyone's lips.

"That's who I saw Cassie with at the party," I answer nonchalantly.

"Not with Steven?" Kurt prompts, clearly assuming I'm confused.

No, pay attention," I scold indignantly. There's a sharp intake of breath on either side of me—apparently, watching someone call out Kurt and survive is another first for the two men flanking me. Kurt looks torn between laughing, crying, and clearing the room to stage an intervention.

"Cassie—or whatever her real name is—was with Judge Simmons on New Year's Eve. I never saw her speak to Steven, or even knew they were acquainted, until I spotted them together a couple of days later—outside the Obsidian, the night I went off on my own to grab a burger. Other than you and me, the only other person I saw Steven talk to at the party was Bear."

If I was hoping for a reaction, I get one. The room's temperature plummets to sub-zero—ironic, considering the fury radiating from the three men is molten—pure heat, enough to melt steel. Their silence is heavy, their stares locked, and I know I've just dropped a bomb. I just don't know what kind, or how devastating the fallout will be.

Chapter 13

"Wait," Blake regains his composure first. "There has to be hundreds of people with that name. Thousands even. Let's not get carried away before we know for certain it's our guy."

I glance around, confused. Kurt's jaw ticks, and the vein in his neck pulses like it's trying to escape his skin. His fists are clenched so tightly his knuckles have gone bone-white. Ace doesn't look like he's faring much better.

Blake turns to me. "Can you describe him to us… Bear?"

"I guess," I murmur, unease prickling at the back of my neck. What if I'm about to paint a target on the wrong man? I think carefully before answering, knowing I need to be as accurate as possible.

"Over six foot, broad build—kinda like you," I say, gesturing to Ace. "Close-cropped brown hair, beard—neatly trimmed, not bushy. Mid-thirties, maybe…" I pause, realizing I've just described half the male population.

All three men stare at me, rapt, waiting for whatever I'm about to say next.

"He had a tattoo," I blurt out. "Across his chest. Script surrounded by roses. I only saw part of it—just a few letters through the open seam of his shirt. It was…" I pause again, the memory sharpening. "V-I-D-I."

"Veni, vidi, vici," Kurt mutters murderously.

"Could've been," I murmur thoughtfully, "I wonder what it means?

Kurt replies without hesitation, "I came, I saw, I conquered."

The silence crashes down, thick with rage. Even I'm too afraid to break it. Blake and Ace are staring at Kurt, waiting for him to emerge from the trance he's dropped into and give them orders.

"Kurt?" I call gently. It's all the prompting he needs.

"Ace. Go find Foxy. Fill him in and wait for further instruction."

Ace leaps to his feet, hesitating only when Kurt calls after him again, voice low and dangerous.

"Stay in the shadows. And if you see him—do not engage. You hear me? Do. Not. Engage."

Ace nods reluctantly, then vanishes.

Kurt turns to Blake and me. "I need to make a call," he growls, and disappears too.

I look to Blake for some kind of explanation.

"How much do you know about what went down last year with your friend Maeve?"

"Pretty much all of it... I think. From her perspective, anyway," I reply. "We've always been close. After everything, she needed someone to listen—and I was there."

Blake nods, but his expression darkens. "But you never knew Bear used to be one of us. That he served with us in the Navy. That when he got out, Josh offered him a job at his firm."

I shake my head slowly as Blake continues.

"Bear was part of our unit when everything went down in Maine. We trusted him to have our backs. We were heavily outnumbered; every move we made was crucial—and he sold us out. Sold Kurt out. Bear was supposed to be gathering intel for us. Instead, somewhere down the line he switched sides and he started selling information to the enemy."

Blake's eyes flick to me. "I assume you've seen the fresh scars on Kurt's torso."

I nod. I never asked him about them. Never had cause. They were just part of him—who he was. They never bothered me.

"Bear may not have inflicted the wounds personally," Blake says, voice low, "but he was just as responsible as the man who did. Thanks to him,

Kurt, Foxy, and I walked into a trap. Kurt created a distraction so Foxy and I could get away and warn the others. Otherwise, we would've been tortured too—or worse."

"Tortured?"

As the word sinks in, nausea settles like lead in the pit of my stomach. I instinctively pat my belly, telling myself it's a reassuring gesture for Nugget—when really, I'm trying to reassure myself. I still want Kurt to give me the open honesty I demanded earlier... don't I?

My emotions must be playing out across my face, because Blake smiles softly.

"He's fine. The man's indestructible. That's why everyone's afraid of him. The rest of us know we have limits. Piss him off, and Kurt won't stop until he finds them, exposes them, and pushes you so far beyond them he'll walk away leaving you a husk of a man."

Blake's voice drops, almost reverent. "That's what Bear has to look forward to when Kurt catches up with him. I'd wager right now he's on the phone to Josh, arguing over which one of them gets to take him down. The whole team wants five minutes alone with him—but Kurt deserves it more than most."

"And to think he hit on me," I murmur, choking back the bile rising in my throat. I press a hand to my mouth, willing the sickness to pass. The memory of Bear's smile—once harmless—now feels like a stain.

He hit on you?" Blake echoes, eyes wide. "For Christ's sake, don't tell the boss that. There'll be nothing left of Bear to find if Kurt finds out he messed with you in any shape or form.

But a word to the wise—when Kurt finally catches up with him, don't stand in his way. Don't try to stop him doing what he needs to.

This is a debt that needs to be settled. And one way or another, Kurt always collects.

Bear won't go down without a fight, and the only chink in Kurt's armour is his feelings for you. Whatever happens, he'll need your support. Feed his strength—going against him will only make him weaker and that could prove fatal."

I nod, but the weight of his words settles heavy on my chest. I asked for honesty—now I have it. And with it, a possible choice I never wanted to make.

I swallow hard. I wanted to be part of this, to stand beside Kurt through thick and thin. But now I begin to wonder if he was right—if I'm really up for the task. Because if I falter, it won't just be me who pays the price.

"Good news!" Kurt announces cheerfully as he re-enters the room, clapping his hands and startling both me and Blake.

If he notices the sombre mood that's descended, he doesn't mention it.

"What's that?" I ask, as casually as I can muster.

"Josh is coming to visit."

Blake and I share a look. If Kurt registers it, he pretends not to.

"It'll take him a few days to get here since he won't let Maeve fly. We thought it'd be good for you girls to spend some time together."

I want to say *while you find Bear and annihilate him*, but I focus on the positives instead.

"Maeve's coming?" I squeal, excited.

"Thought you'd be pleased." Kurt aims a wink in my direction before turning to Blake. "Now you need to duck off. I need to tidy up before Tina's roomy gets home and kicks me out for defacing her wall. Then we're…" he gestures between him and me, "going on a date. And you're…" he points at Blake, "not invited."

Far from offended, Blake chuckles as he stands. "What about Prentice? We kind of got off track a little."

"He can wait. When Foxy gets into the dickwad's systems tomorrow, we'll review his files, see what he's hiding, and plan our next move. I'm going to call Ace and get him to take watch on the hotel to give Foxy a break. When Steven's friend surfaces, I want Ace to tail her and find out what he can there.

"We know Prentice is back in court tomorrow, but if the woman disappears, we won't know where to find her should we need to."

"Wait," I say, panicked, grabbing Blake's arm and shaking it. Both men turn to look at me—though Kurt seems more interested in why I'm clinging to Blake than in what I'm about to say. I ignore his raised eyebrows.

"If Bear used to be part of your team, surely he knows Foxy. If Steven's mentioned Foxy to him, even in passing, Bear could be questioning why Foxy is here. He might have warned Steven somehow. They might already be one step ahead of you. I don't know how close the two of them are, but the night I saw Steven leave the Obsidian with Cassie, he was picked up in a black SUV. At the time, I thought I recognised Bear as the driver, but I only caught a glimpse—I can't be sure. What if it was him? What if Foxy came up in conversation? Bear could be the reason Steven disabled his computer before you could access it. Or worse—what if Bear has been watching you, watching Steven. He might already know you're all here, and he's luring you into another trap?" It's less a conversation, more a frantic unravelling of my own thoughts.

"Babe," Kurt says, trying to placate me as he shoots Blake a look. One that reads: *I only left the room for two minutes, and now look what you've done.*

"She could be right," Blake says, clearly trying to defend the fact he probably let on more than he should've in Kurt's absence.

"Baby, calm down," Kurt replies softly, still glaring at the hand I have resting on Blake's arm. I let go as he continues, measured but sharp. "Blake and Ace only got in a couple of hours ago. They came here straight from the airport. Not even Foxy knows they're here yet, so I doubt Bear does. Foxy's name may or may not have come up in conversation. If it hasn't, Bear won't have warned Steven to be on his guard. And even if it has, Steven won't know that we know he knows we might be onto him. That confusion is our advantage."

"That's easy for you to say," Blake chuckles, but his tone shifts as he adds, more thoughtfully, "If you ask me, I don't think Bear is aware any of us are here yet. He knows he's a marked man. If he thinks one of us has eyes on him, he won't stick around to see who else shows up. He'll vanish without a trace —just like before. Staying would be suicide, and he knows it."

Kurt gives him a slow chin tip, but behind his eyes, I can see he's already working the angles.

"What do you want me to do, boss?" Blake asks.

"Nothing tonight. I want you at the court tomorrow, in the gallery, taking notes. Find out what you can about anything or anyone connected to the Knox case or the attorney who disappeared.

Someone out there knows what happened to him. He could be the key to us working out what's really going on here. Axel's on standby back at base—send him whatever info you get and he'll use his contacts to do a deep dive. Keep your head down. Bear could show at any time, and if he recognises one of us, the jig's up."

Kurt's voice drops to a low, threatening rumble.

"He's not to be touched—not yet. Not until Josh gets here. Understand?"

"Gotcha," Blake says. The word comes easily, but a flicker of unease crosses his face. His body language betrays the truth: he knows better than to brush off the warning he's just been given.

"We'll all meet again tomorrow night, pick up where we left off with any new intel. Time and venue to be confirmed."

Blake nods, then turns to me. "Enjoy your date," he says with a smirk and mock solemnity. "I know it'll be hard spending the evening with him when you know you could've had me."

He shrugs, and the levity makes me smile.

"It's a cross I'll just have to bear," I sigh in mock resignation.

Blake grins and takes off.

"That's twice now," Kurt growls.

"Twice?"

"I've caught you two flirting," Kurt challenges with a raised eyebrow.

"Oops," I tease. "I guess I do need reprimanding after all."

"How long before Izzy gets home?"

I check my watch and sigh in disappointment. It's later than I thought. "About fifteen minutes."

Within seconds, Kurt has swept me off my feet and into his arms.

"Won't be my best work," he says with a smile as he carries me off to the bedroom, "but I'm always up for a challenge.

I arch a brow, teasing. "You say that like I'm difficult to please."

He chuckles, nudging the bedroom door open with his foot. "You are. That's why you're so much fun."

The laughter, the closeness, the rush of what comes next—it all leaves me blissfully spent. I don't remember dozing off, only the feeling of being completely content when I do.

When I wake, Kurt is nowhere to be seen, and Izzy's panicked voice cuts through the air, tangled with banging and crashing from an adjoining room.

I pull on my robe and step into the hallway, tying the belt as I go. "Iz?" I call.

I find her in her bedroom, throwing clothes into a suitcase with frantic precision. Her phone is wedged between her chin and shoulder as she moves.

"I've managed to get some time off," she says decisively before hanging up. "I'm coming home and that's that."

"Iz? What's going on?"

She doesn't stop packing, but when she glances up, her face is tight with concern.

"My mom," she says. "She's had a fall. Apparently she was out in the garden trying to refill the bird feeders while it was snowing—because obviously it's the only place in the world the robins come to eat—when she slipped on a patch of ice she didn't see. She landed awkwardly, slid the full length of the garden and nearly ended up faceplanting in the fish pond. She's at the hospital getting x-rays as we speak."

"Shit, is she okay? What can I do?" I offer immediately.

"Nothing," Izzy replies, smiling gratefully. "But thanks for offering. Dad says it's nothing more than a few bumps and bruises, although she may have broken her leg. I'm heading home to check for myself. If she ends up in a cast, Dad'll need me to stick around and help out for a few weeks."

"Is work okay with you taking the time?"

"They'll have to be." Typical Izzy—always has her priorities in order, damn the consequences. "I'm owed some time," she adds smiling, reading my expression like only a true friend can.

I grin back just as Kurt appears in the doorway. "There's a cab downstairs waiting to take you to the airport."

"Thanks," Izzy says, clearly touched. Then, more tentatively to me, "Is it okay if I send you the money for this month's rent in a couple of days? I had to use some of what I'd set aside for the flight."

"Not necessary," Kurt answers before I can speak. "I'll cover the rent in full for the next six months."

Izzy and I stare at him, slack-jawed, like he's just emerged from a bottle to grant us three wishes.

"It's only fair" Kurt explains reading the room, "You can't expect me to live here for free, and if Izzy isn't going to be here for a bit, she shouldn't be expected to chip in. Besides, if she doesn't mind, Josh can crash here in her room when he arrives." Kurt grins mischievously, "We'll charge him."

"But six months," I murmur in amazement.

"I don't mind at all," Izzy sings. "If you're going to cover the rent for the next six months, you can install a coffee machine and turn my room into your personal war room—I won't stop you. Punch as many tack holes in the walls as you like."

"Don't worry," Kurt chuckles. "I'll repair the damage in the living room."

"You'd better," Izzy replies with a grin. "Since you're staying here now, you're officially responsible for any upkeep—including reinstalling the tap that mysteriously vanished from over the bath."

"I forgot about that," I say, looking to Kurt for an explanation while tapping my foot in annoyance.

"I don't know what you mean," Kurt says, fighting the smirk ghosting the corners of his mouth.

Izzy zips up her suitcase and hefts it off the bed.

"I'll take this downstairs for you," Kurt offers, taking it from her like a true gentleman. Watching him, something warm unfurls in my chest.

Izzy gives me a quick hug goodbye.

"Call me when you get there."

"I will," she promises, already halfway out the door.

Kurt swats me playfully on the behind as he passes. "Looks like it's just you and me now," he says, his voice low and teasing—sending delightful shivers down my spine. "Throw some clothes on and I'll let you take me out to dinner."

"Yes, sir," I reply with a mock salute.

The look he gives me before following Izzy

out is pure predator—sharp, hungry, and entirely insatiable. "Remember this is our first official date, dress appropriately." He calls over his shoulder as he disappears.

I smile, as butterflies swirl in my stomach. It's been so long since I got dressed up for an actual date excitement takes hold. I take a quick shower then try to find something appropriate to wear. Ten minutes later, Kurt finds me curled in a pile of discarded clothes, bawling.

"What the fuck?" He expostulates as he strides in the room. His voice is tight with concern, "Tina what happened? Are you OK?"

"Language," I manage to force out between sobs.

"Then tell me what's wrong. Now!"

"Nothing fits." I wail.

I thought Kurt would have known better than to snigger. Then, to my surprise, he lays on the floor behind me, pulling me close so we are spooning.

We lay there in silence for a solid minute, me relishing the security and warmth of his embrace.

"I wanted to look nice," I manage as my crying subsides.

"You always look nice." Kurt whispers behind me.

"You know—nice nice." I explain.

Kurt's chest vibrates against my back.

"I know you're laughing," I snap.

"I wouldn't dare," Kurt replies, although he takes a second to compose himself before answering. "I thought somewhere in all those bags you bought home yesterday would've been some new clothes you wanted to try out."

"No," I sniff. "I bought you a stress ball though."

This time Kurt doesn't even attempt to mask his amusement as he bursts out laughing. "I'm not sure how I got by all these years without one."

"Shut up," I slap the arm wound round me indignantly. "It's for when I'm giving birth, the woman in the store said you'd need it."

"I think the woman in the store saw you coming," he murmurs incredulously before softening his tone. "Babe, I don't care what you wear, you'll always look good to me."

I snort derisively.

"Remember back in high school when you and Maeve went through that phase of styling your hair like you'd been electrocuted?"

I can't help the giggle that escapes, "It was the fashion."

"Well even though you looked like you'd spent all morning with your finger caught in a live electrical socket, I still thought you were the most beautiful girl in the world."

For a nano second, I believe him. Then I remember all the times he'd joined in when my brother teased me, all our verbal sparring, not to mention all the girls that had warmed his bed on a regular basis. "Right," I scoff. "So beautiful I rendered you speechless and celibate. As I recall you were pain in my ass and you found plenty of others 'beautiful' too."

"Those other girls weren't beautiful, they were just pretty—passing distractions while I waited for the one I truly wanted to notice me," Kurt chuckles.

"Pretty?" I challenge. "Pretty easy more like. I never saw you with the same one twice."

"I didn't want any of them getting too attached," Kurt says seriously. "They knew the score."

"What was, 'the score'?"

There's a long pause, I turn my head to look up at him when he doesn't answer straight away.

"I'd enlisted and was leaving town. I didn't want any of them thinking we could pick up where we left off when I came back. And…"

"And?" I prompt when he doesn't finish.

"And I only made fun of you because I was trying to get a reaction. It was the only way I could get your attention. The rest of the time, you avoided me like I hadn't showered in months."

"Because Maeve was crushing on you—hard,

back then. It was easier to try and ignore you then keep my distance than admit I liked you."

"Fighting with you was the highlight of my day."

"It was?"

"Yeah. Plus, it doubled as a smokescreen for Liam. Your brother made it clear you were off-limits—and he was bigger than me back then." He pauses, then adds playfully, "It's part of the reason I trained as a SEAL, you know."

"Liar," I laugh, knowing he's teasing. It had been a dream of his, Josh's, and Maeve's brother Jimmy's practically since the three of them hit puberty.

"It's true," Kurt insists, failing to hide the fun in his voice. "Well, partly… I knew if I was ever lucky enough to win you over, I'd have to be fit enough to face the consequences. Your brother's always been pretty handy with his fists."

There's a pause as the weight of these seemingly inconsequential admissions settles between us. Kurt squeezes me gently.

"So you liked me too, huh?" He doesn't even try to hide the smugness in his voice.

"Maybe," I answer coyly. "A little." I hold up my thumb and index finger millimetres apart to make my point.

He gently rolls me, repositioning us so he is resting on his forearms, hovering over me.

"You know we could always skip dinner and stay home if you'd prefer," He kisses the tip of my nose before I catch the hand slyly reaching for the belt of my robe.

Although his suggestion has merit, I feel the need to reprimand him "You're insatiable," I groan half-heartedly. "Do you ever stop thinking about sex?"

"Yeah," he grins, "I never, however, stop thinking about you."

I search his eyes and see nothing but the sincerity behind his words. It's maybe the most romantic thing anyone's ever said to me. And it makes me want this date even more. After bestowing a quick peck, I shove him so he rolls off to the side so I can scramble up. Kurt stays on the floor, watching me with his head propped on one elbow as I rummage through my wardrobe with renewed determination.

"Get outta here," I call as I finally find something suitable to wear. "I want to get ready."

"Babe, I've seen you naked," Kurt replies. "More than once!"

"That was different," I say, crossing the room to rifle through my underwear drawer.

"It was?" He frowns, confused.

"Yes," I reply, exasperated. "This isn't about sex. This is our first real date, and I want to look nice before you see me."

"Nice nice?" Kurt chuckles.

"Exactly."

"In that case, I'll leave," he says. I glance over, puzzled when he doesn't move. "After I've watched you put your underwear on," he adds with a smirk.

I whip off my robe and fling it over his head, blinding him just long enough to snatch up the rest of my clothes before retreating into the bathroom.

Men!

With limited options, I'm pleased with the final outcome. What used to be a black oversized jumper dress with a V-neck now hugs my new curves while staying comfortable. Paired with long black boots, softly curled hair, and subtle makeup, I look sexy—but not overtly so.

When I walk into the living room, I see I wasn't the only one who made an effort. Kurt is rolling back the sleeves of his white shirt when he glances up, spots me, and lets out a low whistle.

"I could say the same about you," I reply, taking in the tailored grey slacks and crisp white shirt stretched taut across his broad frame—a far cry from his usual black combats and worn T-shirt. He smells divine, and I make a mental note to find out the name of whatever cologne he's wearing.

"Shall we?" Kurt shrugs on a jacket, then helps

me into a thicker coat and extends an arm for me to take. We make our way down to the street, where he hails us a cab.

"Where sort of food do you feel like?" I ask, assuming that since he's new to the area, he's waiting for me to take the lead.

He smiles softly as a car glides to a stop beside us and he opens the door for me to climb inside. "I hope you don't mind, but I've already booked us a table."

"Where?" I groan. "Please don't tell me it's another place you found that thinks serving an overpriced entrée as a main course qualifies them as a restaurant."

"I learned my lesson," Kurt smirks as he climbs in beside me, taking my hand and resting it on his thigh, his fingers covering mine like he needs reassurance I'm really there. "Besides, this is a date, not an intervention. I've waited a long time for this moment—tonight, I get to spoil you, whatever it takes."

"I *really* like this version of you." I beam up at him, the happiest I think I've ever felt, as the taxi pulls away and merges into traffic.

Half an hour later, we pull up outside a small Italian restaurant nestled in a part of town I rarely visit. The exterior is dark mahogany, broken up by sprigs of realistic faux greenery entwined with twinkling fairy lights. A large illuminated sign in elegant script hangs above the door.

"Giovanni's," I read aloud, as Kurt—ever the gentleman—pays the driver, leaps out of the cab, and rushes around to open my door. As he extends his hand to help me out, the cold air bites at my face. He notices me shiver and wraps his arm around me, hurrying us toward the entrance.

Considering there aren't many amenities in this part of town, I'm surprised to find the place is packed. There are about twenty tables, all dressed in crisp white linen with polished silverware resting on top. Flickering tealights sit in the centre next to slim vases containing a single red rose. Most are set for two and occupied by couples enjoying romantic meals, though four tables have been pushed together at one end of the room to accommodate a raucous group of ten—clearly celebrating a birthday, judging by the colourful balloons tied to one of the chairs.

We don't have to wait. As soon as we step inside, a man in his fifties scurries over.

Kurt, *mio amico!*" the man cries, his voice rich with an Italian lilt. Though he barely reaches Kurt's chest, what he lacks in height he more than makes up for in enthusiasm. He grabs Kurt's elbows with both hands, shaking him as he steps back to admire him — eyes wide, mouth agape, as if beholding a miracle. "You're here! Like the prodigal son returned, si!"

"Giovanni," Kurt nods, a faint smile ghosting his lips. To the untrained eye, it might seem casual, but paired with the warmth in his eyes, it's clear he has genuine affection for the man.

"When I saw the name on the reservation, I hoped it was you. Gabriella said I was being silly—you were thousands of miles away, and even if by some miracle you were in town, you'd be too busy to swing by our little place."

"You didn't think I'd come all this way and leave without saying hi—or filling up on your wife's delicious cooking, did you? Though every time she feeds me, it's like she thinks I'll never eat again. I have to hit the gym twice as hard the next day just to balance things out."

Giovanni smiles. "You could always leave what you can't manage."

Kurt fans himself dramatically. "And offend the second love of my life? Never. Where is she?"

"In the kitchen," Giovanni says, nodding toward a door marked Staff Only.

"May I?" Kurt asks.

"Only after you've introduced me to this charming young lady."

I watch their interaction, entranced. Seeing Kurt so relaxed around strangers is a whole new experience. I only snap out of it when he says my name.

"Tina, this is Giovanni—proprietor and inspiration behind this lovely establishment. Giovanni, this is Tina, the girl I told you about."

Giovanni takes my hand, bows slightly, and kisses the back of it. "Bellissima," he murmurs, making me blush. Then his eyes drop to the swell of my tummy. He looks up at Kurt, eyebrows raised.

Kurt nods, a quiet confirmation that the child is his.

Giovanni claps Kurt on the back in excitement, beaming like he has just been told he is about to become a grandfather for the first time. Then he clocks the absence of any rings on my left hand and frowns.

"I'm working on it," Kurt chuckles. "Perhaps you could put in a good word for me while I go and surprise your wife." He kisses me on the temple before disappearing and leaving me in Giovanni's care.

I say care, but the man doesn't pull any punches.

"Why you no agree to marry this marvellous man?" Giovanni asks, sounding like a concerned parent the moment Kurt is out of earshot. "He loves you, you carry his bambino… what is it, cara mia, that holds you back?"

A squeal of joy bursts from the kitchen, accompanied by the crash of pans hitting the floor.

I glance over, curious, as I reply distractedly, "It's complicated."

But as Giovanni's words sink in, I snap my attention back to him. "Wait—what makes you think he loves me?"

Giovanni gives me a look that screams *Seriously?* Then, with the dramatic flair only an expressive Italian can muster, he waves his arms wildly. "It is written all over his face! He looks at you like you are the last cannoli in Sicily. Plus, he told me."

"What? When?"

"Come," Giovanni says, brushing off my questions. He ushers me to a table at the back of the restaurant, pulls out my chair, and waits until I'm seated before taking the one beside me—ready to resume his interrogation.

"So, cara mia... does he not cook for you?" he asks, folding his hands like a man about to judge a pasta competition.

"Yes," I confirm with a giggle, "He cooks for me —and very well."

"My Gabriella—she is the best cook in Italia, and she taught him plenty when he stayed with us a while. He tells us you live on junk," Giovanni says, shaking his head like it's a personal tragedy. "And I tell him. Go to her! Cook for her! The way to this woman's heart is through the kitchen — cook with passion, serve with charm, and you will be irresistible. The love will flow as freely as the wine." He leans back, satisfied. Then, with a dramatic glance at my expanding waistline, he widens his eyes and nods. "By the look of you, it worked. The love certainly looks like it's been flowing."

"He stayed with you?" I ask quickly, grasping at any chance to steer the conversation away from me and back to Kurt. I quickly realise Giovanni must be hard of hearing—or just stubborn—when he ignores me and presses on.

"And your family? They like Kurt? Or do they think he's too handsome to trust?"

I blink. "They've known him since we were kids and have always liked him," I admit. "Although my brother's on the fence since, well..." I pat my stomach gently. "We haven't told my parents about the baby yet."

Giovanni gasps like I've just confessed to a crime. "*Madonna mia!* You carry his bambino and they do not know? What are you waiting for—the child's graduation?"

I open my mouth, but no words come out. I glance toward the kitchen, silently begging Kurt to reappear.

Giovanni leans in, lowering his voice like he's about to share a state secret. "Tell me, cara mia... is the bambino the reason you're glowing, or is it because he's good in bed?"

I nearly choke on air. *Kurt, where the fuck are you?*

"Wait!" Giovanni flops back in his chair, stunned, like he's just uncovered the answer to a lifelong mystery. "Is it because he's *not* good in bed you refuse him as your husband?"

Kill. Me. Now.

"N... no. Things in that department are more than fine," I stutter, wide-eyed and gasping for breath.

Giovanni looks relieved, like he's narrowly avoided having to give the birds-and-bees talk to a man who could eat nails for breakfast.

"Then it's romance," he declares, slapping his hands on the table loud enough to make the couple beside us turn. "He skipped straight to dessert before you even had a chance to savour the meal. You need more romance in your life. Say no more."

He holds up one hand as if to silence me. I stare at him, confused—well aware I've said nothing at all.

"We Italians invented romance," he declares. I've been happily married for thirty-seven years, and tonight I will show you the reason why. I will help fan the flames of love between you until they burn so bright the stars above will be jealous."

I watch as my self-appointed cupid, dressed in a black suit and armed with a thick Italian drawl, strides away with the purpose and determination of a man on a mission.

I subtly scan the room, making a mental note of the exits—because I'm certain whatever Giovanni's planning is bound to be mildly terrifying... and absolutely not Kurt-approved.

Chapter 14

Giovanni disappears into the kitchen, and I pass the time people-watching while waiting for Kurt to return.

Couples sit hand-in-hand across candlelit tables, gazing dreamily into each other's eyes with goofy smiles, whispering sweet nothings only they can hear. It would be the perfect romantic scene—if not for the largest table in the room, strewn with empty wine bottles and echoing with chaos. Seven of its occupants—five men and two women—are visibly worse for wear, while the remaining women, who I take to be either designated drivers or the responsible ones of the group, look on in stunned disbelief. Their expressions flicker between horror and resignation as the man at the head of the table, egged on by the others, grows increasingly loud and obnoxious.

The woman whose birthday they seem to be celebrating leans over and smacks him lightly on the arm, whispering something that makes him shoot her a glare. He stops holding court, flops back into his seat, and pouts like a scolded child. The rest of the table erupts in laughter, amplifying his indignation at being told off. I catch myself smiling at his sullen expression, wondering how long it'll be before the alcohol starts talking again.

A waitress weaves between the tables, whispering something to the patrons as she removes the vase containing their rose, replacing the void with a complimentary dessert and two spoons. I wonder if the kind gesture is Giovanni's way of enticing people to return—or if I wasn't the only one to receive a pep talk tonight, and Cupid is slinging arrows throughout the room.

"What did you say to Giovanni?" Kurt murmurs in my ear as he returns, settling into the chair Giovanni vacated, adjacent to me. He places a jug on the table together with a dish of olives, knowing I've been craving them. "He's acting strange all of a sudden."

He picks up the jug of water and pours us both a glass, then takes a deep draw.

"Nothing. He did ask me if my reluctance to marry you had anything to do with your inability to please me in the bedroom, though," I giggle, knowing that'll get a reaction.

Kurt's eyes go wide, and he starts choking on his water.

"Excuse," a young Italian waiter interrupts, swooping in to snatch away the olives—including the one I've already speared and am holding mid-air, about to eat.

"What are you doing?" Kurt growls. "Give those back."

The lad takes one look at Kurt and visibly withers. His eyes dart between the closed kitchen door and Kurt's scowl. It's clear he's been given two sets of orders and is weighing which he values more: his life or his pay packet.

"Now," Kurt drawls slowly.

The waiter clearly decides a pay packet isn't much use if you're not around to spend it. He sets the olives back on the table and scurries away.

"Honestly," I chuckle. "I think you just shaved five years off that poor guy's life." I stab another olive. This one makes it closer to my lips before it's snatched away mid-air by Giovanni.

"No, no, mia amica," Giovanni says gently. "Not yet." He winks at me, then scowls at Kurt, flapping his arms in exasperation and muttering, "Stupido. The olive is an aphrodisiac."

He sighs as he takes in Kurt's perplexed expression—clearly dumbfounded, not understanding what's happening.

"Let us not hoist the sail before the boat is even out of the harbour," Giovanni tells him, as if that explains everything. He gives Kurt a once-over, frowns, and disappears again.

The look on Kurt's face is priceless. He starts checking his appearance, smoothing down his hair and shirt. "What is it? What's wrong?" he asks me, as if I'm supposed to know.

I shrug as our young waiter reappears with half a dozen bruschetta, artfully arranged on a slate tile. At least, I think it's bruschetta—I've never seen it baked in the shape of a heart with an arrow shot through before. Whatever it is, it tastes good.

Giovanni breezes past. "Antonio," he addresses the waiter, pointing to the light above our table, "that bulb seems to be flickering. Remove it, come to the kitchen, and I'll find a replacement."

Both Kurt and I glance up at the light, which is in perfect working order.

Antonio grabs the small towel hanging from the pocket of his apron, reaches up, and unscrews the bulb. Five minutes later, he returns—not with a replacement bulb, but with an elaborate candelabra, which he slides into the centre of the table to replace the small tea light. It's far too large and takes up more room than necessary.

He coughs and mumbles as Kurt and I stare at him, open-mouthed. "We seem to be out of bulbs… right now."

"What about fire extinguishers?" Kurt deadpans, making me smile as he eyes the flaming candles.

Antonio blinks, clearly unsure whether it's a joke or a genuine concern. He glances at the towering candelabra, then back at Kurt, visibly calculating the odds of Kurt's spontaneous combustion versus Giovanni's wrath. Without a word, he turns and walks away—presumably to check.

Kurt and I make short work of our starter. Antonio returns to clear our plates, then reappears moments later with a bottle of wine. He fills Kurt's glass first, then moves to mine. Kurt places his hand over the top of my glass, but he's a fraction too late—red liquid spills over his fingers.

The waiter freezes, as though staring down the barrel of a loaded gun.

"She's pregnant," Kurt growls.

Antonio turns the bottle so Kurt can see the label. "It's grape juice," he explains, his tone laced with quiet indignation, as if hurt that Kurt would think otherwise.

Kurt drops back into his seat, chastened.

"Your main course won't be long," Antonio says politely.

"Really? That's funny, because we haven't ordered yet," Kurt replies, dry as dust.

I kick him under the table. He jolts.

"Thank you, Antonio," I say sweetly, smiling as the waiter wanders off.

"Quit it," I giggle to an aggrieved Kurt. "It's not his fault."

Giovanni emerges from the kitchen, a silver platter in hand. He sets it down with a flourish, and Kurt and I stare at it—an array of perfectly presented nibbles, each sculpted into tiny hearts.

"For while you wait. These are best eaten with your hands," Giovanni gushes, returning to hover beside me. "But your hands are like silk—too delicate and soft to stain with sauce. I'm sure your man will feed you?"

"He won't," Kurt mumbles.

"He will if he knows what's good for him," Giovanni replies through clenched teeth and a faux smile, before vanishing again like a warrior with a cause.

As soon as we're alone, I lean my head on my hand, elbow resting on the table. "Feed me," I taunt seductively, licking my lips and opening my mouth in exaggerated expectation.

Kurt smirks, picks up a heart-shaped canapé, and places it gently in my mouth. I kiss the tip of his finger as he withdraws his hand. He gazes at me, something flickering in his eyes—an emotion I don't quite recognise.

"Bravo," Giovanni whispers in Kurt's ear, making us both jump and killing the moment instantly.

Neither of us saw him reappear. He crept up like a ninja—if ninjas wore tailored waistcoats and smelled faintly of rosemary.

I pick up my glass, hiding my smile behind it. We're granted a blissful ten minutes of peace, though Kurt stubbornly insists I feed myself—despite my best efforts to tempt him otherwise. I bat my lashes so hard I start to wonder if I'll have any left by the time we get home.

Our next interruption arrives in the form of a young waitress. She sidles up to Kurt, coughing delicately to get his attention. When he turns, she curtsies—much to our amusement.

"Mr Callahan," she says, trying to sound official, "your presence has been requested in the office."

"Why?" Kurt barks sceptically.

Undeterred, the waitress presses on. "I believe you have a telephone call."

Kurt retrieves his mobile from his pocket and waves it at her. "Nope. Try again."

She glances nervously toward the kitchen, where the door is cracked ajar.

"Plan B, Maria," rasps a voice that sounds suspiciously like Giovanni's.

"Um," Maria falters, "Gabriella would like you to help her with something."

"What?" Kurt folds his arms, standing his

ground.

"I'll check," she says, relieved, and scurries off. From behind the door, we hear hushed voices talking animatedly.

"I'm sorry," Kurt sighs. "This evening isn't turning out quite as I'd hoped."

I roll my lips, trying not to laugh.

"I'll go see what they want and put an end to…" he waves his hand across the table, "…whatever this is."

His chair scrapes across the floor as he pushes out of his seat and storms off. I pick up my grape juice and sip it, resuming my favourite pastime: people-watching. My attention drifts back to the birthday celebrations, specifically to the man who was previously silenced. He's clearly not a happy drunk, still smarting from his public telling-off. I watch as he leans in and snarls something into the ear of the woman who dared to embarrass him in front of their friends.

The rest of the group seem oblivious as he grabs her arm beneath the table, inflicting just enough pain to make her face contort in agony. I consider going over to ask if she's okay, but just as I'm about to stand, Maria appears before me, presenting a folded piece of paper on a small silver tray.

"Mr Kurt," she says shyly, "He asked me to give this to you."

I take the paper, heart pounding. If Kurt left so suddenly and unannounced, this can't be good. I unfurl the note and read:

My darling, your eyes are like night vision goggles — sharp, focused, and able to see through to my soul. You are the mission I never want to complete. Always yours Kurt. xoxoxo

I bite the sides of my cheeks, trying not to laugh, and cover my mouth with my hand. Maria leaves, and Giovanni reappears.

"Kurt sent me to tell you he'll be back in a moment. He's just..." Giovanni coughs and averts his gaze, "tidying himself for you."

"Tidying himself?" I raise an eyebrow.

"Si." Giovanni glances at the note I'm still holding. "What have you there?" he asks, in the manner of a man who already knows the answer.

"It's a note," I reply, attempting nonchalance — though it's hard. Giovanni is bouncing on the balls of his feet like a schoolboy convinced he's about to ace his final in Espionage 101.

"Here, want to see? It's a little concerning, if I'm honest."

"Concerning? How so?" Giovanni takes the note and pretends to read it — all the confirmation I need that Kurt wasn't behind such poetic nonsense.

"Well," I begin, feigning careful thought, "The

handwriting… it's neater than Kurt's."

Giovanni lifts his chin proudly. "Letters of love are declarations from the heart. His writing must have evolved emotionally. A testament to his deep feelings — for you."

"Oh," I nod, suppressing another smile. "But I'm not sure it's something Kurt would actually write."

"No?" Giovanni looks from me to the paper and back again. He flicks the note, clearly affronted. "Who else would make reference to his work in such a way? I think it is exactly what he would say."

Not wanting to offend him further, I relent. "Maybe you're right."

"Si." Giovanni stomps back to the kitchen like a student whose prose just got marked *Must try harder*.

I chuckle and turn my attention back to the woman I was concerned about. Whatever I witnessed earlier seems forgotten — the whole table is laughing and joking again.

I recline in my chair, until suddenly the kitchen door bursts open. Kurt stands in the frame. He looks… different. Aside from the frown and the spray of red roses he's holding, I can't quite place it. Giovanni stands behind him, giving me a proud thumbs-up as he shoves a reluctant Kurt toward me.

I glance at my watch, wondering where Kurt got

the flowers — until it hits me. They must be the ones collected from the tables earlier.

"These are for you," Kurt says, thrusting the roses at me before slumping back into his chair.

"Mamma Mia," Giovanni mutters under his breath. "No wonder this poor girl has doubts." He brushes off Kurt's shoulders and turns to me. "He looks good... si?"

I look at Kurt, who sighs. And then it dawns on me.

"Have you... cut your hair?" It's not vastly different — just trimmed and tidy.

Kurt raises his eyes to mine, giving me a hard stare. Confirmation enough that he had no choice in the matter. Though I'm desperate for more details, I know now is not the time to ask.

"A man should always look his best for the lady he is trying to win," Giovanni declares, aiming a loaded look at Kurt. "Now, for your main course."

"Thanks for the note," Kurt deadpans once we're alone again.

I burst out laughing. "What did it say?"

"If you made romance your battlefield, I'd rappel into your heart without a harness — surrendering to you without negotiation," he sings indignantly, before barking incredulously, "I mean, for fuck's sake, what does any of it even mean? It's not safe or tactically sound."

I snort in laughter as I'm about to take a sip of my drink, and grape juice shoots up my nose. I'm not sure what's funnier — the words themselves or Kurt's reaction.

"Do you want to hear what you wrote me?" I ask, catching my breath.

"No," Kurt replies bluntly.

Which sets me off laughing all over again.

"We'll have the main and then leave," Kurt grumbles. "We'll find somewhere else for dessert."

"That seems a little mean," I reply sniggering, "I mean it's not the worst first date I've ever been on."

"It's probably not the best either," Kurt growls, picking up my hand and kissing my fingers. "I want a do-over."

"Only if you *please* let me choose where we eat next time."

"Deal."

We smile at each other as we are swamped by waiting staff who move a vacant table over to accommodate what looks like a sample from the whole menu. Like before, each dish has been meticulously fashioned with the theme of love and romance in mind. Everything from a heart shaped lasagne, to heart shaped meatballs on a bed of spaghetti are piled up on plates beside us. Looks aside, it all smells and tastes delicious. We tuck in like secret agents on a stakeout, one eye scanning the room in anticipation of cupid's next strategic assault.

Thankfully, our feast goes uninterrupted. Kurt and I make small talk until neither of us can face another bite.

"Now for dessert," Giovanni gushes as the waiting staff clear our plates.

"Can we get it to go?" I ask politely. "You've fed us so much good food—I don't have room left right now."

"B... but... it is the best bit." The man looks genuinely heartbroken. I glance at Kurt, a little panicked.

"I'm sure we could manage just a little," Kurt says, saving me at the last second.

As Giovanni ambles off, appeased, Kurt leans in to whisper, "Judging by the rest of tonight's offerings, he and Gabriella have gone over and above to win you over—for me. It'd be rude not to stay and at least see what it is."

"You're right. And considering it was me who said we couldn't leave when you suggested it earlier..."

I trail off, already hearing Giovanni's triumphant return from the kitchen. Whatever this dessert is, I have a feeling it's going to be unforgettable.

A procession of waiting staff, orchestrated

by Giovanni, arrives bearing dishes, cutlery, a chocolate fountain, and a platter of skewered heart-shaped strawberries interspersed with marshmallows—also heart-shaped, of course—alongside the pièce de résistance: a chocolate fudge cake sculpted into two swans kissing beneath a glittering, heart-shaped sugar moon.

We're so awestruck—Kurt gobsmacked and me speechless—that we don't even notice the waiting staff forming two neat rows beside us.

Kurt and I glance at each other just as Giovanni coughs, then—wielding a ladle that's part baton, part microphone—he begins to sing with the volume and enthusiasm of Pavarotti. As he belts out the opening line of "That's Amore," every eye in the room turns toward us. The waiting staff sway side by side, reluctantly awaiting their cue. Each time the title words come around, Giovanni raises his ladle for everyone to join in.

I've never seen Kurt look so uncomfortable. It's absolutely hilarious. When the entire restaurant starts to chime in, he pinches the bridge of his nose before flopping forward with his head in his hands, looking totally defeated.

Not wanting to offend Giovanni, I stifle my laughter as best I can, clamping a hand over my mouth and hoping he mistakes my mirth for shocked surprise. When the song ends, a chorus of cheers erupts around us, and the tears I was fighting to contain finally start to fall.

Both Giovanni and Kurt notice them. Kurt recognizes them for what they are—a side effect of bottling up my laughter for too long. Giovanni, however, reads the emotion as a woman overwhelmed by love—and by the sheer brilliance of his efforts. He leans down and whispers not-so-subtly in Kurt's ear.

"It is time."

"Time for what?" Kurt mumbles without looking up. "A straitjacket?"

Giovanni slaps him upside the head. He's a brave man—few would dare. It's a light touch, but firm enough to get Kurt's attention. He sits bolt upright, staring at Giovanni like he's sprouted a second head and is about to lose one of them.

Undeterred, Giovanni widens his eyes at Kurt, then nods at his knee and over at me.

Kurt stares back, clueless, as the entire restaurant begins chanting, "Do it," over and over.

For what I bet is the first time in his life, Kurt looks at me like he genuinely doesn't know what he's supposed to do.

With all eyes on us and the chanting growing louder and more intense, I know I need to put him out of his misery. I only hope he realises this is simply a kind gesture to rescue him from an impossible situation—and nothing more.

Much to Giovanni's horror, I slide off my chair and drop to one knee in front of Kurt. It's a struggle to keep a straight face as I take his hand in mine.

"Cara ragazza," Giovanni says, placing a hand on my shoulder. I don't know what the words mean, but I know exactly what he's implying—that it should be Kurt, not me, on the floor.

"It's the twenty-first century," I say with a smile.

Giovanni shrugs, his head bobbing in uncertain understanding. I turn back to Kurt.

Will you marry me?" I blurt out.

Kurt's eyes widen in surprise. He glances around the room, now silent, everyone waiting for his response. Then he looks at me—and the smile tugging at the corners of my lips tells him I'm joking.

"You know I will," he snaps, before leaning in under the pretence of kissing my cheek to whisper, so only I can hear: "When you ask me and mean it." His tone is lost on everyone but me, as the whole room erupts in celebration.

We spend the next hour fielding well wishes and congratulations. Even though he never actually turned me down, the dull ache in the pit of my stomach makes the festivities feel like a hollow victory. I laugh, I smile, I nod—but the question lingers, echoing louder than the clinking glasses and cheerful chatter.

Did I mean it?

I told myself it was a joke, a throwaway line tossed into the air like confetti. But the way he looked at me—like he was irritated it was just a performance—makes me wonder if his feelings for me run deeper than I ever realised. Now, with that look still lingering in my mind, I start to question whether I've misread him entirely. My thoughts swirl, caught between the comfort of the present and the weight of what the future might hold. One thing is clear: if I don't start playing for keeps, I might let something slip away. Something… real.

As Kurt's people skills begin to stretch to their limits, I recognise the signs and start preparing to leave. While he meanders off to say his farewells to Gabriella in the kitchen, I excuse myself and head to the ladies.

I'm just washing my hands when I'm joined by the woman celebrating her birthday.

"Congratulations," she says warmly as she enters the room.

"Many happy returns," I reply smiling, just as the door swings closed and catches her arm. She winces—far more than she should for such a light tap.

"Are you okay?" I ask instinctively.

"I'm fine," she assures me, disappearing into a toilet cubicle and locking the door.

I'm just about to leave when I hear muffled crying. I freeze.

Knocking gently on her door, I call through awkwardly, "Um… is there anything I can do?"

"No… no… I'm fine," she calls back, though it's clear she's anything but.

I hesitate, then slip into the cubicle next door. Climbing onto the toilet seat, I peer over the top of the stall.

She's sitting on the closed lid, her sleeve rolled up to just below the elbow. Her arm is blooming with all the colours of the rainbow—bruises old and new fighting for dominance across her pale skin.

"Shit," I exclaim, causing her to look up. "Did he do that to you?"

We both know who I'm referring to.

"He's not a bad man," she says quickly, horrified to have been caught and scrambling to cover the marks. "Except when he drinks…" Her voice trails off.

"And does he drink often?" The anger in my voice is unmistakable. Her silence says everything.

"Please. Just go," she pleads. "Forget you saw anything. There's nothing you—or anyone—can do."

"Can't you leave?" I ask softly, my heart breaking

for her.

"I tried…" she sniffs, wiping her eyes. "Once. I… it… didn't work. He found me and…"

She doesn't finish, but I can guess the rest. He dragged her back home and made sure she regretted ever trying to escape.

"If you could leave safely… with no repercussions…, would you?"

She looks up at me and nods. "But I can't. I'm hiding in here because he's causing a scene out there right now—refusing to pay. It's humiliating. Everything was so lovely… the food, the staff, everything. But if I don't back him up, it'll only make matters worse. When we get home…"

Her voice trails off.

I offer a small, understanding smile and climb down from my perch.

Back in the main restaurant, I see Antonio trying to placate Mr Angry—who's now demanding to see the manager, the chef, the maître d', and basically anyone else he can name. His face is flushed, either from alcohol or misdirected rage, and the rest of his table watches in stunned silence as he snarls and rants like a man possessed. Not one of them steps in to try and help defuse the situation.

I can't just stand by while poor Antonio takes the brunt of this unacceptable behaviour for no reason. Probably against my better judgement, I march over to help in any way I can.

"Antonio, maybe go get Giovanni," I say gently, pulling the young waiter out of harm's way before the irate customer takes a swing at him. Antonio hesitates, reluctant to leave me alone, but I reassure him. "I'll be fine."

As Antonio scurries off, the man turns on me.

"Who the hell are you?" he spits, wobbling unsteady on his feet. "I want to speak to the man in charge, not the hired help."

"Richard." His wife's voice cuts through the noise as she emerges from the restroom, stern at first, then softening into a plea. "Please."

"Please what? You ungrateful cow," he slurs. "I arranged all this for you, and all you've done is whinge and moan all fucking night. Not to mention you embarrassed me in front of all our friends."

"And she paid the price for it, didn't she?" The words slip out—sharp, unfiltered. "I saw what you did, even if no one else noticed."

"Don't." There's a whisper, barely audible. I feel a hand on my arm and turn to see Richard's wife, her eyes wide, pleading with me to stop.

All eyes are on us now. Richard senses it. He straightens, puffing up like a man who thinks he's untouchable.

"What's that supposed to mean?" he snarls, before shifting his gaze. His voice drops low, laced with menace. "Emily, what lies have you been spreading now? What have you been saying?"

"N... nothing," she stammers, backing away in fear.

"She didn't have to say anything," I say, stepping between them, forcing his attention back to me. The room holds its breath. "I saw the bruises you inflicted. New *and* old."

"What are you insinuating?" Richard roars, incandescent with rage.

"That you enjoy hitting women." *Prove me right, asshat. Right here. In front of everyone.*

"Only the impudent ones."

A collective gasp ripples through the room.

Richard lunges, arm drawn back in blind fury. For someone so drunk, he moves fast. Too fast. I don't have time to dodge. Instinctively, I shield my belly—protecting Nugget—leaving my face exposed. I squeeze my eyes shut and brace for impact.

But it doesn't come.

I risk a peek through one eye—and see Kurt.

Giovanni and Antonio hover behind him. As the seconds tick by, more staff gather—drawn by the tension, waiting to see what unfolds.

Kurt stands beside me, calm but coiled, gripping Richards's wrist—caught mid-air, inches from impact. His arrival was silent, but his presence is thunderous.

"Someone care to tell me what's going on here?" he growls.

His voice is low, even, but there's a dangerous fire in his eyes as he locks onto Richard. Kurt's Controlled. Unflinching. And absolutely not to be messed with.

Richard falters, his bravado flickering. His beer goggles no where near strong enough to prevent him recognising the monumental mistake he has just made.

Kurt doesn't move, doesn't blink. But everything about him screams: *Try it. I dare you.*

I glance around the room. Nobody wants to be Richard right now.

Not even Richard.

Should I feel guilty for riling him up? Probably.

Do I? Not one bit.

I rise onto my tiptoes as Kurt leans down, just enough to hear me whisper what I know. His eyes never leave Richard for a second. His grip never loosens.

"Is that so," he murmurs.

I nod.

And in a flash, Richard is upended—dangling by the ankle like a rag doll. Kurt shakes him with such force that the contents of his pockets begin to rain down: keys, receipts, loose change.

Richard shouts obscenities, flailing, declaring he's about to be sick. But Kurt doesn't stop.

Not until Richards's wallet hits the floor.

"Antonio, I believe this gentleman is offering to pay for his meal," Kurt says jovially.

Antonio snatches up the wallet and extracts Richards's credit card. He hesitates, uncertain, until Kurt gives a small nod. That's all the confirmation he needs—he grabs the card machine and gets to work.

"Remember to add a tip," Kurt calls.

When Richard swears at him, Kurt cups a hand to his ear and sings to Antonio, "He says to make it a large one."

It proves tricky for Richard to input his PIN while still dangling upside down in Kurt's grip. But bless Antonio—ever the professional—he gently guides Richard through the process until the payment goes through.

Only then does Kurt swing Richard upright and deposit him into a chair. Richard slumps forward, looking decidedly green and extremely relieved the ordeal is over.

After a few minutes of heavy breathing and

quiet groaning, Richard lifts his head and croaks at his wife, "We're leaving."

Kurt pulls out a chair, flips it backwards, and straddles it in front of Richard. As he sits, the chair leg lands squarely on Richard's foot.

Richard screams out in pain.

"My bad," Kurt says, not sounding remotely sorry. He shifts just enough to ease the pressure. "That's bound to leave a mark."

As the screams fade to whimpers, Kurt leans in, calm as ever. "Before you go, I'd like to discuss your wife's bruises—and why you thought it was okay to dare try and hit my pregnant girlfriend. Perhaps we should take this conversation outside to avoid disturbing the other diners."

Richard doesn't get a choice. Kurt lifts him by the scruff of the neck and half-drags, half-carries him out into the street.

"Who *is* that?" one tipsy woman breathes while fanning herself with a menu. She's not the only one staring—every female eye in the room is locked appreciatively on Kurt's flexing muscles as he disappears through the door.

"That's my guy," I announce proudly and to no one in particular. If I'm honest, I'm too busy admiring his butt to turn.

Chapter 15

After about five minutes, the diners return to their meals. Then the waiting staff disperse, resuming whatever they were doing before the interruption.

Only Emily, her birthday guests, and I remain fixated on the door, waiting to see what happens next.

Ten minutes later, the door swings open and Kurt strides back in—alone.

He marches up to Richard's table and announces, "Dick told me to tell you—the party's over. You can all leave now."

There's a frantic scraping of chairs as everyone surges to their feet, rushing to grab their coats and disappear through the door. Not a single guest pauses to ask where their host has gone—or to check on his wife.

When the last of the group has left, Emily slumps into the nearest vacant chair, her head in her hands. Kurt crouches in front of her.

"Hey," he says gently. "Are you okay?"

"Yes... No... I don't know," she sighs, unshed tears glistening in her eyes.

"Talk to me," Kurt says.

Emily glances at me, and I nod encouragingly, pulling up a chair to sit beside them.

"Thank you," she begins, her voice trembling. "For what you did. But... but when I get home..."

"Do you *have* to go home?" Kurt asks softly.

"I guess not—except to collect a few personal belongings. I don't have any family around here, and only a few friends."

Kurt snorts derisively. "Friends like the ones who watched you get beaten black and blue and didn't lift a finger to stop it?"

Emily opens her mouth to respond, but Kurt cuts her off, anticipating her defence.

"And don't tell me they never knew. My girl's known you for less than two hours—and she knew. Then she went and threw herself right into the line of fire for you. Where were your friends then huh?" The word 'friends drips with contempt as he utters it. He turns to me, his tone stern. "Something we'll be discussing later."

I roll my lips, trying not to smile. "Will you be reprimanding me again, sir?"

Kurt gives me a long look—one that suggests he'll be 'punishing' me for my impudence, if nothing else. Finally, he sighs, despair creeping into his voice. "Why didn't you come and get me?"

I shrug. "Things just sort of escalated."

He turns back to Emily.

"I tried to leave before... he found me... it was..." Her voice trails off again.

"If I could guarantee your safety," Kurt asks gently, "where would you go?"

"Anywhere," she murmurs. "Anywhere he couldn't find me."

Kurt stands. He seems to like that answer.

Just then, the restaurant door swings open, and I'm surprised to see Blake striding toward us. He looks dressed for war—black combat trousers, t-shirt, and boots. Muscles for weapons. All that's missing is the camouflaged face.

"Blake!" I squeal happily. "What are you doing here?"

Kurt flaps his arms in exasperation. "Seriously? Control yourself, woman."

"I heard there was a damsel in distress who needed rescuing from her date," Blake deadpans. "I thought it might be you, so I rushed right over."

"No," I giggle. "I'm good." I glance at Kurt, who frowns and holds up three fingers. I know what he's getting at—he's misconstrued our banter as flirting and is clearly keeping score. I look back at

Blake and tell him, "For now."

"I'll only ever be a call away," he replies, winking to confirm he's teasing Kurt too.

"When you two have quite finished," Kurt snaps.

"Well, if it's not you…" Blake mirrors Kurt's earlier gesture, crouching in front of Emily. "It must be this pretty little thing right here."

"Um," is all Emily manages, blushing furiously.

Blake chuckles and stands, facing Kurt. "What do you need me to do?"

"She's decided to leave her husband. She'll need an escort home—and someone to stay with her while she packs whatever she wants to take. There's a chance he could turn up while you're there."

"Do I need to be worried?" Blake asks, although he doesn't sound all that serious.

Kurt scoffs, as if the question is absurd.

Blake smirks. "Where is he?"

"A&E, if he's got any sense," Kurt deadpans. "At least, that's where I asked the cab to take him after he fell on my fist, tripped on my boot, and toppled to the floor—smashing his face on the ground."

Blake arches a brow.

"He was drunk," Kurt adds, as if that explains everything. "Anyway, once…" He pauses, suddenly realising he doesn't know Emily's name.

"Emily," I fill in, so she doesn't have to.

Kurt nods and continues. "...Once Emily decides where she wants to go, make it happen. She's had enough of being a punching bag and wants to start a new life somewhere else. I'd suggest somewhere out of state."

"I can't afford to go far," Emily says, her voice small and embarrassed. Both Blake and Kurt turn their attention to her. "Richard handled the finances. He gave me an allowance. I saved what I could, but he made me account for everything."

Blake smiles, raises a brow and says to Kurt, "It'll give Foxy something to do while he's sat on his ass in that hotel room tonight."

Kurt nods. "I'm sure Dick would agree his wife deserves some financial compensation for the way he's treated her. Get Foxy to track down what he's got stashed and transfer it all to her name. If it falls short of what you need, I'll pick up the rest."

"I can't ask you to do that," Emily blusters.

Blake claps Kurt on the back. "You're a good man."

Kurt ignores them both. "One more thing. When I told Dick to stay away from his wife going forward, he was a little dazed."

"The alcohol?" Blake chuckles.

"Must've been," Kurt shrugs nonchalantly. "If he does show up, make sure he got the message."

"With pleasure," Blake mumbles darkly, then offers Emily his arm.

She takes it tentatively letting Blake lead her away.

"So good-looking—a little bird tells me you're recently single," he shmoozes Emily, as he helps her on with her coat. He doesn't wait for her to answer as he rattles on, "You're in luck, because I'm a free agent too. I know, I know, it's hard to believe right? But it makes it easier for us to move into together."

Emily glances over to me her eyes wide with apprehension. I give her a reassuring nod with a smile, and she relaxes a little looking back to Blake as he continues talking without letting her get word in.

"Where shall we go? I hear California is nice this time of year. Don't take this the wrong way but you look like you could use some sun. Right now you could give Casper a run for his money and I like my women to at least look like they're alive."

Those are the last words we hear as he opens the door and gestures outside with an exaggerated flourish.

I sigh and look at Kurt. "He's right, you know?"

Kurt tips his head quizzically.

"You are a good man."

"Good enough to marry?" He challenges, "For

real?"

"Maybe," I smirk back at him.

He grins and throws his arm around my shoulders. "I'll take it." He gives me a light-hearted squeeze. "Wasn't a bad effort for your first proposal, but if you really want to lock this down," he gestures down his body, "I need champagne, fireworks, and you in something that makes me forget how to say no."

"Fireworks?" I chuckle. "How am I supposed to get those?"

He leans in, his voice low and loaded. His fingers trail lightly down my arm, sending pleasurable shivers down my spine. "You dress for the occasion and bring the champagne. I'll handle the explosions. You've definitely got the spark—it just needs the right... ignition." He waggles his eyebrows, and I slap his chest playfully.

"I guess Blake won't be in court getting the lowdown tomorrow now," I muse.

"Meh." Kurt shrugs. "If he isn't back in time, he'll call Ace to fill in."

"And what if Ace is still busy?" I throw back.

"Then," Kurt says, kissing the crown of my head, "once I've dropped you at work, I'll go myself. C'mon, let's get out of here before Giovanni notices we're still around and starts singing again."

Chuckling, we grab our coats and head for the

door.

A quick glance around confirms there are no cabs in sight. The night is cold but clear, so Kurt and I decide to walk a bit to work off some of the calories we just consumed.

"Is that blood?" I exclaim, horrified, pointing at the sidewalk just as we set off.

"Mmm." Kurt nods. "Dick had a nosebleed."

"That must've been some nosebleed." I glance at him, but he won't meet my eye—staring straight ahead as we walk. I don't press. He looks visibly uncomfortable, like he's bracing for a question he doesn't want to answer, one that might make me think less of him. Instead, I reach for his hand, lacing my fingers through his. He squeezes back, glancing down at me with a soft smile—a silent thank-you for letting it go.

When we're able, Kurt flags down a taxi and bundles us inside, giving the driver my address. As we pull away, I suddenly remember the whole point of our evening excursion.

"Wait," I say quickly to the driver, "can you swing by here first?" I give him a new address, then turn to Kurt. "I still need to grab my phone from the office."

He checks his watch. "Isn't it a little late? It's gone ten. Will you be able to get in?"

"Got you with me, haven't I?" I tease. "If I'm able

to rappel into your heart without a harness, surely you can rappel in through a window with one."

Kurt huffs a laugh and smirks. I roll my eyes, realising he thinks I was being serious, and continue, "Ever since that cyberattack, we've had round-the-clock security. Carter's worried that since the virtual breach failed, whoever tried it might attempt a physical one to get whatever they were after."

Kurt starts laughing.

I frown, confused. "What's so funny?"

"Just good to know it's me surprising you this time."

"What's that supposed to mean?"

He flicks his eyes subtly toward the driver. "Ask me again when we get home."

I shake my head, bemused, as the car pulls up outside my office.

Kurt and I look up at the building. The foyer is well lit, but aside from a few scattered lights, the rest of the structure is plunged into darkness. It looks completely different from how it does in daylight—more ominous, more foreboding.

Just inside the main door, a security guard lounges in a chair, feet propped up on the desk, chuckling at something on his phone. He doesn't look like he could fend off a puff of wind in a paper bag, let alone an actual intruder.

"I was going to ask if you wanted me to come in with you," Kurt says, "but now that's a moot point."

"What do you mean? The place isn't deserted—there are lights on. Plus, there's a guard."

Kurt snorts.

"He might have a black belt or something?"

Another snort.

"I'll be fine. In and out in less than five minutes. Ten tops. Wait here so we don't lose the cab."

I reach for the door, but Kurt catches my arm. I watch as he sets the timer on his watch to exactly four minutes.

"Assuming you can distract Buttons there from YouTube long enough to let you in," he says, "you've got four minutes to get upstairs, grab your phone, and text me to say you're on your way back down. That guy's clearly more into scrolling than patrolling—I wouldn't even trust him to guard my Netflix login, let alone a building."

"Seriously?" I scoff.

"Deadly," Kurt replies, not a hint of sarcasm.

"What happens if my phone's out of charge? Say I can't text and you don't hear from me in time?"

"I'm coming in."

I smile and grab the lapel of his jacket, pulling him close enough to kiss him on the cheek.

"What was that for?" he asks, surprised.

"For caring," I say with a grin. "But you're seriously overthinking this."

I exit the cab, close the door, and blow Kurt a kiss through the window.

Kurt's right about the guard. It takes me longer to get his attention than it does for me to get him to open the door. Once inside, I wave to Kurt. He gestures to his wrist pointedly starting the countdown on his watch. I smile back before turning and making my way to the elevator.

A few seconds later, the elevator dings and the doors slide open.

I step out onto my floor and into a heavy, unnatural silence. The building feels unfamiliar at this hour — darker, colder, almost hollow. I've never been here this late before. Normally, sunlight floods the space through the tall windows, or the cleaning crew has already lit up the place. Even when I'm early, there's always someone else around — a distant voice, the hum of a vacuum, the soft shuffle of footsteps.

Tonight, there's nothing.

The hallway ahead is short, leading into the wide, open-plan office with a few rooms branching off. I hesitate, unsure where the light switches are. For a moment, I just stand there, letting my eyes adjust, trying to orient myself. Then I start forward.

Each click of my heels against the marble floor echoes like a judge's gavel in an empty courtroom. The silence swallows the sound and hurls it back at me, louder than it should've been. I feel exposed — like someone unseen is listening.

I shake the feeling off, telling myself I'm overreacting, but I move a little faster, clutching my coat tighter around me. The open office looms ahead, and I'm nearly at my desk when I notice a sliver of light spilling out from beneath Steven's door.

It isn't the light itself that makes me freeze — it's the shadow that flickers across it. Someone has just walked through the beam on the other side.

Kurt and I hadn't spoken about Ace since before the restaurant. He hadn't been assigned to watch Steven, and to my knowledge those orders had never been changed. It was entirely plausible Steven had left the hotel and come back to grab something he needed before court — just as I had stopped off to pick up my phone.

I lift my foot to take another step, but the sound of whispered male voices makes me freeze mid-stride.

"...if anyone finds him, we're finished," Steven snaps, his voice tight with panic.

Then another voice — rougher, but familiar.

"Relax. He's gone, and he's not coming back. If by some miracle he is found, nothing traces back here. And he won't be talking. Not anymore."

My breath hitches. I clamp a hand over my mouth to stifle the sound. The voices stop. Terrified I've been heard, I drop to my knees, scanning frantically for somewhere to hide.

My desk is directly opposite Steven's door — too exposed. If it opens, I'll be spotted instantly. I crawl toward Foxy's, carefully sliding out the chair and wedging myself underneath, trying to reposition everything like it hasn't been disturbed. Being pregnant and full from dinner makes the contortion awkward — and far noisier than I'd like.

As I shuffle into place, a pen rolls off Foxy's desk and hits the floor with a sharp clatter. I snatch it up, heart pounding, breath ragged. The handle on Steven's door turns and it creaks open.

A shaft of light creeps across the floor toward me. I hold my breath and squeeze my eyes shut.

"Where are you going?" Steven hisses. "We need to switch this out. Now."

"Shhh. Did you hear something?" The second voice is low, suspicious.

Footsteps pad across the marble. Seconds stretch into an eternity. Someone stops beside Foxy's desk. I see his boots — polished, heavy —

and the cuffs of dark trousers. Whoever it is—he's big.

Could it be… Bear?

The boots turn to face me. Foxy's chair wobbles. I brace myself, certain it's about to be pulled away, exposing me cowering in the shadows. The tension is unbearable.

Then the man speaks.

"Who did you say this tech guy is?" he growls, pushing things around on the desk above me, tapping keys on a computer that wasn't powered on when I arrived.

Don't say Foxy. Don't say Foxy. The words loop in my head like a mantra.

Steven answers. "I didn't. He's a nobody. Just some half-wit the stupid old fool who runs this place met in a bar."

"If he's a nobody, why are we here doing what we're doing?"

"Because, like you, I don't leave things to chance. Why do you think I hired that dumb bitch as my executive assistant? She was a desperate single woman about to have a baby. I knew she'd be too distracted to pay close attention to me — or what I might be up to. She's just here for the money. Which suits me fine."

Ass.

"So it had nothing to do with the fact she's incredibly easy on the eye?" A low chuckle follows. "I thought you hired her before you knew she was pregnant."

If he knows what I look like... we've met.

Steven snorts, ignoring the jab. "Listen, when the Knox case is over and we get our payday, I'll give her a bonus and send her off on maternity leave early. You know — to recover from all the pressure she's been under. I'll tell her the stress can't have been good for the baby. Anything she knows will leave with her. Just like when I arranged for Robert's minion to be transferred. I'll start fresh. Clean slate. Get someone decent in."

"Someone who won't knock you back, you mean." Another chuckle.

"I didn't see you faring much better," Steven barks.

"I was doing just fine until you cockblocked me at the party."

So it *is* Bear.

Just then, their attention shifts to a low humming coming from my desk.

"What's that?" Steven whispers, panicked.

Bear moves, crossing the room and opening the drawer. The humming grows louder.

"It's her phone. Who's Kurt?"

Fuck. Damn caller display!

I send a silent prayer of gratitude to whoever stopped me from updating my screen saver with his picture.

"Her boyfriend," Steven mutters.

"What does he look like?" Bear asks, cautious now.

"A moron," Steven snaps.

"Do you have a picture?" Bear presses, voice low and sharp.

"Do I look like I'm running a frigging dating service? Of course I don't have a picture. Why the interest?"

"No reason," Bear murmurs. "Just wondered if I knew him."

"He was at the party—New Year's. So if you didn't recognise him there, I'd say no, you don't. Now can we finish what we're doing and get the hell out of here before we get caught?"

I hear my phone being tossed back into the drawer, the slam of it shutting. Footsteps retreat as Bear and Steven head back into the office. They're just about to close the door when the elevator pings.

"I definitely heard that," Steven growls.

"Whoever it is — I'll take care of it," Bear replies, voice dark and deliberate.

I bury my head in my lap, tears pricking the backs of my eyes. I can't let Kurt walk into an ambush. I just can't.

Think, Tina. I will myself. *THINK!*

Chapter 16

"Hello?" A voice sings out.

I release a breath I didn't realise I was holding. My shoulders sag with relief.

It's not Kurt.

"It's the guard from downstairs," Steven hisses. "He knows me. Hide in my office and I'll get rid of him."

There's a grunt followed by footsteps shuffling across the floor. I bet Kurt sent him up when I didn't answer my phone.

"Hello?" the voice calls again, louder this time—and then, all the lights snap on.

"Mr Prentice, I didn't know you were here, sir."

"Sorry, didn't mean to startle you," Steven replies, voice smooth as silk. "I was at home reviewing my notes for tomorrow, and realised I'd left some behind. Thought I'd swing by and grab them now since I have to be in court early tomorrow."

"I didn't see you come in sir."

"I came through the back," Steven sighs, disappointment laced in his tone. "You know the door wasn't locked."

"Shit. I… I mean… I'm sorry. I was sure I'd checked it. I'll get fired."

Panic bleeds into the man's voice.

"Chin up," Steven says, and there's a sound—maybe a clap on the back. "We all make mistakes. No harm done. How about we keep this little slip between us? In return, maybe you could do me the courtesy of forgetting you saw me here tonight."

There's a pause. Something shifts—maybe in the guard's posture, maybe in his face—because Steven feels the need to elaborate.

"If the senior partner finds out I forgot vital notes, he'll probably start questioning my ability to handle this case. I don't want him thinking I'm about to crack under pressure like the last guy. I've almost got what I need. I'll be out of here soon."

"I see." The relief in the guard's voice is unmistakable. "Fine… yes… whatever you say. I'll leave you to it, sir."

As footsteps retreat. I start to relax.

Then Steven calls him back.

"Wait. What brought you up here?"

My heart kicks into overdrive. No wonder Kurt wanted me out of this. None of this stress can be good for Nugget.

"I came to check on your friend."

"My friend?" Steven echoes.

"Yeah, the good-looking one—"

"Oh," Steven draws out the word, stretching it like it explains everything. "You just missed 'em. Left a few minutes ago. If you could keep their presence to yourself as well, I'd appreciate it. Here—take this. Go have breakfast on me when your shift ends."

I hear the rustle of notes being handed over.

"Oh… okay… sure. Wow, thanks a lot. I'll leave you to it, sir."

Footsteps retreat again, this time not stopping. The elevator dings. Moments later, Steven flings open his office door.

"He knows you're here. He saw you," he snaps, voice tight with frustration.

"When?"

"How the fuck should I know? CCTV, maybe."

"I disabled the feed."

"Not well enough, obviously. He knows what you look like. Said you were good-looking."

"I am," Bear chuckles.

"Will you stop mucking around? Finish what you're doing, grab the box and let's get the hell out of here."

The office door slams shut.

The moment it does, I slip out from under the desk and tiptoe toward the exit, careful not to make a sound. I'm just through the main room and obscured by the hallway when the office door creaks open again.

I freeze beside a small stockroom, heart hammering. If I run, the tapping of my heels will give me away. If I take the elevator, they'll see me. If I head for the stairs and they choose the same route, they'll catch me.

They're getting closer. I don't know what to do.

Then—without warning—the stockroom door opens just enough for a hand to shoot out, clamp over my mouth, and yank me inside.

I don't even get the chance to struggle.

"It's me, baby. Quiet," a familiar voice whispers in my ear.

Kurt.

His voice is a balm, soothing every frayed nerve. I melt against him, the tension draining from my body.

Without a sound, he pulls the door closed behind us. Darkness swallows us whole.

Once he's sure I've recognised him, he releases his grip, replacing his hand with a single finger pressed gently to my lips—a silent command to stay quiet.

Footsteps echo past the door.

Kurt gently nudges me behind him, shielding me with his body. He cracks the door open just enough to peer through.

He sees the two men and watches in silence as they reach the stairs, turn the corner, and vanish from sight.

Then he closes the door.

His body betrays the storm inside him. He's vibrating with rage—every muscle taut, every breath sharp.

"It's him." He growls. I know he means Bear. "Wait here. I've a score I need to settle."

"Not now." I fling my arms around his waist causing him to hesitate. "Please," I beg, "Not tonight. I heard them talking. He doesn't know about Foxy or that you and the others are here. We still have the element of surprise of our side."

I press my head to his back. "I really don't want to be left alone again." As the adrenaline from the last few minutes fades, a completely different emotion begins to take its place. Relief at not being discovered, memories of an absurdly romantic evening, and the sensation of being pressed up against the hard planes of Kurt's back in such a confined space all blend together — leaving me feeling a little frisky.

There's a long silence after which I mumble, "I'm getting a little hot."

"Course you are. The coast should be clear now, we can leave." Kurt whispers, totally missing the point. He cracks the door and peeks out just as my hands start to wander down from his waist.

"Not that sort of hot," I murmur.

"Tina, you have to be kidding me?" Kurt sounds genuinely shocked. "Now?"

"Why not?" I challenge fumbling with the belt of his pants. "You said the coast was clear. And you did promise if I ever got horny at work you'd come over and we'd find an empty stockroom. Et voilà."

"They might come back,." Kurt turns, trying to lecture me but I'm only half listening. I'm too focused on finding a way to appease my raging hormones.

"We'd better be quick then," I whisper seductively, climbing Kurt like a tree and kissing him passionately.

His response is immediate, he wraps his arms around me, kissing me back before setting me down on a cupboard in order to relinquish me of my underwear. I push down his trousers and boxers before taking him in my hand, pumping him a few times to make sure he is ready. His reaction is visceral — he groans, grabs my legs and pushes them apart, taking over control. As he crashes his lips back on mine, I claw at his back, dragging him as close as two people can get. My desperate whimpering is all the encouragement he needs to give me what I want.

It's a hard and fast ride, but no less satisfying. The dent in the top of the cupboard? A mystery no one else will ever solve. Our little legacy — a quiet echo of tonight's mischief, loud enough to stir a smile, large enough to remind me of us every time I go hunting for staples or paper clips.

Afterward, we creep out of the building through the rear exit to avoid the security guard. Kurt looks a little flushed, but otherwise doesn't have a hair out of place. I, on the other hand, look worse for wear — ruffled hair and smudged makeup that screams *you've been up to no good*.

I watch, quietly impressed, as Kurt unlocks the rear exit and relocks it again without a key, like it's second nature. It's a small act, but it unveils a deeper layer beneath his commanding presence — a quiet power, ready to rise when called. It makes me wonder how much more he holds back, and what other skills he's mastered that I've yet to discover. There's a calm precision in the way he moves, a quiet confidence that feels almost surgical. He doesn't scare me — not even a little. But watching him now, I can't help but pity anyone who tries to stand against him. Suddenly, he feels more dangerous than I'd ever given him credit for

— not in a reckless way, but in a way that suggests he's capable of far more than I've seen. If he chose to stay hidden, his enemies wouldn't even see him coming before the strike.

When we get home, the events of the evening finally catch up with me, and I'm exhausted. Although I can tell he is desperate to find out what happened before he found me at the office, he doesn't push— he reads the signs and leads me straight to the bedroom. He kicks off his boots, lies on the bed, and pulls me down beside him. We don't bother to undress or climb beneath the covers. Instead, he wraps an arm around me, and I snuggle into the warmth of his body. Safe and content, sleep consumes me.

The following morning, I wake alone, cocooned in a blanket as the scent of a cooked breakfast drifts into the bedroom. Kurt is whistling cheerfully while he works. I glance at the clock— barely six a.m. The alarm isn't due to go off for another hour. I groan, pulling the blanket tighter around me, but the urge to visit the bathroom wins out, and I reluctantly peel myself from the warmth of the bed.

By the time I return, I'm too awake to settle back in. Then, as the aroma of whatever culinary masterpiece Kurt is conjuring reaches me again, Nugget sends a signal to my brain, insisting I investigate because she's hungry.

Kurt stands in his boxers and my apron, fussing over a tray laid out on the counter. There's already a small glass of orange juice, a coffee—presumably decaf—and a bowl of some white, lumpy substance topped with birdseed and a banana, presumably to make it look more appealing.

He hasn't noticed me yet. I watch as he places a small plate beside the rest and carefully loads it with a slice of wholemeal toast slathered in avocado, then crowns it with a poached egg. He adds three rashers of crispy bacon to the side—clearly meant as a treat—then pauses to survey the scene. After a moment's deliberation, he decides two slices of processed meat will be more than enough, snatches up the third, and pops it into his mouth.

"Oi!" I call out. He freezes like a kid caught with his hand in the cookie jar.

"Stop eating my bacon."

"What makes you think this is for you?" he says with a grin.

"Oh please. Unless you've suddenly developed a craving for white goo accompanied by every vitamin and mineral ever recommended for healthy foetal development..." I pat my stomach. "That tray is definitely not for you."

He places a hand over his heart in mock offence. "That 'white goo,' as you so eloquently put it, is oatmeal topped with banana, chia seeds, and almond butter. It's a fibre-rich combo that aids digestion and delivers omega-3 and potassium."

"In other words, I'll be gassy for the rest of the day."

Kurt snorts in frustration. "Get back into bed. I wanted to surprise you."

"Any reason you couldn't have waited another hour? I should still be dreaming about breakfast, not smelling it."

"I'm sorry," Kurt says, looking genuinely contrite. "I know you need your rest, but I really need to talk to you about what happened last night before we head out. Sometimes the smallest detail can make the biggest difference. With Blake out of play, I've got to be in court, and I want to drop you off at work first so you can shadow Foxy while he works his magic on Steven's IT."

"He still hasn't given me a key to his room. He might be trying to stall again."

"Did he lock it when he left last night?"

"He locked it before he left at lunch. As for the evening—I'm not sure. I wasn't paying attention. I was too busy trying to escape without getting caught. He'd be stupid not to lock it. After making the guard promise to forget seeing him, leaving it unlocked would be a dead giveaway that he'd been back."

Kurt shrugs. "If the guard's arrival spooked him,

it could've made him nervous. Nervous people make mistakes."

"Speaking of which, why send the guard up if you were coming in yourself?"

"When your time was up, I was coming in one way or another. I thought I could convince the guard to let me in. He took one look at me and refused."

"Funny that," I chuckle, picturing Kurt looming behind a closed door in the dead of night, demanding entrance.

"I didn't want him to call the cops so we compromised. He said he'd go upstairs to check on you if I waited. I agreed, slipped round the back, let myself in, and took the stairs."

"How is that a compromise?" I laugh.

"It was as much of one as he was going to get," Kurt growls. "When I got to your floor, I heard voices. When I realised one wasn't yours, I ducked into the supply room to figure out what was going on. Your turn. Let's take this back to the bedroom so you can put your feet up." He gestures to the tray. "You eat while you fill me in on what happened before I got there." His tone turns playful. "Then I'll help you shower before work."

"When you let yourself in, was the door locked?" I ask as an afterthought.

"Yeah, why?"

"Steven made out it was left open where the guard forgot to check it."

"Quelle surprise!" Kurt mumbles as I follow him out of the room.

We settle back in the bedroom, and I fill Kurt in on everything I'd heard the night before. He doesn't say a word — just listens carefully as I recall as much detail as I can between mouthfuls of food.

When I've finished, it's almost time to get ready for work. Just as we're about to get up, a thought strikes me.

"Last night, in the taxi, what did you mean when you said it was good to know it would be you surprising me?"

Kurt's lips quirk. "I don't know what you mean," he says, trying to brush the question off — but I know he remembers all too well.

"Yes you do. When I was talking about the security breach and you couldn't stop laughing."

Kurt starts laughing again.

"What?" I demand, impatient.

"The cyber breach. It was us," Kurt finally puts me out of my misery. "The second you told us Robert had gone missing mid-trial, Josh and I started making tentative enquiries — just to make sure you were safe and he wasn't involved in anything that could come back and put you in harm's way. We couldn't find any trace of him from the moment you told us he disappeared. Foxy checked his financials — no card transactions, no cash withdrawals, nothing. Josh and Axel started reviewing his past cases, I started looking into his current one. That's what originally led me to the Knox case and Steven. The deeper I dug, the less I liked what I found. Little discrepancies here and there — nothing significant. We needed an in. Foxy made it look like someone was trying to compromise the firm's systems and security..."

"Then you arranged for him to 'bump' into Carter," I finish. "So let me get this straight: The very guy Carter hired to secure his systems — is the same guy who compromised them in the first place?"

"Yeah," Kurt bursts out laughing. "That's about the size of it."

"Good morning, Mr Fox," I announce cheerfully, tossing my bag onto the desk and shrugging off my coat. "Productive evening?"

"Good morning, gorgeous," Foxy lifts his head from the monitor and flashes me a grin. "Not bad. Caught up with a friend who was in town unexpectedly, then went back to my hotel and played a game of cat and mouse with some jerk's financials."

"Did you win?" I ask, desperate to know the outcome—whether Emily is financially secure or facing a tough road ahead.

"I always win," Foxy smiles. "In case you're wondering, your friend from the restaurant now has enough in her account to get settled somewhere nice before she has to look for a job. That's if she survives Blake's charm offensive in the meantime. How was your night?"

"Eventful." I open my desk drawer and take out my phone, waving it at Foxy and lowering my voice. "I came back to get this and ran into a few complications."

He nods, getting the message loud and clear. "I might just pop out and grab us a decent coffee from down the street."

I know it's an excuse to phone Kurt and get the lowdown in a safer environment. "While you're gone, I'll find out what I can do to get you into Steven's office. He hasn't given me a key yet."

Foxy nods and saunters off.

The first thing I do is power up my computer. Once I'm settled, I log in and check my emails, scanning the list until I find what I'm looking for. Steven sent me a message at seven a.m.

I open it and read a crisp, pointed note:

Key to my office in envelope, bottom left

drawer of your desk. Keep it safe. Lock up when you've finished. WATCH HIM!

I open the drawer and find an envelope tucked beneath a pile of files. Upending it, the key falls onto my desk with a clatter. I immediately head to the office door to test it. I don't know what makes me try the handle first — but I do.

The door opens without the key, and I smile to myself. *So you were rattled.*

I relock the door, return to my desk, and get on with my usual tasks while I wait for Foxy to return.

He comes back about twenty minutes later with two coffees, handing me the one marked decaf.

"Any luck?"

I smile and dangle the key in front of him. He grins in response.

Then he rifles through a bag he must've stashed under his desk when he first arrived pulling out a small device. Turning to me, he says, "Ready?"

I nod at Foxy and unlock the door. I'm just about to step inside when he stops me with a hand on my arm. I glance down at the strange-looking device in his hand — sleek, black, bristling with tiny dials and blinking lights.

He casts a quick look around the open office to make sure no one's watching, then fiddles with the controls, eyes scanning the readout. After a moment, he quietly closes the door and steers me to one side. He rests his arm casually against the wall and leans in close, whispering in my ear. To a casual observer, it probably looks like he's flirting.

"Listen carefully," he murmurs. "My scanner picked up at least one device in there that's not connected to the main network."

What does that mean?" I whisper back, playfully slapping his arm in mock annoyance to keep up appearances.

"It means there's either an unauthorized listening device or a hidden camera in that room. Maybe both. Someone's planted it to keep tabs on what we're doing. If it's a camera Bear's monitoring, he sees my face and it's game over."

My stomach tightens.

"I'm going to try jamming the signal from out here," he continues. "But it'd help if you go in first and do a quick sweep. Just take a casual look around — act like you're checking that Steven hasn't left anything lying around he wouldn't want me to see before you let me in. If you spot anything unusual, don't investigate. Just come back out and tell me."

"What exactly am I looking for?"

"Anything that seems out of place. Something new that wasn't there before. If the office was locked, the cleaning crew wouldn't have been in — so check for patterns in the dust, signs something's been moved."

"I'm not sure about that last part. The door wasn't locked when I tried it — the office might've been cleaned."

"No matter," he says. "Trust your gut. And whatever you do, don't draw attention to what you're doing—someone could be watching."

I nod and step into the office, calling out sternly as I go, just in case anyone's listening.

"Wait there until I've checked that any confidential files have been locked away. Then I'll come and get you."

I fix a frown on my face, playing the part in case anyone other than Foxy is watching. He looks like he's biting the inside of his cheek, trying not to laugh. Then he gives me a subtle thumbs-up.

Inside the office, I glance around. The desk is neatly arranged. The cabinets are tidy. The bin hasn't been emptied, which tells me the cleaners haven't been in. I don't see anything out of place. I listen, but aside from the hum of activity outside, there's silence.

I sit at the desk and try the drawers to my right. They're locked. I try the drawers to my left. The top one opens with ease, revealing nothing but the usual array of stationery—pens, pencils, and the like. I close it and open the second. Half a dozen large, ruled notepads stare back at me, all unused, ready and waiting for action. Sighing, I close that drawer too.

The last contains a thick file. I take it out and flick through it. It's notes on the Knox case, but all very generic and bland. I scoop it up anyway. As I do, a small piece of paper falls out and flutters to the ground. I lean at an awkward angle to pick it up and miss; the paper slips under the desk, beneath the drawers.

I get on my knees and reach under to retrieve it. As I do, the back of my hand brushes against something stuck to the underside of the drawer. I don't look. I just casually grab the paper and pop it back in the file as I stand.

It's then I notice the picture on Steven's desk. It's in a heavy block frame, and it's of a woman I presume is his wife. She's young and looks happy and carefree. For a second, my heart sinks at the thought of her not knowing what her husband may—or may not—have been up to on his recent clandestine visits to the Obsidian.

Then it strikes me: that picture was never there before—nor was the fancy fountain pen standing proud in its holder on the left side of the desk.

Clutching the file to my chest, I call out to keep up the charade as I grab the lining and contents from the waste paper bin and walk back out of the room. "It's okay, we can get started. I'll just grab a drink and bring you in."

Foxy is seated at his desk, waiting when I appear. I roll the chair from mine over and sit beside him, leaning in so I can speak discreetly while making it look as if he's showing me something on his monitor.

"There's something taped under the drawers on the left side of the desk," I murmur, sounding like an extra from a spy film. "There's also a picture on his desk that's never been there before, as well as a fountain pen—which is odd."

"What's odd about it?" Foxy leans in, mimicking my tone and smirking. I know he's teasing me, thinking my behaviour is slightly OTT.

I still can't help looking around covertly before answering in a soft voice, fully aware I'm acting like I've just stepped out of a Cold War thriller. "Well, he hates fountain pens. He can never refill them without getting ink everywhere—not to mention the time one leaked in the pocket of his Armani suit. He went postal. Also, it's on the left side of the desk."

Foxy quirks an eyebrow, waiting for me to explain why that matters.

"He's right-handed. Surely you'd keep it on the side that's easier to reach. Oh and there's this…" I wave the file I'm still clutching at him, "It's labelled Knox and is thick enough to look like it's important. But there's nothing of any value in it. I think it was left as a decoy.

"What's that?" Foxy gestures to the small sack I'm holding.

"His rubbish. I thought we could go through it like they do in the movies."

Foxy lets out a deep chuckle. "Well done, Sherlock. The boss been giving you lessons in reconnaissance?"

I ignore him. "What next?"

"I've found two frequencies transmitting that aren't part of the firm's network. Once I jam them, it'll probably draw attention. We need to work fast so whoever's monitoring them thinks it's just a glitch—not a deliberate attempt to disable them. Here's the plan."

I lean in, eyes wide—probably looking like I'm about to cram for my finals. Foxy smiles and shakes his head slowly before he replies.

"I'm going to jam the signals, go in and check out what you've found, do a cursory sweep myself, disable any devices, come out and unjam the signals. Then I'll run a second scan with this gadget here…" He picks up the same little black box he used earlier, waves it, then places it back on the desk. "…to confirm we've found all the tech that may have been hidden. If we have, I'll re-jam the signals, reconnect the devices so they're live again, and once I've seen them and have a better understanding of what we're dealing with, I'll formulate a plan."

"What if we haven't found all the devices?"

"Then we're screwed until we have." Foxy taps a couple of keys on a laptop that has appeared alongside all the other technology, before calmly sliding out from under his desk, and disappearing into the room with a wink and a smile.

Meanwhile, I'm left sitting at the desk, watching him vanish like he's about to defuse a bomb with a paperclip.

Foxy works quickly and with precision, I stay out of his way, waiting on the sidelines ready to run interference if we are disturbed. After what seems like a walk in the park for Foxy and a tense few minutes for me. He is back a satisfied smirk on his face.

"Thanks to your keen eye, we're almost ready to rock. There's just one more thing I need you to do."

I grab a notebook and pen off the desk, waiting for further instruction.

Foxy leans in, eyes twinkling. "Best not write it down—unless you plan on eating it after."

"Course," I mutter, facepalming as I toss the notebook aside and scooch close, bracing myself. I whisper, "What is it?"

"Don't worry. It doesn't involve lasers, disguises, or rappelling from the ceiling. The boss would kill me." Foxy chuckles.

I exhale witheringly.

"So disappointing," I joke, flopping back in my chair.

"Wait!" I exclaim, sitting bolt upright again. "Is it legal?"

"Probably," Foxy deadpans, pretending to consider it. "Maybe." He grins. "Let's just say—in the fight between good and evil, you're a portal with a memory leak and a flair for plausible deniability."

Great. Just what I need—espionage with a side of improv.

"I don't want to have this baby in prison," I warn.

"Relax," Foxy sniggers, "that's the boss's child, it will probably be born ready for combat, with enough brains to plot your escape or enough attitude to have you thrown out within the hour." There's a pause, a slight shrug then, "That's if his dad doesn't break you out first."

Chapter 17

As it happens, the job I'm so apprehensive about involves little more than 'creating more space for Foxy to work' — which means turning the photo on Steven's desk so it faces the bizarrely placed fountain pen.

Two hidden cameras are 'accidentally' repositioned so the only thing they film while Foxy infiltrates Steven's computer is each other. Neither is equipped to pick up audio — that's reserved for the basic bit of kit under the desk.

To avoid arousing suspicion, Foxy leaves all the devices operational, which means we speak as little as possible while he works. And when we do, it's little more than an act.

It doesn't take Foxy long to do what he needs, but the whole time he wears a constant, confused frown I can't decipher. It's like he's found something totally unexpected. After we evacuate with a performance worthy of an award, I lock the office back up and turn to Foxy expectantly. "Well?" I'm itching to know the results.

"Later. Keep your phone switched on and with

you," is all he says, hurriedly packing up his desk before vanishing for the rest of the day — doing nothing to appease the curiosity bubbling away inside me.

I throw myself into my usual routine, ticking off daily tasks while glancing at my phone every few minutes, expecting it to ring with information or details of an exciting new mission. But the day drags, and I'm left waiting for a call that never comes.

By the time I get home, I'm seething. Even more so when I find Foxy and Ace lounging on my couch with a coffee in hand, and Kurt inspecting a brand-new whiteboard—clearly bought to avoid making any more holes in my wall.

I stomp past the three musketeers, announcing, "I'm going to get changed."

Three pairs of eyes snap toward me, catching the bite in my tone. They track my movements warily as I sweep past and head to the bedroom. I hear soft footsteps behind me—Kurt follows, closing the door behind him.

"Babe?" he says, eyebrow raised. One word, a thousand meanings. What's happened? What did I do? Why are you pissed? Do I need to make someone pay?

"No one called me?" I yank a pair of sweatpants and a sweater from the wardrobe and toss them onto the bed. "I get you in, I give an Oscar-worthy performance to throw off suspicion, I feed you intel every chance I get..."

"Intel?" Kurt echoes, amusement lacing his voice. I ignore him and keep going.

"...and you..." I jab a finger into his chest. "You told Foxy not to give me anything, didn't you? He left me hanging—alllll day!" I rip off my work clothes and start pulling on my loungewear. One leg in the bottoms, mid-hop, Kurt chuckles.

"I didn't, I swear." He holds his hands up in surrender.

I freeze, one leg suspended in the air. I wobble, and he catches me before I fall.

"I don't believe you. You've been here having your little meeting, hoping you'd be done before I got home so I'd be none the wiser. I saw you trying to dismantle the whiteboard." I pause, then add, "Thank you for not putting any more pinholes in the wall, by the way."

"You're welcome." Kurt grins. It's unnerving how often he's been smiling lately. He used to walk around like he'd just been slapped in the face with a wet fish by Josh—aka the only guy on earth who'd survive telling that tale. "And I was just setting up. All I've told them is what happened when we went to pick up your phone. Since you were there, you already know about that. We were waiting for you before we started on the other stuff."

"You were." I beam at him, suddenly aware of how unhinged I must've sounded. Izzy was right about my mood swings. Note to self: get a handle on them. I finish dressing, walk over, and reach up on tiptoes to give Kurt a peck on the lips. "Sorry."

He crouches and places a chaste kiss on my belly, whispering, "Cut your mom some slack, will you buddy? We're all suffering out here."

I burst out laughing. "Am I really that bad?"

Kurt widens his eyes and lies—badly. "No."

"Wait," I frown. "If you didn't tell Foxy to keep quiet, then he ghosted me on his own?"

"I guess," Kurt murmurs cautiously.

I stomp out of the bedroom and past the living room. Ace and Foxy watch my every move.

"I'm just grabbing a drink," I say, motioning to their mugs but avoiding eye contact with Foxy—who's just made it onto my hit list. "Then we can get started."

In the kitchen, I grab a mug and a herbal tea bag. While waiting for the kettle to boil, I spot Kurt's latest baking effort: a pumpkin pie topped with piped cream, ready for dessert later. The longer I stare at it, the angrier I get. This is the second time Foxy's withheld information. I try to fight the impulse building inside me… but something snaps.

I grab the pie and stomp into the living room.

Kurt has just finished setting up the whiteboard. He stands and sees me coming—his eyes go wide. Ace and Foxy notice his expression and turn, alarmed, to see what could possibly rattle the one person who's never fazed. Their chuckles die the instant the pie lands squarely in Foxy's face.

Kurt and Ace erupt into laughter, teetering on the edge of hysteria. Foxy sits frozen, cream dripping from his jaw, while the tension inside me melts away. I stroll into the kitchen, grab my tea, and return to the living room. Calmly, I wedge myself between the still-giggling Ace and the stunned Foxy.

Turning to Kurt, I say with practiced nonchalance, "You can begin now."

It actually takes twenty minutes to get started. Foxy disappears for a quick shower and re-emerges in one of Kurt's shirts. Kurt scrubs the sofa clean of Foxy's creamy aftermath. I make Nugget some snacks. Ace, meanwhile, needs the full twenty minutes to stop laughing.

Once we're all settled, Kurt clears his throat and begins.

"Right. Since it's obvious Tina thinks we're deliberately keeping her out of the loop, I suggest the three of us"—he gestures between himself, Foxy, and Ace— "go first. Then, if she has anything to add, Tina can jump in at the end. That way, we might avoid another food fight. Sound good, babe?"

I nod, smiling around a mouthful of popcorn I've just shoved in rather inelegantly. Ace's hand strays too close to the bowl in my lap and earns a sharp smack and a muttered, "Get your own." He raises his hands in surrender, grinning, and turns his attention back to Kurt.

"Ace. What've you got?"

"Not much. The woman with Prentice at the hotel—her real name's Cassandra Monroe. She left at exactly eight forty-two last night…"

"That's precise," I mumble, still chewing.

Ace flashes a grin. "It's good to be exact—that way the boss thinks I'm focused… when really, I'm just calculating how cute you are."

I blush and nudge the popcorn bowl toward him. He grabs a handful with a wink.

Kurt clears his throat, unimpressed. Ace snaps back to business.

"Prentice wasn't with her. Foxy had left by then, so I tailed the woman like you asked. No clue when Prentice left, or where he went, until you filled me in on your escapades. Monroe went straight to an apartment in Manhattan and didn't leave the rest of the night. I got Axel to run a check—it's definitely her registered address, and the only one he could find. She had a gentleman caller from midnight to six a.m. I sent Axel some pictures, but the guy doesn't seem to be a person of interest."

"Can I see the pic?" I ask.

Ace pulls it up on his phone and hands it to me.

I study the image for a while. When I look up, three pairs of eyes are locked on me expectantly.

"Nope. Don't know him."

"Useful," Ace teases, nudging me playfully with his shoulder. He continues, "I stuck around until ten a.m. and bumped into one of her neighbours…"

"Fortuitous," I say, unable to hide the disbelief —because we both know that kind of encounter is never accidental.

"I thought so," Ace replies with a grin. "Apparently, she's not a morning person. Rarely leaves her place before evening unless she's got a 'lunchtime appointment.'"

We all know exactly what kind of appointment that implies.

"So I headed back to my hotel for some shut-eye. Didn't have any toys on me to tag her, but if you want me to, I'll go back later."

"Foxy." Kurt passes the baton with a nod.

Foxy shoots me a nervous side-eye. I flash him a grin — the kind that says *revenge served, grudge lifted*. He clears his throat and begins.

"The system was clean," he says. "Too clean. No documents. No encrypted volumes. No recent user activity. No backups to the central mainframe. Just a calendar, a few meetings, and some lunch reminders. I couldn't retrieve any deleted data. None of it made any sense. I uploaded some spyware, but I had a hunch — so as soon as we wrapped, I left to check it out."

He casts me a sideways glance. I feel a flicker of guilt and offer him some of my popcorn as a peace offering.

"I'll take some — but only to stop you throwing it at me," he grumbles, then continues.

"I checked the machine's credentials — MAC address, device ID, registry keys, the works. They matched the room, but not the history on the mainframe. The box containing the hard drive was swapped out."

"Bear was carrying a duffel bag when he left last night," Kurt adds. "Three guesses what was inside."

"Now that he thinks he's in the clear, I'll bet Steven plans to swap the decoy drive back out — after he's copied what he needs and wiped anything incriminating off the original."

"Dammit," Kurt snarls. "If he wipes it, can you recover anything?"

"Depends how good he is. Deleted data can

linger until it's overwritten. But once that happens…" Foxy trails off.

"We need eyes and ears in that room," Kurt growls.

Foxy smirks. "We've got 'em."

"We have?" Kurt and I say in unison, then exchange a grin.

"Once I was sure what cameras and mics he and Bear had planted, I was able to hack the feed. We can see and hear everything they can — straight from their own devices."

"What if they shut them down, convinced you've finished what you went in to do?" I ask.

Three pairs of eyes turn to me. Kurt grins and arches an appreciative brow.

"Now you're thinking like one of us. Foxy?"

When I disabled their feed, I slipped in some of our own tech. There's a bug in the light fitting above his desk. Two micro-cams — one in the air vent, covering the door and anyone across the desk, and one under the lip of the plant stand by the entrance, catching the opposite angle. I embedded our signal inside theirs — same frequency, same modulation. If they scan for bugs, all they'll see is their own gear. And if they shut it down, I get an alert to my phone and our ghost protocol kicks in, rerouting our tech through encrypted fallback channels."

"Nice," Ace whispers, nodding as Foxy continues.

"I'll get a notification if the room is breached. Someone could go back in tonight to swap out the bogus drive. So my question is: should I keep monitoring remotely, or do you want eyes on the ground?"

"Remotely," I blurt out instinctively, then slap a hand over my mouth as all eyes swing toward me. The room erupts in laughter.

"Care to explain?" Kurt asks, his voice laced with amusement.

"Well," I begin, flustered by my outburst, "if anyone does go in tonight, the box you need will already have been wiped. There's nothing left to gain—assuming anyone even shows up. What's the point of someone sitting there, watching an empty room, waiting for something that might never happen?"

Kurt nods smirking, "remotely it is."

I beam, feeling like I've just been bumped to the top of the class.

Foxy leans in whispering, "See, smart as well as beautiful."

I offer him some more popcorn for his compliment. He sniggers and takes some while Kurt cups an ear and barks, "What was that?"

"I said smart as well as unavailable," Foxy

replies, shooting Kurt a cheeky grin. Ace, who clearly caught the original line, chuckles from the other side of me.

"What about you, boss? Get much today?"

"Prentice spent the entire day challenging the testimony of the prosecution's final witness—Samuel Doyle, a junior subcontractor with a conscience who had worked on Ramirez's building before she moved in. Doyle claimed he was pressured to use cheaper insulation and substandard wiring, compromising the building's safety. He also alleged he was incentivised with a cash bonus to complete the work under a tight deadline, suggesting the reward was tied to cutting corners."

"How much?" Ace cuts in.

"Five grand. Almost exactly what he needed to clear his student debt," Kurt says. "He also claimed he had internal emails and texts showing the cost-cutting was deliberate and concealed. But when asked to produce them, he couldn't. Swore he had them saved, but they'd vanished from his account. He said he'd already given a copy to the prosecution, who supposedly forwarded a duplicate to Robert Taylor for review—shortly before Taylor vanished.

Prentice argued that the messages had never been included in the case file he received. Since their legitimacy couldn't be verified, he pushed to have them ruled inadmissible. The prosecution, whose case is hanging by a thread, countered that the forwarded copies should suffice. They accused Steven of deliberately stalling and claimed he couldn't have reviewed the file competently. To back this up, they produced read receipts for all the information sent—not just from Robert Taylor, but also from Carter Shaw—a detail that visibly unsettled Steven. Sensing his unease, they went further, boldly accusing him of exploiting Robert's disappearance to bury evidence, unaware that Carter also knew the documents existed. Looks like the emails went out separately, not in the same chain, so Steven could've easily assumed Robert was the only one at the firm who got them. Tensions rose, prompting the Judge to call a recess.

The issue resurfaced after lunch when Steven miraculously "found" the missing communication. He argued that the copies Doyle had originally provided weren't part of a verifiable email chain with timestamps; instead, they had been attached to a standalone message after the trial had already begun. Prentice claimed the documents were forged to discredit his client.

Doyle also alleged the building inspector was on Knox's payroll and falsified parts of his report to ensure the building passed inspection. The inspector, of course, denied it. And with no hard evidence, it's just one person's word against another's.

I did find out that one of the neighbours reported electrical issues in their unit a week before the fire. An engineer was sent to check it out. His report said everything was fine and blamed it on a faulty fuse. But the resident said he was there for less than ten minutes and barely looked at anything—he basically dismissed the complaint. Again, there were no other witnesses.

Prentice also submitted documentation showing Ramirez increased her home insurance two weeks before the fire—the minimum waiting period before a claim can be made. He's arguing that, as a single mom on a low income, she tampered with the fuse box intending to start a small fire and file a false claim. Unfortunately, due to the unexpected surge, the fire quickly spiralled out of control.

I get the feeling the judge doesn't like Prentice very much. He called a forty-eight-hour recess so the prosecution had plenty of time to thoroughly review the insurance documentation."

Ace leans forward, his forearms resting on his legs as he looks at Kurt. "So, what's next, boss?"

Kurt scratches his head, thinking. "We could really do with Blake right now," he murmurs.

I raise my hand.

"Babe, will you quit doing that?" Kurt laughs. "If you've got something to say, say it."

"You didn't come to me."

"What?" Kurt frowns, confused.

"You said you'd come to me at the end to see if I had anything to add."

"I said you could jump in at the end if you had anything to add," Kurt counters. Seeing my expression, he concedes apologetically. "Tina, do you have anything you want to add?"

"No," I say with a smile, hoovering another handful of popcorn. "But thanks for checking."

Kurt sighs heavily as the other two men stifle a chuckle.

"Oooh," I suddenly pipe up excitedly. "What about the rubbish bag I took from Steven's office? I stowed it in my desk drawer. Want me to bring it home for you to go through?"

All three men avert their gazes and try to hide their smiles.

"If anyone laughs, they'll live to regret it," I growl.

Everyone snaps to attention.

"Put it back where you found it," Kurt replies. "I don't think he'd be stupid enough to toss anything of interest."

I snort, clearly disagreeing, and shrug.

"Anything else?" Kurt presses.

"Is there anything I can do to help until Blake gets back? You sounded like you could use an extra pair of hands." I ask, knowing he'll either say no or assign me something mundane just to keep me safe and in one place.

Kurt thinks for a moment, then lays out his orders.

"Foxy. Call in sick tomorrow."

"What with?" Foxy asks automatically.

"Food poisoning?" Ace quips — a sly dig at either Kurt's cooking or my previous act of violence.

Kurt pins him with a hard stare as he continues talking to Foxy, "Whatever will buy you a couple of days. Follow the electronic trail, see if you can dig up anything to support Doyle's claims. Check out the insurance policy that was supposedly taken out by Ramirez. If Steven goes into the office tomorrow, keep tabs on what he's up to remotely. If you're not about he might relax a bit more and let something slip. Before you go have a look in your bag of tricks, I want a small tracker that can be hooked up to my phone."

"Boss," Foxy acknowledges, since Kurt is still staring at Ace.

"Ace."

"Boss?" Ace is clearly trying not to laugh.

"The neighbour who filed the complaint about the electrics — track her down. Put that quick wit and charm to good use for a change. Get a first-hand account of her story. If anything feels off, dig deeper. Try to talk to Camila Ramirez's brother — after all, he was the one who got the ball rolling on Knox's arrest. See what he has to say. And then, if you can, have a chat with Doyle. I don't need to tell you we need to tread very carefully. There are some powerful people in play here, and we're walking a fine line, the last thing we need is to draw attention to ourselves."

Ace nods.

"Tina."

I sit bolt upright, surprised he's even remembered I'm in the room.

"Since Prentice won't be in court the next couple of days, he should turn up at the office. I want you to keep an eye on him from there."

Quelle surprise.

Kurt must read my mind — or my sour expression.

"It's an important job, babe. We only have eyes in his office, not the whole building. He might let something slip in the break room or take a call by your desk that is out of range from Foxy. He'll give you details of his schedule but he might not stick to it. Keep a timeline of his actual movements. That alone might be enough for us to take him down later — if he claims to be in one place and turns up in another."

"You could go through his bin, look for clues," Foxy teases.

"How's she going to explain that if she gets caught dipshit," Kurt immediately cuts in, frowning at Foxy before turning to me. "Do. Not. Put. Yourself. At. Risk. More important than any of this is keeping you and our baby safe. Do you understand?"

"Fine," I grumble. "What are you going to do?"

Kurt's expression darkens. "I'm going to try and locate our friend Bear."

My face falls instantly. Kurt spots it.

"Don't worry," he says, trying to placate me. "I won't be engaging with him. Yet. I spoke to Josh earlier and promised I'd wait for him to arrive. He and Maeve are already in Oklahoma City. Depending on how many stops she needs for the restroom, he anticipates getting here the day after tomorrow. I've told him Izzy said they can stay here. I just want eyes on Bear. I don't like the idea that he's out there and unaccounted for. He could spring up at any time and blindside us."

"Can't you find him?" I ask Foxy hopefully.

He shakes his head solemnly, "I've tried. Problem is, he knows how to disappear. He's had the same training we have. Ever since he ditched us in Maine, he's known we'd be hunting for him.

He'll expect us to have all the usual channels flagged—bank accounts, travel records, old burner phones, the works. Anything he touches will light up like a flare.

He must've stashed a decent amount of cash or set up an alias to handle his financials. Right now, he's a ghost. The only reason we know he's here is because of you."

Kurt swiftly changes the subject, "I also want to figure out where Miss Monroe fits into all this. I feel like we're missing a vital piece of the puzzle, but I can't work out what it is. Is she just a bit of fun for Prentice, or is there more to it? It seems a bit too much of a coincidence that she was also seen cosying up to Judge Simmons."

"But he isn't the judge on the Knox case," I point out. "Judge Fletcher is."

"I know. I just don't believe in coincidences. I asked around yesterday—Simmons doesn't have a reputation for playing away from home. By all accounts he's been a loyal husband for over thirty years. So why didn't he take his wife to the New Year's party? No one I spoke to hinted at trouble in paradise, yet there he was—flaunting his connection with Monroe like it was nothing.

He's acting like a man in love, and that doesn't happen overnight no matter how good she is in bed. He's a man ready to risk everything—and he doesn't give a damn. I'd say she's been working him for a while to have that much influence. But why? Purely for financial gain? Status? Protection? Or something darker. Did they start hooking up before or after she started meeting up with Prentice?"

The whole room pauses for thought. After about a minute, Kurt claps his hands, snapping everyone's attention back to him.

"Right, meeting adjourned. We all know what we need to do. Keep in touch, and if we can, let's meet back here tomorrow—same time."

Ace and Foxy relax into their seats.

"Don't get comfortable," Kurt admonishes. "You've got work to do, and I need to debrief my girl."

"What about dinner?" Ace whines.

"Since dessert's off the menu, I suggest you try Giovanni's." Kurt grabs his mobile. A few seconds later, Ace's phone pings. "That's the address. Tell them I sent you."

"Shall we go too?" I ask, a little too enthusiastically.

Kurt shoots me a warning look. "After last night? I think I'm suffering from PTSS."

Ace and Foxy say their goodbyes and head out, but not before I catch Foxy slipping Kurt a small device—pulled from one of the bags he brought in.

Once we're alone, Kurt turns to me. "So, do you want to be debriefed now or after dinner?"

I think for a moment. I'll probably lack concentration after eating.

"Now, I think," I reply. "Do I need to take notes? Should I grab a notebook and pen?"

"You can take notes if you like," Kurt says, flashing me a wicked grin, "but some things are better learned through hands-on experience."

And just like that, I realise with a smile—he's not about to unpack the meeting. He's about to unpack me.

Chapter 18

"Where's the tech guy?" Steven hovers at my desk on his way to his office at nine o'clock the next morning.

"Carter swung by, said not to expect him, called in sick apparently," I reply nonchalantly.

Steven smirks. "Grab us both a coffee, would you, sweetheart? Then come into my office. You can fill me in on what happened yesterday."

I mentally replay the conversation he had with Bear while I was hiding under the desk—especially the part where he called me a dumb bitch. My fingers twitch with the urge to slap him. Instead, I plaster on a fake smile and decide that tampering with his drink will have to do. "Sure."

Ten minutes later, I'm sitting across from him at his desk, watching as he takes a large swig from the mug I've just handed him. It takes effort not to laugh as he coughs and splutters, showering his pristine white shirt in coffee.

"Something wrong?" I ask, feigning surprise.

"I think you accidentally put salt in my coffee

instead of sugar," he mutters, blotting the spill with a tissue.

"Oops. That was a dumb thing to do," I say sweetly. He gives me an odd look. I shrug. Justifying myself with, "Baby brain."

"Yes... well... what happened yesterday?" Steven leans forward, resting his forearms on the desk.

"Not much," I say with a bored expression. "Once I found the key you left, I came in to make sure there was nothing confidential lying around. I found a file on the Knox case in an unlocked drawer, so I took that and cleared away your rubbish. Foxy came in and did whatever he needed to. Didn't take long. He said your system was clean and he was moving on."

"Moving on where?"

"I didn't ask. Another floor, I guess, now that he's happy this one's secure. Are you here all day?" I ask, digging for information. "Your schedule says you're supposed to be in court, but since you're sitting in front of me now, I guess that's changed."

"Judge called a recess. I'll be in the office for the next couple of days—on and off."

"On and off?" I prompt, hoping for more detail.

"My plans aren't finalised. I'll update my calendar once they are." He glances at me. "That'll be all."

Heeding his dismissal, I stand and head for the door. But my heart leaps into my throat when he calls me back.

"Yes?" I turn, hoping I haven't slipped up somehow.

"Drop the Knox file back in, would you? I want to review it."

"Sure." I grab the folder from my desk drawer, return it to him, then close the door behind me and flop into my chair.

My phone chimes with a thumbs-up emoji from Foxy. I smile, send one back, and dive into my inbox.

Halfway through, a notification pops up: Steven's schedule update. I skim the entries and fire off a quick text to Foxy:

> *Steven's out of the office this afternoon from 1, and tomorrow from 3. Diary says he's working from home both days.*

Seconds later, Foxy replies:

> *Definitely not working from home. He just booked a suite at the Obsidian —champagne, the works. Charged it to Knox's account. Sent a text right after. No clue who he's meeting. Probably Monroe.*

I pause. With Steven out, no one would notice if I slipped away. And if they did? I could always say I was sick, it would be plausible enough with Foxy already absent.

Want me to find out? I could tail him —since you're short-handed.

I barely hit send before I get a reply. I'm surprised to see it's from Kurt not Foxy:

NO!

How the hell did he know what I sent? I flip both Foxy and Kurt the middle finger emoji, toss my phone face-down, and get back to work.

At 12:30, Nugget starts demanding I go for lunch. I grab my bag—then remember I need to ask Steven something before he disappears. I knock and step into his office. He's hunched over a pile of papers.

"Tina?" Steven straightens. "What can I do for you?"

"I found this the other day." I hand him the paper I'd reprinted after discovering it wedged in my drawer. "I couldn't find anything that goes with it, so I figured it's old news—but thought I'd better check before I ditch it."

He takes the paper and stares at it a beat longer than necessary.

"I don't recognise it," he says, though I get the distinct impression he does. "Leave it with me. I'll get rid of it later."

"I could trash it for you now."

"No." His reply comes a little too fast. "Best I'm

certain before either of us destroys it."

"If you're sure." I force a smile.

"I am." He leans back in his chair, eyes drifting to my stomach. "You're really starting to blossom, aren't you?"

"I'm not sure 'blossom' is the right word," I reply, patting my expanding waistline.

"Are you getting enough rest?"

"I think so. Why? Do I look tired?" A little thrown, I pat my cheeks, trying to coax some colour into them.

"I was thinking—since I'll be working from home the next two afternoons, maybe you'd like to do the same."

"Really?" I sound surprised, even to myself. It's totally impractical. "How would that work?"

Steven shrugs. "I take it you've caught up on all the admin I gave you?"

I nod.

"Then I'm sure the office will survive without you for a few hours. Can you check your emails from home?"

I nod again. "I was set up with remote access in case you needed me for external meetings. I've never actually used it."

"Well, here's your chance. Keep your mobile on in case I need you, but otherwise I should have everything covered. Just meet me here tomorrow morning so we can show face and handle anything we can't do off site.

"What abut Carter and the others?" I ask a little worried about what they might think.

"I'll square it with Carter. Don't worry, as long as I bring the Knox case home for him, he has given me free reign," he answers a little smugly. "Why shouldn't I look after the people who look after me?"

I blink. It's a harmless enough line—on the surface. But something about the way he says it makes my skin prickle. It feels more like a veiled bribe.

Like the money still sitting in my desk drawer. Untouched. The wadge of notes he tried to give me. Has he seen it in there? Is this his way of nudging me to take it?

"If you're sure," I say, hesitantly.

"I am." He stands, ushering me toward the door. "Go grab some lunch, then home to put your feet up. I'll see you in the morning."

The door clicks shut behind me. My phone vibrates on the desk.

I don't need to look—I already know it's Kurt. And I have a pretty good idea what the message says before I even read it.

I'm not wrong:

Don't get any bright ideas about playing detective. Go straight home and EAT SOMETHING HEALTHY.

I send him a GIF of a compliant soldier saluting a sergeant major.

He sends one back—a woman laid over a man's knee being spanked.

I smile and text back:

That's more of an incentive than deterrent.

I end the line with a winking emoji, then I power down my phone and make the conscious choice to chase a sudden craving for a Flippin' Scrumptious burger — not my fault the place just happens to be exactly opposite the hotel my boss is heading to.

Since I leave before Steven and manage to catch a cab right away, I'm tucked into a booth with a burger and a clear view of the hotel doors across the street by the time he arrives. He climbs out of a taxi, extending a hand to help whoever's beside him.

Cassandra Monroe slides out, all elegance and gloss.

I pretend to check my messages, angling my phone just enough to snap a photo. But just as I'm about to tap the screen—it goes dark.

I look up.

Kurt is looming over me, blocking the shot like an irate bouncer at a nightclub.

"What the hell are you doing here?" he snaps, eyes narrowed, arms folded across his huge chest.

I flutter my eyelashes as I stare at him. "Lunch?"

He doesn't budge. "I said healthy."

I shrug, lifting the top off my bun. "Pretty sure there's lettuce in here somewhere."

"And this was the only place you could think of to get a lump of processed meat sandwiched between two slices of bread?" He glowers.

"Didn't you read the sign when you came in? *Flippin' Scrumptious*," I argue, smiling around the mouthful of burger I've hurriedly shoved in—just in case it's about to be confiscated.

"And what were you doing with that?" Kurt nods at the phone I'm trying to nudge under a napkin.

"Multitasking," I say instantly.

He sighs, pinches the bridge of his nose, and slides into the booth opposite me like a disappointed dad at a parent-teacher conference.

"I've stood up to cartels less dangerous and unpredictable than you," he mutters, more to himself than to me. "Babe, you promised you'd behave—listen, follow instructions, stay out of it when I told you to. You could be putting yourself —and our baby—in danger. What kind of example are you setting here?"

"How to be independent and think for themselves," I mumble, suitably chastised but still a little defiant. He's right. I know he's right. I rest a hand on my belly and whisper, "Sorry," to both of them.

Kurt slouches back in his seat. "I knew it was a bad idea, I don't know what I was thinking, letting you get involved in the first place. Liam will have my balls in a vice if he ever finds out. I think it's best if we go back to the way things were."

"No, please." I reach across the table and grab his forearm. "I'm sorry. I really am. Don't shut me out—I was just trying to help."

"The people I work with follow orders because they know what happens if they don't. They're trained to expect the unexpected, and how to survive it." He trails off, eyes darkening. "If anything were to happen to you…"

"It won't," I say quickly, pressing one hand to my heart and raising the other. "I swear I'll be good from now on. Besides, Maeve will be here tomorrow—we'll go out, grab lunch, get our hair and nails done. I want to show her the sights, the Empire State Building, Rockefeller Centre, Central Park. It'll take us a whole day to do Bloomingdales and Macy's alone. I'll probably be too busy to help you anyway."

He studies me, dragging the silence out until the tension is almost unbearable.

"Last chance," he says finally. "You pull something like this again, and you're out. Plain and simple."

"Agreed," I confirm with a relieved smile. "Do you want to take me home and spank me now?" I add, throwing in a teasing eyebrow wiggle for good measure.

Kurt gives me a long-suffering look, but the corner of his mouth twitches.

"Perv."

"Takes one to know one," I say sweetly.

He shakes his head, already reaching for his wallet. "Come on then, let's get you out of here and find you something to eat with actual vegetables in it. And no, ketchup doesn't count, tomato is a fruit."

I gasp, clutching the last of my burger like it's a wounded comrade. "You take that back. Ketchup is a clearly vegetable. It's cooked, it's squishy, you don't have it for dessert…ever, and it goes with chips. That's science."

Kurt raises an eyebrow. "That's delusion."

"Tomayto, tomahto," I mutter, stuffing the rest of the burger in my mouth before he takes it.

He stands, waiting for me to slide out of the booth. "Let's go before you start arguing that chocolate milk is a protein shake."

"Don't be ridiculous," I say indignantly, grabbing my bag. "It's clearly calcium."

Kurt snorts and grabs my hand. "Keep your head down and keep walking."

He leads me away from the restaurant and hails a cab. On the ride home, I glance over at him.

"How did you know I was there? I switched my phone off."

"The minute it went down, I knew you were up to no good. I tailed Monroe to the hotel, saw the place opposite and came straight across the road to find you."

"Shouldn't you have stayed to keep watch?"

"No need. I've incentivised one of the receptionists to let me know when either she or Prentice leaves."

"Incentivised?" I raise an eyebrow. "How much did that cost?"

"Who said I offered her money?" he replies with a smirk.

My jealousy spikes. "Her? What did you offer?"

"Something I wouldn't be able to if I were married," he quips, avoiding eye contact as he tries not to laugh. "Anything you want to ask me right now?"

"Don't mess with a hormonal pregnant woman, jerk," I snap. "I asked you last night and you turned me down."

"Because you didn't mean it." He cups a hand to his ear, waiting. "And I didn't exactly turn you down."

"Fine," I huff. "Will you marry me?"

He considers it for a moment. "Nope. Still not feeling it."

"Ass!" I exclaim, as he bursts out laughing, draping an arm around my shoulder and pulling a reluctant me into his side for a hug. He presses a tender kiss to my temple.

"Better luck next time," he says with a wink. "Third time's the charm."

"Just remember we're exclusive until then," I scowl, though I'm trying not to smile.

We get home and cuddle up in front of the television for an hour, then Kurt gives me the most amazing foot massage before I help him set up the whiteboard and prepare some nibbles, arranging them neatly on the coffee table — much to his amusement.

"The guys are here to work, this isn't a social call," he sighs when he sees the spread. "No wonder they're all crazy about you."

"Crazy about me, huh?" I giggle. "Good to know."

Kurt realises he's said more than he meant to. He snaps his mouth shut and busies himself with the notes and photos that were previously pinned to the wall, now securing them to the whiteboard with magnets. There's nothing new in the notes — we've already discussed them — but the photos catch my attention. There are a few covert shots of Cassandra Monroe and Steven going about their day, and an old photo of Bear that's been defaced — someone's drawn a pair of horns on his head and a target over his chest. There's also a lineup that includes Judge Simmons. I recognize a few of the faces, but not all.

"Who are these guys?"

"They're all judges. That one there is Fletcher," he says, pointing. "We're still checking out the rest. Apparently, they meet once a week for a poker game at one of their houses. It could be something. It could be nothing."

He pauses, then continues.

"It came up when we first started looking into Robert's disappearance and the case he was working on. Fletcher was presiding, so that's where we began. Then Prentice became our priority, and Fletcher got pushed to the back burner. When the connection between Prentice, Monroe, and Simmons surfaced — even though the link from Simmons to Fletcher is tenuous — we figured the overlap was worth digging into, just to make sure we weren't missing anything. Axel's working that angle back at base, but it's slow going. If we get caught... these guys literally have the power to lock us up and throw away the key."

Do you have their names?"

"Sure, I'll show them to you later. Why? Should I be worried?"

"No," I chuckle. "I'm mostly office-based, so I'm not great with faces from court. But I'm pretty sure I'll recognize some of the names. I might be able to offer something useful."

Kurt pulls me in for a kiss and just as things start heating up — there's a knock at the door.

"That'll be our guests," I say excitedly, pulling away to let them in.

"Babe, they're not guests. They're liabilities with impeccable timing," Kurt grumbles.

"They're guests," I call back. "And since they're so crazy about me, it's only right I don't keep them waiting — I should hurry to welcome them with open arms."

I hear Kurt mutter something under his breath, but it's too low and I'm too far away to catch it.

Chapter 19

"Wow, is this all for us?" Ace asks, eyeing the spread of food I've laid out.

"Since you two were helping yourselves to my popcorn last night, I figured I'd better lay out extra snacks for tonight," I say with a smile.

"I hope there's no pie," Foxy mutters, peering over our shoulders. He drops his laptop case and bag, gives me a quick hug, and flops onto one end of the sofa.

"There's more in the kitchen, so don't be shy," I tell them.

"I'm never shy," Ace murmurs, planting a peck on my cheek before grabbing a handful of chips and settling on the other end of the couch.

"Can I get you both drinks?" I ask sweetly, slipping into full hostess mode.

"When you are all quite ready!" Kurt exclaims, loud and sharp.

He's standing by the whiteboard, arms crossed, foot tapping impatiently. He looks like a headmaster trying to quiet a room full of unruly children—one whose patience is dangling by a thread.

I'm not the only one who notices.

"Perhaps after the meeting," Ace says in a low voice with a wink. "Looks like someone's getting their panties in a twist."

I giggle and wedge myself between the two men, who shuffle to make room.

"Who wants to start?" Kurt says, his tone clipped.

I begin to raise my hand, but Ace catches it midway and gently lowers it. "I think Tina has something to say, boss."

Kurt sighs. "Go ahead."

I clear my throat, glance at the snacks, and say, "Well, first off—there's definitely pie. Key lime. It's in the kitchen, so you'd all better behave yourselves. Secondly, I thought I'd go first since I haven't got much to add—and this will probably be my final contribution."

"Why? You going somewhere, or did the boss roast you?" Ace smirks, and I catch Foxy smiling on the other side of me. I give him a pointed look—just enough confirmation that it was, indeed, the latter.

"Anyway, Steven left the office at one. He's leaving early again tomorrow. He said I can work from home both afternoons, which doesn't make much sense. Apart from a few generic emails I can respond to, everything I need is back at the office. Feels like he's either setting me up for a future favour or wants me out of the way. Maybe he's wiped the hard drive he took and wants me gone so he can return it. I don't know. But I do know that when he left today, he picked up Cassandra Monroe from an unknown location and took her to the Obsidian."

I mime zipping my mouth shut and tossing away the key.

"I thought you were the one tailing Monroe, boss?" Ace says playfully to Kurt.

Kurt exhales sharply through his nose, eyes narrowing. "And I thought you liked this job," he counters.

Ace grins. "Nah, I'm just here to see who's getting the pie tonight. How did you get on?"

"Fine. In and out like we planned. The place was clean," Kurt replies, making me frown.

"In and out of where?" I ask.

Kurt looks at me like he's weighing how much to say. After an extended pause, I quirk an irritated eyebrow at him. He sighs. "Prentice's place."

"His place as in his home?" I bluster.

"Bet I know who's getting pied tonight," Ace whispers to Foxy behind my back making him chuckle.

"What if he'd had an alarm?" I cry.

"He did. I disabled it," Foxy answers calmly on Kurt's behalf.

"CCTV?" I flap my arms at Kurt in exasperation.

"Yep. That too," Foxy replies.

"What if his wife was home?" I yell at Kurt. "You could've been caught. She could've called the police and had you arrested!"

"She wasn't," Ace says.

"How do you know?" I shout at him.

"She was having coffee with me."

I don't have an answer. I just sit there, stunned, as Kurt picks up the conversation like he hadn't just witnessed my mini meltdown.

"Anyhow, like I said, the place was clean. The drive wasn't there—I'm betting Bear still has it. There was nothing to indicate where he's hiding either. And for someone claiming to work from home, the place was suspiciously devoid of paperwork. His office was unlocked and looked barely used. I booted up his system, uploaded the software Foxy gave me, and left.

I spent a couple of hours checking out the usual type of haunts Bear's known to frequent, trying to get a handle on his whereabouts, but came up dry. Then I headed over to Monroe's at one-thirty. Watched her place until Prentice picked her up in a taxi at quarter to two. They went straight to the Obsidian and holed up in room 128.

I've paid one of the receptionists 250 bucks to keep an eye out—to contact me either when they leave or if anyone visits their room. I told him I'd give another 250 for any credible information. So far, no word—but I know he's not the most reliable source.

Still, we know where Prentice will be tomorrow morning, and Monroe's address is no longer a mystery. So I'm not too worried."

"He?" I growl, realising Kurt played me so I'd get jealous and propose.

Kurt rolls his lips, trying not to laugh. "Ace, what have you got?"

"Edna Margolyes. Eighty years old, sharp as a tack. Makes a mean brew. Said I reminded her of her son—he should call more often," Ace begins.

"Anything useful?" Kurt cuts him off with a sigh.

Actually, yeah. She was the one who reported the electrical fault. Said the lights in her flat flickered every evening, and the washing machine kept tripping the fuse. The technician—Malcolm Swift from BrightSparks, a subsidiary owned by Urban Future—came during the day. He told her she was imagining the issue with the lights and blamed a faulty machine for the fuse trips. He replaced the fuses, did little else, and signed the work off as complete.

When the problem wasn't resolved, she hired an independent contractor. He found multiple issues with the wiring. She paid him to fix it and sent a handwritten letter of complaint to Urban Future Initiatives with the original work order and receipt enclosed. They reimbursed her without question—and sent her a luxury hamper as compensation."

Kurt raises an eyebrow. "Please tell me she kept a copy of the paperwork."

Ace grins. "And the card off the hamper—signed by Knox himself."

Kurt exhales, satisfied.

"Foxy?" Ace prompts him to jump in.

"I've started a dossier," Foxy says, flipping open his laptop. "A copy of both the work order and receipt's in there. Since Edna sent the original to Urban Future, I figured it was long gone. But I managed to get hold of the contractor's accounts —including his electronic sales log for that day. It shows the date, time, and sequential issue number of the paperwork he issued. So if anyone tries to erase the evidence later, we've got proof it existed."

I lean forward, squinting. "How'd you get that?"

Foxy smiles innocently. "I must've hit the wrong key and got misdirected to his files."

Ace snorts. "You mean you hacked it."

Foxy shrugs. "Semantics."

Kurt nods, then gestures for Ace to continue.

"I also managed to touch base with Ramirez's brother. Bit of a hothead—he just was mouthing off, no hard evidence, just grief. He wanted someone to blame for his sister and nephew's death, Knox was the obvious target.

The whole thing probably would've fizzled out if Doyle hadn't seen him on the news and recognised him. Turns out they went to school together. Doyle always had a soft spot for Camila. When he realised what he'd been part of, the guilt got to him.

He went for a few drinks at a bar round the corner from where he lives, confided in a mate about what he'd done—and that he planned to come forward. The very next day, the trail started getting scrubbed. My guess, someone in Knox's pocket knew Doyle was getting twitchy and was tasked to follow him, or maybe he just got unlucky —someone overheard his plans and took the info straight to Knox hoping for a quick payday.

Fortunately, he'd already penned the email to the prosecution and sent it—without realising they'd need the full chain. Of course, when they asked for it, it had been erased. They forwarded the new evidence to Robert Taylor. The last call Foxy traced from him was to their office. He didn't show up for work the next day.

"And Steven was drafted in," I finish for him, dread pooling in the pit of my stomach. "You don't think something's happened to him, do you? No," I answer myself quickly. "I think he took off. If he found out he was defending a guilty man, it wouldn't have sat well with him. I bet he went to Carter and asked to be removed from the case. And if Carter could only see dollar signs he must have tried to talk him out of it, I bet Robert walked—distanced himself so someone with more questionable ethics would take over. He's probably sunning himself somewhere, waiting to come back when this is all over. Right?"

When Ace and Foxy stay silent while looking to Kurt for an answer, I know it's not going to be good.

"You're probably right," Kurt tells me softly. I ignore the look in his eyes that tells me I'm wrong.

Kurt clears his throat. "Foxy?"

"I'm still following the financial trail on the building supplies. Knox has been good at covering his tracks—on the surface, everything looks legit. But the volumes are off. I think they've been cross firing between the businesses. I just have to prove it.

I believe Knox has been ordering high-end materials for the Urban Future building projects, then transferring the stock to the Knox

Development builds. He replaces what he takes with substandard products, probably bought with cash from the cheapest supplier he can find to keep costs down.

A cursory glance at Knox's finances suggests he's not nearly as wealthy as he pretends to be. As soon as one of his luxury pads is completed, he's forced to sell it fast — injecting capital back into the business just to keep it afloat. He expanded too quickly, without a proper financial cushion. His outgoings are astronomical, and the kind of clientele he caters to won't part with their cash until every detail is exactly to spec.

His latest offering, Sapphire Heights, is causing major problems. It's triggered a serious cash flow crisis he's been desperately trying to keep a lid on. Knox poured nearly all his liquid capital into the project, supplementing it with funds from some pretty hardcore investors.

Built on prime real estate along the banks of the Hudson, Sapphire Heights boasts a rooftop terrace with a bar, pool, and helipad—exclusive to residents—and offers unprecedented views of the river and the Manhattan skyline. Seven storeys high, it includes a secure underground parking facility, a full ground-floor reception with on-site concierge, several compact staff apartments, and five sprawling private residences above. The top level houses a maintenance zone and the crowning feature: the rooftop terrace.

Each floor has been custom-designed for its resident, offering the kind of privacy only the ultra-elite can afford when in such close proximity. Glass elevators ascend through the heart of a colossal, world-record-breaking aquarium that spans the full height and width of the building. Each resident has their own designated lift, programmed to access only their floor, the roof, reception, and garage. Every apartment also includes a private fire escape, allowing owners to evacuate discreetly if needed.

The aquarium itself is a living sculpture — home to some of the rarest marine life on Earth, including the elusive blacktip tiger shark. Residents experience a cinematic journey through the shimmering blue depths every time they rise. From bioluminescent jellyfish to endangered reef species, every creature has been hand-selected by Knox for its rarity and visual impact.

All five apartments were sold off-plan, and the revenue from those sales should have more than covered the outlay — delivering a generous payday for everyone involved. But Knox was arrested before the deals could close. One buyer pulled out, and the others are stalling. He's now haemorrhaging money he doesn't have, just to maintain the aquarium alone.

The cash bonus Doyle claims he received didn't go through his bank account, but I can prove his student debts—$4,895.88—were settled shortly after the job on Ramirez's place was completed. I'm working on tracing the origin of those funds.

If I can prove the building inspector was on the take, we've got him as well as put another nail in Knox's coffin. I've found several deposits into his account, all consistent with what you'd expect to see. But his outgoings suggest several sudden lifestyle changes, including a new vehicle recently. I ran a check with the DMV—he's upgraded from a second-hand Ford to a Porsche Cayenne. There's no bill of sale in his name that I can find. I'm checking to see if Knox gifted it to avoid leaving a more incriminating financial footprint. I'll run the same checks on that Swift guy from BrightSparks see what that turns up."

Foxy leans forward. "One more thing—I'm positive Camila Ramirez never took out the building insurance that was presented. It was taken out after the fire and then backdated. Sloppy job. The database it's stored on has high-end encryption; it scrambles and updates regularly. Whoever arranged the policy clearly couldn't get back in a second time to cover their tracks. The timestamp metadata doesn't match the policy date, and the access logs show a single entry—no follow-up edits, no cleanup."

Kurt's jaw tightens. "So they forged the policy and then hoped no one would dig deep enough to notice."

"Exactly," Foxy nods. "Now we've got a digital footprint they can't erase. The next step is figuring out who actually did it. The company has CCTV —I'm working on getting that footage to see if it caught the perp. If it did, I can start digging into their financials… or someone can pay them a visit, see what they've got to say for themselves."

"If it's so tough to hack, how did you get in?" I ask.

Foxy smirks. "I won't dignify that question with an answer." He shifts in his seat. "Not much happened with Prentice in the office. Every time someone knocked, he acted busy—really, he was just killing time until he could leave to meet Monroe. He spent most of it checking the feed from the cameras he installed, making sure no one had been in his office without his knowledge. Two outbound calls: one to his wife, saying he'd be working late and not to wait up. The other to book the hotel room. One text, which we know was to set up the meet with Monroe."

Foxy turns to me. "The only thing that was odd was the way he looked at that piece of paper you handed him before you left for lunch. He was definitely rattled. What was on it?"

"Nothing really. Just lines of numbers. I found it stuck in my drawer. I was going to bin it —I couldn't correlate it with anything I'd been working on—but I thought I'd better check with him first. It was ripped, so I retyped it the other night before showing it to him."

"Do you have a copy?"

"I can't remember if I saved it. I'll grab my laptop and check."

I head to the bedroom, log on, and find the document still sitting in my files. I print it off and hand it to Foxy.

"Thanks," he says with a grin. "You never know—this might just save the day."

"AWD," Kurt calls.

I look over, flummoxed. "Don't you mean AOB—any other business?"

"Too formal," Kurt grins. "We prefer 'Are we done.'"

I chuckle, but Foxy's tone sobers the room again.

"I'm confident that once I reach the end of the financial trail, we'll have enough to put Knox away for a long time. His arrogance — believing he's untouchable — has led to mistakes. He tried to cover his tracks, but not well enough for me to miss them.

I've already uncovered an offshore account he thought was invisible. It's registered under a shell company, with his wife listed as the beneficial owner. She's authorized him as a signatory, giving him full control of the funds. The account was opened in her maiden name — a detail easy to overlook unless you're actively searching for it.

I've seen a copy of the account opening documents, and I'm fairly certain her signature was forged. Honestly, I'd be surprised if she even knows the account exists.

There are transfers linked to that account that tie Knox to multiple deals he's flat-out denied knowing anything about on the stand. I just haven't found anything linking him directly to the Ramirez case yet.

I will, but time's against us. I'm aiming to have everything neatly wrapped and handed to the prosecution before court reconvenes on Friday. They're struggling and Knox will walk if we don't give them something. Once things start to unravel for Knox, people will either be out for blood or scrambling to cover their tracks. Prentice included.

We need to find the hard drive Prentice pulled from his office. Whatever's on it ties him in—I'm sure of it. And I bet it implicates Knox even further. He never gets his hands dirty; he pays others to do that for him. Who knows what records he passed along while trying to get Steven to clear him. We have to get to it before it's wiped and I lose any chance of recovering the data. Which means we need to find Bear."

"What makes you so sure Prentice is involved?"

I ask. "I mean, I know the man's reprehensible, but that doesn't mean he operates outside the law."

Foxy and Ace both look to Kurt again, and I swallow hard as I wait for him to answer.

"Let's just say, if his history is anything to go by, there's not much he won't do to advance his career. And leave it at that for now, shall we?"

"Sure," I say quietly. Some questions are best left unanswered.

Kurt smiles at me softly before snapping out of it and addressing the room, "Foxy, you just worry about getting the information the prosecution needs to bury Knox. Camila Ramirez and her son deserve justice. We…" he signals between himself and Ace to ensure everyone is aware I'm not included, "will concentrate on finding Bear and the missing hard drive."

A knock at the apartment door snaps every head toward the sound.

"Expecting company?" Ace asks.

Kurt and I both shake our heads. Kurt starts toward the door, but Ace, being closer, intercepts him. "I got it," he mutters, hauling himself up and wandering off.

We listen as Ace opens the door and exchanges greetings. Moments later, he returns, grinning like a cat with feathers in its teeth—Blake trails behind him, along with a guy I don't recognize. The newcomer is tall, fit, and olive-skinned, the kind of complexion that whispers Mediterranean ancestry and good lighting.

"Blake!" I squeal, launching myself at him. He's too tall for a kiss, so I jump—and to my surprise, he catches me. I grin as I wrap my legs around his waist, then cling to him like a koala while I plant a smacker on his cheek.

"Beh, ciao bellissima," the stranger purrs. With Blake still holding me, he takes my hand, bows slightly, and kisses my knuckles. His voice is velvet-wrapped in a thick Italian accent. It's the kind of sexy that can make your panties drop without you even realising. "If I'd known such a welcome awaited, I would've made sure to be the first through the door," he drawls, tossing me a wink. "Sono Nico, al tuo servizio."

My face heats up just as Kurt barks from across the room, sharp and loud. "Cut the crap, Nic. You're from New Jersey. Blake, if her feet aren't on the floor in ten seconds, you're fired."

I roll my eyes at Blake, who chuckles and sets me down gently.

"When did you get back? How's Emily? Is she okay? Where is she? You didn't leave her alone, did you?" I fire off questions like an overcaffeinated interrogator.

"Just now. She's adapting. She's fine. She's at my place in L.A. And what was the last one?"

He pauses, thinking. "Ah—right. I've got someone watching over her."

"She's at your place?" Kurt asks, suspicion dripping from every syllable.

"She couldn't decide where she wanted to be, so I told her she could house-sit until I got back. Then we'll figure out something more permanent. I wanted to be here for..." He glances at me, voice trailing off. "You know, the reunion."

"Nic was at a loose end," Blake continues, "so he asked to tag along. I figured, why not? Get the whole Maine crew back together. We cleared it with Axel—he wanted in too, but..."

"Someone had to stay at base," Kurt finishes. "Good to see you, Nic."

Nico smiles and nods. "Boss." His accent vanishes like smoke—pure Jersey now.

"So, who's going to catch us up then?" Blake scans the room. "Oooh, snacks. I'm starving."

"I'm pretty hungry myself," I say, met with a chorus of murmured agreement. I stroll to the front of the room and stand beside Kurt, motioning for Blake and Nico to grab whatever seats they can find. Kurt's hand lands gently on the small of my back, tracing soothing circles as I start barking out orders.

"Right. Here's how this is going to go. I suggest we order in." I announce this with full authority, ignoring the amused glances being exchanged around the room. "Chinese food okay with everyone?"

Silence. Everyone stares at me, then at Kurt, then back at me again.

"Erm... hellooo?" I say, dripping with sarcasm. "Cat got your tongues?"

Finally, I get a "Fine by me," a "Hell yeah!" laced with chuckles, and two nods from Ace and Foxy, who are clearly trying not to burst out laughing. I glance at Kurt, who's staring at me like he can't quite believe I've just hijacked his entire meeting. Since I already know he likes Chinese cuisine, I carry on regardless.

"Kurt, you take down what everyone wants."

"No." He barks incredulously. "I'm not a fucking waiter."

I give him the stink eye and murmur, "What happens if we don't know what people want?"

"*People* go hungry or *people* order in them-damn-selves." He murmurs back pointedly, loud enough for everyone to hear.

"Foxy." I sigh, changing focus.

"Yes ma'am!" He sits bolt upright giving me his undivided attention, clearly trying to be funny. I ignore him and the sniggers which surround us.

"I'll get you a menu and you can type up a list of

what everyone wants so it's easy for me to read out down the phone."

Foxy raises his hand. I roll my eyes and shoot Ace a warning look—apparently, that simple gesture has him on the verge of losing it.

"Yes?" I ask sternly.

"Why don't I just pull up the menu on my laptop and order online? That way I can bump us up the wait list."

"Oh… yeah… right. You do that," I say, annoyed I didn't think of it first. "Although don't push us forward in the queue—we wait our turn like everyone else."

Someone snorts.

"I mean it." I growl menacingly. Foxy nods dejectedly and I feel it's safe to continue, "Okay, order a sharing starter for Kurt and me. I'll have the sweet and sour chicken; he'll take the chicken chop suey. Two egg fried rice. And we'd better throw in a side of stir-fried vegetables—gotta keep him happy I'm getting my greens…"

"Got it," Foxy calls, cutting into my flow while glancing at Kurt, clearly thrown that he let me order for him.

"Wait, I'm not done yet. Nugget…"

"Who's Nugget?" Nico interrupts, brows raised.

I pat my belly. "She'll have a side of chow mein,

crispy shredded beef, barbecue ribs, better throw in a few wontons—and make sure they don't forget the fortune cookies. Got that? Oh, and maybe some extra spring rolls."

Foxy's fingers fly across the keyboard as he tries to keep up. When he finally stops, he flashes me a thumbs up.

"You sure you've ordered enough?" Blake chuckles.

I pause, genuinely considering it. "I think so. I'll grab my card you can put the whole order on there." But before I can move, Kurt tosses his over my shoulder. Foxy snatches it mid-air with a smirk.

"Ace." I call.

"Present," he replies, like a kid answering roll call. *Wiseass.*

You fill Blake and Nico in on what's been happening. Kurt." I shoot him a pointed glare. "You and I are going to have a little chat about your manners—while you help me make drinks in the kitchen."

Before he can protest, I grab his arm and march him toward the door. He follows, dragging his feet like a sulky teenager knowing he is about to be sent to detention.

"Damn she's hot when she's feisty," someone murmurs as we walk away. "I think I just got hard."

A chorus of unrestrained laughter fills the air. Furious, Kurt spins around to go back, his jaw clenched, hands balling into fists at his sides. I block his path and silently usher him into the kitchen. There's going to be no blood spilled in this apartment tonight. Not on my watch!

Chapter 20

I eat so much I have to have a lie down straight after dinner. So, after telling all the men to play nicely, I leave them all to it. Kurt comes to check on me just as I'm dozing off. I feel him brush a loose strand of hair away from my face before pulling the covers up and over my shoulders. I thought he left until a few minutes later he rests his hand gently over my tummy as he kisses my temple.

I wake in the early hours of the morning missing the warmth of his body wrapped round mine. I can't hear the distant rumble of chatter I fell asleep to so I get up and go in search of him.

As I walk past the living room, I see the profile of a man hunched over a laptop. He looks up when he hears me and his face is clearly illuminated from the light of his screen.

"Foxy? Not that I mind, but what are you still doing here?"

"I'm still collating info on Knox."

"Where's Kurt?" I ask, looking around as if he

is about to spring up from behind the couch or similar."

"He and Ace have gone out looking for Bear."

"Now?" I say surprised.

"The sort of people they need to speak to only usually come out at night." Foxy sees my face fall and rushes to reassure me. "Don't worry. Ace will make sure he comes back in one piece. He is too afraid of being pied if he doesn't."

I smile apologetically, "I'm sorry, since I've been pregnant, I feel like I get taken over by an ogre at times."

"That's the boss's genes," Foxy jokes. "I won't hold it against you."

"Speaking of, he told you to stay here and keep an eye on me, didn't he?"

Foxy smirks. "He did suggest I might be more comfortable working here than back at my hotel. Blake and Nic are still here as well."

"You need that much back up?" I laugh. "Where are they?"

"Boss told them to get a few hours shut eye so they could take over from him and Ace at seven if they're unsuccessful in locating Bear. Kurt wants to be back in time to take you to work. He said they could crash in the spare room. Last I heard they were fighting over who got the bed and who got the floor."

"Who do you think won?"

"Well, it's a close call, but my moneys on Blake." Foxy admits with a smile.

"Shall we check?"

"Foxy and I creep down the hall to the spare room and gently push the door open enough for us to peek inside. Both Blake and Nico are asleep on Izzy's bed a wall of pillows between them. Blake has the covers over him on his side, while poor Nico is in his boxers, the pile of bedding pooled on the floor beside him suggests he started out on the floor and crept onto the bed when Blake fell asleep. If he took a blanket with him, it has subsequently slid off him and back to the ground.

"You were right," I tell Foxy. "Looks like Nic got the short straw."

He huffs out a laugh. "Don't they look peaceful?"

I chuckle mischievously, "Wait there."

Foxy watches me bemused as I dash off to grab my mobile. When I return I hand it to him before pressing a finger to my lips signalling him to be quiet as I creep past him and into the room.

Blake and Nico are both lying on their sides and facing each other. I carefully remove the pillow buffer before pushing back the sheet covering Blake's legs. I carefully lift his shin hooking it over Nico's. Then I take Nico's arm and gently drape it over Blakes waist. I hear Foxy sniggering and shoot him a warning look as Nico stirs. We watch as he shuffles to get comfortable, inching closer to Blake in his sleep, it's more than I was hoping for.

I grab my phone off Foxy and take a few shots before sneaking back and wrapping both men back up under the same blanket. Foxy holds his hands up backing away while sending me the clear vibes of *I'm not taking the blame for this*.

We go back to the living room and review the pictures. We are both laughing so hard we are bent double.

"You've got some balls, I'll give you that," Foxy wheezes.

We stare at each other before the irony of the statement sets us both off again. Suddenly we hear "WHAT THE EVERLASTING FUCK?" bellowed from the adjoining room followed by a thud then some kind of skirmish punctuated with expletives.

I squeal and rush back to bed leaving Foxy literally pinching the tears from his eyes on the sofa. Once I'm back in bed, I take a picture of the empty spot beside me sending it to Kurt with the message:

I miss you.

I'm reassured when he texts me back immediately:

Go back to sleep baby, I'll be home soon.

I smile and put my phone on the bedside table before snatching it back up:

Be safe, stay out of trouble.

I follow it up with a heart emoji.

You to.

Kurt isn't one for adding unnecessary decoration to his messages, so I'm shocked to see the little round face blowing me a kiss at the end of his words. My heart floods with warmth as I clutch the phone to my chest. After minimal consideration I send one final text back attached to one of the pictures I just took of the men next door in bed and cuddling.

I'll try x

I thought he'd find it funny. But seconds later, my phone rings.

I answer it, still laughing—only to be met with a loud crash and a terse, "What the hell were you doing in there while they had no clothes on?"

"Um... they were in their underwear?"

"Were you?" Kurt snaps. "I don't want them looking at you like that."

Another crash followed by the sound of glass shattering. Metal rattles. A faint "oof!" echoes in the background.

"Relax," I sigh. "I'm hardly every guy's dream right now, am I? I swear, every morning Nugget pushes my belly out another inch. Pretty soon I won't be able to walk—you'll just be rolling me everywhere."

"You're being ridiculous," Kurt barks. "You're my dream girl. And you're beautiful. Even more so because you're carrying my baby."

There's a definite tussle going on behind him. I hear Ace shout, "A little help here!"—followed by a sound that could only be a body slamming into a wall.

"Really?" I coo, smiling—until Ace's voice cuts through again, louder and angrier.

"You Motherfu—!"

"Kurt! What's going on?" I ask, panicked.

"Ace is playing with some new friends," Kurt chuckles. Then, "One sec." A loud crack. Knuckles hitting bone. A groan followed by the sound of a body slumping to the ground. Then Kurt bellows, "I'm on the phone, moron!"

"How many are there?" I cry.

"Not many."

"How many?" I yell.

"Only six. Ace isn't as young as he used to be and he's obviously out of shape—he's making a bit of a meal of things, if I'm honest."

"Six?!" I scream.

Ace sounds like he is being strangled as he

grits out, "Fuck you!"—right as another barrage of angry shouts and crashes erupt.

"Make that five." Kurt says nonchalantly before shouting, "Language," presumably back at Ace. He drops his voice to a whisper, "I'd better go help him before he throws a hip out. Be home soon baby. Love you."

The call disconnects.

I whisper a stunned, "Be safe," to no one, the words catching in my throat. Did he really say that? I know he did—I heard it, clear as day—but it feels unreal. Like I dreamed it. Like it's too much to believe.

'Love you.' Two words I've silently longed for, feared even, and now they're here—quiet, powerful, and impossible to ignore. Unless... unless he wasn't even aware they slipped out. He was under attack, not thinking clearly.

The words loop endlessly in my mind, making sleep impossible. And when I finally do succumb, it feels like the alarm goes off only minutes later.

The only thing that gets me out of bed is the thought of having a half day. Still half asleep, I saunter into the kitchen and snap on the kettle for my morning brew. While it boils, I drift into the living room.

Foxy is hunched over his laptop again, this time on the floor his back resting against the sofa, while Nico stretches out on the couch above him, snoring lightly. I giggle, imagining Blake banishing him from the bedroom.

"I'm making coffee. Do you want one?" I whisper to Foxy.

When I get no answer, I step closer and realize he's asleep too—clearly having drifted off mid-task. Smiling to myself, I fetch a couple of extra blankets. After gently lifting Foxy's laptop and placing it on the coffee table, I cover both men and tiptoe back into the kitchen.

I'm just making some toast when the front door opens and a bickering Kurt and Ace tumble in.

"I'm just saying, they weren't even that big, and there weren't that many of them. You're losing your touch. Maybe it's time to retire?" Kurt teases.

"Says the guy who got floored by a pie," Ace volleys back. "Chocolate cream, wasn't it?"

"It was," I answer for him as Kurt strides over, giving me a hug and a kiss on the crown of my head. He doesn't have a mark on him other than the knuckles on his right hand which look slightly pinker than they should. Ace, however, wasn't so lucky—there's a cut just above his eye, which is red and swollen, a welt across his neck, and a split lip. Altogether, he looks a bit of a mess.

"Sweet Jesus," I exclaim, rushing to wet a cloth and fuss over him. "What happened to you?" I ask, examining his wounds.

Ace smirks at Kurt over my head, clearly pleased to be the centre of attention.

"Erm... babe?" Kurt calls, a hint of annoyance in his tone.

"Yeah?" I reply, not turning around. The next thing I know, the cloth I'm using is whipped out of my hand and tossed at Ace, who bursts out laughing.

"Get your own nurse," Kurt tells him, taking my now-free hand and gently pulling me along behind him.

"Where are we going?" I throw Ace an apologetic look as he watches us disappear.

Kurt leads me to the bedroom and closes the door behind us.

"What about my injuries?"

"You're jealous?" I snort, amused.

"No," Kurt answers petulantly. "I'm in pain and in urgent need of medical attention."

"Is that so?" I giggle, examining his face and arms—without finding a single scratch. "Where?"

In one smooth, fluid action Kurt drops everything he is wearing from the waist down before pointing to his twitching dick. "Here, I think if you kiss it better it would help."

I shake my head, trying not to laugh. "Seriously?

We have company."

"I did tell you I loved you," Kurt murmurs, sulky and soft.

The air thickens as I stare at him. His pupils are dilated, and sincerity seems to ooze from every pore.

"You remembered?" I whisper, wide-eyed, warmth flooding my chest.

"Of course I remembered," he snaps playfully. "Other than my mother, you're the only woman I've ever said those words to."

Unable to speak, I maintain eye contact as I slowly drop to my knees to show him just how much I love him back.

Of course, that makes me late for work — again.

Steven's office door is closed as I guiltily slide into my chair, fifteen minutes behind schedule, hoping he'll assume I've been here all along. When he emerges at ten with some documents he needs copied, I'm relieved he doesn't mention my tardiness. I presume it's gone unnoticed.

He is leaning over my desk, explaining what he needs me to do, when his mobile buzzes. He straightens, pulls it from his pocket, and frowns at the screen before answering with a curt, "Tell me it's ready."

He clearly doesn't get the answer he's hoping for. Dragging a hand through his hair in frustration, he half-yells, "That's not good enough."

He notices me watching and steps away from my desk. Instead of retreating to his office — where I know Foxy will hear his conversation — he strides off toward the restroom. I follow discreetly, just in time to see him veer away from the toilets and head for the lift, barking, "Hang on."

The elevator opens, but when it's not empty and no one steps out, he swerves into the stairwell of the fire escape. I catch a glimpse of him pacing behind the frosted glass pane, though I can't hear a word.

Without thinking, I dive into the lift before it closes, ride it up one floor, and slip into the fire escape from there. I'm now directly above Steven — and this time, I can hear everything. Not that what he's saying makes much sense. I've clearly missed the start of the conversation and can only hear his side.

"No, you idiot. It's got sensitive information on it I need. That's why it has to be copied before it's wiped."

A pause. Then a frustrated growl.

"That wasn't the plan, you son of a bitch. I didn't get where I am now just to let you start calling the shots. I've come too far to turn back. I may have eradicated a certain obstacle at the beginning, but you still helped dispose of the evidence. That makes you an accessory after the fact."

A pause. Whoever's on the other end is speaking.

"Don't you dare threaten me. I've got enough pull to bury any charges before they stick— especially if I offer up someone else in my place."

Another pause. Then my blood runs cold.

"Is that why you won't tell me where you hid the body? All that crap about plausible deniability — really, you were just covering your own ass. If I go down, you can be sure I'll be taking you with me."

I'm holding my breath so long I feel myself starting to turn blue.

"I want that drive, Bear. I need to get it put back before anyone realises it was missing."

Silence.

"None of your damn business."

Another pause.

"Look. If the prosecution finds anything off with Ramirez's insurance documents, Knox might not be out as fast as we planned. I've got almost everything I own tied up in the Sapphire deal — and unless he's acquitted of all charges, that deal's going south.

That's why you're here. We hoped it wouldn't come to this, but it has. If things don't go as planned tomorrow, we implement Plan B over the weekend. Monroe thinks she has Simmons whipped. But, if he refuses to play ball, she's got photos she can use to persuade him.

You just need to keep your mouth shut, do the job you've been paid to do — and leave. BUT NOT BEFORE I'VE GOT THAT DRIVE BACK."

One more pause, then: "You'll get the other half when the job's done like we agreed. Fine. I'm leaving here at three. I'll come straight over and we can discuss it then."

Steven hangs up, curses under his breath, and strides back into the office. I finally release the breath I'd been holding, dash back the way I came, and reappear at my desk with two coffees — handing one to Steven, who's clearly wondering where I've been.

"Sorry, you were gone a while so I made us both a drink," I say smoothly, offering a smile. "Don't worry — I remembered not to add salt this time."

Steven takes it gratefully. "Got anything stronger?"

"Problem?" I ask, feigning concern.

"No... no." He waves the question away, and I maintain cover by returning to the paperwork we were discussing before his abrupt departure.

I point at the documents on my desk, but Steven isn't listening. He's distracted, staring off into space.

"Steven?" I nudge him.

"Yes... what?" He blinks, then scoops up the papers he'd left earlier. "Something's come up. This can wait. I need to make a few calls. No need for you to hang around — you were leaving early today anyway."

"You want me to go now?" I ask surprised.

He's lost in thought again.

"Steven!" I raise my voice just enough to snap him out of it.

"Yes... yes, you can go," he replies distractedly, retreating into his office and closing the door.

I plonk myself back at my desk, snatch up my phone, and head straight to the restroom. Locking myself in a cubicle, I call Kurt. He answers on the first ring.

"Babe?"

"Can you come and get me?" I whisper.

"Now? What's wrong? Are you alright?"

"I'm fine. But something happened. And before you say anything — I didn't go looking for trouble. It just kind of... unfurled in front of me. I don't want to talk about it here. Someone might overhear."

His response is instant — no questions, no hesitation. "One of us will be there in ten. Wait downstairs in the foyer until we get you."

It's a clear instruction, and Kurt doesn't wait for

a reply before hanging up.

I power down my computer and begin packing up my desk. As I shove some papers into a drawer, I spot the rubbish I removed from Steven's room — I'd forgotten to get rid of it. Something compels me to snatch it up and shove it into my bag before leaving.

By the time I reach the foyer, Kurt is already there. I rush over, and he takes my hand, leading me outside to a black SUV. Ace is waiting at the wheel. We climb in without a word and head home.

Foxy is waiting when we arrive.

"What happened?" Kurt asks once we're inside and I'm settled comfortably on the sofa.

I recount everything — except the part about actively following Steven. I make it sound like my presence on the fire escape was nothing more than a fortunate coincidence. I'm not sure any of them buy that part, but they hang off my every word regardless.

"We need to get to that drive," Ace says decisively when I've finished.

Kurt tips his head in acknowledgment, but his mind is clearly elsewhere. He turns toward the whiteboard, eyes fixed on the row of judges' photos neatly aligned across the top. The room falls silent as we watch the gears turning behind his eyes, each of us trying to guess what he's seeing.

"Boss?" Foxy ventures.

Kurt doesn't respond right away. His voice is low when it finally comes.

"I think we've got a bigger problem than the missing hard drive."

He turns back to face us, slowly—his expression dark, ominous.

"Get Blake and Nico back here. Now."

Chapter 21

Kurt disappears into the bedroom to make a quick call to Axel back at base. Twenty minutes later, he returns. Blake and Nico have arrived, been briefed, and now we're all lounging around—chatting, sipping drinks, waiting.

When Kurt strides back in, the room falls silent. All eyes turn to him.

"What do all these people have in common?" he asks, pointing to the lineup of faces he'd been studying earlier.

I start to raise my right hand, but Ace grabs it and places it on his thigh, covering it with his own. I glance at him, surprised. He nods and winks, urging me to speak.

"They're all gamblers," I say, thinking of their regular poker games.

Kurt's eyes narrow. "Anything else?"

I try to lift my right hand again, but Ace holds it firm. I switch to my left—only for Foxy to mirror Ace's move, catching it before it's barely left my side.

"They're all judges," I say, stating the obvious.

"And this one," he says, tapping a picture on the board behind him, "is the Chief Judge. He oversees a lot of court functions, including administrative operations. He's the one responsible for deciding whether a replacement judge can be assigned to a trial already in motion—and who that replacement should be. If anything happens to him, he flicks another picture on the board this one takes over."

Kurt tips his head, as if that explains everything.

"Back in Coronado—where we underwent training," he adds for my benefit. "—Bear was top of the class in one particular discipline: long-distance firearms. That's why we took him to Maine when we did. He could stay hidden, eyes on the terrain, covering our backs from afar."

"Holy shit. Plan B," Foxy blurts, the first to catch on. He locks eyes with Kurt, and something passes between them—silent, but unmistakable. Kurt's expression confirms it: Foxy's right.

The rest of the team glances around, puzzled.

Kurt sighs. One by one, the realisation dawns across their faces.

Until I'm the only one still in the dark.

"Tell me," I nearly scream, frustration bubbling over.

No one answers. All eyes shift to Kurt, who's weighing the cost of letting me in.

"If we tell you," he says, arms crossed, voice like steel, "you have to quit your job. Effective immediately."

His stance makes it clear—this isn't up for debate.

"But I need your decision now. We have to move."

Everyone's watching me. I hesitate, torn until my curiosity wins out.

"Deal," I mutter, hoping I can talk him down later.

"I won't change my mind," he says flatly, reading me like a book.

"Fine," I sigh. "So I start maternity leave a couple of months early. What am I supposed to do with myself?"

"I'll buy you a jigsaw," Kurt deadpans.

"Tell me," I growl back.

"The Knox trial is already deep into proceedings —jury's seated, evidence presented, media circus in full swing. Once Foxy hands over the evidence he's collecting, Knox and Prentice will do whatever it takes to stop it from landing. Prentice could try to force a mistrial, but that's risky, expensive, and slow. He needs Knox out fast—so the Sapphire deal closes and everyone gets paid."

Kurt pauses, then adds, "Now imagine something happens to the presiding judge."

"Judge Fletcher?" I ask, frowning.

He nods. "What happens then?"

I think. "If the judge is incapacitated, the court can declare a mistrial. But under a certain rule—I don't remember which—if the judge can't proceed, a replacement can be assigned. Only if the new judge certifies they've reviewed the entire record and both parties' consent."

"Exactly. And what if that replacement's already been lined up?" Kurt leans in. "Say a young, persuasive woman's been whispering in his ear—during certain… extracurricular activities—nudging him to influence the court's internal politics in a social setting. Like a regular poker game." He pauses, letting it sink in. "So if Fletcher's removed, he could push for the trial to continue and get himself installed as the new judge without it being too obvious. Then the woman, for arguments sake we'll call her Cassandra Monroe, will be right there, through all the stress, using her charms to guide his rulings to get the outcome she wants."

I gasp trying not to swear. "Oh… cock-a-doodle-doo."

A few eyebrows rise at my odd declaration.

"You think Knox or Prentice has paid Bear to take out Judge Fletcher—so Simmons gets the bench, having already been compromised by Monroe, who's been playing him from the start?"

The words tumble out, breathless.

"Bingo." Kurt smiles, a flicker of pride in his eyes—pleased I connected the dots.

Ace and Foxy each give the hands they're still holding a quick squeeze—silent congratulations for impressing the boss.

Then Kurt snaps back into command mode.

"Foxy, is Prentice still at the office?"

Foxy checks the feed from his hidden camera and nods.

"Nic. Blake. I want you back there. We know he's scheduled to meet Bear at three, but we can't risk him leaving early and missing him. Tail him. I want eyes on Bear. The moment you spot him, I want to know. And don't forget—we still need to locate that missing drive."

"Boss." Both men peel out of the room and vanish.

Foxy's fingers start to work overtime across his keyboard.

"Ace, find Judge Fletcher. Watch him like a hawk. Don't raise alarms unless there's an imminent threat to life. Check in every hour. Stay sharp—Bear could be hiding in the shadows, some distance away. If his relationship with Prentice is breaking down like the conversation Tina overheard suggests, he might start working to his own agenda. If I don't hear from you, I'll assume you're down and come in all guns blazing."

"Gotcha."

"Here." Foxy hands Ace a slip of paper. "Fletcher's home address and the golf club he frequents."

"Thanks." Ace studies it. As he heads out, Kurt calls after him.

"As soon as Josh gets here, one of us will join you for backup."

Ace tips his head and disappears.

"Foxy, where are you at with Knox?"

"Close. Just tying up loose ends. I'll upload everything to a flash drive and hand-deliver it anonymously to the prosecution tonight—give them time to review before court tomorrow."

"Great. Once that's done, get some sleep. I want you in court tomorrow watching the chaos unfold."

Foxy grins, "I love this bit."

"Babe."

I jump, startled.

"As soon as Prentice leaves the office, I'm taking

you back to collect your things and hand in your resignation."

"But I have to give four weeks' notice. I can't just walk out." I whine. "And I'll lose my benefits."

"Walk or be carried. Your choice. I'll be with you to make sure anyone who objects understands it's in their best interest to let you go. I'll also take care of you financially so you don't lose out."

I roll my eyes dramatically.

Foxy catches it and smirks. "It's been a pleasure working with you. I'll ask Carter to write you a glowing letter of recommendation. You can leave your stapler on my desk."

I curl my lip at him, which only makes him chuckle.

"What's next?" I ask Kurt, who's standing there looking far too smug.

"I'm going to make you some lunch. Then we wait," he replies with a nonchalant shrug.

"Nothing too heavy," I say, rubbing my belly.

Both he and Foxy furrow their brows, concerned.

"What's wrong?" they ask in unison. Kurt casts Foxy a bewildered but grateful look for his concern, while Foxy drifts back to his laptop, continuing whatever it is he was doing.

I roll my eyes again. I really need to stop

doing that—I'm going to give myself a headache. "Nothing serious. I think I overdid it last night. Bit of indigestion."

"Indigestion usually hits your chest, not that low down," Foxy comments without looking up.

"We should get you to the hospital," Kurt says, reaching for my arm.

I shrug him off. "No. I'm fine."

"If you were fine, you wouldn't have mentioned it," Kurt insists, reaching again.

"I've got gas, alright!" I shout, shaking him off. "It's embarrassing, so I was trying not to draw attention to it."

Both Kurt and Foxy press their lips together, trying not to laugh. Kurt's phone rings, and he uses it as an excuse to escape before he bursts out laughing.

"It's nothing to be embarrassed about," Foxy says once Kurt's gone. "But are you sure that's all it is?"

I know he won't let it go unless I prove it. So, I raise myself slightly and let one rip. The relief is overwhelming after keeping it bottled up for so long.

Foxy's face is amused. I stare at him, mortified. "Pretty much, yeah," I mumble.

Between the uncontrollable rage that leads to

pieing unsuspecting men, the sudden bouts of nymphomania that strike without warning, the nausea that ambushes you at the worst possible moments, the complete strangers poking around in your business every five minutes to make sure the baby isn't about to fall out — and now, the gas — I've come to terms with one undeniable truth: My dignity is long gone.

Pregnancy is the worst.

"Josh isn't going to get here for another few hours," Kurt announces as he walks back into the room. "What's that smell?"

I shoot Foxy a death stare.

"Last night's Chinese I reckon," Foxy quips, clearly not picking up on my silent plea to ignore the question. "He's taking his time, what's the holdup?"

"His wife," Kurt deadpans.

I miss the sarcasm and immediately panic. "Maeve? What's wrong?"

"Nothing," Kurt says, with just enough sincerity to be believable. "Between her constant need to be fed, stop for the restroom, and jump his bones —combined with his driving like a ninety-year-old with cataracts—they're running behind. He still thinks they'll make it today, just later than planned."

He claps his hands together. "So, on that note,

will you two be alright waiting here if I go help the others?"

"Sure. I'm confident I can handle making a light lunch," Foxy says. "I can even take your girl back to clear out her desk and tender her resignation—save you the trip."

"What about Knox?" Kurt asks.

"It's in hand. I'll leave the programs running and collate the data when we're back if I have to. We won't be long. Besides, it makes more sense —Carter loves me. And I can be a little more diplomatic if he refuses to let her go."

Kurt gives Foxy a hard stare. Foxy nods in silent understanding. Whatever telepathic exchange just happened between them, I'm completely in the dark.

"Okay then," Kurt concedes, walking over and grabbing my hand. "A quick word."

He leads me into the kitchen. I follow like a lamb to the slaughter. Once inside, he closes the door and turns to face me. I brace for a lecture — but instead, he lifts me into his arms and kisses me with unrestrained desire. My body quakes, craving more within seconds. He knows exactly what I need, but pulls back with an apologetic look.

"Baby, I have to go." He says softly, dragging his thumb across my swollen bottom lip.

"What?" I pant and pout simultaneously — a

difficult combo, but proof I can multitask under pressure. "Why kiss me like that then?"

He shrugs. "I couldn't help myself."

"Good to know the mighty Kurt Callahan has a weakness," I tease.

He sets me down gently and smiles. "Be good for Foxy while I'm gone. Josh knows most of what's going on — when he gets here, fill in any gaps you can and have him call me."

"I will," I say, smiling back. "When will you be home?"

His gaze drifts. "Honestly, I can't say. We need to find Bear ASAP. He's shrewd and already on the run. It could have already reached him that Ace and I were out looking last night. If it has, he'll go even deeper underground."

He pauses, then continues, voice low and urgent. "From what you told us, it's safe to assume Bear hasn't received all the money he was promised. The question is — has he made enough to disappear now, or will he stick around to finish what he started? We've got one shot at picking him up if he meets Prentice as planned. If we miss it… who knows how long it'll be before we find him again." He hesitates. "Or who might pay the price."

The thought of Judge Fletcher meeting an untimely end casts a shadow over the room. I give Kurt a quick peck. "Go. I'll be here waiting when you get back."

"You'd better be," he says with a wink. "We've got unfinished business to take care of." He swats my ass playfully on his way past. "Later!" he calls to Foxy as he heads out. "You know what to do."

I end up making lunch for Foxy and me while he continues working. We've just finished eating when his laptop starts flashing and beeping like a Vegas fruit machine hitting the jackpot.

"Finally," Foxy exhales, plugging a flash drive into the side.

"What?" I ask, intrigued.

"All the proof we need—Knox is corrupt. Whoever he hired to cover his tracks was good, but not good enough. We've got irrefutable evidence he paid an insurance agent to falsify Ramirez's documents. There's also CCTV footage showing exactly who accessed the system at the precise date and time the policy was created. It won't be hard to track him down—then one of us can 'persuade' him to testify. And that's just the beginning."

He leans in, voice low and charged.

"There's more footage of Knox meeting with an unlicensed contractor, money changing hands. I've uncovered a set of undisclosed accounts linked to a ghost file. We've got proof that quality building supplies were swapped for inferior ones

—and not only did Knox know about it, he was instrumental in the transaction himself. We can prove his back is against the wall as far as his finances go, a solid motive for risking everything."

He clicks through a few files, then pulls up a grainy photo. "Then there's this, we've even got a picture of the woman who opened the offshore account in his wife's name. Look familiar?"

Even though the image is blurry and she's in disguise, I recognize her instantly. "Cassandra Monroe!"

"She'll be going down for fraud, if nothing else, when this is all over. We've also found a hidden log of 'gifts' bequeathed to various individuals — all coinciding with shady services rendered. Including the brand-new Porsche Cayenne the building inspector received."

He grins. "Best of all, you helped me start linking everything to Prentice."

"I did? How?"

"That paper you found lodged in your desk — the rows of numbers corresponded to a date followed by an amount. I can link almost every line to either a cash bribe or a material item Knox gave to someone to smooth the way or buy their silence. Look here." Foxy pulls up a copy of the paper I gave him, pointing to a line. "This amount — that's the cost of a brand-new Cayenne. Now, this is the date…" He moves his finger along the line, then flicks a couple of keys. "And here — same date, same amount, on a sales invoice for a car of the same make and model the building inspector now claims he owns. The purchase agreement bears Knox's signature, and the registration matches the vehicle the inspector has insured and is currently driving. If Knox tries to worm his way out of it, claiming the signature on the sales docket was forged, I'm sure I can dig up CCTV or phone records to prove it was him."

"I have questions."

"Shoot."

"You can't prove Prentice knew about the paper I found. Sure, he looked like he recognized it — but that alone isn't proof. He denied knowing what it was and it wasn't even found in his office."

"True," Foxy nods. "But it's a start. Once we get our hands on that hard drive, I'm confident this will show up—hopefully with a more detailed breakdown. And who knows what else might tie him to Knox... connections that stretch far beyond any proper attorney-client relationship I'll bet.

Ever since you overheard him mention he was in on the Sapphire deal, I've been digging into his financials to see what turns up. Every visit he makes to the Obsidian gets billed straight to Knox's account there—no questions asked, no deductions on any his invoices for any of the stays before submission. And the charges he racks up are outrageous. He's bleeding money on room service, always ordering the most expensive food and drinks on the menu. That reeks of either a bribe or payment for services well outside the usual scope."

"That's if the drive hasn't already been wiped by the time we find it," I remind him.

We fall silent for a few seconds. Then Foxy asks, "You said questions — what else is on your mind?"

"Why does Kurt want you observing in court tomorrow? In case the prosecution isn't that great and needs you to dig up more to back their case?"

Foxy smiles. "Yeah, that — and he knows I like watching the takedown. Makes what I do feel even more worthwhile. The boss knows it doesn't always sit well with me, fracturing the occasional law to get what we need. He wants me to see that the risk is far outweighed by the gain. It gives me peace — knowing that even if I bent the rules, I did it for the right reasons. You know what I mean?"

I nod. "Although I'm not sure getting my whole building evacuated just so Kurt could stop me from taking a bath really qualifies on that score."

Foxy bursts out laughing. "He threatened to drown my laptop if I didn't help him, possibly while I was still holding the damn thing."

"Oh, did he now?" I say with a forgiving smile. "I'm curious, why do you call him 'boss'? It's Josh's business. I know he offered Kurt a partnership, but he turned it down. Doesn't that mean you're all on the same level?"

Foxy shrugs. "Josh is still hoping he'll change his mind. Slow down a bit—especially now, with a baby on the way…" He trails off, then continues more quietly. "Kurt's always been Josh's right-hand man. But more than that—everyone looks up to him. Fears him a little. And he's proven, more than once, that if he's got your back on a job, you're making it home that day." He pauses, voice steady. "He wasn't given the title. He earned it."

A moment of silence settles between us before Foxy speaks again, voice low and cautious. "You could do a lot worse."

"Sorry?" I blink, not quite following.

"Marrying the boss. He's crazy about you. None of us have ever seen him this gaga over a woman—ever."

"Because I'm carrying his baby."

"No. Because he's in love with you. And I think he has been for a long time."

"I asked him to marry me—twice. He said no."

"Did he? He actually said, 'No, I don't want to marry you'?"

"Well… not exactly."

Foxy raises an eyebrow. "I really think he wants what Josh has."

"Maeve? She used to like him when they were younger, but she swears it was just a crush and those feelings have long gone."

Foxy sighs, long and deep. "For someone I've called smart and beautiful more than once, you're in danger of losing half the title. Look—I've known Kurt a long time. We've been through some pretty intense situations together. You learn a lot about someone when you're not sure you'll ever make it home.

He's not the type to get emotional. Thinks it shows weakness. But even so, he used to mention a particular girl— a lot. Someone from back home, where he grew up. His whole face would light up when he talked about her. I could tell he had feelings, but he brushed it off, told me he never thought she'd want him. Said she never gave him the time of day when they were young.

From what I understand they ran into each other one night not so long ago. One thing led to another. They hooked up. He left before she woke —couldn't bear to see regret in her eyes. He was supposed to leave town the next day, figured he'd never see her again. But his plans changed. He tried to stay away, but he couldn't. They hooked up again. And again, he ran—because this time, he really did have to leave.

He saw her again at Josh's wedding. Thought something between them had changed. They spent the night together. But when he woke up, she was gone. And all his worst fears were confirmed—she didn't feel the same."

I sit in stunned silence, absorbing every word.

Foxy leans forward. "I might be wrong—and you can tell me to mind my own business—but I think he's on unfamiliar ground. The man who's never known fear is suddenly terrified of screwing, whatever it is you two have going on, up. He doesn't want you to be with him out of duty, guilt, or the fear of ending up alone. He wants you in this for the long haul. To fall for him the way he fell for you—years ago.

A man like Kurt? He'll only get hitched once and when he does, for him, it will be for keeps. He never does anything by half measures. When he finally walks down that aisle, that woman—she'll get all of him and she'll never want for a thing. But to get him there, he needs to be certain she feels just as strongly as he does.

So if you're still worried he's only here because you're pregnant, I can tell you—you're wrong. Everyone sees it. Maybe everyone but you. That's why we all take such joy in ribbing him. He always swore adamantly he'd never fall in love and settle down. He was so convinced the only woman he could ever love would always be just out of reach."

My mouth opens and closes like a goldfish, not quite sure how to respond.

A ping sounds. Foxy smiles and removes the flash drive from his computer.

"On that note, will you be okay if I go drop this off? I want to give the good guys as much time as possible to review it before tomorrow."

"Sure, but can't you just forward it to their email?"

"Theoretically, yes. But this is faster—and safer. I haven't had time to clean up all the metadata properly, and I don't want to leave any links that can be traced back to me. Plus, I want to make sure it ends up in the right hands. I've looked into the lead attorney for the prosecution—he seems legit. But we don't know how far Knox's reach goes. I'd rather not risk an email mysteriously vanishing before he even sees it. I shouldn't be too long, and Josh will be here soon. Just kick back and relax for a bit. When I get back, I'll take you in to see Carter like I promised."

I groan. "I suppose I could use the time to look for a new job. Though who's going to hire me now?" I gesture to my belly. "Getting someone new to agree to let me work for a few months before I leave to have the baby is going to be tough. Especially around here."

Foxy shrugs on his jacket. "Maybe you should expand your horizons. I hear L.A. is nice this time of year." He grins, and I grin back, slowly shaking my head.

"Get out of here." I throw a couch cushion at him. It bounces off his back as he disappears out the door.

I thought I'd enjoy the peace and quiet, but ten minutes into a movie, I'm bored and missing the constant pandemonium of the last few days. I grab my bag, hoping for a candy bar, and instead find the bag of rubbish I'd stuffed in there earlier. With nothing better to do, I empty it out onto the coffee table.

"What have you been up to, Steven?" I murmur, sorting through the mess.

There's not much. A few scribbled notes, some empty crisp packets, and a printout—illegible, clearly the loser in a fight with a dying printer. Then I spot them: torn scraps of paper, handwriting scrawled in what looks like Steven's messy script.

I piece them together, rotating and nudging until the words start to form.

B – ready to move from Friday. North C.

Sapphire 5.

The message loops in my head, over and over. What does it mean?

I reach for my phone to call Kurt—then stop. Who knows when Steven wrote this? I can't risk sending Kurt on a wild goose chase, not with at least one life already hanging in the balance.

I decide to wait for Foxy. I tape the scraps together and leave them on his laptop, then try to sink back into the film I was watching. But my eyes keep drifting to the note. My brain won't let it go.

Sapphire. Could that mean Sapphire Heights? Both Knox and Steven have ties to the place.

B – ready to move from Friday. Could "B" be Bear? Is that where he has been hiding? Is he planning to leave Sapphire Heights tomorrow?

North C. No clue.

5. A floor? An apartment number? A time?

If Bear *is* hiding out there, it makes sense. The project's finished, but the units haven't officially sold yet. The whole place is empty—apart from maybe the odd maintenance worker. Perfect for someone who doesn't want to be found.

I grab my phone again. What if I'm wrong?

I check the time. A cab could get me to Sapphire Heights in twenty minutes. If it's deserted, no harm done. I'll be back before anyone notices. But if I *do* see something—if Bear's there—I won't engage. I'll call Kurt, keep my distance, and wait for backup.

I pull on a coat and grab my bag. Just as I'm about to leave, I freeze.

If I turn off my phone, Kurt will think I'm hiding something and come looking—like he did before. But if I leave it on, and he or Foxy check my location for peace of mind, they'll see exactly where I'm headed. Either way, a vital resource gets wasted trailing me, and that defeats the whole point of me wanting to check the place out alone.

I growl under my breath and toss the phone onto the side table. With GPS spoofing, it'll show I'm still at home.

Just in case, I make sure I've got Kurt's number memorised. If I need to reach him, I'll find a way—pretend it's a baby emergency, flag down a car and borrow someone's phone, whatever it takes.

Not that I'll need to, I'm not expecting to find Bear. I just need to *know*. So when I show the others the note and tell them he's not at Sapphire Heights, I'm certain. Then they can focus on more credible leads.

I'll be fine. There and back before anyone even notices I've gone.

What could possibly go wrong?

Chapter 22

Sapphire Heights is a true architectural masterpiece, oozing grandeur and grace. It doesn't take a mastermind to see why anyone with the means would fight for the bragging rights that come with such an exclusive address.

Two large aquatic maintenance vans are parked outside the towering glass doors that lead into the grand foyer. The doors open and close with a gentle swoosh as the crew meanders back and forth, clearly packing up their kit. As I approach, I catch a glimpse of the back wall—teeming with exotic marine life. I'm so engrossed in trying to get a better view that I'm caught off guard when a man leaning against his van, cigarette in hand, calls out to me.

"Can I help you, miss?"

"Uh, I thought this place was empty?" I reply, thinking on my feet.

"It is. We're just here to take care of the aquarium. I doubt the new occupants would appreciate moving in with a bunch of dead fish stinking up the place."

"So there's no one in any of the apartments?" I ask, I know Bear wouldn't want to draw attention to himself—but that doesn't mean he wasn't spotted.

"Not a soul. Don't you watch the news?" he says. "The bloke who built it was arrested. Unless he pulls a get-out-of-jail-free card, no one's moving in anytime soon. We were given access by his attorney to look after the wildlife while he works on getting him out."

"Have you seen inside the apartments? I bet they're amazing," I gush, trying to gauge whether he's absolutely sure no one's hiding there.

"Nah, we weren't given any of the entrance codes. We can only use that lift there—the boring one," he jokes, nodding toward the only elevator not made of glass. "It takes us to the maintenance floor. That's where the hatches are."

"Hatches?"

"Yeah, the ones divers use to clear the tank. Or the ones we use to feed the fish."

"I don't suppose…" I flutter my eyelashes, trying my best to look alluring before coyly turning away, feigning embarrassment. "No… you probably don't have the authority."

"What?" I'm not sure if it's the stranger or his ego talking now as he stubs out his cigarette.

"I was just wondering if I could take a

quick peek. At the aquarium, that is. I've always found marine life fascinating. But if you're not allowed…" I trail off, sounding despondent.

When he puffs out his chest, I know I've got him.

"Five minutes wouldn't hurt," he calls, waving me in through the doors.

The far back wall stretches high and wide as we approach. A massive treasure chest sits at the centre of the tank, its lid gently rising and falling slightly as trapped air escapes in a flurry of bubbles, helping to oxygenate the water. We stand side by side, admiring the sheer scale of the aquarium, until I shudder—several sharks glide languidly past, weaving among their smaller, vibrantly coloured companions. The largest is about five feet long.

"Blacktip reef sharks," my guide explains. "I don't know how he got them. From what I understand, he applied for some kind of preservation certification, which doesn't make much sense. They're classified as vulnerable, not endangered. Honestly, they'd be better off being monitored in their natural habitat. This tank might be big, but it's no ocean."

"Are they dangerous?"

"Any wild animal is dangerous. But these aren't known to be aggressive unless provoked or threatened. The divers are safe as long as the sharks are well-fed—so they don't mistake them for food. If you're bleeding, though, I wouldn't recommend taking a dip. They can get feisty if they smell blood and think you're serving yourself up for supper."

I laugh nervously, pretending to be more fascinated than unsettled. He seems pleased with the attention.

"You know," he says, glancing at his watch, "I've got to help the others load up. We're behind schedule as it is."

"Of course," I say, feigning disappointment. "Thanks for the peek. It's incredible."

He hesitates, then shrugs. "You can hang back for a few minutes if you want. Just don't touch anything. I'll be right outside."

"I promise," I say, already scanning the room for any sign of Bear.

As he disappears through the swooshing doors, I'm alone—watching the sharks circling behind glass, I hope I'm suddenly not about to find any two-legged ones my side of it.

As the flurry of activity from the workmen subsides, I hear someone call out, "That's the last from upstairs." The maintenance lift doors slide shut, and the final few men disappear out front.

Not thinking about how I'll get back out if the building's locked tight, I seize the moment. As soon as I'm alone, I hit the call button and slip inside the lift the workmen were using. There's only one button. I press it and begin to ascend, hoping the man who let me in assumes I've already left when he can't find me.

The elevator opens into a tropically steamy room, lit by sunlight pouring through a glass dome overhead. Seven doors are spaced evenly around the perimeter. The one directly opposite is labelled **Roof Access**, flanked on one side by a clearly marked **Fire Escape**—both appear to open from this room. The remaining doors are simply numbered **1** through **5**, and are flush with the wall, lacking any visible handles or fixings. I assume they can only be opened from the other side.

There is the gentle hum of a generator and one wall is lined with large fuse boxes bearing high-voltage warning stickers. Cupboards stand tall next to them, I presume they contain cleaning equipment and possibly diving gear since oxygen tanks are neatly labelled and stowed beside them. A whole section is dedicated to food bins and chilled cabinets filled with supplies for the marine life.

Four massive hatches dominate the floor, each sealed with large bolts and fitted with clear lids. I peer through the condensation on one of the windows into the depths of the water below, then quickly step back as a wave of vertigo washes over me.

I barely have time to steady myself before an arm clamps around my torso, tight just beneath my bust, yanking me backward with a force that's almost brutal—albeit measured, not careless. I slam into a wall of muscle that's unyielding, hot and alive. A large hand smothers my mouth before I can scream, fingers pressing into my cheek hard enough to sting.

A voice, low and gravelly, curls into my ear like smoke.

"Well, well, well... who do we have here?"

My heart jackhammers against my ribs. I can't move. I can't speak. My breaths come in rapid, sharp bursts as I struggle to fill my lungs. The sharks behind the glass suddenly seem less threatening than the predator holding me now.

I try to tilt my head, eyes wide with fear, my whole body trembling. *Bear.*

He smiles—slow, victorious—as he growls, "If I let you go, do you promise not to scream?"

I nod. His hand slips from my mouth, and I gasp, dragging in air like I've been drowning. He releases his grip around my middle—slowly, deliberately.

"Don't even think about it," he snarls, catching the flicker in my eyes as they dart around the room, already trying to plot my escape. That's when I notice one of the sealed doors behind me has been pushed opened. Door number 5. That's where he must have sprung from. Five, just like on the note I found.

Our eyes lock and I know he's about to ask for an explanation for my presence.

"What brings you here?" he asks, voice low and suspicious, eyes narrowed.

It takes every ounce of strength to mask my fear. I straighten my spine and meet his gaze.

"Steven can't make your three o'clock," I say, lying as smoothly as I can. "He sent me to pick up the hard drive."

Bear recoils slightly, stunned. His eyes flick to the hatch I'd been peering into before he grabbed me, then back to my face.

A slow, disbelieving smile spreads across his lips. "I'll just phone him to check, shall I?"

He pulls his mobile from his back pocket. My pulse spikes, but I keep my expression neutral.

"You do that," I bluff. "Then you'll really be in trouble."

He laughs, low and dangerous. "Trouble? How?"

"Why do you think he sent me?" I shoot back, answering his question with one of my own. It throws him—just enough to buy me a few precious seconds to scramble for a cover story.

"Enlighten me," Bear growls.

"The tech guy at the office is onto him," I

say, letting urgency creep into my voice. "Steven's backed into a corner. He told me to let you know the guy's good—he already suspects Steven switched out the hard drive in his room, but he can't prove it. Steven stayed behind to stall him and sent me here. I need to get back before anyone starts asking awkward questions."

Bear still doesn't look convinced. I push harder.

"How else do you think I knew where to find you?"

"Why didn't he call me?"

"He was supposed to. Maybe he couldn't. He gave me your number so you could let me in when I arrived, but I left in such a hurry I forgot my phone. Here—check if you want."

I upend my bag, scattering its contents across the floor. Then I turn my coat pockets inside out.

"When I got here, I didn't know what to do. Luckily, I found a maintenance worker who let me in. Then I had to figure out how to get to apartment five to find you. That—" I jerk my head toward the maintenance elevator, "was the only lift I could use."

I can see the wheels turning behind his eyes. I don't want to give him too much time to spot any holes in my story, so I throw him another question.

"How did you know I was here?"

He jerks his head toward the apartment. "Security camera in the foyer feeds back there. Visitors get flagged. I hooked it up when I moved in to prevent any unwelcome surprises."

"So…" I say quickly, desperate to get out of here. "Can you give me the drive so I can get back?"

"No," he growls.

He turns, calling over his shoulder as he starts walking back through the door he materialized from.

"Tell Steven—nice try sending a cute piece of ass to charm me into handing it over. But I'm keeping the drive as insurance. When this is over and I've got my money, then maybe."

"What about Steven?" I blurt out automatically, instantly regretting it. He was about to let me go. I could've called Kurt and the team. But no—I had to try and take down an elite ex-SEAL sniper solo. Stupid. Stupid. Stupid. I would've facepalmed if it wouldn't have blown my cover.

Bear turns back slowly, his expression flat. "What about him?"

"He said he'd make you pay if you didn't hand it over."

Bear throws his head back and laughs—a deep, mocking sound that echoes off the concrete.

"He did, did he? And how, pray tell, is he going to do that? Steven thinks he's playing in the majors, but he's barely out of the minors."

His voice drops, cold and deliberate.

"Did he really think I wouldn't check the files he asked me to copy? That I'd go on to just erase the rest without question—because *he* told me to? Like his word means anything to me? Idiot. He owes me money. Of course I looked. And what I found on that drive? It could put him away for more than one lifetime. It's packed with all sorts of little treasures."

He steps closer, eyes gleaming.

"A list of every witness he ever intimidated. Every piece of evidence he made disappear. Every bribe. Even CCTV footage—clear as day—showing him pulling the trigger to eliminate his competition when they couldn't be bought. Knox made Steven an offer he couldn't refuse to guarantee he walked free, and Steven pulled out all the stops to make sure he was in the right position to deliver."

He pauses, voice low and deliberate.

"But none of it ties back to me."

"Robert?" I force out, nausea surging through me as bile burns the back of my throat. "Steven killed Robert?"

Bear lets the revelation hang in the air, letting it sink in.

"He may have used my gun, threatened to turn it

in to frame me—but without a body, ballistics are useless. And now with the footage, I can prove it wasn't me."

He steps back, arms splayed to indicate the building around us.

"Rumour has it Knox is struggling to pay his bills. If he doesn't pay Steven, Steven can't pay me —not since he sunk every last cent into this place."

His eyes narrow.

"And I need that money, doll. So you tell Steven —no money, no dice. And you might mention I'm not happy he told you where to find me. Let him know we'll be discussing the meaning of discretion when I see him in person."

Bear turns, voice clipped.

"Now if you'll excuse me, I need to pack."

He turns to leave again—and I know if I let him disappear, it could be fatal. I say the only thing I know will make him pause.

"Steve Fox," I blurt out, adrenaline flooding my body, spots dancing in front of my eyes.

"Foxy?" Bear whispers, spinning on his heel.

Before I can react, he's closed the gap and his left hand clamps around my throat, lifting me almost off the ground. His grip is firm—enough to hurt, not enough to silence.

"What about him?" he grits out. There's a flicker

of panic in his voice.

"He's the tech guy that's onto Steven," I choke.

"And you too." Foxy's calm, familiar voice slices through the air. "I'd strongly suggest you let her go."

Bear's eyes snap up, then widen. He releases my throat—only to spin me, pinning my back to his chest, his arm locking across my neck.

I can see Foxy now, casually leaning against the frame of a door opposite, looking relaxed, like he's catching up with an old friend.

Bear snorts, but I feel his body stiffen behind me. He's rattled, trying not to show it.

Relief floods me at the sight of Foxy, and tears spill freely down my cheeks. "I'm sorry," I cough against Bear's grip.

"Let her go," Foxy repeats, with a hint of menace.

"Or what?" Bear volleys back. "You think you can take me down on your own? You've spent too long out of the field, hiding behind a keyboard. Your combat edge is gone, Foxy. You're not the fighter you used to be—and I'm not the kind of problem you can solve with code."

"Oh, I think I'd be able to hold my own," Foxy counters smoothly. "But who said I was alone?"

One by one, doors fly open.

First Nico appears. Then Blake. Finally, Ace.

Bear's grip tightens in fear. He takes a step back, dragging me with him. I claw at his arm, desperate to loosen it enough to breathe.

Blake shakes his head slowly. "You really don't want to make matters worse, Bear."

I feel the body behind me tremble with restrained tension as I thrash against the ironclad hold he has on me.

"Relax, honey. Breathe," Foxy soothes from across the room. "Fighting like that's not good for the baby."

Bear laughs—a low, cruel sound—and tightens his grip deliberately, making me cough and struggle harder.

"So it's your baby," he sneers.

I'd heard the phrase *it makes your blood run cold*, but I'd never truly felt it—certainly never through someone else. I didn't think it was possible... until another door creaks open.

And there he is.

"No," comes a low, ominous growl, thick with fury. "It's mine."

The words ripple across the room like a shockwave. The temperature of the body holding me seems to drop ten degrees in an instant.

"Fuck," Bear breathes—barely audible.

Even through the terror and the trauma, my heart sings at the sight of him. My soul reaches for him instinctively, even as my rational mind screams for him to vanish — to get out, to be safe, to be anywhere but here.

That's when it hits me.

This isn't just fear. It's not adrenaline or panic. It's love — deep, undeniable, and absolute. In that instant, every doubt, every hesitation I ever had dissolves. I would do anything to protect him. Anything. And I know, with a certainty that steadies me, that he would do the same.

Kurt takes a step forward.

A thin vein pulses violently at the side of his neck, betraying the fury simmering beneath his deceptively calm exterior. He stands tall, a formidable silhouette clad in black combat gear stretched taut over muscles coiled for action. The room seems to shrink around him, his presence pressing in like a storm front. Bear feels it too— I feel it in the way he gulps for air behind me, as if the oxygen itself is being consumed by the heat radiating off Kurt's barely restrained rage.

Bear reacts fast. His hand jerks behind him, and suddenly the cold, round barrel of a gun is pressed to my temple.

Kurt freezes mid-step.

"One step closer," Bear warns, voice sharp with

panic, "and I paint the walls with her."

"Then what?" Kurt counters, taking a slow, deliberate step forward.

The others follow suit. Ace, Blake, and Nico raise their weapons, aiming squarely at Bear, who does his best to shrink his massive frame behind mine.

"You'll have to take me next," Kurt says, voice low and lethal, "or so help me, you'll spend the rest of whatever life you've got left wishing you had. And by the time you're done with me, the others will have you hog-tied and gift-wrapped—ready for delivery to the boss."

He glances at his watch.

"Who knows you're here by the way and should be arriving…" he drawls, "…jusssst about…now."

There's only one man Kurt ever calls *boss*.

And right on cue, another door swings open.

Josh steps through — towering, calm, his presence swallowing the room. His anger is palpable, another quiet storm ready to break.

I pray he didn't come straight here. I pray he dropped Maeve off first.

"Give it up, Bear," Josh growls. "There's nowhere you can go where we won't find you."

Behind me, I feel Bear cock his head. "Maybe," he says quietly. "Maybe not."

The next few seconds stretch into slow motion.

Bear shifts the gun from my temple to Kurt.

"Noooooo!" I scream, thrashing with everything I've got. I manage to knock his arm just as the first shot rings out.

A second follows — I hear it but I don't see where it lands as Bear grabs the collar of my coat, twisting me as he yanks me backward, dragging me through door number five, which he slams shut behind us.

He flings me against the wall, taps something into an electronic pad. A light flips from green to red. Fists pound the door from the other side. I can hear shouts. Footsteps. Chaos.

"Move!" Bear bellows.

He shoves me down a corridor, across a marble floor. I barely register the towering windows and the sweeping view beyond. My focus narrows to survival — and that second shot. Where did it go? Is the man I love lying wounded because I couldn't stay out of it, because I didn't listen?

We reach an elevator. He throws me inside, waving his gun in my face to subdue me. He's screaming, but the words blur into noise. All I can hear is my own heartbeat, pounding with guilt and fear.

I brace for the foyer, praying for a chance to break free. To run.

But when the doors open, we're in an

underground car park. A black pickup truck waits nearby. Bear forces me to run even though I can hardly see through the torrent of tears streaming down my face. He grabs a key stashed on top of the rear wheel, unlocks the door, and shoves me inside.

"Buckle up, darlin'," he snarls. "You could be in for a bumpy ride."

I reach for the seatbelt, but he floors it before I can get fastened in. I fumble with the buckle, trying to hold the lap strap away from my belly as I bounce in my seat, terrified for my baby. Tyres scream. Rubber burns. We rocket out of the garage and into traffic. Bear's eyes flick to the rearview mirror. He curses, veering onto the pavement, blasting through a red light making pedestrians scatter.

"Please," I beg, tears streaming as I grasp the handrail above my head in a bid to minimise the way I'm being jostled. "Let me go. Drop me anywhere. I don't care. You can disappear without me."

"I can't," Bear mutters. "Now I've lost the hard drive, you're the only leverage I've got."

He glances at me — a flicker of sadness and regret in his eyes before he shouts, "Look there, out the window."

I turn, expecting to see Kurt. Or any of the others closing in.

I don't realise it's a distraction until it's too late.
My head slams against the cold glass.
"I'm sorry doll," he whispers as I groan.
And just like that everything goes black.

Chapter 23

When I come round, I'm lying on dirty white sheets that cling damply to my skin. The bunk beneath me is narrow, barely wider than my body, bolted to the wall like an afterthought. The room is tiny — more coffin than cabin — and the air is thick with mildew, diesel, and something metallic. Rust. Or possibly blood.

A single bulb swings overhead, casting erratic shadows across the peeling walls. Pipes run along the ceiling, dripping steadily. Each splash echoes in the silence. There's no window. Just a dented steel door with a porthole too grimy to see through.

I've no idea how long I've been out or how I got here. My head throbs. My mouth tastes of salt and fear. I try to sit up, but the bunk groans beneath me, and nausea pins me down. As the fog in my brain clears, I realise I must be on a boat. The rhythmic purr of the engine. The slight tilt of the floor. It's enough for me to know we're moving.

Where the hell am I?

Bear's an expert in not getting found. My

stomach drops. Wherever we're headed, it's bound to be remote. Somewhere off-grid and untraceable.

I swing my legs off the bunk and try to sit again, pressing a hand to my temple. There's a lump, but no blood that I can tell. After a few minutes, I drag myself upright. The floor is flooded — an inch of ice-cold water. I wade to the door, expecting it to be locked.

I'm surprised when it creaks open.

I creep up a step and into a small galley. Rubbish litters the floor — empty beer bottles, sandwich wrappers. A narrow flight of stairs leads up to a trap door which I presume opens out onto the deck. Thin windows run along both sides of the galley. I peer out.

There's nothing but blackness. The sky is stormy, thick with clouds that smother any trace of moonlight. No lights I can see. No markers. Nothing to tell me where I am.

I tear through the tiny cupboards and drawers, frantic for anything I can use as a weapon. Cutlery. Tools. Anything sharp. My fingers close around a small black box wedged behind a stack of greasy plates.

I flip it open. A flare gun. My heart leaps—then crashes. It's Empty. No flares. I toss it aside just as the engine cuts out. Silence swells, thick and ominous, before slow, heavy footsteps echo above me.

Suddenly, the trapdoor bursts open. Bear descends the steps, deliberate and slow. His fierce eyes lock onto mine.

"You're awake," he growls.

He steps fully into the galley and I instinctively back away. He notices and pauses.

"Relax. I'm not going to hurt you."

My hand automatically flies to the lump on my temple.

"Hurt you again," he adds, catching the gesture.

I just stare at him, too afraid to speak.

He pulls a small crate from beneath a counter—food and bottled water. He grabs two sandwiches and two bottles, tossing one of each to me, then gestures toward the bench along the wall.

He sits opposite, unwraps his sandwich, and takes a hearty bite.

"Eat," he growls.

But I've got no appetite. My eyes flick to the open door. He notices and huffs a smile.

"Go for it," he says, gesturing toward the exit. "You won't get very far. We're in open water. Unless you're an Olympic swimmer with a built-in compass and a resistance to hypothermia, there's nowhere to go."

"You're a dead man," I whisper.

He chuckles darkly. "What are you gonna do, doll?"

"Not me. Kurt," I say, firm and cold.

His face pales.

"Gotta find me first, doll," he mutters. "I couldn't figure out how he found me hiding out at the Sapphire. Then it hit me—he didn't. He was tracking you."

"He couldn't," I say, smiling. "I didn't have my phone, remember? He was onto you then—and he'll be onto you now."

Bear returns my smile with one of his own. "He wasn't using your phone, doll. He slipped one of Foxy's little gadgets into your bag. I saw it when you dumped everything out for me. Didn't register at first—in amongst the junk you women carry—but once I thought about it, it was obvious. You ditched it for me, though. Appreciate that. Hope you don't mind, but while you were asleep, I checked to make sure you weren't hiding any others..."

I shiver and check myself over, relieved all my clothes are intact. He must've just patted me down. Thank God.

"I wasn't asleep," I snap. "I was unconscious."

Bear shrugs. "Well, anyway. I'm in the clear."

"Let me guess—you left from North Cove," I say, recalling the note I found and trying to rattle him.

He falters, just slightly, then masks it. "Steven tell you that? Did he also say I'd be on the *Bravura*, by chance?" He gestures around the cramped interior. "Does this look like one of Knox's fancy superyachts? Always good to have a Plan B, doll. Since I'm leaving earlier than planned, we left from somewhere else. Odds are, your boyfriend's looking in the wrong place. That's if he's even looking at all."

"Oh, he's coming for me…" I snap, then drop my voice to a low, threatening growl, "…and for you."

"Like I said, it's always good to have a Plan B. I'm assuming you've been feeding him intel on your boss. In which case, he'll have figured out what the original plan was…"

"To assassinate Judge Fletcher so he can be replaced in the Knox trial," I say, filling in the gap.

Bear arches an eyebrow, clearly surprised by how much I know.

"Very good," he says, giving me a slow, mocking clap. "Steven knew from the start there was always a slim chance I'd have to bail with little to no notice. We planned for that from the start. He's in too deep to let my disappearance derail his future. The player may have changed, but the game remains the same. He'll push forward, with or without me."

He leans back, chewing over his next words.

"I don't know how he'll take out Fletcher without getting caught. He won't be able to do it long-range like I was going to. But he'll find a way. He's saved a lot of creeps from doing time, maybe he'll call in a favour. Hopefully, between trying to figure out his next move—and working out where you are—everyone will be distracted just long enough for me to vanish again."

He shrugs.

"Unfortunately, Steven won't want to pay me now I can't deliver. Without the hard drive I had to bargain with, you've just become my next meal ticket. Once I'm in the clear, I'll ask your man to pay me for your location. Worked out pretty well, I think. With Steven's finances hanging by a thread, Callahan's the better bet."

"He'll never pay."

"I say he will. With the boat sinking, I'd say you've got an hour—two tops—before you become fish bait."

"We're sinking?" I ask, panic rising. I remember the water pooling on the floor when I climbed out of the bunk.

Bear stands. "Yeah. Sorry about that."

His devious smile says he's anything but sorry. He tosses his half-eaten sandwich aside.

"Time for me to go."

He disappears up the steps, slams the hatch

shut, and locks it from the outside. I rush after him, screaming, but he's nimble for such a large man. I don't make it in time.

My pleas fall on deaf ears. Above me, I hear Bear moving around on the deck.

I wait for the engine to start.

Instead, there's a whooshing sound I can't place—then silence.

A heavy splash follows—something large hitting the water. Then, smaller rhythmic sounds. Oars, maybe, propelling away... until the sharp strike of a motor igniting, before it purrs off into the distance.

I pound on the trapdoor. The hinges rattle, straining against my desperation. Water begins to seep across the galley floor.

"Bear?" I scream.

Nothing. Just an eerie, suffocating silence.

The fear of being alone engulfs me. The lights flicker—a sure sign I'm about to be plunged into darkness. I scramble down off the steps, ignoring the numbness creeping in from the freezing water now ankle-deep. I search frantically for a torch, matches—anything to provide light later.

Nothing.

I do find a few simple tools rolling around the back of a drawer. At first, I discard them—they're not what I need. Then I realize: the trapdoor hinges are on my side, built that way to protect them from the elements. If I can get up on deck, there might be a dinghy. Or something I can use as a raft. It's a long shot—but I have to try.

"Don't worry, Nugget. We got this," I whisper, grabbing a screwdriver and paddling back to the door. Climbing the steps, I lift my feet out of the water, a brief respite from its icy grasp.

The tool's head is the wrong shape—not a good fit—but it's all I have. I fumble tenaciously, trying to loosen screws that have welded themselves tight over time. My focus is laser-sharp. I don't notice how high the water has risen until it claws at my feet again.

Panicking, I push harder. One screw. Then another. Finally, with a valiant shove, the door flips open and I drag myself out of the galley.

Cold air instantly bites at my skin. My eyes widen at the grim realization that the deck is nearly level with the waterline. The boat rears as a wave crashes over the stern. I slip, landing hard on my tailbone, sliding toward the murky depths trying to claim me.

My feet scramble for purchase on the slick deck. I grab blindly until my hand catches a stray rope. I almost let go when it moves with me, but then it goes taut. I cling to it, pulling myself toward the bow, grabbing whatever I can as the boat fights to level itself.

My hand lands on a large metal box bolted to the floor. I pray there's an inflatable inside. I flip the lid, it's empty, except for two large cartridges rolling at the bottom.

Flares.

I'm cold. Exhausted. But while there's a breath left in my body, I won't give up.

Carefully, I make my way back to the galley. Just before the lights die, I spot the small metal box I'd discarded earlier. Without hesitation, I plunge into the water, grab it, and scramble back out.

The deck pitches violently in the choppy sea. I stagger, clutching the flare gun—mostly dry, protected by its case. I pray it works.

I load the gun, steady myself, and fire.

The flare shoots skyward, exploding like a firework. For a second, the sky lights up—and I see a shadow on the horizon, far in the distance.

The boat rears again. This time, I'm ready. I've already grabbed a rope tied to the bow. As the stern begins to slip beneath the waves, I drag myself forward, wrapping the rope around my arm for stability.

I load the last flare and fire it with a prayer to the heavens.

"Please," I sob into the air. "Please help me and

protect my baby."

Then I hear it—the distant roar of an engine. Lights slice through the darkness, hurtling toward me. A familiar figure stands at the bow, poised to dive.

"Kurt," I whisper through my tears. The relief at seeing him alive overwhelms me.

As the freezing water starts to climb up my body, the engine cuts. I hear a splash then someone powering through the waves toward me. Strong arms wrap around me, untangling the rope I'd used to anchor myself.

"I've got you, baby," he whispers, pulling me free.

The boat he arrived on bobs a few feet away. He urges me to lie back against him, then uses one arm to powerfully backstroke toward it. When we reach the side, someone grabs my wrists and hauls me aboard with ease.

"Josh? Where's Maeve?" I ask, breathless and shivering, worried for my best friend.

He chuckles. "Only you would ask that right now. You'll see her soon, I promise."

He wraps an arm around me, pulling me into the warmth of his body while Ace helps Kurt climb aboard. Kurt hits the deck and the boat surges forward, slicing through the water at warp speed.

Josh steadies me until Kurt takes over, guiding

me into a tiny cabin.

"We need to get you dry and warmed up fast," he says, stripping off my soaked clothes, wrapping me in a towel and gently rubbing me dry. He finds a grey sweatshirt and a pair of joggers—far too big—rolling up the sleeves and legs until they fit. Then he bundles me in a blanket and tends to himself.

We don't speak. He's focused, methodical. When he finally sits beside me pulling me onto his lap, fatigue overtakes me. My head rests against his shoulder, safe in his arms I let my eyelids flutter closed.

"I thought I lost you." He murmurs into my hair, his voice catching slightly. "I'm so pissed at you right now."

"I'm sorry," I whisper.

A beat passes. Then, softer still:

"I can't believe you planted a bug in my bag."

Kurt exhales, amused. "What makes you think it was me?"

I smile faintly, eyes still closed. "I saw Foxy hand it to you a while back.

"Maybe, it just fell in there."

"You're lucky I'm too tired to punch you."

"I'll take my chances," he chuckles. "I can't believe you ditched your phone and ran off to save the day without me—after promising you wouldn't."

"Truce," I murmur.

"Truce," he sighs into my hair, pressing a kiss to my temple—just before exhaustion claims me.

Chapter 24

I'm woken the moment the boat moors, scooped into Kurt's arms and transferred to a waiting black SUV with Foxy at the wheel. We're driven straight to the hospital so I can be subjected to a thorough check-up even though I demand to be taken home all the way there.

Kurt doesn't even have to argue with me—Josh, Ace, and Foxy pick up that mantle for him. I might have a little sway with Kurt, but Josh is having none of it. Ace and Foxy try to act apologetic, claiming they can't go against him since he pays their wages. But honestly? I think they're too scared to even want to try.

I'm outnumbered. Kurt just sits back, watching the battle unfold with an amused look on his face.

All four of them follow me around the hospital like I'm a flight risk. With that kind of entourage, people start sneaking photos, convinced I must be either famous or dangerously unstable. Honestly, the way they hover and fuss, I'm less likely to be pushed over the metaphorical edge than to leap of my own free will — just to get a break from them.

After hours of waiting, my vitals and bloodwork come back clean. A fresh scan shows a strong heartbeat and no signs of distress for the baby, so I refuse to stay overnight.

I'm given fluids, cocooned in warm blankets—and then, against my protests, Kurt scoops me up and carries me back to the car.

When we get home, I'm tucked into bed like a child. A security guard is stationed at the foot of the bed to make sure I stay put.

"Knock, knock." Just as I settle in, a familiar voice—low and teasing—calls out. The bedroom door creaks open, and Maeve peeks around it.

"Maeve!" I cry, delighted to see my oldest and best friend.

She steps into the darkened room just as I try to launch myself at her for a hug.

"Stay there," a voice barks from the shadows. Maeve jumps about a foot.

"Jeez, Blake," she says, clutching her chest. "What are you doing lurking back there?"

"Following orders," he replies, kissing the top of her head.

Even in the dim light, I can see Maeve slowly shaking her head as she crosses to the free side of the bed. She pulls back the covers and slides in beside me. I shuffle to make room, then wrap her in a hug.

"I've missed you so much," I whisper.

"Me too," she murmurs.

"Please tell me you two are about to start making out," Blake chuckles. "It'd be way more entertaining than watching that one scowl at me."

"Blake, go join the others instead of standing there like a creeper," Maeve says.

He hesitates.

"Where's she going to go?" Maeve sighs. "She'd have to walk past all of you to get to the front door."

"Rumour has it she's some kind of Houdini," Blake grumbles. "She lost the Boss and Foxy more than once. If I lose her, I'm toast—and I'll never get to remind them how useless they are."

"She won't lose *me*," Maeve says firmly. "So go away, or I'll start talking about menstrual cycles and mucus plugs right in front of you."

Blake makes a gagging sound and raises his hands in surrender. "Okay, okay. But keep a close eye on her. If she sneezes, the Boss wants to know."

Maeve taps two fingers to her temple in a mock salute as Blake slides out the door.

"How are you?" Maeve starts just as Foxy, Ace and Nico appear.

"What?" She asks them tersely.

"Nothing," Ace mumbles. As they walk away one

of them calls out.

"Blake you liar. They're not making out"

"If I catch any of you perving at my wife there'll be hell to pay." Josh yells from the kitchen making us both snigger.

"What's going on out there?" I nod towards the bedroom door.

"Usual." Maeve shrugs. "They're all drunk on testosterone and vying with each other to come up with the best punishment for Bear when they get their hands on him. All except Kurt."

That makes me sit up a little straighter.

"Why not Kurt?" I ask worried. "Is he Okay?"

"Depends on what you mean by Okay. If you're asking if his is injured physically No. If you're asking if he is quietly contemplating how he is about to reign hell down on someone…"

"Crap."

"Don't worry. Josh has him in the kitchen trying to talk him down from doing anything stupid" Maeve's voice falters. "At least, I hope that's what he's doing. Anyhow, back to you? How are you feeling?"

"Physically, I'm fine," I tell her honestly. "Mentally…" I trail off. "I really thought that was it for me. I keep thinking—what if Kurt hadn't found me in time?"

"I don't think that was ever an option."

"What do you mean?"

"Well, as I hear it, Foxy came back to the apartment and found you missing, with your phone left on the console by the door. He called Kurt, who went ballistic and activated a tracker he'd slipped into your bag. Gross invasion of privacy—which I told him, by the way."

"Thanks," I smile at my best friend. No matter how good his intentions were, I know she gave Kurt hell.

"You're welcome," she grins, then continues. "When Foxy saw the note you left on his laptop and Kurt realised where you were headed, he wasn't sure who was closest. So he told everyone to drop what they were doing and get there fast. Josh happened to call at that moment to say we were only five minutes away. Since Kurt was frantic, we diverted to the same location instead of coming straight here.

Josh made me promise to stay in the car, but I'd been sitting for so long I got out to stretch my legs. I'd heard about the Aquarium and wanted to take a peek, so I walked around the building to look through the window. Next thing I know, this black pickup comes hurtling past—and I saw you inside, looking terrified. I didn't think. I just threw my phone onto the flatbed as you went by.

Then Kurt came sprinting past me like his ass

was on fire. He shot into the road and started chasing you down the street on foot. Bear must've spotted him, because he veered onto the sidewalk and blew through a red light to get away. The last I saw of Kurt, he was yanking a driver out of his taxi, shoving him into the back seat, and shouting, "I'm driving!" before tearing off after you in a cloud of black smoke.

Josh was worried the cabbie would phone the police, but Kurt said the guy didn't even charge. Called it the most exciting car chase he'd ever been in—though apparently, he did keep criticizing Kurt's driving."

"I bet that went down well."

"Right." We both start sniggering as we imagine Kurt not taking kindly to being told what to do.

"Bear lost him near Battery Park. But the note you left Foxy had "North C" on it. Kurt saw a sign for North Cove Marina and detoured there, thinking that's where you were headed.

He called Foxy, who checked the boat listings and found one registered under Knox's name—the guy this all revolves around, right?

I nod.

"The name started with a B, I can't remember what it was exactly. Kurt wouldn't wait for backup —he stormed the place like a wrecking ball, demolishing anything that got in his way. He was unstoppable, tearing through the boat then the marina looking for you.

Meanwhile, I was struggling to get anyone to listen to me. Men!" Maeve rolls her eyes dramatically, and I nod in sympathy. "Eventually, I managed to let Foxy know what I'd done. He traced the GPS on my phone to a remote dock a few miles downriver. It was tucked behind a crumbling warehouse and half-hidden by overgrown fencing. That's where Josh and Ace found the truck—abandoned, engine still warm.

They were pretty sure Bear had a boat stashed there and had taken you aboard. The problem was, they had no idea which direction he was headed.

Josh called Kurt, who 'borrowed'—well, commandeered—a cabin cruiser from the marina. He swung by to pick up Josh and Ace, and the three of them set off to find you.

Kurt left Blake and Nico behind in case they were wrong and needed someone able to react quickly on the ground. He asked Foxy to work the electronic angle—trying to figure out what kind of boat Bear was using, where he might be headed, and whether any unexpected radio transmissions could offer a clue to his whereabouts.

Josh said he'd never seen Kurt lose his cool like that before, and that searching the water in the dark was agonizing. Kurt was frantic—scanning the horizon, gripping the wheel like it was the only thing keeping him grounded. Every minute that passed without a sign of you chipped away at him. He kept muttering under his breath, blaming himself, replaying every decision, every second he might've been too late. He wouldn't listen to anybody... not even Josh.

Then—finally—your boat pinged on the radar.

He didn't even wait for confirmation. He gunned the engine, eyes locked on the screen. Josh said he looked like a man possessed—hope and fear battling across his face.

And when those flares lit up the sky, Kurt let out a sound Josh couldn't describe. Relief, rage, heartbreak—all tangled together. You were alive. You were fighting. And nothing was going to stop him from reaching you."

"Wow. It all sounds kind of romantic when you put it like that," I gush.

Maeve flops back against the pillows, utterly nonplussed. "It's what you do when you love someone."

"Wait." I sit bolt upright. "So Bear never got his money?"

"What money?" Maeve blinks at me, confused.

"Get dressed," I tell her.

"Why?"

"We're going out."

"It's half three in the morning. Can't it wait a few hours? I think you've had enough excitement for one night."

"No—we need to leave now."

"Good luck with that," she laughs. "You'll be lucky to get past the human wall camped outside this door."

"They can either come with me, or I'll lose them. And we both know how well that went last time." I say defiantly, even if this time I know I don't want to go alone.

Maeve groans and throws off the covers. "Fine. Where are we going?"

"Back to the Sapphire. I just need to convince the others to let us tag along."

Five minutes later, Maeve and I are dressed and ready. I'm head-to-toe in black, no makeup, and hair that looks like it lost a fight with gravity. Maeve, meanwhile, is catwalk-ready in a neon pink fluffy jumper and blue maternity jeans, her hair sculpted into an ornate updo and her face fully made up. We stride purposefully into the living room, looking less like a tactical duo and more like the opening act of a very confused fashion show, where all the men seem to be deep in strategy mode.

Every head turns as we enter.

"What are you doing out of bed? And why are

you dressed?" Kurt tries not to yell—but doesn't do a great job of it.

"Now, before you go off the deep end," I start casually, hands raised in mock surrender. "And having learned from previous mistakes..."

I trail off as five pairs of eyes lock onto me, each one more concerned than the last. Maeve nudges me sharply in the ribs.

"I just wanted to say... I'm popping out."

The silence that follows is deafening.

Kurt's jaw tightens. Josh raises an eyebrow. Blake and Nico actually choke on their drinks. Foxy's already reaching for his gun. And Ace—Ace just looks like he's bracing for impact.

Maeve sighs. "Smooth."

"The hell you are," Kurt growls.

"And I don't know where you think you're going, missy," Josh says, turning to Maeve.

"What could possibly go wrong if you all come with me?" I throw my arms wide. "You want me to stop running off solo—this is me trying not to do that. So I'm asking nicely: will you all please come with me?"

All eyes shift to Kurt. He exhales a long, suffering sigh—the sound of a man who knows he's already lost.

"You're going to be the death of me, woman," he

mutters.

I smile. That's as good as a yes.

"Everyone gear up," he snaps.

The room explodes into motion—tactical gear flying, boots thudding, weapons checked with practiced precision.

Halfway through, Kurt raises a hand. Everyone freezes.

"Wait... we're not just going for ice cream, right?"

"Right," I giggle.

He lowers his hand. The chaos resumes.

"You're not coming," Josh tells Maeve flatly.

"I'm not being the only one left behind," she fires back. "What if something happens while you're all gone?"

"Like what?" he volleys.

Maeve folds her arms. "Like..."

"Like the fire alarm going off and the building needing to be evacuated," I offer, quirking an eyebrow at Foxy, who dips his head to hide a smile.

Josh opens his mouth, then closes it. He knows I've got him. He rescued Maeve from a house fire years ago and still bears the scars. Not that he wouldn't do it all again to keep her safe. Just planting the seed of her being alone during something like that is enough to make him cave.

"Fine," he barks begrudgingly, casting a dopey, love-struck look at his wife. "But you stick to me like glue unless I say otherwise."

"Can't think of anyone else I'd rather stick myself to," she gushes.

The two of them gaze at each other like they're about to rip each other's clothes off, while the rest of us silently debate whether we should give them some privacy.

"Right, listen up," I bark, clapping my hands and stepping into the only spare space at the front of the room. Fitting six huge men, my pregnant best friend, and myself into my apartment's tiny living room is a logistical nightmare. I don't even realize I'm standing beside the whiteboard like I'm about to run a seminar until Foxy and Blake call shotgun on the sofa, sliding down on either end. Maeve squeezes between them just as Josh and Kurt each grab the collars of the seated men, trying to steal their spots.

"Oh no you don't," I shout, halting them mid-heist. "You should've moved faster. You can stand behind them."

Josh mutters something to Kurt—too low for me to catch—and when Kurt huffs out a laugh, I narrow my eyes.

"Something you'd like to share?" I challenge.

Foxy and Blake look up at them with matching shit-eating grins.

No one answers. Josh frowns, while Kurt gives me a heated look that makes my knees go weak. Nico crouches on one side of the couch; Ace sits cross-legged on the floor on the other. Once everyone settles, I begin.

"Babe," I say, addressing Kurt.

Josh's eyebrows shoot toward his hairline. "This is how we address each other in meetings now, is it, honey?" The last word drips with amused sarcasm as he goads his friend.

Kurt's cheeks tinge pink. Maeve catches it and leaps to his defence.

"Buttercup," she teases her husband, whose head snaps down in her direction. "Please be quiet. Tina has something important to say."

"I don't remember putting her on the payroll," he volleys back.

"But you do remember marrying me," she replies seamlessly. "And I'd like to hear what she has to say—so cork it."

No one in the room dares make a sound, but the shaking shoulders and barely contained snorts make it clear Josh's crew finds the whole exchange between the four of us hilarious.

"Tina, go on," Maeve encourages.

I open my mouth, but Josh whispers to Kurt—unfortunately, not as quietly as he thinks.

"Why the hell aren't you up there?"

"Because I don't know where this is going," Kurt whispers back at the same volume.

"Why not?" Josh challenges, like he's about to fire him.

"Quiet, please," I say authoritatively.

Josh opens his mouth again, but Maeve shoots him a warning look. He closes it, though he doesn't look happy.

"And I thought Kurt was the grumpy one," I mutter to my best friend, who smiles back at me while Blake clutches his stomach, wiping a tear from the corner of his eye.

"Kurt," I say, trying to regain control. I glance at Josh—no endearments this time—and he seems like he's about to let me continue without interruption. I pause to be sure. He mimes zipping his mouth closed, so I go on.

"When I was... missing, did Bear contact you to ask for money in return for my coordinates?"

"No," Kurt replies. "But he wouldn't. He knows if he asked for a wire transfer, Foxy would bait him with a honeypot or sneak in a trojan, tracing every withdrawal like it was a game of cat and mouse. Without expert help, we'd find him within minutes. Even with help, Foxy would have his location nailed within hours."

"Thanks, Boss," Foxy beams at the unexpected praise.

Kurt continues, "And if he asked for cash, it would have to be a meticulously planned drop—because he knows we'd all be there to greet him when he picked it up. He wouldn't have had time to plan for anything like that. Why? Where are you going with this?"

"Bear kept saying something that's been on my mind." Multiple pairs of eyes turn to me, expectant. "He kept saying, 'It's good to have a plan B.'"

Confused glances ripple through the room as I continue.

"He also told me the hard drive he was holding for Steven contained enough evidence of Steven's misdeeds to put him away for a long time. He also —" I gulp hard, "—said it had footage of Steven disposing of Robert.

During the trial Robert must have uncovered how shady Knox really was, maybe he had suspicions before the prosecution sent him that damning e-mail. I think he changed his mind about defending him, and when he couldn't be bought, Knox hired Steven to eliminate him and take his place on the trial so he could keep out of prison. Knox is a charmer—we've all seen that in the media. I'm betting with his cash flow as it is, whatever he offered Steven, he promised to triple it if Steven joined the Sapphire deal instead of taking payment up front.

I think Steven took the best offer and poured all his equity into the deal. Knox must have been laughing. Not only did he get a cash injection to tide him over for a few more weeks, he had Steven over a barrel—he made sure Steven would do whatever it took to keep him out of prison. Because if Knox went down, Steven would lose everything."

I glance around. No one moves.

"I don't know how Bear knew Steven was in a financial crisis, but he did. He was holding onto the hard drive as leverage—to make sure he got paid once the Fletcher job was complete. But when you found us and Bear took off with me, he was in such a rush he left the hard drive behind.

Afterwards, he told me he had to disappear now that you were all onto him. Since he couldn't risk going back to finish the job he was being paid for, he came up with a new plan: extort money from you in exchange for my location." I pause. "But if he never asked you for any money…"

Kurt's eyes lock with mine. He reads my mind instantly and exhales.

"Fuck."

"Would someone like to clue me on to what's

going on here?" Josh crosses his arms and rocks back on his heels just as the penny drops. "Fuck," he breathes.

Maeve raises her hand.

"What are you doing?" Josh asks her confused.

"I wanted to ask a question," she tells him.

"Well just ask," Josh barks at her.

"I didn't want to be rude," she replies, "and don't snap at me. These guys…" she waves her hand around the room at his team, "are paid to put up with it. I, however, am not."

"Sorry, babe." He mumbles contrite.

"Babe? Is that how we address each other in team meetings now?" Kurt mocks as he side eyes Josh.

Josh growls and drags his hand down his face. "After today no more wives in team meetings," he mutters.

"I don't have a wife," Kurt replies pointedly while staring at me.

"You will soon enough," Josh growls.

I open my mouth to ask him what he means by that but am interrupted by Maeve huffing, "Can someone please just tell me what the hell is going on?"

"I think Bear was bluffing," I tell her. "I think he plans to go back for the hard drive. Either he is going to use it to extort money from Steven, or he is planning on finishing what he started and he still needs the drive as insurance. Maybe he actually wanted me to go down with the boat so everyone would be kept too busy searching for me to notice what he was really up to. But just in case I did get rescued, he planted the idea that he was about to go on the run—so no one would think to look for him around here.

I just hope he's been laying low long enough that we're not already too late. We need to get back to the Sapphire and find that hard drive before he picks it up."

If there's even the slightest chance we might run into him, you should stay here," Kurt says. It's not a suggestion—it's a command.

"No can do, I'm afraid," I reply sweetly.

"Give me one good reason to take you, and I will." He smirks, confident I won't be able to.

"How about this—I think I know where he stashed what we're looking for." I flash him an angelic smile, watching his expression darken. "And if you want to know what I know, you'll have to take me with you."

"That's a good reason," he growls, reluctant but cornered.

"Well, you sure as hell aren't going," Josh snaps at Maeve, hands planted firmly on his hips.

Blake helps her up from the sofa, and she strolls over to her husband. She kisses Josh on the cheek and says mischievously, "Meet you in the car." Then she bolts before he realises what's happening. When he does, he chases after her, yelling for her to slow down before she trips.

Kurt steps in, taking control. "Babe, you're with me. Blake, you ride with us—watch her." He points to me.

Blake grins, points two fingers at his eyes, then at me. "Got it."

"Ace, Nic—you're with Josh. One of you keeps Maeve in sight at all times."

"Boss," they say in unison, peeling out of the room.

"Foxy," Kurt calls. "Where's the best place for you to work your magic?"

"I hacked the system last time we were there. I've got full access to the building. If I station myself out front, I can deploy a couple of drones to monitor the perimeter while you're inside. That way, I can give you a heads-up if our friend shows."

Kurt nods and tosses him a key fob. "You drive. Drop us at the door, then get into position."

Foxy nods. We all start to move, but Kurt catches my arm, holding me back. The others vanish. As soon as we're alone, he spins me around and kisses me like a drowning man reaching for air.

"Please stay here," he pleads. "Let me go without you. Tell me where to look—we'll be there and back before you know it."

"I'll feel safer by your side than left here alone," I whisper, anxious.

"Then give Josh the info, and I'll stay here with you and Maeve."

I shake my head. "You're a key part of the team. They need you. I won't get in the way, I promise. I just want this to be over. I'm done with all the drama." I cup his cheek, and he leans into my touch. "I want to relax and focus on our future—just you, me, and our baby. But I don't think I can until this is sorted."

He kisses me again, then takes my hand and leads me toward the car.

"Just don't tell your brother what you've been up to," he sighs, then shudders. "Or you can definitely knock having more kids off the itinerary—Have you seen some of the tools he keeps in that garage."

"I laugh, thinking he's joking. But one look at his face wipes the smile from mine—he's dead serious.

Chapter 25

The regal presence of the Sapphire feels different as we pull up just after four in the morning. Although the moon casts a pale glow, the air is cold and damp, clinging to our skin like a warning. The building looms ahead, its sleek facade shadowed and silent. The full moon slips behind a thin veil of cloud, and for a moment, the structure looks abandoned by time—haunted not by memories, but by the absence of them. It was a masterpiece designed to dazzle, to be filled with life and light, not left hollow and waiting, like a stage set for a show that never premiered.

Everyone climbs out of the two vehicles—except Foxy. While Kurt works on disabling the barrel lock on the door, I hang back to have a quick word with Foxy.

"When you two are quite ready," Kurt hisses, catching us mid-chinwag. Foxy taps a screen on the tablet he brought, and the electric doors swoosh open.

Kurt, Josh, and Ace slip inside immediately, weapons raised. Blake and Nico flank Maeve and me, hands poised over the guns holstered at their waists. They communicate via the earpieces Foxy handed out before we left home. Once we get the signal that the interior is secure, Foxy heads off to scout a location to deploy his drones while the rest of us gather in the foyer.

Maeve and I drift casually toward the aquarium —Nico and Blake hot on our heels— so we can watch the marine life that hover in space or glide languidly through the water. It's a stark contrast to the usual daytime bustle. A few dim lights illuminate the tank, casting eerie shadows that make the scene feel more unsettling than if it were plunged into total darkness.

A shark cruises by, close to the glass, its mouth ajar, rows of razor-sharp teeth on full display. Its black, unblinking eye watches us from the other side of the barrier.

I shiver, grateful for the glass between us. For a moment, I wonder—if Kurt hadn't arrived when he did, would I have become shark fodder a few hours earlier?

"Are there sharks usually found near Manhattan?" I ask Maeve absentmindedly—my friend, the seasoned veterinarian.

"A few. I'm no expert in aquatics, but definitely bull sharks. Maybe the odd basking shark, and a few others." She pauses, and in that silence, my mind begins to drift into places I'd rather not go.

"Do fish ever really sleep?" she asks, tilting her head.

"I don't know. You're the vet—you tell me," I chuckle.

She whacks me gently on the arm, snapping me out of my spiralling haze.

"What's next?" Kurt asks, appearing beside us.

"Upstairs. Back to where Bear snatched me," I whisper.

We head toward the elevator, pausing when Maeve doesn't follow. Nico silently steps beside her.

"Is it okay if I wait here?" she asks Josh, who looks torn between going and staying.

"I got this," Nico says.

Josh nods and joins us at the elevator—a quiet testament to the trust he places in Nico to watch over his pregnant wife.

We can't all fit on a single run. Josh and Ace go up first to secure the area. I follow, squeezed between Kurt and Blake. When we step out at the top, the first thing I see is my discarded bag—its contents scattered where it was left.

"You okay?" Kurt whispers, throwing his arm across my shoulders and pulling me into his side.

"Yeah. Just exorcising past ghosts," I say with a weak smile.

"That's my girl." He gives me a gentle squeeze before he and Blake help gather my things to take with us when we leave.

I can't resist teasing Kurt when I find the bug he planted, waving it in front of his face as he crouches beside me.

"I don't recognise this," I say, pretending to muse thoughtfully.

"Course you do," he replies with a grin. "It's mine. I was positive I left it on the kitchen counter—I wondered where it had disappeared to. Must've toppled off into your bag."

"Sure it did," I reply, pulling my best faux-angry face.

"Helped save your bacon, didn't it?" he jokes.

I pretend not to hear him.

"Where now?" Kurt asks once we're done.

Everyone gathers around me, listening intently.

"Just before Bear grabbed me..." I begin. I see everyone's stance stiffen, so I push on quickly. "I was gazing into that hatch there." I point to one of the large, glass-bolted windows. "I wasn't looking at anything in particular—just being nosy. I wanted to see if I could spot any fish from up here. But Bear caught me peering down, and for a split second... he looked worried. Not startled—worried. Like I'd figured out something I wasn't supposed to.

That's what I wanted to check with Foxy just now—if it would be possible for Bear to hide the hard drive down there." I point to the glistening depths below. "He said it would. Bear could easily get his hands on the same military-grade gear you guys use. If he sealed the drive in a Pelican case, threw in some silica gel, maybe even vacuum-packed the whole thing in plastic... there's no reason the data couldn't survive."

"Do you think he would?" Blake asks, glancing at the others. "Sure, he can dive—but it wasn't exactly his favourite pastime. I always figured he preferred dry land, didn't you?"

"I think Tina's on the money," Kurt says.

"Why?" Josh looks at me and winks. I know what he's really asking—he's checking that Kurt's thinking with his head, not a different appendage.

Kurt knows it too. He squares off to Josh, jaw set. "Because he'd pick the last place we'd think to look. He hated diving. He didn't like sharks. He'd assume we'd take one look at this tank and say 'no way.' And we probably would've—if Tina hadn't given us pause."

"I agree," Josh says briskly, drawing an arched eyebrow from Kurt. "Just checking." He grins.

"So who's going down there?" Blake asks as he, Josh, and Kurt flip open the hatch and peer into the water.

"I think the best diver should go," Kurt announces. "There's got to be some gear around here somewhere. I'll get suited up."

"I think you've missed your chance," I say, barely disguising the relief in my voice.

The three men glance up to see Ace already stripped down to his briefs, and about to slip into a diving suit he found in the cupboard next to the oxygen tanks.

The man is built, and Kurt clearly notices me staring. He slaps a hand over my eyes and barks, "Put your tongue back in your mouth, woman—Ace is feeling objectified."

"No I'm not," Ace chuckles, strolling over and zipping himself up. "This place is massive though. Might take more than little ol' me to check it out."

There's nothing little about you, dude. I think to myself.

"Why thank you," Ace replies, grinning like a Cheshire cat.

My face glows brighter than a beacon when I realise I must've said it out loud. One quick glance at Kurt's face confirms my suspicion.

I roll my lips and look away as the conversation shifts back to the tank—strategizing how many men and how long it would take to perform the search.

"It's going to take a while," Josh sighs. "We might

have to take shifts. It could be anywhere down there—hidden in the coral or buried under the sand. We don't even know where to start."

I cough to get their attention. "I might be able to help you out on that score," I mutter, embarrassed to once again know more than the experts.

Josh groans and drags a hand down his face. "Back in school, you were more interested in studying the football team than your textbooks. Now you're like Sherlock bloody Holmes—and not one of you," he gestures at the rest of the team, "knows enough to be her Watson. What am I even paying you all for?"

"Well, I know you keep me around for my good looks," Kurt quips.

"More like your sense of humour," Ace counters.

"Or the fact your girl keeps saving our asses," Blake adds.

"Well, in fairness, you all saved my ass not so long ago," I chip in.

"It's a very nice ass," Ace chuckles. "It was worth saving."

"Back at ya," I giggle, having just copped an eyeful.

"Really?" Kurt growls, clearly not amused by our banter.

"So where am I looking, oh wise one?" Ace

schmoozes, completely ignoring Kurt's pissed-off expression.

"Well... Bear made a reference to the hard drive holding all kinds of treasure. I might be wrong, but..." I bite my bottom lip.

"You think it's in the chest at the bottom," Ace finishes for me. "Then that's where I'll start."

He shrugs on his tank, checks the respirator and oxygen levels, then crouches to wet his mask so it won't fog up underwater.

"Want one of us to come with you?" Josh asks.

"Nah, no point if I find the thing where Tina thinks it is. I'll go down, do a quick recce. If it's not there, I'll come back up and we'll rethink."

Josh gives him a chin tip.

Ace pulls on his flippers and sits on the ledge of the hatch. A dark shadow glides beneath us, and I panic—grabbing his arm just as he's about to slip into the water.

"Wait," I cry. "What about the sharks?"

All the men chuckle like I've just warned them about a kitten on the loose.

"I've heard they hunt at night," I mutter, a little offended.

"In the wild, yes," Ace says, trying to reassure me. "But in here? They've probably been hand-fed more than they've ever had to hunt. Besides, I've faced bigger and more aggressive animals."

"Where?" The word tumbles out—half shock, half fear.

"Every day at work." He throws Kurt a pointed look as he slides into the water with practiced ease.

"Smartass," Josh chuckles.

"Can I go down and watch with Maeve?" I ask Kurt.

"Blake," Kurt says, his eyes never leaving the water.

Blake extends his arm for me to take. "May I have the pleasure of escorting you this evening?"

"You may." I take his arm, and we make our way back downstairs just as Ace comes into view.

Blake and Nico laugh as Ace showboats in front of Maeve and me, pretending to dance to music only he can hear. I clutch my chest and point frantically as a small shark—probably about two feet long—glides over to investigate the new lifeform invading its habitat.

Ace gives it a gentle nudge on the gills, and it retreats, drifting off on its merry way.

He reaches the treasure chest and begins to pry it open.

As he does, I notice a shadow move to the side of him.

From behind a coral outcrop, Bear emerges—

silent, sudden, lethal. His eyes glimmer, hard and unyielding, the cold intent of a man with nothing to lose etched within them.

Panicking I pound on the thick glass, frantic to warn Ace. He spins at last, but Bear is faster. Blake barks into his comms behind me as the water erupts in a flurry of bubbles and limbs. Bear and Ace grapple, twist, and strike—two ex-SEALs locked in a brutal ballet of underwater combat. Bear slams Ace against the tank wall, knocking the regulator from his mouth. Ace scrambles, snatches it back, but Bear is already on him again.

A knife flashes. Caught off guard, Ace jerks away too slow. A gash opens across the top of his arm, then his side. Blood blooms in the water like ink on paper.

The scent rouses the sharks, excitement rising at the promise of a hunt. Maeve screams. Nico swears as two more figures plunge into the chaos —Josh and Kurt, fully clothed with the portable oxygen tanks they grabbed the moment Blake raised the alarm.

They signal quickly, dividing the mission with sharp hand gestures. Ace falters as Bear circles, confident, ready to land the final blow. The sharks close in. One sinks its teeth into Ace's shoulder. He jerks in pain. Josh drives a jab into the predator's eye, forcing it to release. He seizes Ace, dragging him upward toward the top of the tank.

Meanwhile Kurt slices through the water like a missile, ramming Bear mid-spin and sending him tumbling. The fight resets—Kurt versus Bear this time, no distractions, no escape. It's vicious, desperate, the clash of two men bound by history. Kurt knows every recent scar carved into his body leads back to Bear. It's time for him to pay the price for his betrayal. Bear lunges with his knife, but it's an awkward move driven by fear and Kurt strips it away in seconds. The blade drifts uselessly to the floor as Bear drives a fist into Kurt's ribs. Kurt absorbs it, as if the blow is the permission he's been waiting for. Their eyes lock. Fuelled by something deeper than pain, Kurt answers with a brutal elbow to Bear's jaw—the strike echoing like a sentence about to be passed. Bear reels, biting down hard on his respirator until it tears apart. Bubbles burst around him, desperation flooding the water as he fights for one more breath.

From beyond the glass, I can do little more than watch, my fists pressed white against the glass, my thoughts torn between terror and hope. For Kurt, this isn't just survival—it's the reckoning, the moment to finish a vow he made long ago.

Bear lunges for Kurt's breathing apparatus ripping it away.

Kurt retaliates, catching the oxygen tank and driving it into Bear's gut, then slamming it upward into his chin and hard against his temple. Bear's body goes limp, bubbles streaming from his mouth. Kurt seizes him, still holding his own breath as he kicks upward.

"We need to get up there!" I shout, sprinting for the lift before anyone can stop me. I dive inside and punch the button, but as the doors slide closed, an arm wedges through, forcing them back open. I brace for a fight—only for Nico, Maeve, and Blake to push their way in beside me.

At the top, the doors part. Maeve rushes to help her husband, who is crouched over Ace's body sprawled across the floor, his hands frantic as he fights to stem the bleeding from his wounds. Blake and Nico haul Kurt and the unconscious Bear out of the tank and onto the floor. Kurt lays Bear flat, checking for vitals. Nothing. No breath. No pulse. He signals to Nico, whose eyes widen in disbelief before he drops to his knees and starts CPR.

Bear coughs violently, water spraying from his mouth. He groans, eyes fluttering open.

"Didn't think I'd let you get off that easily, did you?" Kurt whispers, his voice deadly cold.

Bear groans again as Nico and Blake flip him over, binding his wrists and ankles with cable ties before dragging him away.

I drop to my knees, hugging Kurt in relief and showering him with kisses. "Are you alright?"

Ace groans. "I get sliced, and he's the one who gets the kisses."

"Not my fault your reflexes are slow old man," Kurt counters humorously.

I grin and blow him one, as Maeve leans in to press a peck on his temple. "We need to get you to a hospital," she insists.

"Nah, I'm fine. Looks worse than it is. You can just stitch me up when we get home," Ace says.

"No, I can't," she retorts, horrified. "I'm a vet, not qualified to work on humans. And you were bitten — who knows what kind of bacteria is in that water. You'll need shots."

"I'm planning on having some," Ace assures her. "Definitely a couple of tequilas later."

"Josh?" Maeve looks to her husband for backup. "The knife wounds aren't deep, but the laceration on the shoulder is deep enough that I can see bone."

Josh hesitates. "It might be hard to explain if we turn up to the ER with a shark bite victim at this hour. Do you think you could help us out, just this once?"

Maeve's eyes widen. "Seriously?"

Ace nods, wincing as he presses a hand to his shoulder. "Please."

"On one condition," Maeve growls. "If it isn't healing properly within a couple of days, you let me take you to the ER myself."

"Deal." Ace offers his good arm for a handshake.

"I haven't finished," Maeve says sternly. "And you're getting shots tomorrow regardless."

"I don't need to. I'm up to date. Mr. Mom over there," he jerks his head at Josh, "makes us have regular physicals if we want to keep working for him."

"Glad to hear it," Maeve smiles at Josh, who leans forward and kisses her.

"More kissing," Ace groans. "Cut it out, I could be dying here."

"If you were, you wouldn't be so vocal," Josh shoots back.

"One day you'll find someone you want to kiss all the time, then you'll understand," Maeve laughs, cupping her husband's face and pulling him in for another smooch.

"Not likely," Ace says firmly. "You two"—he gestures at Maeve and me—"are trouble with a capital T. And those two"—he points at Josh and Kurt—"are at the mercy of their gonads. Whipped doesn't even begin to cover it. I actually used to look up to them, you know?" He rambles on, distraught, while the rest of us try not to laugh. "They were some of the strongest men I knew before they got tangled up with you two." He waves at Maeve and me again. "Now look at them—always following you around with gormless grins plastered on their faces. You," he points at Josh, "I get it—sort of. I mean, you were obviously spiralling—too many whacks to the head I reckon. Who creates a company and then promotes a five-year-old to CEO? But you"—he turns to Kurt, shaking his head sadly—"I never thought I'd see the day, caught lying naked with a rose between your teeth just to impress a girl. One of us has to keep thinking with his head and not his…" He glances between Maeve and me before finishing. "No siree. Not happening to me. I like a woman's company as much as the next man, but you don't have to sacrifice your dignity for it. There's no reason two consenting adults can't spend a mutually enjoyable evening together then move on. I'm fine on my own—totally in control of my own life, happy, thriving, and planning to stay that way."

"Whatever you say," Maeve teases.

Ace shifts uncomfortably and changes the subject. "So, who's going back down there? We still need the hard drive, and since me going in would be like ringing the dinner bell right now, I'd rather pass."

"Wuss," Kurt chuckles. "I'll go."

"What? No!" I exclaim.

"I'll be fine." Kurt gives me a reassuring wink before suiting up, while I pace nervously on the sidelines.

He slips into the water and vanishes. Every second he's gone ratchets my anxiety higher.

Just as I'm about to rush downstairs to check the tank, he bursts back through the surface, thrusting a black case at my feet before hauling himself out. He rips off his mask, eyes locked on Josh.

"We have another problem."

A metallic click echoes across the room.

"Make that two." Steven snaps, stepping from behind one of the unopened doors, a gun levelled at Kurt's head.

Chapter 26

"I guess it's payback time," Steven chuckles, eyes locked on Kurt.

Kurt doesn't flinch. He folds his arms, scoffing. "Hardly payback. I was unarmed when I took you down. Want a shot at the title? Put the gun down and face me like a man."

Steven hesitates, ego bruised. His smile falters. "You'd like that, wouldn't you? With all your friends here ready to jump in."

Josh steps forward, mirroring Kurt's stance. "If you two girls want one-on-one, take it to the roof." He jerks his head toward the door. "We'll wait down here."

"Do you think I'm stupid?" Steven roars, voice cracking with rage.

Josh and Kurt exchange a glance, then shrug in unison. "Pretty much," they say together, laughing at their joint response.

Steven's face twists. He swings the gun toward me. Kurt instantly steps forward, forcing Steven to jerk it back to him. "I gave you that job in good faith," Steven snarls.

"No, you didn't," I growl. "You gave it to me because I was a 'dumb bitch,' a desperate single woman about to have a baby. Too distracted to notice what you were really up to."

Steven flinches, the familiar insult hitting home. "How did you—" He cuts himself off, shaking his head. "Never mind. Throw me the case!" His bark echoes, but Kurt doesn't move.

Steven's knuckles whiten around the gun. "You've got until I count to five. Then I pull the trigger. One... Two... Three..."

When Kurt still refuses to budge, as Steven counts, "Four," he swings his aim so it's pointed at my belly, or more specifically Kurt's baby.

My hand covers my stomach as I stare at Kurt, petrified. His eyes flick between me and Josh, lingering long enough on his best friend to hint at a silent agreement I can't decipher.

As Steven counts, "Five." Kurt lunges, shoving me aside just as Steven pulls the trigger. I stumble, tripping over the lip of the open hatch, and plunge into the deep water with a gasp.

Chaos erupts above, another shot rings out, but I can't focus. Panic grips me as the aquarium's largest shark glides toward me. I thrash, desperate to reach the surface, but the fall knocked the breath from me. My limbs feel heavy, sluggish. A whimper escapes before I clamp my mouth shut, fighting to keep the water from flooding in.

The shark nudges my foot and my terror spikes. Then—arms wrap around me from behind. Strong. Steady. A kick lashes out, striking the shark, driving it away. In an instant I'm rocketed upward, bursting back into the air.

I choke in fresh oxygen, blinking through dripping hair. On the platform, Steven writhes, screaming, blood pouring from a gunshot wound in his shoulder — the precise countermeasure of a marksman's aim, designed not to kill but to sever his grip and force his weapon from his hand.

I spin, ready to throw myself into Kurt's arms—only to find Josh instead, soaked and panting, the one who leapt in after me.

"Where's Kurt?" I gasp, shoving wet strands from my face.

Josh's pitying look makes my stomach drop. He jerks his head toward a body sprawled on the ground, lifeless in a pool of viscous red. Ace and Maeve kneel over him, frantic, pressing hands to wounds I can't see, Ace's broad frame blocking my view.

"Kurt!" I scream as Josh propels me out of the water. I stumble to his side, clutching his cheeks with trembling hands. Tears blur my vision. "Wake up, baby. Please… just wake up."

The world around me dissolves into haze.

Foxy and Blake rush in. Maeve tries to hold me, but I barely register her touch. Foxy hauls Ace to his feet, and together they seize the pelican case, dragging Steven away. I don't care where they're going. My focus is Kurt—his chest rises, shallow and ragged, but he doesn't respond.

Blake and Josh lift him gently, draping his arms over their shoulders. Blake keeps pressure on a blood-soaked cloth against Kurt's torso. As they move toward the elevator, Josh murmurs something to Maeve, then pries Kurt's hand from mine.

"No..." The word escapes me, hollow and broken, as his cold fingers slip from my grasp.

Maeve clutches me tight while I sob into her shoulder.

"Tina." Josh's voice cuts through, firm yet steady. I force myself to meet his eyes. 'He needs you strong right now. Trust me—I've got this. You'll see him soon. I promise."

The elevator doors slide shut, taking with them Kurt—and a huge piece of my heart.

It's been two days since the incident at the Sapphire. Kurt lies in a hospital bed, heavily sedated, recovering from emergency surgery to remove the bullet—the one meant for me, and for our child.

I haven't left his side since Maeve and I reached the hospital.

Josh and Blake didn't wait for an ambulance. They bundled Kurt into a car while Foxy broke every speed limit to get him to a private hospital in New Jersey. The other car had vanished with Ace, Nico, Bear, and Steven, leaving Maeve and me to scramble for a taxi. That forty-five-minute ride was the longest of my life. By the time we arrived, Kurt was already in surgery.

Maeve ran straight into Josh's arms, and he held her close. Blake pulled me against him, whispering, *"Indestructible, remember?"* as my tears soaked through his shirt. His words were a lifeline, even as fear clawed at me.

The bullet had torn through vital tissue, causing massive internal bleeding. Somehow, Kurt survived the operation. Now we wait—every hour stretching endlessly—hoping he'll wake.

When I saw him being wheeled on a gurney to a private room, I rushed to his side and haven't moved since. The doctor tried to insist I leave, but Josh 'persuaded' him otherwise. For that, I'll be forever grateful.

The others keep vigil in shifts outside. Whenever I drag myself to the ladies' room, I find

Josh and one or more of them slouched in the hard chairs, dozing fitfully, their loyalty etched in every weary line of their faces.

"Pizza?" Maeve appears beside me, the familiar waft of melted cheese invading my senses.

I look up and manage a weak smile. I'm so exhausted I hadn't even heard her come in.

"You need to eat," she says gently, then leans over Kurt as if he were wide awake. "I made them load it with vegetables, but if you don't open your eyes and stop me, tomorrow I'm bringing her nothing but carbs and greasy comfort food, and we're going to sit here and eat it right in front of you."

I chuckle, and together we wait for Kurt to rise to the challenge. Nothing. My appetite vanishes, and I push the box away.

"Please, T," Maeve urges. "Just a bite."

"Too tired," I whisper.

A nurse slips in to check the monitors. "You can't eat that in here," she tells Maeve kindly. Maeve sighs and leaves.

"Any change?" I ask. The nurse shakes her head with quiet sympathy before disappearing again.

Careful not to disturb the wires, I climb onto the bed and curl myself around Kurt's sleeping body. I place his hand on my stomach, holding it there. "He's here, Nugget," I whisper. "Your daddy's here, and he's going to be fine."

I tilt my head, speaking low into Kurt's ear. "I love you, you big selfless oaf. I don't think I really realised how much until the moment I thought I'd lost you forever. Marry me? Let's move to L.A., knock out a few more sprogs, and rope our friends into babysitting while we sneak off to fool around on the beach. I promise I'll do anything if you come back to me. Just. Wake. Up."

Unable to fight it any longer, the rhythmic beeping of the machines lulls me toward sleep. Just as I drift, I swear I feel the faintest twitch of the fingers resting beneath mine on my belly.

In my dream, he turns to me, his voice hoarse and raw. "Yes, baby. I'll marry you." The words ignite a smile I can't contain. In that moment, I am the luckiest woman alive. If only it were real.

When I wake, the bed is empty. Josh sits at the bedside, leaning forward, arms braced on his knees, watching me stir. His face is grave, and panic surges as I scramble upright.

"Where is he?" I cry, desperate, fearing the worst.

Josh's expression breaks into a grin. "Christ, you had me worried there for a minute."

"Me?"

"Thought he was going to kick my ass for not keeping a close enough eye on you. Your blood pressure spiked because you weren't eating, and you were dehydrated. You were so exhausted you didn't even stir when they put that in." He nods toward the drip in my arm. "The nurse caught it during her rounds when she checked in on our boy and saw you lying there."

Suddenly, a commotion erupts outside the door and a familiar voice cuts through.

"Will you stop fretting!" the roar is sharp, impatient. "I will not burst my stitches again."

Whoever he's shouting at doesn't answer — either too calm or too intimidated to respond.

Then comes another bellow: "I'm not going anywhere until I've checked on my woman. She should be awake by now — it's been nearly twenty-four hours. She needs to eat."

I glance at Josh, and we exchange grins just as the door swings open. Kurt strides in, hospital gown flapping, balancing a tray with exaggerated care. A doctor follows close behind, wheeling the drip still tethered to Kurt's arm.

"Oh good, you're awake," Kurt says flatly, before flicking his head toward the doctor. "You can leave now."

Josh huffs out a laugh and rises. He escorts the

doctor back to the door, whispering something low as they go. The doctor sighs, nods, and disappears.

With theatrical force, Kurt sets the tray down in front of me.

"Eat!" he commands. "I went to the kitchen and made it myself."

"I can tell," I reply, raising an eyebrow as I sift through the heap of limp greens, searching for anything remotely appetizing. A burger, a hot dog — even a scrap of cardboard would be an improvement.

"I'll leave you two to it. Time to let the others know she's back with us." Josh chuckles.

Kurt murmurs something to him at the door, but I don't catch it. My attention is fixed on the unmistakable glimpse of his bare backside peeking through the loose ties of his gown.

A giggle bubbles out of me, unstoppable. Relief floods in—he's here, alive, fussing over me. He turns at the sound, hands on his hips, frown etched across his face, and I laugh harder.

"What are you laughing at?" he grumbles.

"I hope you didn't storm into the kitchen like that," I tease.

He glances down, confused.

"Your butt's hanging out," I laugh. "That

couldn't have been hygienic."

"Meh." Kurt flashes a crooked smile before his expression hardens, signalling I'm the one in trouble. "You need to look after yourself properly. You can't fall apart every time I take a quick nap."

"Quick nap?" I arch a brow. "And are you sure you should be up and walking around? You still look pale."

"I do feel a little woozy," he admits, then smirks and nods toward my bed. "Room in there for two?"

"Three," I correct, flipping back the sheet.

He climbs in beside me. Space is tight, and the medical equipment makes it a challenge, but we shuffle and wiggle until we find a comfortable position — him on his back, one arm around me, my head nestled against his chest. The tray of food balanced across his lap. A drip hanging either side of us.

In silence, he feeds me the tasteless vitamin feast he prepared while I slept. Each bite is offered with such tenderness that my heart melts beneath the weight of his gaze. He winces every time he stretches, the cannula tugging at his hand, but still he doesn't stop.

When I've eaten every scrap, he sets the tray aside and leans further back against the pillows. I snuggle in close, a deep certainty settling over me — he's going to be alright.

We lie in comfortable silence for a few minutes before I finally ask the question that's been gnawing at me. "Is it over?"

I expect an answer, not a bellowed, "Help!" The shout sends Josh and Maeve rushing in.

"What?" Josh scans the room, ready to drop-kick an intruder if he finds one.

"Tina wants to know if it's over," Kurt chuckles.

Maeve presses a hand to her chest, relieved it was a false alarm. Josh folds his arms, glaring. "You could switch the TV on yourself," he snaps.

"I've been shot, you idiot. I'm supposed to be resting so I don't split my stitches," Kurt volleys back.

Josh throws his arms up in exasperation. "He can wander around the hospital to whip up a—" he air quotes, "nutritious meal for the mother of his child — but he can't press the teeny-tiny button on the remote?"

"I can't reach it," Kurt grins.

Josh snatches the remote from a side table and lobs it across the room. Kurt catches it mid-flight with a smug smile.

"C'mon," Josh mutters, grabbing his wife's hand. "I need a drink."

"The coffee machine's out of order," Maeve says, confused.

"Not that sort of drink," he growls, tugging her out the door. Seconds later, Josh's head pops back around the frame. "I think you'll find today's news… interesting."

I glance at the clock — the broadcast should just be starting. Snatching the remote from Kurt, I flick on the TV and scroll until a reporter appears outside the courthouse where Knox's trial was being held. A bold red banner scrolls across the screen:

Knox trial halted as second attorney goes missing; new evidence leads to further indictments.

I turn up the volume, transfixed by the exchange between the anchor and the reporter on location.

Anchor: "So Charlotte, after the disruption in court on Friday, what's next for Knox?"

Reporter: "Well, as you know, Knox's current attorney, Steven Prentice, failed to appear on Friday. Many believed he was aware of new evidence about to be presented by the prosecution and stayed away in an attempt to stall proceedings. However, after repeated efforts to locate him over the weekend, authorities have now officially declared him a missing person, and a statewide search is underway.

This development follows the discovery of Knox's previous attorney, Robert Taylor, whose body was found concealed inside a chest at the bottom of the huge, record-breaking aquarium connected to Knox's newest venture, Sapphire Heights."

I gasp, my hand flying to my mouth.

Anchor: "Was Knox involved?"

Reporter: "Nothing can be confirmed at this time, since Knox was in custody when Robert Taylor was killed. Sources say that following an anonymous tip-off about a faulty aeration pump, the body was discovered while the tank was undergoing routine maintenance Saturday morning. Forensics are now on the scene trying to recover anything that might shed any light on how it got there. What we do know is that Taylor died from a single gunshot wound to the head. Knox denies any knowledge of the shooting, saying he simply sought new representation after deciding Taylor was no longer the right man for the job.

Now, with Steven Prentice also missing and substantial new evidence being presented against Knox, Judge Raymond Fletcher — who is presiding over the case — has had no choice but to adjourn proceedings while the new charges are prepared."

Anchor: "Can you tell us what those charges are likely to be?"

Reporter: "At this stage, we haven't been given full details. However, rumours suggest the new charges could be extensive, potentially including several federal counts. Everyone is now waiting to see if — and when — Steven Prentice reappears, and whether he will be able to challenge or refute any of these new allegations."

"He won't," Kurt chuckles.

I tilt my head toward him. "Won't reappear? Or won't be able to refute the charges? Where is Steven?" My voice trembles, afraid of the answer.

Kurt nods toward the TV. "Keep watching."

On screen, the reporter is describing the fire that claimed Camilla Ramirez when a black transit van — no plates, windows tinted — screeches to a halt just feet away. Gasps ripple through the crowd as the camera swings to capture the scene.

The side door slides open. Two men in black, faces hidden behind balaclavas, shove Steven Prentice onto the street. He's barefoot, dressed only in a white T-shirt and briefs, his hands bound behind him despite the swathe of bandages binding his shoulder, his mouth is taped shut. He thrashes, trying to shout against the gag.

But it isn't just Steven that shocks the crowd — it's the oversized manila envelope strapped to his chest. Scrawled across it in thick red letters: **"Arrest me. Evidence inside."**

As the news team and bystanders rush forward, the van doors slam shut and the vehicle roars away in a cloud of dust.

"They looked familiar," I murmur, side-eyeing

Kurt.

"Did they?" he replies casually. "Can't say I recognised them myself."

"Sure you didn't." My suspicion sharpens. "Where are Foxy and the others?"

"On the road, I suspect," Kurt says with a smile. "Job's over."

He switches off the television and pulls me close. "Rumour has it there's enough evidence strapped to Prentice's chest to put him and Knox away indefinitely. Alongside countless other revelations, the idiot unbelievably documented the plan to hire a hitman for the judge. Foxy found it right there on the drive we recovered. Bear's name wasn't mentioned which makes life less complicated. I don't know how those two became acquainted. And just in case that envelope disappears, copies have already been sent to the local PD, the FBI, and to Carlos Ramirez — should he wish to bring additional charges of his own. Monroe took off before we could catch up with her. She's in the wind but there's a warrant out for her arrest. Not even Simmons will be able to help her now."

I settle against him, comforted. "What happened to Bear?"

His body stiffens. "That's a whole new story," he mutters. "One for another day."

I don't press. He needs rest, not questions. For now, I sense we're safe, and that's enough. Wherever Bear ended up, I'll learn in time.

"Yes," Kurt murmurs into my hair, breaking into my thoughts.

"Yes what?" I ask, confused.

"Yes, I'll marry you. And I kinda really wish I was on the beach making out with you right now."

I chuckle. "I don't think either of us have the energy for that." Then the realisation hits, and I push up on my elbow. "Wait—you heard me?"

His smirk deepens. "We'll discuss what I did and didn't hear on the way to my place in L.A."

He closes his eyes, one hand behind his head, looking maddeningly relaxed. I gape at him, mind racing through the repercussions of the promise I made. He cracks one eye open, glancing at me with a mischievous grin.

"How many sprogs were you thinking of?"

I roll my lips, then deadpan. "Four or five."

I expect shock at the inflated number, but he only pretends to mull it over before replying, "Doable."

I gasp, and he tugs me back down until my head rests on his chest. Silence stretches, then he breaks it with a sly edge. "When you promised to do anything if I woke up... were there any caveats to that statement?"

"Why?"

"I'm compiling a list."

I snuggle closer, breathing in the familiar scent of him, letting the warmth of his body seep into mine. The near-loss cements what I already know: he's everything I'll ever want, everything I'll ever need.

There were..." I begin, lips twitching, "but since you took a bullet for me, I guess I owe you. So fine—marriage, sprogs, sunsets in L.A., late-night pizza raids, and every ridiculous adventure you can dream up—it's all yours. Just promise me that if we ever end up here again, you'll keep your hospital gown tied tighter next time, I don't want you flashing all and sundry—that ass is mine."

He lowers his hand, giving my butt cheek a squeeze. "Right back at ya."

I yelp, looking up to find him staring down at me.

"I love you," I say, serious now. "You're it for me." I need him to know it's real — not whispered through exhaustion or a medicated haze, but clear, deliberate, and true.

He leans in, and I brace for a kiss, but he pauses just shy of my lips, murmuring against them. "You know that list I'm compiling?"

"Hmmm," I hum.

"It just got decidedly dirty."

"Glad to hear it," I smile, tugging him closer and giving him a taste of exactly what our future will look like.

Epilogue

"I still can't get over this place," I say, dropping my last moving box just inside the door of Kurt's huge, swanky L.A. apartment. "I can't believe we get to live here."

The whole place is tastefully decorated and furnished, except for the master bedroom and one of the spare rooms. I'd always imagined Kurt in a tiny bachelor pad with little more than a bed and a microwave—not a four-bedroom condo with sweeping views of the Pacific Ocean in Malibu and a vast open-plan kitchen, dining, and living space.

Kurt slings an arm around my shoulders. "I can't take all the credit. Sure, I bought the place as an investment, but I had help decorating. It was an empty shell for a while. After we hooked up in Vermont, I dared to hope I might persuade you to visit one day. I wanted it to feel like somewhere you'd want to come back to, so I called in some help. When the apartment next door sold, my new neighbour was struggling with some heavy furniture. I offered to help, and in return she helped me design the interior."

"Why not finish the last two rooms?" I ask.

"The master was never on the list. That's too personal. If I was ever lucky enough to share it with someone..." He squeezes me and gives a knowing look. "...I wanted them to put their own stamp on it. As for the other room, I left for New York before it was finished. Now I figure it would make a great nursery."

I tilt my head, and Kurt leans down to kiss me tenderly.

Knock, knock.

"I'll get it." Kurt reluctantly lets me go and heads for the door. "Kat, hi."

I freeze. Is this the woman he was seeing before me? If she wants to pick up where they left off, she's in for disappointment. I brace myself as he leads her inside.

She's tall and elegant, dressed casually in fitted jeans and a blue silk blouse. Her long blonde hair swings from a high ponytail. Far from distraught, she actually looks delighted to see me. She rushes over and scoops me into a hug.

"I can't believe you're actually here," she gushes, as if I'm her long-lost friend. I glance at Kurt, bemused. She catches the look.

"I'm sorry—it's just that I feel like I already know you. Kurt's talked about you nonstop."

"He has?" I raise an eyebrow.

"All the time. From the moment he helped me move in, he was always talking about you. Then one day he's shifting this mammoth unit in my living room when you phoned..."

"Helping?" Kurt snorts, eyebrow raised. "I don't remember you breaking a sweat."

"You wouldn't let me. Insisted you could do it on your own. What was it you said, 'You can be director of operations and I'll be manual labour.'" She rolls her eyes, "Anyhow, his mood flipped instantly." She clicks her fingers for emphasis. "I knew something was up, but it took me ages to pry it out of him. He finally admitted you walked out on him after the wedding. I told him he should talk to you, tell you how he felt, but..." She shrugs, exasperated. "You know what he's like."

I glance at Kurt—he's actually blushing. Kat beams at me. "Then when he said you were in trouble and he took off to New York like a sailor on shore leave, I was hoping..." She looks at me all doe-eyed before sweeping me up in another hug. "...and now here you are."

"What's going on?" Josh strides in carrying a pack of beers and two bottles of grape juice.

"How did you get in?" I ask automatically.

"I have a key," he replies.

"No, you don't," Maeve counters crossly.

Josh just grins. "I left the door open. We have a

surprise for you."

"Your unexpected intrusion wasn't enough?" Kurt deadpans.

A tall, willowy brunette saunters in to join us.

I look at Josh. He seems just as confused as I am.

"Tash," Kurt greets her with a kiss on the cheek before introducing her. "Everyone, this is Natasha—"

"Tash," she corrects.

"Sorry, Tash to her friends," Kurt amends. "Kat's girlfriend."

She wiggles her left hand in the air as Kat goes to her side and plants a kiss on her cheek. "Try fiancée. And as of next week, your other new neighbour."

"You did it!" Kurt scoops them both up and spins them around as they giggle and beg to be put down. Setting them back on the floor, he grumbles, "Wait… does this mean I have to shift another load of stuff?"

Maeve and I gape at each other, mouthing *"Fiancée"* before bursting into fits of giggles. Just like that, I know I'm going to get along famously with the girls next door.

"Hello?" Another familiar voice calls.

"Liam?" I throw myself at my brother for a hug. He drops his bag and willingly obliges before standing back to look me over. Unlike Maeve, who has a cute little baby bump and doesn't look much different from her pre-pregnancy days, my waistline has shot out at least another two inches since I last saw him.

"Jeez, it's not gonna suddenly burst out of there, is it?" he says seriously, gazing at where my navel would be. "Keep growing at this rate and you'll be as wide as you are tall by the time this kid decides to put in an appearance."

"You'd think with the number of women you've befriended over the years, you'd know babies don't actually arrive from the belly button," Kurt jokes.

"Not that I'm not happy to see you, but what are you doing here?" I ask.

"I came to make sure you're here of your own volition and he hasn't kidnapped you." He jerks his head at Kurt.

I laugh, but my brother looks so serious I have to stop and question him.

"Of course I'm here because I want to be. Why would you think otherwise?"

"The same reason I asked him if he knocked you up on purpose."

I must look confused, because Liam feels the need to explain.

"He's always had a thing for you. It was obvious when we were kids. I told him you were not an option, and you never used to encourage him, so I never thought I'd have to worry. Then I show up and you're pregnant with his child. I needed to be sure he didn't engineer the situation for his own benefit. Because if he had..." Liam squares up to Kurt, who refuses to be intimidated.

"Not this again." I step between them, tugging the front of my brother's T-shirt so he tears his eyes away from Kurt to look at me. "Liam, I love him. I really do. He's the one for me. We're getting married, having a baby together, and we're going to live happily ever after."

My brother's eyes soften. "Well, okay then." He takes a step back. "Then I give you my blessing."

"Okay, Dad!" I tease, rolling my eyes.

"As long as he keeps you out of whatever trouble he gets into at work," Liam adds, giving Kurt a pointed look, "or else there really will be trouble."

Josh coughs to break the tension, and we all glance anywhere but at my brother. All except Kurt, who of course refuses to back down. Before Josh can speak, another voice cuts in.

"Here she is." Ace strolls into the room, closely followed by Blake, Foxy, and Nico. They each stop to kiss me on the cheek before working their way around the rest of the room. "We heard you were arriving today and thought we'd stop by to say hi."

"How did you get in?" Kurt barks.

"Door was open," Ace retorts.

Kurt glares at Liam, the last to arrive, as Blake chuckles. "No, it wasn't."

"How are your injuries?" I ask Ace.

"Fine." He looks at Josh. "I'm ready to get back to work."

Josh crosses his arms and stares him down. "No."

"But I'm better, see." Ace rolls his shoulder, trying to look stoic, but when he winces it's obvious he's still in pain.

"I told you," Josh says firmly. "Your second lot of stitches only came out yesterday. I'm not putting you back on duty until that shoulder has fully healed. That means taking a few more weeks off. If you'd listened to the Maeve, then the doctor, in the first place and rested when they told you to, you would've healed faster and been back at work already. You didn't — so here we are."

"More time off? That's just code for slowly continuing to die of boredom. What am I going to do with myself?" Ace pouts, whining.

"I don't give a damn," Josh shoots back, not budging. "You must have a hobby. Do that."

"I can't," Ace replies sullenly.

"Why?" Josh demands.

"You won't let me," comes the surly response —

much to everyone else's amusement.

"You know what they say," Maeve sings, "all work and no play makes Ace a dull boy."

Ace doesn't look amused.

"What do you do to relax?" she presses.

"Work," he replies flatly.

"Look, I have a suggestion," she begins carefully. "You know my brother is currently staying at my place in Vermont?"

Ace nods.

"Well, he's going out of town for a few weeks, so the place will be empty. Josh and I were going to visit, but since he doesn't want me flying right now, and Tina's just moved here so I want to stay with her while she settles in... why don't you go in our place?"

Ace still doesn't look convinced, so Maeve continues.

"You'd be doing me a huge favour. I don't like leaving the place empty for too long. Especially this time of year. I even got Jim to advertise it for a short-term rental, but there weren't any takers. Not many people like staying there because it's a bit remote. You could really kick back and relax until you're back to full strength. Go fishing. Hiking. Swimming. There's plenty to do that will help you rebuild. You could also check in on Aiden and the business for me, I feel bad I've not been back since Josh and I got married. Please. A change of scenery will do you the world of good." She pauses. "It's got to be better than moping around here bored. What do you say?"

Ace huffs out a breath. "Fishing? Great. Me, a stick, and a lake. Riveting television."

"Use a grenade," Blake jokes. "That'll liven things up."

"There's a hot tub," Maeve adds coaxingly. "Think of the therapeutic benefits."

"Of shrivelling up like a raisin?"

"Yeah, careful," Blake chuckles. "His tackle's not that big to begin with — you wouldn't want him to lose it altogether."

Ace glares at him.

"Don't worry, I know that's not true," I tell Ace with a wink.

"How do you?" Liam roars from the sidelines.

"Please," Maeve bats her eyelashes as she pleads with Ace.

"Sure. Why not." Ace grumbles. "Might as well sit in a hot tub in Vermont doing nothing as opposed to sitting here on my couch doing nothing. Guess I'll go play hermit in Vermont. Maybe I'll write a memoir: *How to Do Nothing and Hate It* — it's a bestseller guaranteed."

"You don't need to go to Vermont to write that,

you could do it anytime from your desk at work. Just tweak the title: *How to Do Nothing and get paid for it.*" Blake needles him.

"Great!" Maeve claps her hands in glee. "I'm sure you'll have a wonderful time chilling and being away from all the drama for a couple of weeks."

Ace snorts, unconvinced. "I'd rather be back in the action."

No one senses the subtle shift in the atmosphere as fate bends low to whisper: *"Oh, Ace... be careful what you wish for."*

Bonus

"Get in."

Nico shoves Bear forward, but the bindings around Bear's ankles make movement clumsy. He stumbles, slamming into the back of the black transit van with a groan. His shoulder ricochets off the open door before he faceplants onto the metal floor.

"Oops. My bad." Nico chuckles. He and Ace each grab one of Bear's legs, upending him and heaving him fully inside before slamming the doors shut.

"Well, the Boss was clear," Ace says, nodding toward the van. "That one goes back to L.A. We deal with him later." He jerks his chin toward the car they arrived in, where Steven is still writhing in agony. "That one stays here and faces the music. So—what's your poison?"

"I don't think you're in any fit state to drive to L.A," Nico replies. "You need stitches in that shoulder. Probably your arm and side too."

"Meh." Ace shrugs, then winces as pain shoots down his left side.

"Give me the keys," Nico says.

Ace hesitates, then hands them over.

"I'm heading out now," Nico continues. "Roads are quieter. I'll get a few hours under my belt, find a motel, grab some shut-eye. You get patched up and keep vigil with the others at the hospital. Keep me posted on any changes."

Ace nods. "What am I supposed to do with him?" He jerks his head toward Steven. "He's a screamer. Hard to stay under the radar with that one. If he draws attention and I lose him, a few stitches will be the least of my problems."

"Here." Nico hands him a small vial. "Give him a shot of this and stick him in the boot for now. Ask Josh where he wants him held and the plan moving forward."

"What is it?"

"A sedative. Fast-acting. He won't be a problem. I'm giving Bear a dose before I leave."

"Good idea. It's a long drive, and you'll need eyes in the back of your head if you're taking him alone. He's a slippery bastard. Why not wait until one of us is free to go with you?"

"Who knows how long everyone's going to be parked at the hospital. After that, Prentice still has to be gift-wrapped for the authorities. Boss wants Bear out of the vicinity and locked down ASAP, before anyone twigs he was involved"

Fifteen minutes later, both Steven and Bear are unconscious. Ace claps Nico on the back as Nico climbs into the driver's seat of the van and starts the engine.

"Good luck, my friend."

Nico grins. "See you back in L.A."

Traffic is light, and Nico makes good time. After a few hours on the road, he pulls into the cracked parking bay of a motel on the outskirts of Pennsylvania, right near the Maryland border. He opens the back of the van. Bear is still out cold.

Once he's checked the locks—twice—Nico books a room under a forgettable name and heads inside. He doesn't bother undressing; if he needs to bolt, he wants to be ready. He sets an alarm for two hours to check on Bear, texts Axel his location, and lies back. Sleep hits him instantly. In his line of work, rest isn't a luxury—it's a switch he can flip on command.

An hour later, back in the van, Bear stirs. Early sunlight spills through the open doors, slicing across his face. A hand clamps onto his shoulder and shakes him hard.

"Wake up. We don't have much time."

His eyelids feel like lead, but he forces them open. A lone figure hovers over him, backlit by the morning glare. A blade flashes—then the plastic bindings around his wrists and ankles snap free.

He stretches, sluggish and disoriented, the drugs still fogging his system. When his vision finally sharpens, he recognises her.

"Monroe?" His voice is hoarse, and he suddenly realises how badly he needs to pee. "What are you doing here?"

"I was at the Sapphire with Steven. Hiding outside. I saw them drag you out," she whispers, eyes darting toward the motel. "I tailed the van. The guy who brought you here went into one of the rooms and hasn't come out. He could walk out any second, so we need to move. Now."

"And go where?"

"I was hoping you'd tell me. I need to disappear for a while, and rumour has it you're an expert."

Cassandra Monroe slings one of Bear's arms over her shoulder and hauls him upright. It's like trying to move a tranquilised bear—fitting, given his name—and the fact his coordination is shot. After a tense, breathless struggle, she manages to get him into her car.

She slams the door, jumps behind the wheel, and peels out of the lot.

"Where to?" she asks.

Bear is already drifting again, eyelids drooping.

"Bear!" Cassandra snaps, shaking him. "Stay with me."

"Head to Michaux State Forest," he slurs. "We'll find a cabin... hole up for a while. I need to—"

But he's gone again, head lolling to the side as sleep drags him under.

Cassandra glances at him, then at the road ahead. Michaux is huge—miles of rugged terrain, old fire roads, abandoned ranger stations, and seasonal cabins scattered deep in the trees. No neighbours. Patchy cell service. Easy to lose a tail. If Bear says it's the place to disappear, she believes him.

Back at the motel, Nico's alarm blares. He jolts upright, heart pounding, heading straight for the van before even thinking about a shower or something to eat. The moment he steps outside, his stomach drops.

The lock on the back door hangs twisted and broken.

"No. No, no, no..."

He yanks the door open. The van is empty.

All the blood drains from his face. His hands shake as he fumbles for his phone and dials Axel.

The call is answered on the first ring.

"I've fucked up," Nico blurts, voice cracking. "He's gone—I think he had help."

A heavy silence stretches. When Axel finally speaks, his voice is low.

"You still in Penn?"

"Yeah."

"Then I'd put a few more miles between you before you call the Boss and tell him. I'll start checking, see what I can find. There must be some traffic cams that have caught something."

Nico swallows hard. "Right."

He hangs up, staring at the sky for a moment as if a prayer might help. Then, with a resigned breath, he scrolls through his contacts and taps the number he's been dreading.

The call he'd give anything to avoid.

Twenty-four hours later, Bear sits on a fallen log outside a cabin, staring into the dense forest surrounding him. The cold bites at his skin, but his thoughts run hotter than the air around him.

Cassandra appears in the doorway of their temporary hideout, cardigan wrapped tight around her. "It's freezing out here," she says, stepping onto the porch. "What are you doing?"

"Thinking," Bear replies.

"And you can't do that inside?" Her tone is sharp, but it softens almost immediately. She needs him—more than he realises. She's in deep, deeper than she ever meant to be, and Bear is now the only thing standing between her and prison… or worse. There are things she hasn't told him, things she's not sure she ever will. Whatever he's heading into, she intends to be part of it. He's the only one who can teach her the skills she needs to vanish properly, to stay ahead of the people already looking for her. "Come to any conclusions?"

"Yeah." Bear rises slowly to face her.

She lifts an eyebrow. "Care to share?"

"The way I see it, I've only got two options."

She waits, arms folded, breath fogging in the cold air.

"There's nowhere I can go where Josh Stone and his crew won't find me. New York proved that. And if Callahan pulls through... if I wasn't a dead man walking before, I am now. He'll make it his personal mission to hunt me down after what I did to his woman. So I either hand myself in—take my chances in jail, where it's harder for him to touch me..."

"I'm not sure I like that suggestion," she mutters, her motives entirely selfish. "Or...?"

"Or... I take him out before he does me."

"I'd go with that option," she says with a smirk.

"It's not going to be easy. Even if I get him alone, the others won't be far behind. And if they figure out it was me, I'll have Stone on my back all over again. I need a way to take Callahan down without implicating myself."

"Come inside. We can come up with a plan."

"We?" Bear tilts his head. "I work alone."

"You need me— not to mention you owe me. Don't forget you'd still be unconscious in that van, heading to who-knows-where at their mercy, if I hadn't pulled you out." She turns, her voice dropping into a slow, sultry drawl. "Besides… I think we could work well together."

She casts a deliberate smile over her shoulder as she steps back into the warm glow of the cabin, her movements confident, controlled—an invitation and a challenge wrapped into one. The cardigan slips from her shoulders. Her dress follows.

She lingers in the doorway, wearing nothing but her heels and a black lace thong, the light behind her highlighting the soft curves of her silhouette. She ignores the cold air biting at her skin; it's a small price to pay for the promise of freedom. She watches the realisation of her offer settle in his eyes—something shifting there, something she can use. Bear's expression hardens with intent, and he starts toward her with purpose.

Men, she muses as he closes the distance. A slow, knowing smile curves her lips as she fights the urge to roll her eyes. So predictable. And so easy to steer. Getting him to do what she needs is going to be a breeze.

If you skipped the dedication at the beginning as many people do:
Thankyou for choosing this book to read.
I hope it made you smile, please pass it along for someone else to enjoy.
If you're able, please share a review on Amazon, a fun pic on your socials:
#anovelchallenge,
or simply try one of the other books
in the series.
Any one helps more than you know!

Thankyou.
D

Fb: Anovelchallenge
Keep 'em peeled for the next in the series.

Books By This Author

Stone's Security Series:

When danger and desire collide, love can prove to be the most unpredictable threat of all.

>Marked by Stone
>Unbelievably Kurt

Healing Hearts Series:

When love and laughter collide, sparks fly, hearts heal, and Hollywood's brightest stars learn that fame is no match for fate.

>Healing Hollywood Hearts
>Meeting Mitchel's Match
>Lovin' 2 Leading Ladies

Marked by Stone

Josh Stone isn't a man to be messed with. Ex-Navy SEAL. Highly trained. Highly skilled. A code of ethics so unshakable, the good guys always come out on top.

Now, he's building his own elite security firm—backed by a network of operatives with lethal expertise and a relentless drive for justice. The firm's growing fast thanks to its rock-solid reputation for getting any job done. Crossing him isn't just a mistake—it's a lesson learned the hard way. Feared by many. Respected by all. But to those lucky enough to be in his inner circle, Josh is more than a weapon—he's a protector, willing to fight to the end for the ones he loves.

So when childhood friend Jimmy Mercer begs for help, desperation lacing every word, Josh listens. Jimmy needs him—or his best friend, Kurt—to protect his estranged sister. Maeve Mercer. The woman Josh once wanted so badly, he stepped aside, knowing her heart belonged to Kurt.

Before he can demand answers, Jimmy vanishes.

Hot on his trail, Josh faces Maeve, determined to assess the danger. He won't let her become collateral damage for any of Jimmy's mistakes—

but the emotions he buried years ago refuse to stay hidden. As long kept secrets start to surface, so does a shadowy figure from Maeve's past. When it seems that he's entangled in Jimmy's disappearance, Josh's protective instincts ignite.

Thrown together by fate, danger and desire collide. And as Josh edges closer to the truth, only one thing is certain—anyone who threatens Maeve, or the people he loves will pay the price.

They may not live to regret it, once they've been...

Marked by Stone.

Meet Josh and Kurt for the first time in:

Lovin' 2 Leading Ladies - A book dedicated to every parent that has ever endured the never-ending battle against glitter.

Printed in Dunstable, United Kingdom